It's You

Dee Dee Welch

It's You

Copyright © 2022 by Dee Dee Welch

All rights reserved. No part of this publication may be reproduced, distributed, or transmitted in any form or by any means, including photocopying, recording, or other electronic or mechanical methods, without the prior written permission of the author, except in the case of brief quotations embodied in critical reviews and certain other non-commercial uses permitted by copyright law.

ISBN
978-1-956529-76-0 (Paperback)
978-1-956529-75-3 (eBook)

Contents

Chapter 1	1
Chapter 2	17
Chapter 3	29
Chapter 4	45
Chapter 5	61
Chapter 6	87
Chapter 7	99
Chapter 8	113
Chapter 9	125
Chapter 10	131
Chapter 11	135
Chapter 12	141
Chapter 13	149
Chapter 14	153

Chapter 15	173
Chapter 16	183
Chapter 17	189
Chapter 18	199
Chapter 19	211
Chapter 20	217
Chapter 21	227
Chapter 22	239
Chapter 23	249
Chapter 24	263
Chapter 25	277
Chapter 26	295
Chapter 27	313
Chapter 28	327
Chapter 29	343
Chapter 31	359
Chapter 32	371
Chapter 33	393
Chapter 34	413
Chapter 35	435
Chapter 36	459
Epilogue	464
Authors Note	467
Book Club Guide	468

THE PRESENT

Chapter 1

Chiffon muttered to herself as her footsteps tapped onto the payment. "I can do this. I can do this. I'm going to knock 'em dead." This was her best, and perhaps only choice. Why did she doubt herself? She continued to walk with a brisk stride toward the high-end, all-glass skyscraper.

She hesitated at the curb and watched a hoard of workers pass her like a swarm of bees to honey. Her start date finally arrived after an exhaustive round of interviews. You name it; she did it, competency tests, phone screenings, and an entire day of in-person interviews. She'd won everyone over; so much so, she received an offer on the spot. It happened fast.

This new job had to work out. There was no turning back now. Her head shook back and forth. Did I accept this role too fast? she fretted. Something had been gnawing at her insides as if it might be too good to be true, but it was too late now. She would stop this ridiculous nonsense.

Within recent weeks, she relocated to her hometown of Chicago. She had been in Atlanta for the past three years.

However, recent circumstances prompted a swift departure. After a tedious search, she found a humongous condo in a high-rise building on the North Shore. Her lips upturned just thinking of her new place. She loved being home again, familiar landmarks, favorite restaurants, and life-long friends.

Her eyes soon clouded over with a familiar, dark, brooding emotion. She shook it off, refusing to allow herself to go there again. Her stomach sank at the recollection. Plenty of time for that later, as always. That man was imprinted onto her skin as if a tattoo artist decorated her body head to toe. She finally accepted it. It wasn't possible to get away from her own damn skin. She gave up the attempt to ignore cruel reality months ago.

She shivered and rubbed her hands over the blanket of small bumps that coated her arms. Would she ever get him out of her system? It was as if he'd secured permanent residence in her heart. No matter the hurt, she couldn't shake him off. Her nights were spent tossing, turning, longing for him. Those hands, those eyes, and his incredible tongue all over her... "Unt umm!" she cleared her throat as she felt smooth warmth creep up her legs landing at her center. Shaking her head rapidly, she continued her brisk stride. This torture had to stop.

Staring up at the massive glass building and back down to the entrance, she inhaled deeply and pushed through the revolving door. Here it goes! She put on a smile and headed into her new life.

The new position was a dynamic one full of new enterprise initiatives to absorb. Over the next few weeks, she realized she was in her element indeed.

The end of her fourth week arrived, and her best friend, Tam, would be coming over to help her finalize her unpacking. She couldn't wait to see her again. Although they spoke almost every day, she hadn't seen her friend, her sister, in almost a year now.

She and Tam had been inseparable ever since Lit' Mikey put a frog down Tam's t-shirt in 2nd grade. Chiffon was there to help fish it out, and they bonded over how to get back at his little badass. Tam agreed to be her plus one at a company-sponsored "meet and greet" that evening. It would be a chance to mingle with the firm's partners and thank them in person for her quick hire.

Deep in reflection, a half-smile infiltrated her features. She felt proud of herself for landing this job with such expediency. She wanted to implement as many new initiatives as possible. Not only to prove herself but keeping busy equaled no extra time to think. In that department, she needed all possible help.

She dove into the various emails in her inbox, but as always, about 20 minutes in, she began to reminisce. So often, visions of him danced through her head. His broad, muscular frame, his smoldering, dark sensuality, his soft lips, and those damn eyes. Oh, how she missed him.

She shook her head. "Stop it!" she ordered herself and then almost jumped out of her skin when her cell rang out in a loud chime. Her left hand went up to her chest as she retrieved her cell from her pocket. Her phone didn't ring very often. She only provided her number to individuals whom she could trust.

She peered at the phone, an unknown number. Here we go again, she thought. Someone had been calling her new number periodically since she got it, not uttering a sound. She considered it could be her ex calling, but that just wasn't his style. Besides, he would never force himself on her without making sure she knew it was him. This clown was just playing on the phone. She hated to change the number again, but she would if she had to.

"This is Chiffon. Can I help you?" Silence greeted her on the other end.

"Hello?" she muttered, feeling a familiar frustration creep up her spine. This calling and just breathing was getting old. She'd had enough. Again, nothing on the other end.

"Who is this, please? Do you have anything to say? I'm sure you've figured out you have the wrong damn number by now!"

She tried a new tactic and said, "Please stop calling me. This is my new number. You are harassing the wrong person." Still, all she heard was breathing.

She rose to her feet, "When are you going to stop calling this number saying nothing? You creepy pervert!"

"Whenever you stop running from me," he spoke in a cool, even tone.

Time stood still around her. Hairs prickled at her nape. It couldn't be. Her mouth gaped open as her eyes widened. It was, that was, it was Joshua's voice.

How on earth had he found her? How did he, how could he get this number? Her pulse raced frantically. It had been months.

"We have unfinished business, my Sweetest. Resolution is in order. I deserve it, and I will have it, baby. Nothing good comes from decisions made in haste. Wouldn't you agree?"

She swallowed the lump in her throat. "How...how did you get this number, Josh?"

"From the moment we met, I've had your number." She detected the smile in his voice. "Surely you haven't forgotten it or forgotten me." he continued, "I certainly haven't forgotten you, baby."

She was positive she stopped breathing. She gripped the phone tighter. His voice sent electric currents throughout her body. How long had it been since she last saw him? Who was she kidding? She knew precisely how long, three months, two days, and about 12 hours since she'd spoken to him, felt him. A flood of memories threatened to overwhelm her. She trembled, finding it difficult to hold the receiver to her ear.

"I-I," she closed her eyes and tried to calm her pounding heart. This havoc he wreaked, she inhaled deeply, so unfair.

"Yes?" he prodded her on.

"I-I-um..." she couldn't find the words. She still loved this man so completely, and so desperately, although she had no right, she reflected bitterly. Silent tears escaped down her cheek.

"Fonn," he called out to her, both pleading and commanding. The way he uttered her nickname caused her stomach to somersault into knots.

"Did you think you could just leave me, just disappear on me? Did you think I wouldn't move mountains?"

"Please stop," she managed to get out.

He exhaled into the receiver, "The time has come for you to talk to me, baby. It's been long enough now. You have made your point."

"I, I…" No words would come—his voice, so deep, so smooth, so familiar. After a bout of silence, she decided to ask the only question she needed him to answer. She prayed silently and exhaled, "Are you still married, Josh?"

A lengthy silence ensued before he responded, "I need to see you, sweetheart, face to face."

More tears escaped the well she was trying to hold back. Eyes closed; she felt the sharp sting of daggers penetrating her heart. He was still married. If it weren't so, he would have told her. Not knowing what to say, unable to get her bearings, she pushed the disconnect button and turned her phone off. Damn him and the hold he still had over her. He knew it too - that cocky, arrogant bastard.

She drew in a deep breath. Did he know where she was right now? "Oh, my God!" She exhaled, frantically glancing back and forth around her office. Still quivering, she rose to her feet to shut her office door. Wringing her hands, she leaned her head back against it. Damn! She couldn't handle it, handle this. It was too soon. She needed more time away from him. She wasn't strong enough yet. She put her hands up to her temples. Dammit, he'd found her.

She accepted this new position under an assumed last name. She did everything she could think of to disappear. Still, he found her. Was she a fool to think he would let her escape? She often wondered if he'd gone back to be with Candice, his wife. The thought made her cringe inside.

A sharp knock startled her. She wiped her under her eyes to remove the moisture. She glared toward the door. She was primed for a heart attack today. Eyes blinking rapidly, "Come in," she invited, taking a few steps back. The door opened to muted sounds of various conversations mingled with phones ringing and printers whirling in the background.

Isaac sauntered in with a stack of papers. "Good morning, Chiffon," he smiled at her. "Here are the docs you requested while your assistant is out." He extended the stack of papers in her direction. "I thought I would drop them off myself so I could see how this week is wrapping up for you," as his smile brightened. Warmed by his presence, she almost smiled too.

Isaac Ruiz, the VP of Mergers and Acquisitions, appeared to be a nice guy. She liked him immediately after they first met. He wasn't hard on the eyes either. In fact, he was damn fine. She appreciated his willingness to aid her as she maneuvered the unchartered waters of the company. She felt an instant connection with him since day one, and it comforted her.

She smiled warmly, "Thank you, Isaac," as she took the papers he held.

He glanced at her quizzically, "Are you ok, Chiffon?" he asked, brows wrinkling.

She was startled as his words caught her off guard. Her lips trembled, "I... um, yes, of course, I am," she stuttered out a little too quickly. One of his eyebrows raised, and for some reason, she didn't want to lie. Maybe she just needed an impartial someone she could confide in. "No...no, I'm not," she said as she glanced from his eyes to her watch, then down to the floor.

He turned to close her office door, shutting out the noise. Clutching the papers for dear life, she remained immobilized, standing there like a child. He removed the papers out of her tight grip and sat them down on her desk. Turning toward her, he outstretched his arms. Not thinking twice, she walked in.

His strong arms encircled her, and she lay her head down on his shoulder. He patted her back. Boy, did he smell good. Cool, and crisp like a waterfall splashing on rocks below. "There...there," he muttered softly into her hair. God, it felt good to be comforted, to be in a man's arms again even though she didn't know this man very well. "Are you overwhelmed with the new job?" he said sympathetically.

She closed her eyes tightly, "I-I'm so sorry, Isaac. This is embarrassing. I don't know what to say."

"Shhhh... it's ok. I wish someone comforted me when I started at this crazy ass place. We all need a hug sometimes." She smiled to herself, unwilling to divulge the true cause of her distress.

After a long beat, he stepped back from her and held both of her hands in his. "If you want to talk about anything, I'm here. If you want to talk about nothing, I'm still here," he grinned boyishly.

"Thank you, Isaac. I get the feeling I will take you up on it."

"No problem, I'll be around. Reach out to me if you need me, Chiffon. I mean it." He embraced her again, squeezing her to him. What was that intoxicating cologne? She could have stayed right there in his arms, inhaling him.

"Will you be ok now?" he wanted to know as he looked down into her eyes.

"Yes, yes, of course, Isaac, thank you so much." She shook her head, a little embarrassed by the rather intimate encounter with someone she barely knew.

"Good girl," he said as he squeezed one of her hands. "Remember, don't hesitate." He then turned and departed.

Feeling better, she glanced at the open doorway. Isaac had a certain presence about him. He was tall in stature with a shock of dark, wavy, almost too long hair. Latino mixed with Afro-American, she thought. He was almost pretty. She tapped her manicured nail on the desktop and wondered what it would be like to run her fingers through his sexy, unruly hair. Oh, Lord! What was she thinking? She needed to stay far away from Isaac. She didn't need that kind of trouble.

It was just, something about him felt so cozy and so, so well..., familiar. She couldn't put her finger on it like they'd crossed paths in the past. If so, she would have remembered him. Maybe they were just meant to become friends. Lord knows she could use one right now.

She could tell Isaac carried a bit of a torch for her. On several occasions, she caught him checking her out, including the way he just tenderly comforted her. However, the last thing on her mind was another man or any relationship. Because, despite her protests, she knew she was still in one.

The rest of the day rolled by in a cloudy daze of meetings, calls, and emails. Glad to get home, her phone remained buried deep in her purse but she refused to look at it.

At a vigorous pace, she jumped into unpacking her home office. As she placed the last book on the shelf, she turned abruptly toward the front door. Although the music was blaring, she thought she detected a loud banging at her front door.

"Oh, my God!" she stood motionless. "Joshua?" she whispered to herself. Did he know where she lived? Could he be at her door? Not knowing what to do, she turned down the stereo and waited.

Part of her wanted to run to the door and jump into his arms, delighted he finally came for her. The other half wanted to hide and scream out how she would never get the chance to start over and forget. How did he get past the doorman downstairs? She was supposed to have the opportunity to accept or reject all visitors. She chose this building for security reasons.

She inched closer to the door. The knocking grew more intense. She attempted to calm down by closing her eyes. Should she open it? Blinking frantically, she contemplated calling for reinforcements. She approached the peephole but found it blocked. Her hand rose to her chest, trying to still her palpitating heart. A clamminess crept over her skin. She did not want to face him, not now, not yet, but the banging remained persistent.

"Who is it?!" she finally yelled out but no answer. She unlocked the door, snatched it open, and almost passed out from relief. Tam stood there with her arms crossed and lips poked out. "Oh, Tam!" she cried, rushing into her friend's arms.

"Chi-Chiffon girl. What's going on with you?" Tam returned her friend's hug, confused at the emotional display.

"I-I thought,"–

"You thought you would leave me out here knocking on this door forever. Girl, do you know what I had to do to get security to let me up to surprise you?" Chiffon released her friend and smiled with relief.

"I showed him photos of us as kids and blood samples and everything!" Tam grabbed at her bag and walked in, trailing the scent of wildflowers behind her.

Chiffon peaked out into the hallway and looked down both corridors before going back in, shutting, and locking her door.

"You don't know how glad I am to see you, Tam." She gave her friend a quick tour of the place. "This room is where you will stay," she said, as she pointed into the guest room.

Her friend looked around with a broad grin. "Real nice Chi," her friend used her childhood nickname. "This place is gigantic. I love it. I hope to spend lots of time here."

"I hope so too," she patted her friend on the shoulder.

Tam dropped her bags on the floor and plopped down on the bed. She patted the place next to her, motioning for Chiffon to join her. She sunk down into the mattress next to her friend.

Tam turned to face her, "I'm so glad you came back home. You look fantastic, Chi, and your place is da bomb," she laughed aloud. "I might never leave."

"I might never want you to," her voice darkened.

Tam stared at her, eyes narrowing, "Ok, what's going on Chi? You are obviously disturbed about something. I've been trying to call you all evening. You know, as you instructed me to do when I was on my way," as she shook her head in annoyance. "Didn't you get any of my calls or messages?"

She stared at her friend with apprehension. "I'm sorry, Tam. I..., I've been um, I...," tears burst from her eyes. In shock, her friend grabbed her and held her close.

"Chi, my God! What's going on with you?" her voice laced with deep concern. "What the hell happened since yesterday?"

She released her. "It's that dammed Josh, isn't it?" her friend seethed. "What happened now?" Tam rose to her feet in disgust. She knew Tam did not like Josh very much, and she'd never even met him. It's one of the reasons she never shared the entire sordid story with Tam - just bits and pieces.

"He found me, Tam," as she shook her head in disbelief again.

"You mean he's here in Chicago?"

"Well, I'm not sure where he is exactly, but he called me today. It seems he's the caller who has been holding the phone over the past several weeks."

"So, Josh is your stalker guy? No way. How did he ….."

"He finally spoke today and instructed me to stop running from him."

Her friend put her hands up to her temples, "That damned Joshua! Well Chi, the good news is, he may only have your number. We don't know if he knows exactly where you are."

"Hmmm," Tam had a point. She felt herself start to relax a little. If she ever dealt with Josh again, she made up her mind that it would be on her terms, not his.

"So, what, you turned off your phone?" Tam questioned after hearing the rest of Chiffon's troubling day.

"Yes," she nodded.

"So, where is it?" Tam headed out of the room.

"In my purse. Why?" Chiffon followed her.

Tam retrieved her phone and held it up. "Turn it back on, Chiffon."

"What?" as she shook her head in disagreement.

"Chi, look at you. You're a wreck."

"I-I thought you just said I looked great," she smirked at her friend.

"I'm not talking about your outside Chi. I'm talking about your inside," as she looked her up and down. "It is clear you have not been doing well, and you're turning into a bag of bones."

"What? Ok, now I'm confused, she squinted. You don't even like Josh."

Chiffon took a seat on the ivory, leather love seat and mindlessly twisted a lock of her hair. Her friend came to stand in front of her, "But you love him. Look, Chi, I didn't want you to go through the same kind of hell I went through with Terry. "Terry was single," she admonished her friend.

"Yeah, single and womanizing over several states. He didn't end up being worth everything I went through, but I don't think it's the same with Josh. I think you should at least hear him out. Maybe he's right, and the running should stop."

She stared up at her friend in complete disbelief. She couldn't stop running. Didn't Tam understand? If Josh ever caught her, she would be done for. "I will take it under advisement." She rose to her feet and grabbed her phone – leaving it off. "Let's eat!" she smiled.

"Always a perfect answer to any question, she laughed. No more talk of Josh."

They spent the night eating, reminiscing, decorating, and giggling, but Chiffon still had a restless night. She tossed and turned and memorized the number of ceiling tiles again. Maybe one day, she would sleep peacefully again. Maybe.

Chapter 2

They breezed through the next day. Tam created one of her culinary masterpieces for lunch. They watched two of their favorite movies, Beaches and the 1st Transformers.

She loved having her friend nearby again. "We better start getting ready, don't you think?" as she stood in her office, breaking down an empty box. She did a quick once over of the room. It looked good. All crisp and clean. Professional chic. Everything was either black, white, or red. There wasn't much left to unpack. Progress was king.

Tam headed to the guest bathroom, and Chiffon went into her bedroom. She chose her outfit as if she had backstage passes to see her favorite artist. She showered and put on a blush-colored chiffon cocktail dress with a black satin sash. It fit her in all the right places. Her black and rose-colored heels matched to a tee. After applying her makeup and putting her hair up, she felt sexy.

Her friend knocked on her door and, upon opening it, did a slow cat-call whistle. "Damn, you clean up nice."

She laughed at her friend, "You don't look half bad yourself." Tam looked great in her black mini dress with gold and black heels. She always admired Tam's fair skin color and brown eyes. A no-nonsense beauty who never took herself too seriously. Chiffon loved that about her. "Let's go, girlfriend," as she grabbed Tam's arm and headed out of the building to hail a cab. Chiffon wanted to drink freely tonight. No driving!

They arrived amidst other guests and were ushered into a large reception hall. It was dimly lit with many tall, round tables with crisp, white tablecloths. She glanced at how the chandeliers twinkled and cast a dim glow throughout the space. The wallpaper had an aged antique look. Classy.

A tall woman with a clipboard asked for her name and pointed down a list with her finger until she located it. "You're at table 1." Then the woman did a low whistle to herself. "You're sitting with the big wigs," she uttered under her breath.

"The big-wigs?" Chiffon repeated, confused.

"Please follow me," she said as she led them through hordes of people standing around laughing and drinking.

They closed in on a table where two impeccably dressed distinguished caucasian gentlemen sat with their guests. The men rose to their feet as she approached. "You must be Chiffon." The older of the two held out his hand, and she shook it.

"Yes," she smiled.

"Finally, we meet. I'm George Baker, and this is my wife, Brenda," as he motioned to the lovely lady next to him. Brenda smiled and waved at Chiffon and Tam.

"Hi Chiffon, I'm Maxim Reynolds." She shook the other man's hand, realizing she just met the owners of the agency.

"This is my friend Raceil," as he turned to his guest. Raceil stood up and shook her hand as well.

"It so good to meet you all. I didn't know I would be sitting with you this evening." She then smiled again at everyone and said, "And this is my friend Tam. Tam, these are the owners of the advertising firm, The Reynolds and Baker of Reynolds and Baker." Tam flashed her warmest smile. Good girl, Chiffon thought to herself as they sat down.

"Well, Chiffon, we have heard nothing but wonderful things about you." She lightly smiled as she eyed the four remaining empty seats at the table. Would they have more guests?

"Thank you," she mused. "I love the job."

She exhaled and found herself relaxing a bit. They small talked and ate hors d'oeuvres. She found out more about how the company was established and the vision of the owners. She hung onto every word of the story Raceil shared with the group, when she suddenly felt a hand rest lightly on her shoulder. She turned and saw Isaac smiling down at her.

"Hey," she laughed with surprise. Isaac and his date sat down.

She introduced Tam to him, and her friend's eyes lit up. Isaac chose to park himself in the empty seat right next to Chiffon. She smiled warmly at him. The group continued their former banter. She eyed the two empty seats at the table directly in front of her and wondered again who had yet to arrive.

She laughed aloud at something Isaac said and caught his 'guest' giving her a quizzical look. Oh geez, she thought just as one of the girls from accounting came up to say hello to everyone. She wanted to introduce Chiffon to some people.

She rose to her feet and motioned for Tam to come with her, but she could tell Tam only had eyes for Isaac, his date be damned. Chiffon smiled to herself. She could see them as a nice pairing, but there was the matter of the woman seated next to him. Isaac didn't seem to be very into his date, so Tam might have a good chance.

"Come on, girl." Chiffon reached for her friend, and they headed off into the crowd.

Before any introductions could be made, someone asked Tam to dance, and she disappeared. Chiffon smiled and waved goodbye to her. Now, this was fun. It was so nice to have something enjoyable happen for a change. Clutching her purse tightly, she thought she heard her phone buzz, but that was impossible, as it has been off for some time now.

Wait staff walked around with varieties of delicacies and wine. There had to be at least 100-150 people in the crowd. Over their heads, she could see the night sky glistening with bright stars through the large wall of picture windows. Two birds caught her eye as they appeared to dance, fluttering together near the clear pane—what an adorable sight.

She made her way to the powder room then walked around introducing herself to more people. She never had a problem mingling. She wouldn't meet everyone tonight but as many as she could muster. She vowed to keep it stress-free tonight.

Her pretty heels started to become a little uncomfortable, so she decided to head back towards her table and take a load off. The heavenly aroma of roasted beef and sautéed potato whiffed through the air as she tentatively took each step. Through the clamor of voices and rhythm of the music, her stomach grumbled.

She almost made it back to her table when she wondered how inappropriate it would be to take off her shoes and walk back in her bare feet. She stared down toward her now throbbing feet. "Why these shoes again?" she said to herself and shook her head with a slight grimace.

When she glanced back up, all movement in her body halted. The warm blood seeped out of her veins as if the suction from a vile was attached to her soul. Her eyes riveted. There was a new man sitting at her table. She knew that silhouette anywhere. Dear God, Almighty! It was him. Her Joshua sat right there next to George. He literally stole her breath. How dashing he appeared, in a dark, tailored suit. Jesus, how could she forget the visual impact of witnessing him in the flesh. Her heart peeled open and ached.

She closed her mouth, which gaped open of its own accord. She blinked, trying to decipher if her imagination was running wild. Did she miss him so much she conjured him? He couldn't really be there, could he? She stood stark still, not knowing what to do next, should she run, and which way?

He suddenly laughed aloud at something, which erased any doubt. How did he get here? How was he already acquainted with her colleagues? It didn't make any sense. Oh, God! What could he be saying about her? Nothing about this was good.

She turned to eye the dance floor until she located Tam. She could walk backward, ease back into the crowd, snatch these damn shoes off, and run. She managed to take one step back when his gaze turned, met, and locked on hers. Everything else dimmed around her. She saw him and only him.

She lost her grip, literally. Her purse, newly collected business cards, and anything else she held in her hands exited her grasp and splattered to the floor. Isaac noticed and came over to her, stooped down, and assisted her as she unsuccessfully tried to pick up the contents of her purse with shaky fingers.

"What would you do without me?" Isaac flashed a smile her way as he continued to pick up the items.

"Thank you, Isaac."

Everything replaced, he reached out his hand to help her to her feet. She smiled weakly.

"You ok, Chiffon?" he asked as she took his hand.

Josh then came to stand directly in front of her. She had no words - held captive in those eyes of his.

"I might ask the same question," his greenish-gray eyes penetrated hers. Unprepared, her bottom lip trembled. She swallowed, as the connection between them was still as strong as ever, like no time had passed at all. The pounding in her chest grew stronger. She couldn't tell if he was angry, pleased, annoyed, or what.

With raw nerves, she started, "How did you…" – then her voice trailed off.

Isaac glanced back and forth between the two of them. "Chiffon, do you remember Mr. Abbott?"

"Mr. Abbott..." she repeated, barely audible.

"Yes, we know each other quite well," Josh answered for her. She stared daggers into him. She didn't understand what was happening here, but she knew Josh had a huge hand in its orchestration.

"Ms. Hartwell and I were in Atlanta when she worked for an organization I had an affiliation with." His lips curved upward slightly. "Hence, I knew she would be a perfect fit here," he said, as he spoke to Isaac, but his eyes never left hers. She nodded, unable to say another word. What did she just hear? What in the hell was going on? His slight grin turned into a full-on smile as he placed a scorching hand on her bare shoulder near her neck and led her back to her seat. Isaac sat back down as well, and Josh held out her chair for her.

"It's good to see you again, Ms. Hartwell," as he leaned in close to her ear. "Umm, thank you," she said as she and realized everyone was watching her intently.

"Chiffon, glad you're back," George called to her, breaking the awkward silence. "You remember Joshua Abbott, don't you? You two have a previous acquaintance, correct?" Before she could answer, he went on, "He recently joined us as a senior partner at Reynolds and Baker."

"He what?" she cried out, unable to stop herself. "I, I don't understand," she said, shaking her head in dismay.

"I made them an offer they couldn't refuse," he stated, with his eyes never leaving hers across the table. Speechless, she found herself lost in those magnificent eyes. He was spinning his web around her. Transfixed, she stared without blinking. Apparently, everyone found him quite humorous, everyone but her.

"He's right, Max interjected, still laughing, but we are the fortunate ones. Josh brings an expertise that will take us to the next level and beyond," he beamed.

"The timing was truly amazing," George chimed in. "Everything came together with such expediency. We didn't plan to branch out this soon, but this is a fantastic move for this company. Your family is iconic. We are the fortunate ones indeed," he nodded at Josh.

Josh grinned, "I never let opportunities of a lifetime pass me by. This was clearly a move I had to make. I never let anything, obviously meant to be a part of my future, slip through my fingers. Sometimes your destiny is obvious, wouldn't you all agree?" as his gaze remained locked on her.

Chiffon cleared her throat and took a deep breath, unsuccessfully trying to slow her rapid pulse. No one answered, and an awkward silence engulfed the table. Isaac saved her, yet again, by asking about timing on an upcoming press release. She had to stay calm. She didn't quite understand what was going on but knew everything she'd believed so far had been a bold-faced lie.

She inadvertently started to twist a lock of her hair, a nervous habit when ill at ease. He looked at her hand, and then to her eyes and back again, so she immediately dropped her hand into her lap. He knew the effect he was having on her. Didn't that bastard need to blink? Didn't he care that everyone could clearly see he was fixated on her?

"Um, I'd better get Tam," she announced, rising from the table. She didn't wait for any reactions, just retreated into the crowd.

She had to get out of there. She felt the hot tears well up in her eyes. No matter what she tried, she couldn't get away from him. He haunted her thoughts in the daytime, her dreams in the nighttime, and just when she thought she had a bit of freedom from him, he appeared in the flesh.

She needed some air, some time to compose herself. Her new management must think she belonged in the psycho ward. Thanks, Josh, she thought sarcastically. Wait a minute – he was her boss too now, right? Jesus, take the wheel. She let out an exasperated breath.

Walking down a long corridor, she opened the first door she came to, where another smaller banquet room appeared. The lights were off, and she was glad. She wiped at a few stray tears. She would become dehydrated from all the tears she'd shed over this man. How could he do this to her, blindside, and ambush her like she were some sort of... of... toy? "Ok, Chiffon, I'll just trick you into believing you have control over your own life," she spat out, mimicking his deep voice.

She hated him, hated him as much as she hated the sense of relief she felt knowing he never let her go. "Damn him," she choked out tremulously. She refused to let herself bawl uncontrollably like she wanted to. She had to keep her composure.

Plopping down at one of the empty tables, she took off her damn heels. She rubbed her feet and placed her shoes on a nearby chair. With a light push of the glass, she stepped out onto a nearby terrace. The warm, gentle breeze made her loose, soft curls bounce around her head. The riser was low enough to faintly detect the scent of freshly mowed lawns but high enough to see the tops of the adjacent, low-level stone rooftops.

She closed her eyes and held onto the railing. For a fleeting moment, she thought about jumping. Better to be dead than to suffer and be played like a fool. She took short, ragged breaths. Light perspiration dampened every inch of her skin. She pressed her palm against her breast to calm herself. She had to relax, or she would never make it through the remainder of this crazy night. What kind of life was it to love someone you could never have and could subsequently never escape?

She knew she was thinking crazy. Of course, she wouldn't jump. For one thing, she wasn't up quite high enough. She would probably just land on the awning, break her damn back and end up in a wheelchair. She laughed aloud at her observation of her luck.

"Can I be in on the joke – or am I already a participant?" His deep, rich, familiar voice tumbled through her insides. She turned and let his full magnificence fill her gaze. She unwittingly inhaled his familiar fresh rainwater scent, a masculine, powerful force of beauty, a strong elegance of a man. His face she should slap.

Chapter 3

"How did you find me Joshua?"

His eyes narrowed on her. "How did I find you? You're asking the wrong question, baby. What deserves an answer is why you needed to be found in the first place? Didn't you realize I would make every effort to locate you? Vanishing without a trace was simply an invitation."

The little hairs on her neck prickled, her fight or flight reflex on high alert. He rubbed over his chin and widened his stance.

She pointed a manicured nail at him, "How could you set me up like this?" she hissed. "You just made me look like a complete fool, Joshua."

"Hummmm," he murmured, "Now we can safely say we match. You think you look foolish?" his brow crocked. "You think you're the one wronged? It seems to me you appear to have landed quite well, my sweet. You are the unbelievable conniver here, not I." His eyes narrowed to slits. "When I consider the meticulous preparation on your part. How did you manage to disappear with such expedience?"

Before she could reply, he continued, "I knew you would never answer my calls, but when I showed at your place, just a few days later, it was empty. Every single trace of you, gone," he shifted, "It was as if you never existed. So efficient you were. Had you always planned to leave me? Was what we had just a joke to you?" his voice rumbled. "You've been angry and stopped speaking to me before, but never something so drastic. This was no impulsive decision. It had to be pre-planned."

"What?" she cried out in exasperation. She couldn't believe he thought she was the villain here. "How could you imply...? I never played with your..." she quieted as his gaze turned to steely ice.

"Did you think there would be no repercussions, and I would allow you to just get away with it?" he seethed, brow-raising.

"Allow me?' She took a shaky step back. "I didn't have some evil plot against you." When his eyes narrowed on her, she spat out, "You think you're the only one who can do exactly as he pleases? What I decide to do and when and where I decide to go is my choice, not yours!"

"Oh, I beg to differ," he inched closer. "The first thing you need to do is drop the 'y' on the word 'your'. Once we pledged our love to each other, every single subsequent action automatically involves the other person." He stared at her quietly, waiting for her to respond. His eyes hardened, "Go ahead, deny it, I dare you. Tell me, with each other, we aren't absolutely affected. You feel it in your bones right now, don't you?" he dared her.

She wished there were a bit more room on the terrace. She wouldn't waste time denying it. She knew he was right. "Dammit Joshua! I was trying to protect myself," her voice rose an octave.

"From what? From me?" he asked in disbelief.

"You're the biggest threat to my sanity, Joshua!"

"Oh, I haven't threatened you yet, sweetheart."

She recoiled at his tone. How dare he invade her... her... well, everything. She blinked cautiously. "So, you found me just to punish me, for this um, for… for this!" she motioned around herself.

He didn't respond.

"Am I about to lose my job now?"

He stared at her with a slight smirk. He's enjoying this, she thought. She was about to jump out of her skin, and he was enjoying every minute. When he remained silent, she asked again, "Will you take my livelihood away as some sort of retaliation? Is that your plan?"

"Oh, contraire mademoiselle," he finally spoke, "This situation is more about your retaliation, not mine."

She noticed, out of the corner of her eye, what appeared to be the same two birds from earlier, but they were no longer dancing. They seemed to be fighting over something the bigger one held in its mouth. She swallowed hard and returned her attention to Josh.

"So, you managed to become a partner in this company to make me suffer for leaving you? I never imagined you could stoop so low."

In continued silence, his eyes blazed into hers. "Say something, dammit, Joshua!" she shrieked. Without this job, she didn't know how she would make ends meet. She'd already made it clear she would never be his mistress. He had to be there to bring the pain, she surmised.

He cocked a brow, finally stating, "Is the security of your job what matters the most to you right now, Fonn? Is that the first thing you're considering upon seeing me again?" He stood just inches away from her.

She swallowed. She couldn't retreat further because the railing was at her backside.

"Of course not. A million things are going through my head." She hesitated, "But I... I need this job, Josh. I gave up everything to be here."

He smiled a slow, languid smile at her. "Yes, yes, you did. I can't think of a single thing you didn't sacrifice."

When her eyes widened, the corner of his mouth raised slightly, mocking her. "Put your mind at ease. I'm not here to interfere with your job." He leaned closer still, and her breath caught. His heady masculine scent stroked her insides. It should be against the law what he did to her senses. Dammit.

Her heart thumped out of her chest. The intensity of the emotion she felt for the man, made her feel weak, barely able to remain standing. How did she manage to ever leave him? Damn his handsome, arrogant ass. She swallowed and exhaled. This is exactly why she ran from him. She had little resistance to the chiseled, hard muscle that silently called out to her. Not to mention those damn eyes of his; they always seemed to stare into her soul and read her thoughts no matter what she said. He knew it too. She knew that he knew that she knew that he knew.

With his eyes locked on hers, he'd already touched every part of her. Huskily, she breathed out, "What are you planning to do to me, Joshua?"

"What do you want me to do to you, Fonn?" They stared at each other in silence. She wanted him to do everything to her, everything he always did, and much more.

He didn't blink, daring her to answer him.

Breaking the silence, she exhaled, "I know you're upset —"

"Upset doesn't even begin to describe how I feel, Fonn."

She swallowed again. All she could think of was how much she loved and missed this man. They shared such a wonderful bond and friendship once. Clearly, the man looming over her could not be considered a friend. Lord, why was love so complicated and painful? Why? She found it all so unfair and so very cruel.

Her fight already left the building, but she had to muster up some strength from somewhere, or she would lose herself again. She was this close to begging him to make her lose herself again. She inadvertently shook her head. This had to be how his wife, Candice, felt, why she wouldn't release him from their marriage. Both multi-faceted and multi-layered, being tangled in Josh could be mistaken for a delicacy.

She recalled the loving connection she and Joshua shared and what a wonderful addition he'd been to her life. He fit right in, bringing with him hope, excitement, and challenge. But even more, he offered an all-consuming love. They spent almost every waking moment together.

Hand in hand, they explored new venues, sang off-key at concerts, took in art galleries and theater. Although his hectic schedule made it difficult, he always made time for her.

When she had to cram for her Project Portfolio Certification, he helped her study, sometimes calling to spring pop quizzes on her. How he made the time, she still didn't understand, but she felt grateful. He listened to her when she needed to vent and made countless unsuccessful attempts to just listen and not advise. He wined her, dined her, and gave her beautiful gifts. With him, she felt precious, special, and cherished. He was her everything. Yes, he was before the truth slapped her in the face.

His haunting eyes burned into hers. She couldn't believe he stood right there. She could reach out and touch him now, when up until a few days ago, she thought she'd never see him again. No man had ever gone to such lengths to be with her if being with her was his goal.

She started to speak but felt his single finger rest solidly against her lips. "Hush now, don't speak," he demanded. "Not a word." He held her gaze for a lingering moment, then lowered his finger. "I have moved heaven and earth to find you. You covered your tracks so well, it was quite challenging to secure an audience with you again, but challenges motivate me."

She glared at him, "I can't believe what you've—"

He lifted her chin, "I told you to remain quiet."

"I know you didn't just…

"Shhhh. His finger rested over her lips once more. "Stop talking and listen," he said. She quieted.

"I don't give a damn what you thought you discovered; you should have never disappeared on me." He shook his head in disbelief. "I still can't believe you up and left everything we had. Everything we were building."

He began to say something else but struggled to find the words. Clearly overcome by emotions, he pointed toward her and choked out, "You will never understand what you have put me through, woman." Her stomach clenched when she detected moisture in his eyes. She never witnessed this level of vulnerability from him, and it was breaking her already broken heart.

Oh my God! What had she done? What had she solved by running away? He was right. Her behavior had been borderline irrational and no doubt unfair. So raw and so real, his pain. It coiled itself around her and squeezed at her heart. She realized he wasn't there to hurt her; he was there because he was hurt.

"Oh Josh, I didn't even consider the magnitude of –"

He raised a hand, "Please, I need to say this to you. She quieted once more.

"Your behavior has been unacceptable and unjust. I simply didn't deserve it, Fonn. I thought we'd become much closer than you making such a final decision in confusion and haste." His voice crumbled, and her heart seized. "I wouldn't treat an enemy the way you have treated me, treated us. You never even gave me a chance to explain. You ran, after you promised you would never do that again. We already endured a difficult separation in this relationship. This is not the first time I've had to hunt you down."

She remained silent, waiting for him to get it all out.

"This time, not only wouldn't you answer calls, but letters were returned, emails rejected. Hell, I couldn't even get you to Facebook or Tweet." She smiled faintly at him then. He knew she didn't tweet. She couldn't feel more foolish, though, like a reprimanded child.

"I don't care what I might have suspected of you. I could never vanish without at least confronting you. How easy it seems for you to have left me behind to start your new life. Not a word nor hint, he faltered. Didn't I, didn't we mean anything to you, Fonn?"

She wrapped her arms around herself, shaken by his emotional plea.

"Didn't I rate a goodbye at the very least? You may have been confused about everything else, but you had to know the depth of the love I had for you. There were no lies or omissions regarding our love. I thought you knew, Fonn."

Remorse coursed through her. She turned away to face the view. She didn't know what to say. She never thought she would get called out on her shit. He used the term love in the past tense, 'the love I had for you.' Was he saying he no longer loved her?

She had been so wrapped up in her own pain, her own anger, she didn't consider his. At the time, she doubted he even experienced any pain. He represented a debonair playboy without feelings – a form of low-level varmint who deserved whatever the fallout.

Now, she felt ashamed of her rash behavior. "You're right," she turned back to face him. "I-I shouldn't have, I mean to say, well, I could have handled everything better, Joshua," she lowered her head, feeling hot tears stream down her cheeks. Hurting him wasn't intentional. His feelings ended up collateral damage in her effort to save herself.

She never wanted either of them to end up like this. He had the power to turn her world upside down, more so now than ever before. Her entire future lies in his disappointed hands. Situations like these, when her impulsiveness trumped rhyme and reason, filled her with the most regret.

His eyes softened on her, and he wiped at the next tear that escaped down her cheek. She let her eyes close for a moment, enjoying the feel of his touch against her skin. "I didn't know what to believe, Josh." She gazed at him, "I may have overreacted," she admitted.

"The situation I put you in was unfair, he acknowledged. Believe me; I'm doing everything in my power to make it right again for you, for us. I will make it right, Fonn, but I'll never get it accomplished if I'm spending precious time tracking you all over the country. He folded his arms, "My time and focus will be utilized more efficiently from this point forward because this is ending right here, right now." Her brow raised as it started to sink in, what Josh wanted, needed, and expected. He wanted blind faith. This man explained nothing but asked for everything.

Before she could ponder the next thought, his lips smashed onto hers in a kiss meant to rediscover and reacquaint. His arms encircled her, and she melted into him. Instantly she was gone to pent-up desire and yearning. How she'd missed the feel of him, the smell of him, the taste of him. His soft lips and expert tongue had her entire body humming a sweet love song of renewal.

His tongue collided with hers more fiercely. Could she take this man at any cost? A low groan escaped his throat. "Fonn, my sweet, sweet, Sweetest." He leaned back, breaking the contact between them. Liquid fire coursed through her veins as she struggled to catch her breath.

"Dammit, woman, I want you to think about everything I said tonight and everything my lips just made you feel. My mouth has many more plans for you, sweetheart. I have missed every part of you." She gasped as he kissed her forehead and let his lips linger. To prevent herself from grabbing him, she gripped onto the back railing with both hands.

"I'd better head back before things start looking more suspicious," he decided. "I think we were quite the spectacle earlier."

"No thanks to you," she mumbled.

A slight grin came to his lips, accompanied by a glint in his eye. "You will thank me later." He brought his mouth down close to hers again and breathed out against her lips. "When you participate in an action, you automatically become a participant in its inevitable consequence. I am your consequence," he said as he stepped back, eyes gleaming.

She smirked, then frowned. She was caught somewhere between disbelief and dismay at his actions. She needed more answers right now, "Why Reynolds & Baker, Josh? There had to be a less embarrassing way for you to accomplish this, she waved her hands up, to make me um…"

"Collaborating in this agency was a business move, but you brought me here, Fonn. I will be wherever you are, so running away from me is pointless," he said tersely.

"So, you think you can just come here and..."

Her response was interrupted by the soft, wet feel of his tongue pushing into her mouth again. "I could kiss you all night." he breathed into her. He nibbled, sucked, and ravaged her mouth, leaving her panting for breath. He pulled away from her slowly and held her bottom lip between his teeth, tasting her until it fell from his grasp. "I am here to get you back, Fonn. You belong with me, sweetheart, and I'm not leaving this company or this town without what I came for." She let out a moan dropping her head onto his shoulder.

Regaining her wits, she took a step back. How easy it was for her to get lost in him knowing nothing changed. He was still married.

"How did you find me, Josh? How did you manage to infiltrate this company? I can't believe what you've done."

With a slight grin, he explained, "My expertise will take this company to the next level in sales and branding. Decisions were made to grow our marketing/acquisitions arm. I would have purchased into Reynolds or a firm exactly like it in this quarter. However, to answer your question, you are the main reason. I ran the numbers on every company where you had 2nd or 3rd interviews scheduled. My family agreed that buying into Reynolds was an excellent investment choice."

It's You

Her eyes squinted, "So, you had a detective following me? You couldn't possibly have known where I applied or my interview status." She couldn't believe him. What about her sense of privacy? What a joke leaving him had been. All this time, she thought she was escaping Joshua. What a fool. Nobody escapes Joshua. Not unless he allows it.

A wry smile came across his features. "I didn't need a detective."

"So, I only secured this job offer because of you?" She thought back to the exhaustive interview process. She would be pissed to find she didn't need to work that hard. "You were behind it all." she deduced in disbelief.

"Management wasn't under my instruction, well… he hesitated, your name did come up. I let them know of your excellent work in Atlanta. The rest was up to them – and of course, you. To avoid any suggestion of impropriety, I recused myself from final decisions. Then, fate intervened."

She shook her head in suspicion, "You were willing to risk me declining this job, and still you bought in? You partnered in a company based on your gut feeling or some hope?"

"That is what faith is, Fonn – the substance of things hoped for, the evidence of things not seen. You should try it sometime." She winced at his biting words.

"I was pleased when you accepted the role, as it ensured my path in front of you again."

All she could do is continue to shake her head in disbelief.

"No more running from me, from us, Fonn. I need to know you are all in. You might not appreciate or cosign my tactics, but you know everything I've done has been out of love for you. You believe me, don't you?"

"I don't condone what you've done. You crossed the line in so many ways, Josh, but yes, I know it," she nodded. She never doubted his love for her. She knew it was real. It was everything else that remained at issue.

"Good, then understand this as well. Trust between us is not optional. It is not a yes or no checkmark for you to pick at random. You need to trust me, period. I want you to offer it freely."

Her brows creased. What in the hell did that mean? Was he planning to take it if she didn't give it to him willingly?

"We love each other, Fonn. We can get through anything if we are together. Not apart, together. You," (he pointed to her), "And me," (he pointed back to himself), "Together." He reached out and pulled her into him, encircling her in a solid embrace. She could feel the rapid pulse at his neck. She inhaled his wonderful scent and fought back more tears. What an awful position he had her in.

He backed up and studied her eyes without speaking for a while. A tidal wave of emotions stirred between them. Their gazes held a million words and just as many promises left unspoken. "Give me a chance to show you I'm for real, that this love is real. You can trust in me, Fonn. You can trust in us again."

He placed his hands on her shoulders, and she felt as if her legs would give way.

"Give me a chance to prove it to you." It came out like a question, but she knew it was a command. He pressed his lips against her jaw and rubbed his face up and down her cheek, letting her feel the light stubble prickle against her skin.

He gazed at her for a moment, then turned and headed off the terrace just as suddenly as he appeared. She stared at his retreating frame until he disappeared into the dark banquet hall. Speechless, she wondered when she'd be able to breathe again. He looked just as good walking away as he did on approach.

She took a deep breath and placed a hand against her throbbing chest. She still didn't quite understand how he managed to accomplish all this under her nose. He obviously had resources she wasn't aware of. They didn't talk about his family much, so she had no idea what kind of wealth he came from.

He'd said, 'An excellent investment choice,' as if referring to a blue sky or a green forest - very matter of fact. Damn, did she know this man at all? He didn't even mention how he would deal with his wife. Nary a word, he just expected her to step out on faith – believe in him completely. She wished she knew how to do that.

The only other man she tried blind faith with failed her miserably. Never again, she vowed. She watched her mother wait in vain for her father to come back to no avail. Her father's betrayal still hurt. She turned again to face the night sky.

She shut her eyes and thought again of his lips against hers, holding him again, inhaling him, although briefly, penetrated to her core. How could she give him what he wanted? He was still married, and for all she knew, he wanted to have his cake and eat it too – like a bull in a china shop – the cost be dammed.

All the while, she would be tied in knots, waiting for a divorce that might never come. He couldn't make her deal with that kind of treachery by force. She bristled. It was her decision, not his. As much as she cared about him, she refused to participate in this song and dance of a relationship for good reason. He needed to come correct or not at all. She vanished to prove her point. How cruel of him to show up after all this time wreaking havoc yet, still unavailable.

Also, what footing did she have to compete with his wife? If she went back to him now, she would just be his… well, his mistress. She remained steadfast and immovable in her vow, in the pledge she made after her father cheated on her mother. She refused to knowingly take part in an affair. Never. Exhaling deeply, she wondered what led him to devise such an elaborate plan. That energy would have been better spent getting a damn divorce! She took a deep breath and rejoined the party.

Chapter 4

Once inside the terrace doors, she slipped her feet back into her tight ass shoes. Upon entering the reception hall, she headed straight to the dance floor. She found Tam and motioned her off immediately. Her friend sensed the seriousness of her demeanor and approached. "What up girl? This party is fantastic right? Are you having a good time?"

"He's here, Tam!"

Her friend's eyes widened, "He is? He who? Not Joshua?" Tam looked around to see who Chiffon was referring to.

"Yes, Joshua. He's sitting at our table, he bought into the company, he wants blind faith, he expects me to…"

"Wait a minute, hold up." Her friend stopped Chiffon's tirade, holding up her hand. "Do you mean Joshua is physically here at this function tonight?"

"Yes! Not only is he here," Chiffon turned her friend around to face the table, "He's sitting right there at our table."

Tam blew out a low whistle. "Oh my!" she stopped short, "Lord have mercy. Girl, that's Joshua? I mean, I've only seen pictures, but what a specimen he is in the flesh, she panted. Girl – um… um… um… damn and damn!" she shook her head, mesmerized with the view. Chiffon rolled her eyes at her friend.

"Oh, I'm sorry Chi. I know you don't need to hear that right now. What are you going to do?"

"I don't know."

It's You

"You said he's part-owner now?"

"Yes, he bought a stake in the company."

"Wow! Does anyone know what's going on between you two?"

"No, I don't think so. Isaac may have noticed something but not for sure."

"Damn girl, your man went and bought into the company you work at; to get close to you again, just to be in your space. He's serious. He's not giving you up. It's obvious; he must really love you. That is just too damn sexy!" she clapped her hands together.

"Tam!" she snapped her fingers at her friend. "I need you to focus! Help me get out of here, please. I can't stay; I'm too shaken up. I'm afraid I have already made a fool of myself, and Joshua is still married. He didn't come back to me divorced. I don't care what he does. I can't claim him as mine. I wish he would just leave me alone. I need to find a life without him."

"I don't think a life without him is much of an option. Do you? Maybe hear him out. See what he has to say for himself."

"What is it with you wanting me to talk to him all the time? Besides, I did – I'll tell you all about it later. Right now, I need you to help me get out of here," she choked up, hot tears approaching fast. "Please, Tam. My world is falling apart again."

The loss of their relationship had been more than painful. The finality was pure anguish, something a-kin to despair. How could he think leaving him was easy? It was anything but. Without him, nothing felt worth it. She missed him so much that it hurt even to remember; no eating, sleeping, just endless sorrow. He had no idea.

"Ok, Chi – I'll get you out of here." She grabbed her hand and headed toward the table. Joshua's eyes fixated upon her as she returned. He didn't even try to be subtle. Anyone at the table could feel the electricity, the tension between them. It was so thick, so overpowering, a knife could slice through.

Tam spoke out to the group, "Thank you so much for having us tonight. Unfortunately, we must cut it a bit short. I hurt my ankle on the dance floor and need to go soak it immediately."

Chiffon gave her apologies, gathered up her belongings, and turned to leave with Tam. She purposely did not make eye contact with Joshua. He never uttered a word, but she felt his eyes searing into her even as she waked away.

They couldn't move fast enough. Outside, they hailed a cab. She kept looking back at the entrance thinking he would come and try to stop her. He'd made it clear; he'd come to get her back. She was positive her exiting abruptly wasn't a part of his overall plan. Her friend draped an arm around her shoulder, and their heads touched. She didn't want to talk, and thank God Tam knew her well, no pressure.

When they arrived at the apartment, Tam went into the guest room talking on her cell phone. Chiffon drew a hot bubble bath, removed her clothes, and slipped into a robe. She took her phone out of her purse and stared at it. When she turned it on, she had 17 missed calls and 14 voicemails.

She didn't check them. She placed her phone on the charger and headed for the tub. She slid down in the hot water and closed her eyes.

Soon there was a soft knock at the door. "Hey Chi," her friend called out through the closed bathroom door. She cracked it open a tad and said, "I'll be back a little later. Are you going to be ok?"

"Where are you going?"

"Mike wants to talk, so I told him I'd meet him for a drink."

"Ok, then have fun. See you later."

"Try to get some rest, Chi. We'll talk more tomorrow, ok?"

"No problem, Tam, go on. I'll be fine. Are you going to be all night?"

Her friend hesitated.... "Umm, I don't know. I don't think so."

"Ok, well, grab the spare keys out of the bowl at the door and tell Mike I said hello." Chiffon glanced at the clock on the wall. It was already past 10 pm. What a night, the water felt so good. It was just what she needed. She let her body relax and closed her eyes again. She must have drifted off.

Her eyes fluttered open when she heard what she thought was a soft knock at the bathroom door again. "Tam, girl,

I thought you were long gone by now," she uttered aloud, closing her eyes again. The water was still hot and delicious. She heard the knock again. "Just come on in, girl! I can't hear what you're saying through the door." She moved the bubbles up under her chin. The door opened. "So, what happened, did Mike piss you off or cancel on you?" She heard nothing. "Tam? What's wrong?"

She opened her eyes, and Josh stood over her. No mistaking him. He loomed over her, silhouetted by the candlelight dancing around his frame. "What the!" she shrieked and jumped to her feet, splashing bubbly water everywhere. Unaffected, he began unbuttoning his shirt, never taking his eyes off her shaky frame. She put her hands over her breasts to cover them. Her body tingled all over at the very sight of him. "What are you doing here? How on earth!" she said in utter shock. "You can't be here, Joshua!"

"Oh, but I can, baby, and I am." A sinister grin took over his features.

She shook her head in disbelief. "You know where I work, and you know where I live. You are just too much. I need to get dressed! Get out of here!" her heart raced. When he remained standing there, she shouted, "You are stalking me!"

He smirked, "Such a brilliant, little girl. I'm surprisingly good at it, yes? We can add it to the myriad of things I do well." He let his shirt drop off, exposing his muscled frame. His t-shirt came off in one quick motion. Her eyes transfixed on the ripples of his washboard abdominal muscles. Her hand rested between her legs and the other across her breasts. She couldn't cover much with an arm, but at least her long, solid nipples weren't visible.

"How is this poss…where is Tam?" she exclaimed. "How did you get in here? What did you do to her!" she swallowed hard.

"Tam is fine, don't worry about her. She's a smart girl; she let me in on her way out." She shook her head in disbelief, not understanding as he proceeded to unbuckle his belt.

"What are you doing?" she shrieked. "You, you can't be in here!"

He chuckled with cynicism.

She glared around wildly. Completely naked, she needed her towel. His eyes followed her hungrily as if she were on the menu for tonight. She stumbled out of the tub. "Joshua!" she yelped as he dropped his pants and stood only in his boxers. Every single tight muscle of his chiseled frame calling out to her. She flushed with embarrassment when she felt her nipples getting more solid under his gaze. He happened to be standing on the towel she placed on the floor of the tub. The other rack holding dry towels stood far behind him, out of her reach. She slowly backed herself up against the farthest wall.

"You know what, baby?" he said in a quiet, controlled voice. "For months, I tried this your way." Her pulse raced as he came closer to her wobbly frame. "I've waited and waited for you, but you refuse to get it. I also tried calling you again tonight to let you know I was coming here for you, but again, you didn't answer."

"I - I…" her words trailed off as he smiled a wicked, seductive smile. "You want to know what I'm doing here? I will tell you. I'm done waiting for you to come to your senses." The smile dropped from his face. He stood toe to toe in front of her. She quaked under his penetrating gaze. His heady scent of sandalwood, with a heaping dose of anger, infiltrated her nostrils. Her breath came out in short pants.

"Put your hands down. Let me see what I have been missing so desperately," he said gruffly.

She didn't move. He seemed irritated, not himself. She didn't want him like this.

"Put your hands down," he demanded. She held her ground. How dare he invade her privacy like this. Just who did he think he was?

"Fonn," he let out an exasperated breath. "I said let me look at you," he spoke in a softer but still no-nonsense tone. "I need to see you, all of you. Stop this hiding from me. Why are you so afraid of us, of me? I think you have always known there is no real marriage between Candy and me."

His head crocked slightly to the side as if something suddenly dawned on him. "My non-existent marriage is just an excuse." He peered closer to her. "Now, you feel justified to remove yourself from this relationship and give up on us." He shook his head, "You're so afraid I'm a womanizer like your father; facts don't matter? Well, I'm not him. What else can I do to convince you I'm serious about you? I don't want anyone else," his hand shook out to emphasize each word. She blinked rapidly.

"I see your strength, Fonn, but vulnerability is also a strength. Loving me hasn't been easy and I'm sorry I hurt you. You must understand I will never leave you like your father did. This is not your childhood revisited." Her eyes widened. He leaned in closer, "If you recall, you're the one who left me in this scenario baby. I didn't leave you."

He reached out to caress her face, "Everything is ok now. We can put an end to the pain we've both been suffering."

Her head shook again, tears welling. "Our situation is anything but ok, Josh. What could be ok about a mess that started with a lie and ended the same way?"

His eyes turned into icy metal. "I have had it!" He held up his hand. "I'm done with this nonsense. You're about to stop fighting me right now," he stated succinctly.

"Listen, to me, Josh, please." She wanted to reason with him, to appeal to his common sense. This could not work between them, not like this. He continued to stare at her, unmoving. Her nudity made it difficult to make a serious plea. Joshua wanted her like this, she thought; completely dependent on him for everything in her life. It was fine to leave her with no job, no morals, no clothes, or resistance.

It was unfair of him to come at her when she was at her most vulnerable. Eyes cemented; they held each other's gaze. She felt caged and trapped. It was clear; he wasn't going anywhere, and he was certainly not letting her leave. Without much choice, she lowered her gaze and cautiously dropped her hands. She could feel the water dripping down her naked body, splashing to the floor beneath her.

"So damn beautiful," he mumbled out as he reached out to brush his finger across one of her nipples. It stiffened at his touch, and she let out a quiet whimper.

"Josh, please don't do this to me. I'm begging you."

"Shhhh," he directed. "Enough with this hide 'n' go seek." He stepped closer, "No more fighting me." His lips brushed against her cheek. "Turn around and put your hands up on the wall."

She stared up at him in disbelief, "What?"

"Turn around," he demanded. "Do it now," he instructed. She felt the hairs prickle all over her body. Who did he think he was? She hesitated for a moment, but they both knew she had little recourse. She did as she was told and placed her hands up and flat against the wall. His hot breath suckled at her neck, planting scorching, wet kisses there. She closed her eyes and felt herself drowning. No matter her fight, her body was sinking underneath the stormy sea that was Joshua.

"You are mine, baby—all mine. We are one. You know it. I know you feel it." His lips burned kisses along her shoulder. He cupped her breasts from behind her and massaged them with expert precision.

Her body arched backward, and she felt his solid manhood beneath the thin layer of his boxers. Her breath caught in her throat as he twisted and stroked each nipple.

"Please, Josh," she purred against his assault. "Why can't you just leave me alone? Please let me get over this thing with you. Hot tears spilled from her eyes.

"This thing?" he repeated gruffly against her hot skin, continuing to suckle at her flesh.

"You do not belong to me," she squeezed her eyes together, "It's unfair to act as if you do. Please, I don't want to love you, Joshua." Trying to steady herself, she used one hand to grab onto the empty towel rack to the side of her.

"But you do, he murmured, so stop fighting me," he breathed against her damp skin. She bent her head back to rest on his shoulders as her body involuntarily responded to his expert caresses. "You think you don't want to love me, but it's not true. You want to love me darling and you want me to love you. I want to hear you say it." His hands slid down the sides of her body as he bent to trail kisses down her back.

The fire began consuming her now, and shivers engulfed her. Her need for him fired in her belly. How difficult not to melt into him, not to give in.

Every part of her that didn't want him wanted him desperately. Of course, he was right; she didn't want him to go. Not ever. Having him back in her arms surpassed her good sense. She removed her hand from the wall and turned around to face him. He got down on his knees and placed her thigh over his shoulder. Moving in, he teased her most sensitive bundle of nerves with his tongue. Tentatively, he tasted her. "Sweet baby," he muttered. She grabbed his head and pulled him closer. Receiving her cue, he added more pressure, lapping and twirling his tongue up and down her center. "Love you, and I love this baby he whispered as he continued to suckle. You are so sweet, so delicious."

"Joshua, oh my," she let her head fall back against the wall. Her hand grasped his head, pulling him closer still. It had been so long, and she missed him, missed how wonderful he made her feel.

Sensations coursed through every inch of her body. "Oh yes, baby. So good!" ripped from her throat. She felt her body begin to vibrate against his tongue. When he ultimately slid two fingers deep inside her, she detonated. A guttural cry escaped her lips, and she tightened her clutch on his head. Her body spasmed in ecstasy. Pure, delicious bliss is what she felt. He lapped at her as though she were his last meal.

When he righted himself again, their eyes locked in silence. Torturous aftershocks rocked through her core, and she squeezed her legs together.

"There's only you and me, he whispered. You believe me yet, baby?" He smiled his beautiful smile at her, and she was gone. He could do whatever he wanted. Under his intense gaze, she was putty. It was difficult to remain calm. He slid his boxers down, and his beautiful, solid staff stood at attention. She stared at it in delight. His lips upturned, and he reached out and lifted her onto his hips. Her arms encircled his shoulders, and her legs folded around his backside. He turned and leaned her against the wall, positioning himself at her entrance.

"I'm going to take you now, Fonn," he groaned. "You are so deliciously wet for me," he breathed out huskily. "Is it ok, baby? Can I have you now?" he trembled. She felt him rub himself slowly against her clit. "God, I have missed you, woman." His eyes squeezed together.

No fight left, she murmured, "Yes, yes, please. Do it now!"

Without hesitation, he entered her, pressing her back against the cool, drenched wall. His lips overtook hers again. Inch by inch, she took him in, tightening her muscles around his hard cock. She cried out his name as he picked up the pace filling her steadily and repeatedly. "I do love you, Joshua," she whimpered.

"I know, I know." He lifted his gaze to meet hers. I had to have you, baby," he rumbled as he pumped away inside her, filling her with what she longed for. "I couldn't wait another damn day to feel your tight walls around me again," he huffed. Sometimes slow, sometimes fast, hard delicious strokes were taking her to the edge.

"You are all mine, Chiffon Hartwell, and I'm not asking permission anymore," he grunted. He knew how to make her crazy with desire. He squeezed her ass cheeks, and she clutched onto his muscled arms. Nothing in this world compared to Joshua, his tongue, his hands, and her love. Her body bounced up and down rhythmically, meeting each deep thrust. He lowered his head to begin to suckle on her nipple.

"Baby!" she cried out, feeling a familiar electricity start take over her senses. Harder and harder, he pumped delectably into her heat. He whispered naughty things as he hammered away inside her.

Then, when she heard him pant, "Nothing has felt this fucking good in my life. Your hot juices surrounding me. It's all I want, all I need. There's no place I'd rather be." She completely lost it. Her fingernails bit deeply into his flesh as her world shattered around her. She collapsed, crying out as the intensity overtook her mind, body, and soul. Unbelievable.

Soon he joined her in climax, bellowing out as he exploded deep within her. He pulled her securely against him. They held each other for what seemed like an eternity while continuing to gyrate and throb from the volatile orgasms.

Finally, he let her sweat-soaked body slide down off his hips. "I missed you, sweetheart," as he planted kisses all over her face.

"I missed you," as she held him close to her. Could she believe he was all hers now? He took her hands in his and bent down to kiss her slightly parted lips again.

"Tell me what you want, Fonn. Anything. I'll give it to you. Just stay with me, baby, trust me and stand by me."

He dropped to his knees and pulled her body to his, hugging her lower half. She felt his tongue swirl inside her belly button, and she yelped. He chuckled and rose to his feet. "Some things never change," as he looked down at her adoringly.

"You mean it, Josh? You will give me anything?" her eyes searched his.

"Yes, of course. Anything you desire. If it's in my power."

"I want," she hesitated, and he raised a brow. "I just want you. It's all I've ever wanted."

A look of surprise appeared on his face, "You already have me. I'm here."

"No! I want to know I'm the only woman in your life. I want you to myself, for myself. If you can't give that to me, I don't want anything else." His brow furrowed.

"I mean it, Josh. I can't survive on just bits and pieces. I'm not willing to share you. It's as simple as that. If you think I'm going to fool around with you while another woman calls you husband, you are mistaken. I'm not fighting your wife over you. I deserve better. It's very painful knowing you married someone else and..."

"Shhhhh," he quieted her. He slid his hand under her chin and rubbed a thumb over her cheek. Gazing into her beautiful brown eyes, it hit him; just how much he loved this woman. She didn't understand. She already had what she asked him for.

Closing her eyes, she never felt so vulnerable, helpless, and utterly possessed by someone else. Some of him would never do. It would never, ever be enough for her.

He bent down to pick up a towel and proceeded to dry himself off. "I would never ask or expect you to share me," he solidified.

"No, but you let me believe I was the only one in your life."

"You are."

"I'm not!" her voice rose. "We keep coming back to the same place, and it's becoming a broken record."

His brow raised. "So, let's take it off repeat, Fonn. The time has come to change our tune together."

Chapter 5

Folding her arms, she exhaled, "We're in complete agreement, Josh, the time for a significant change is upon us." Taking in her angst, he murmured, "I apologize Sweetest," his t-shirt slid over his head. "After I found the scattered papers on the kitchen floor, I knew exactly what prompted your departure. You never," he paused, visibly trying to keep his tone down, "You shouldn't have seen that. She is delusional."

They moved into her bedroom and sat down on the bed. Silence hung in the air between them. He glanced around, "You have a nice place."

"Thank you," she said quietly. "I never expected you would see it."

Hurt clouded his eyes, "Look. I know this hasn't been easy for you. I know you read the letter, which I'm still not sure how you found since I threw it out like the garbage it was."

"I didn't rummage through your personal items Josh if that's what you're insinuating. A crumpled-up picture was on the floor. I wanted to see who it was and why you balled it up for trash—"

Hard lines appeared around his jawline, "I owe Candy nothing! She must have been smoking something. She damn sure wasn't about to move in with me. I spoke to her a few weeks prior to the letter arriving about visitation. She was talking out of her head then, so I ended the conversation.

"Enough about poor, little disillusioned Candice. The essential point here is, if you want me, you must get a divorce. Plain and simple. I will not continue going through this hell with you. It's too much to ask. She has to be out of the picture if you want me in the picture."

His brow furrowed, "Ok, that's fair, baby, but I'm dealing in a hostile environment, and I want, no," he corrected, "I need you by my side. No more being apart for us," he said vigilantly with his eyes flashing at her.

"Explain," she requested.

"We are going to accomplish all of our future achievements together, side by side. You can stay here in Chicago, or you can come back to Atlanta, but we will be together - live together from this point forward."

"You want us to do what?" she shrieked.

"You heard me, woman. You can come back home to Atlanta and move in with me, or I will come here, but no more being apart. I mean it, Fonn. No more. I'm done chasing you."

"But, but... you're still married," she stammered.

"I will file. I don't need her approval to have her served. I will handle my end. Your job is to decide where you want us to live."

"Seriously?" she asked in dismay. "What about your position in Atlanta? Don't you have to be there for work?

A slight grin came over his face. "Sweetheart, haven't you figured this out by now? I don't have a regular j-o-b. By the time I turned 18, my father had me well versed in international business operations. I worked for and learned from him throughout college. Over the years, I have gained holdings all over this country as well as abroad. I am not stationed at any one location.

I reside wherever I choose and go where and if I'm needed. Ownership means I hire people to be there daily. I stay apprised regarding operational matters. I have a board of directors when I can't be there in person."

She moved her head back and forth in dismay. "But wait, I thought ..."

"That's one of the things I love so much about you, Fonn. You didn't even realize it. I'm independently wealthy baby. I work by choice, not because it's necessary. As I told you previously, I come from, as they say, old money."

"Yeah, but I thought you were talking about your family's money, not yours."

"I have managed to make my own fortune, sweetheart. I have been blessed."

"Fortune?" she repeated and shook her head again in disbelief. "Independently wealthy," she repeated. "So, you're saying you don't have to work?"

He smiled genuinely at the love of his life. Her innocence was so appealing, so untainted. "Money is not an issue in my life. You are my issue, sweetheart, not dollar bills."

She squinted at him, not believing they never had this conversation in depth. "So, all this family money came from advertising?" she inquired, still not quite understanding what he was trying to convey.

"No, not advertising exactly. I dabble in advertising. They, meaning my family, have been in electronics and the mergers/acquisitions arena for over 75 years. I've wanted to branch out from them, but I guess it will be impossible to disengage fully. Wealthy families tend to be very controlling of their offspring. I don't conform to that paradigm, so I made sure I would never have to go to their coffers. I can live wherever I choose. If it's with you, I don't care where we go."

She studied him closely. She wanted to believe him again. So much. "You have a wife and a baby, and I'm just supposed to wait until you get divorced one day." She removed her hand from his. "She doesn't want to let you go, Josh."

"Listen, baby. I explained the situation I'm in with Candy. I told you everything before you disappeared. On the financial front, I made sure the prenup Candice signed was iron-clad. The settlement between us won't be an issue. This is what I've been trying to convey. Filing for a divorce has never been the problem. I never wanted or planned to "stay" married to her. The real issue has always been timing and Candy and my son's safety. I will not allow him to be hurt by the insanity his mother brings."

It was a bit unsettling to hear him say, "my son". She still had to come to terms with the fact he considered Candice's child his own.

She knew Candice had been in a volatile relationship with her baby's father, and that's what prompted her to strike a deal with Josh. "What if they are never safe from him, Josh? What if this Terrance guy never wants to let go? I can tell how much you care for this baby. Would you stay married to her and live in a lie in perpetuity or until the child turns 18? No wonder she is so confused. You have served as her guardian all these years. She thought you would be there to protect her always, especially once you married her. I'm starting to see things more clearly."

He gave her a thoughtful look and said, "I realize I have played a major part in this mess, and I'm going to handle it."

"How do you think us moving in together is going to work for Candice? If she freaked out about you dating me, so much so that there was a confrontation between us, what's going to happen when she finds out we live together?" she folded her arms.

"I don't give a damn what Candy thinks about my life, he said gruffly. Especially given the crap she has pulled. I'm not going to lose you, not over this, not over anything. This," he motioned around the room, "Won't ever happen again."

Her brow creased, "So you think moving in together will solve all of our problems?" she couldn't believe it.

"When do you think this cohabitation should take place?"

"Well," he said thoughtfully, "I want us together now and forever more," without blinking, he stared at her.

Could he be serious? What a huge step to take in what was already a mess of a situation. "You don't have to move in with me, Josh, to prove your love. I know you care about me."

"You still don't get it. I'm not angling to just be a boyfriend. That's for children. I want to sleep with you in my arms every night and to wake up like that every day from now on. You are going to be my wife one day when we can do it properly. I want it all with you," he paused, "Everything."

Tears threatened. Boy, did he know how to melt her heart.

He took her hands in his. "I want you to understand you are not alone in your feelings for me. I love you just as much, probably more than you love me, baby. There's nothing I wouldn't do for you, for us. Tell me what else you want? I will make sure you have it, but you need to return the favor." She felt her already shaky defenses begin a slow descent around her again. She believed there was nothing he wouldn't do all right. He traced his finger over her bottom lip. Damn him. He knew the effect it had. Her eyes fluttered closed.

When she reopened them, she blurted, "I don't know what to say."

"It's pretty simple, baby," he said with a hint of humor in his voice, "Say yes. We both know we belong together." He traced his finger over her nose and then her lips again. He sang softly to her, 'The time has come for us to stop messing around, 'cause don't you know that I like having you around in my life. Oh, baby – he sang an old school jam to her. My heart is yearning for your love. You can't keep running in and out of my life.'

How torn she felt between her love for him and her ability to trust him. She never resided with a man before, and she always expected it would be with her husband, not somebody else's. Where was the actual marriage proposal? Did he just want to shack up with her, and for how long? She sighed to herself; how could they possibly discuss marriage when he wasn't even divorced yet?

A million questions besieged her; where would they live? What happens after the divorce? What about his son? Were they officially getting engaged? She couldn't believe she was even considering this. What about her job if she stayed? She would be living with one of the owners of the company. Nobody would take her seriously anymore. Did she want him to have that much control in her work life? Their relationship would have to remain a secret. He wouldn't like it, but they couldn't tell a soul—

"I'm flying back to Atlanta tonight," he interrupted her thoughts. "I dropped everything to come here to find you. I have business to take of. I will return on Monday."

Not paying attention to him, her mind continued to race with a million thoughts. She liked her new job, her new co-workers; she wanted to be respected there. Would she have to lie to them to keep their trust?

"I'll pick you up after work Monday."

"What?" she said in surprise. "Pick me up? Where? At Reynolds?"

"I can expect you to be there Monday?" he asked.

"Yes, but you plan to pick me up? Where? Like inside the building?"

He smiled at her hesitantly and raised an eyebrow. "Sweetheart, my office is on the 15th floor in the executive suites; I don't think it will raise suspicion if I'm in the building. I own it now, remember?" he said smugly.

Her mouth dropped. His arrogance was unreal sometimes. "I still can't believe you did that, Josh. How intrusive you have been. There had to be another way. I still can't wrap my head around it," she said irritably. "You just think you can do whatever you want when it suits your purpose. Damn the wreckage in your wake."

He stared at her for a long moment and turned to walk into the bathroom to grab the rest of his clothes.

"Would you really like us to discuss acceptable and unacceptable behavior, Fonn?" He zipped and buttoned his slacks. "Do you want to do that right now?" he irritably asked as he walked out of the bathroom to stand in front of her. He glanced down at her and started buttoning up his shirt. "You should have never left me like you did either, but what's done is done, isn't it?" he said wryly.

She rose to her feet. "You are such an arrogant, smug bastard. You think it's perfectly fine to exercise this… this complete control over me," she fisted her hands in frustration as she looked him eye-to-eye. He looked down at her, gawking at her defiance.

"I want you to take me seriously, Joshua," she demanded.

"Oh, I take everything regarding you seriously. You can believe that sweetheart." They stared at each other, both a bit miffed.

He broke the silence, "What did you pick up from all this Fonn?" He folded his arms across his chest, crossing his leg at the ankle.

"What are you talking about?" she asked in irritation.

"Just what I said – tell me what you have learned from the situation we find ourselves in today," as his hands motioned around them.

"The lesson, hmmm…well let's see," she placed her finger against her forehead as if deep in thought, "Oh yes, I've learned to perform a background check on everyone you meet, else you could contend with a great deal of dishonesty," she raised her voice in disdain.

A smirk covered his handsome face, "Touché, but, let me help you dig a bit deeper." She raised her brow. "First of all, it's a very bad idea to disappear without a word and go on to ignore my attempts to reach you," his voice tinged with anger. "It accomplishes nothing and just pisses me off. When I'm pissed off, I don't react well. You have a nasty habit of running when the going gets tough. You're going to discontinue that behavior with me from this point forward," he stated unblinkingly.

"Is that another threat Joshua?" her hands fisted at her sides.

He flashed a dazzling smile. "Promises, threats, suggestions – call it what you will." Narrowing his eyes, they raked over her t-shirt clad body, the change in temperature between them apparent. She had a sudden urge to cover herself more.

"Well, you can't force me to be with you if I don't want to," she added.

"Have I ever forced you to do anything?" he asked with a hint of menace in his tone. She didn't respond. "Have I?" He baited her. She didn't know how to answer because he hadn't 'forced' her per se to do anything, but he made it difficult, no, impossible, to escape him.

"You forced me to see you!" she said in frustration. "You won't let me move on with my life."

"So that's what you're calling this?" he said with disgust.

"Yes," she answered, "Yes, an attempt."

"So, you never wanted to see me again? Ever? You wanted a life without me in it?"

"Yes, I…I mean no. I just didn't want to hurt anymore," she puffed.

"And how has that been working out for you, Fonn?

How much did your pain recede from your antics? All you accomplished was making us both hurt."

Well, that felt like a slap to her face. She winced.

He shook his head, "You should be thanking me."

"What?" she said in amazement.

"My arrival here has made it possible for you to face your true feelings, but never have I forced you to do anything you didn't want. Have you already forgotten? Not 30 minutes ago, your legs were wrapped around me as you screamed my name in ecstasy. You said you wanted me deeper inside you, how it was where I belong. Were you lying to me, Fonn? Did I force those words out of your mouth?" She flushed all over.

He stepped closer to her. "Did I force myself inside you, or did you grant me permission and open wide for me like you always do?"

She gasped, and her mouth dropped open. "Joshua!" She cried out. She couldn't believe him.

"Secondly, it is pointless to try to leave me. It would better serve you to talk to me about your feelings because I will track you down wherever you go, and I will do whatever it takes to get you to be reasonable. I don't give a damn what you call it. I don't consider it forcing you because we belong together. You need to face it and accept it as I have. I know it like I know my own name. Stop trying to pretend something that is, isn't. It will only prove futile and rather exhausting for us both. I have lost countless work hours because of this already," he ranted.

She was about to reply, but with the way he glared at her, she decided against it. She kept her mouth shut for this chastisement.

"I advise you never to do anything like this again. If you do, I will make it my life's work to dismantle anything you build up to keep us apart. I'll do it because it's difficult to live, to even breathe, without the person who has your heart, Fonn. I have yours, and you have mine. Don't ask or expect me to stay away from you because I can't. I tried, and I can't, so I won't. A flimsy, meaningless piece of paper will not keep us apart. He leaned in towards her. You are stuck with me and everything that comes with me."

"Oh really?" she interrupted sarcastically.

"Absolutely, you automatically signed up the moment you let me taste that." He pointed to her sex, "And it is all mine. Every delicious drop of it belongs to me just like you do." Her muscles clenched together down there, tightening at his mere suggestion. She couldn't believe he was speaking to her like this, and it was so damn hot she almost leaped up off her feet and jumped him.

"Nobody will ever take it away from me again, including you, Fonn," he continued, "When I'm deep within those hot, tight walls, you know it as much as I do." She gasped and covered her mouth with her hand again in shock.

"You know me, probably better than anyone else in this world. Many have tried and failed to take away what belongs to me. Suffice it to say, it didn't end well," he said briskly.

"You don't have to keep threatening me, Joshua. As you can plainly see, you are not in the boardroom; you're in the bedroom," she railed.

He didn't skip a beat, "I don't tolerate it in business or in pleasure. That is why I'm here now. This," he motioned around the room again, "Ends today." He stuffed in his shirttails and sealed his belt.

She shook her head, "Surely you don't expect me to just —"

"Enough, woman!" He raised his voice and his hand up to stop her. She was effectively startled into silence. Her heart thumped in her chest. "I'm not fucking around with you, Fonn. All the bullshit and games end today. I have humored you long enough. I'm not some toy you can pick up and put down at your leisure. We are doing things my way moving forward."

"I…" she started to reply but shut her mouth abruptly when his eyes narrowed on her. Wow, she thought to herself, Joshua never spoke to her like this. Irritation flapped about him like a cape in a wind tunnel. She couldn't understand it, he was extremely upset, but she only tried to preserve a family, his family. Maybe she would have chosen differently if he would have been honest with her at the beginning. He could have saved them both a lot of heartaches. She acted with the limited knowledge she had, limited because of his damn secrets.

He glanced at his watch, exhaling deeply, "Unfortunately, we must finish this later," he said softly, changing his tone completely. He didn't want to fight with her. In fact, if he only had the time, they wouldn't be spending their last moments arguing. They would be doing exactly the opposite.

It wasn't easy for him to be extremely stern with her, the dismay in her beautiful eyes nearly broke him. It was necessary to let her know to let her know he was damn serious about this.

"I've got to get out of here, baby, or I'm going to miss my flight. I'll call you when I arrive."

She nodded, suddenly feeling an overwhelming sense of sadness. He made her so angry, but she didn't want him to leave.

His soft lips grazed her cheek, her forehead, then the corner of her mouth. "I can give you what you want, Fonn," he whispered against her skin. "I will give it to you, I promise, but you have to trust me." He stepped back, stared into her sad eyes, and sighed, "Yes, I went through the motions, but I have never been married before, Fonn. Never truly, baby." She felt those damn hot tears at the back of her eyes again. He glanced again at his watch. "My driver should be outside." He picked up his wallet and keys off the nightstand near her bed.

"Wait a minute, Josh, a question before you go."

"Yes, baby?" he stopped and waited.

"How in the world did you get Tam to let you in here?"

That infamous smirk took over his features again. "Unlike you, sweetheart, Tam understands true love has to bend the rules a bit. She knows how we feel about each other and figured we needed a chance to talk."

"I'm going to kill her," she muttered under her breath.

"Don't be too hard on her. She only wants your happiness. Just as I do."

"Uh-huh," she said aloud.

He smiled and kissed her lips again, sucking at her bottom lip. She moaned. Their lips parted, and he gently rested his forehead against hers. "I love you, baby. I'll call you later. I'm out." With that, he departed.

She heard the front door close in the distance. She would give Tam a real piece of her mind. How very deceitful to trick her that way. She left her vulnerable and literally naked with a man who had too much control over her willpower. How does Josh convince all her friends to trust him like that? I mean, they are willing to present her on a silver platter as if a hungry man would not devour her. She made a mental note to keep him away from all her girlfriends.

She yawned and rubbed her eyes. She lay down across her soft bed and fell into a deep sleep. She opened her eyes briefly to the beep of a text from Joshua, telling her he landed safely, he loved her, and he would call her later.

The next morning, she floated deliciously into consciousness to the aroma of eggs, bacon, hash browns, and biscuits. Her stomach growled. She left the party in such a hurry last night; she missed dinner altogether. That damn Tam, she smiled to herself. Food wasn't going to work this time, but she was famished after the crazy night she'd had. She grabbed a quick shower and changed into some jeans and another t-shirt.

She walked out into the dining room, where the sun blazed through the open windows. Tam loved the fresh air. She'd opened all the blinds in the living room and cracked each side window open. A light spring breeze gave life to the sheer window treatments. They swayed to the sounds of the city below. The dining table held two plates piled high, along with orange juice, milk, and ice water. She glared at her friend sitting there with her lips poked out.

"Don't you dare give me that damn sad face, Tam. I'm going to kill you." She sat down at the dining table and grabbed up a piece of delectable bacon.

"Please, don't be mad at me, Chi," her friend pleaded. "I made breakfast for you guys."

She started to say quite a few things, but her friend held a hand up and stopped her. "Chi, let me explain first, please, then I'm at your humble mercy."

She smiled cautiously at her friend, "Josh is not here, Tam. He had to catch a flight." Shock registered on Tam's face. "Don't let that stop you. Go right ahead and explain. I'm listening."

"Please eat the rest before your food gets cold," her friend motioned to her plate, "I'll tell you everything." Chiffon dug in.

"So," Tam began, "When I got downstairs, I saw him. Joshua was sitting in the lobby. I was stunned to see him. I recognized him immediately; he was the prettiest thing in the vicinity." Her eyes took on a dazed, reflective look. He changed into tan shirt and trousers, adding tan and brown shoes. Damn! I had to stop Chi, if only to get a better look at him. His eyes even appeared tan." Chiffon rolled her eyes.

"He spotted me just as I was walking nearby. He rose and called for me to join him. He said he only wanted a quick minute. I told him you would kill me if I spoke to him without your knowledge, but he told me you would kill me if I didn't. He is very convincing, Chi."

"Umm," she nodded and took a sip of orange juice, her eyes never leaving her friend's.

"Well… she went on, he told me just how awful the last few months have been, all the mistakes he'd made, and how much he needed your forgiveness. He apologized for any pain he caused. Dammit, Chi! Those gorgeous eyes teared up."

"Say what?" Chiffon asked skeptically

"Those amazing eyes transfixed me. I witnessed such raw emotion for you. He loves you, Chi. He made me believe. I know you refused to hear him out. He needed to meet you on your turf. After a few minutes, I was leading him up to the apartment. I knew you would be mad, but I think you two deserve a chance despite my better judgment. He spoke from his heart. He convinced me if I didn't help, it would take weeks or possibly months to accomplish what he felt could be done in a night."

"Ok, fine, I get it, Tam, but you didn't even warn me. I thought it was you opening the bathroom door."

"I know Chi, please forgive me. He wanted to talk to you privately, and I knew you wouldn't speak to him otherwise."

Chiffon squinted at her friend, "Well, he didn't just want to talk. I was dripping wet and naked!"

"I'm so sorry, Chi. I didn't think it all the way through, but I knew you could handle yourself."

She couldn't believe her friend; she'd ended up putty in his hands just like her. Damn all his charm and charisma. No one was safe when those clutches sank in. Suddenly, just like that, she was no longer upset with her friend. She knew the wand the man wielded, and lucky for Tam, she wasn't the object of his affection.

"Forgive me, Chi," her friend pleaded, eyes starting to water. "Your happiness means everything to me. I apologize if I messed up," she sniffed.

"It's ok Tam," she got up from her seat and hugged her friend. "I know you love me and want me to be happy."

Her friend grabbed a napkin off the table and dabbed it under her eye. "So, what happened last night? I see you are still in one piece."

"Yes, one precarious piece." she smiled a half-hearted, unsettled kind of smile. She unloaded the details to her and almost giggled at her friend's jaw-dropping gasps while she described the night.

"Wow! Tam put her hand up to the side of her head. That damn Josh," she shook her head. "What are you going to do?"

She shook her head wistfully, "I don't know, but I'm tired of fighting a losing battle. She sat back down. They write songs about the ardor that consumes. I understand it now, and I don't even remember how to stay away from him anymore.

When our relationship began, I tried to enjoy our time together without taking it too seriously. We had a lot of fun. It was lighthearted fun at first, but he just kept chipping away at my barriers, proving himself worthy. Then it happened. One day, I was completely smitten with Joshua Abbott.

He represented my one safe place in this world. We got along so well. I believed I found my soulmate." She smiled introspectively and then quickly frowned, snapping back to reality.

Tam eyed her with compassion. "You thought you found your happily ever after."

Yeah, until this woman comes raging at me, telling me, he was her husband. I've never felt so embarrassed and ashamed. She let me have it, and nothing has been the same since.

And just when I began to have hope for us again, I find a letter detailing more lies. She wrote how he promised her he would let me go. She wanted to know why he didn't drop me like all the others.

"What?" her friend gasped.

"Yeah, I felt like a fool again. I was done. With nothing more to say, I left everything behind. I ran for my life because I refused to break up his marriage."

"Why didn't you share any of this with me before, Chi. I'm your best friend, and you shouldn't have gone through it all alone."

Chiffon grabbed Tam's hand across the table, "I couldn't even breathe, Tam. I had no voice. I didn't want to relive it. I was a depressed, miserable, hot mess."

"I don't judge you, Chi. You know that. I could have been your voice. I could have come out there and broken out his windows or something." Chiffon giggled aloud because she knew Tam was serious.

Tam didn't laugh. Nobody was going to hurt her sister. "So, you decided to come back home to get away from him, not just because you landed a great job?"

"That was part of it. I primarily wanted to do what it took to create distance."

"I understand," her friend agreed, "But he didn't intend to let you go without a fight."

"No kidding. When I saw him at the table last night, I thought it was a dream. Like moths to a flame, I'm helplessly drawn to him. He has this, this thing about him that makes you yearn to be near him, to talk to him, to touch him. He has magnificently mesmerizing down to a science."

She shook her head in disgust, "I didn't just haphazardly do this," she motioned around the condominium. "I had to for my sanity," she wrung her hands together and took a breath. "It seems we can't stay away from each other, or I should say, I can't stay away from him, not staying away from me," she scoffed.

"So, the bottom line is, Josh, is beautiful, obsessive, and loaded? What a lethal combination," her friend surmised. "And his mucho dinero adds layers to this situation. Why the secrecy, though? I know you had no idea."

"Right, not to the true degree anyway. Imagine my surprise to find he could afford a partnership into a major corporation. George and Max weren't searching for a 3rd partner. Joshua decided he was going to become one and invested enough to make it happen. According to him, this kind of thing is done regularly. I'm convinced I've only witnessed the tip of the iceberg regarding his financial state."

Her friend whistled low. "He's quite the catch, hun?"

"Yea, if you call married with children a catch," she shrugged her shoulders.

Tam bit into a biscuit, "Seems to me, it won't be much of an issue."

Chiffon's brow creased, "Come again?"

"So, assume he is telling the truth," Tam swallowed. "If he is, it means he is married in name only, and he doesn't have any biological children. This Candice woman is just a minor obstacle for you all."

"Oh, I don't know about that Tam, I don't think she's walking away without a fight."

"Let her swing all she wants to. He doesn't want her. He wants you. He used extreme measures to prove it."

She smiled at her friend then. It was nice to hear someone else say it. Warmness blanketed her with satisfaction. She started to cautiously have hope again.

Rising from the table, she started to pace, "It's just this job situation is going to be a real problem." She fiddled with the napkin in her hand, shaking her head apprehensively. "I want to stay here in Chicago, but I think I'm going to end up looking for a new job."

"Why? So, he can buy that place too? Don't waste your time, girl."

"He wouldn't," Chiffon reasoned, "If he bought into Reynolds only because I wouldn't speak to him, surely he wouldn't..."

"Chi!" she held up her hand, interrupting her, "Do you hear yourself? This man purchased a rather large stake in a huge corporation because you might get a job there. Oh, and you would not return his calls. God only knows how much he is willing to do, to spend, to have you. I don't care what he told you. I think you are underestimating him.

If you like your job, you might as well stay there. He will only use his power and influence to keep close tabs on you wherever you go. I get the sneaky suspicion; he will do it by any means necessary."

Chiffon shook her head in disbelief. "He wouldn't dare purchase every company I decide to work at to keep me under his control. He couldn't do it."

Her friend stopped chewing. "You're fooling yourself, Chi. It seems to me Josh is about getting what he wants, and my friend, he wants you."

She grappled with that reality for a long moment. Surely everything would go back to normal once they were officially "on" again. However, she couldn't be positive about the lengths he would go. They would discuss it. He would listen to reason. Maybe he could become more of a silent partner in the firm or sell his partnership? They would figure it out. Currently, they had bigger fish to fry, like his damn wife and kid.

She clapped her hands together, changing the subject. "Since this is our last day before you head home, let's make the most of it."

"Right on," her friend made a fist, and they finished the delicious breakfast. They went on to unpack more stuff, shop and made dinner. After finishing, Tam prepared for her departure. Chiffon gave her a note in an envelope and told her only to read it after getting home.

"Are you breaking up with me?" Tam half grinned.

"No, silly," she grabbed her friend's hand. "I just wanted to express my appreciation for having you in my life. I love you, Tam, although I want to kill you sometimes."

"I know – I'm sorry Chi, I love you too," they embraced.

"I'll call you later." Tam blew her a kiss and headed out the door.

Later, when Josh called to check in, she had to admit it was good to have him back. She'd been in love before but nothing like this all-consuming, gut-wrenching, heart-constricting love. Sometimes when she closed her eyes, she could still feel him deep inside her, becoming one, caressing her inner-most places. The physical connection was unlike anything experienced before him. It was overwhelming and raw. "Don't let me down, Joshua." she prayed. Keep your promise and get the damn divorce, please.

Visions of the events that forced her to drop everything and run back to Chicago danced around her head. Her mind was on replay for some reason. She couldn't shake reliving that painful experience. Her eyes wide open, she stared at the ceiling. Was she making a mistake putting her trust in Joshua yet again? Lord knows he let her down before. She wouldn't survive another scene like the one that led to her painful departure from Atlanta. As much as she tried to fight it off, it came rushing back to her in vivid detail.

The Past

Chapter
6

She stood stark still, staring into the eyes of the man she loved. Too bad his miserable life was about end. She'd stepped inside the patio door to retrieve an item for the party host. Dusk fell, and the living room was bathed in an orange, smoky hue. Nightfall was upon them. He was the last thing she expected to encounter standing in her colleague's living room. She did a quick scan of the room for a weapon. She was going to kill him.

"Fonn, sweetheart, we need to talk." He approached her cautiously, and she took a step back. She was at a coworker's house for backyard dinner. She was confident no one at her current job knew Joshua. So how on earth did he get in here? No matter, his lying, cheating ass was right there—the nerve, tracking her down.

"What are you doing here, Josh?"

"I need to speak with you. Will you talk to me, Fonn?"

She couldn't find anything within arm's reach to end his lousy life with. The kitchen cutlery was too far out of reach—murderous venom shot through her veins.

"Talking to me right now is not the best idea," she uttered menacingly. "I knew I shouldn't have come here," she spat out, glaring around the room. She smelled a setup. What should have been a cozy dinner had turned into a mission to trap Chiffon. Who had he paid off? She was so done with Joshua and his manipulative, duplicitous ways.

However, as angry as she felt, a liquid warmth threatened to override the venom at the sight of him. Joshua Abbott was a thing of beauty. Panty dropping submission remained a hairs breath away whenever he was in view. Everything about him delicious to the sight as well as the touch. Her pulse raced uncontrollably in her chest, and a light mist of dampness covered her skin.

She despised the physical reaction to him. He made her knees weak, and her heart ache, but more than that, she felt so hurt and angry.

"You don't have the right to force yourself on me! Her hands balled into fists. Where I go and what I'm doing is none of your lying, cheating, whorish business!"

He visibly winced at her words; his warm eyes hardened on her. "You!" he stated boldly, "Will always remain my business."

"And You! You! will always remain married to somebody else! Your wife is your business, not me!" she growled as a waterfall threatened. "Not anymore! You, deceitful bastard!" she accused him as her voice raised several octaves. "You have lied to me repeatedly. You're a filthy, disgusting LIAR!" Her finger waved judgmentally at him. "How could you live with your own triflingness-ness!"

He rubbed a hand over his short crop of soft, curly hair. He almost smiled at her made-up word. He found her adorable even though his life hung in the balance here. His blue, gray, green, whichever color they presented today, eyes trained on her soft-brown, red-rimmed ones. He breathed out softly, "You don't know the entire story. Can we please go somewhere private to discuss this civilly?"

She took another step away from him, "You're disgusting!" She started to shake violently. "I hate you for doing this to me, Joshua." She clutched onto the back of the nearest armchair. "I trusted you with, with everything, and you broke my heart," she whimpered in misery.

He felt the painful, burning sting of her words in his eyes. He couldn't believe it, tears threatened, and he never cried, not even at his GrandMere's funeral, and he worshipped his Gran completely. Ah, but Fonn, this woman touched a place in his heart no woman accessed before or since. Never had he seen her so lost and broken. The blame rested at his feet. Remorse twisted in his gut.

Fonn provided life to his soul and breath to his body. If she would just give him a chance to explain this horrible mistake, this terrible misunderstanding, he could alleviate some of the agony she was in; but she was stubborn. He had to find a way to convince her to leave with him so he could talk some sense into her.

"She, she said you have a baby," her face contorted, "Are you really married to her, Joshua? Is she your wife? Do you have a baby together?" Her eyes widened frantically, "Do you?" When he didn't answer right away, a guttural cry escaped from her throat. She started to wail uncontrollably then, pure anguish overtaking her.

"Oh, my God! she cried out, "It's all true! Oh my God!" She shattered into a million pieces. She wanted to die. He really was married. That woman who approached her and screamed at her was really his wife. No longer able to stand, she crumbled to the floor, burying her sobbing frame into the cushions of the nearest chair.

Violently, she beat her hands into the pillows. Over and over, she screamed, "Damn you, Joshua! I hate you! I hate you! I loved you and trusted you!"

"Fonn, baby, please, you've got to calm down. I'm so sorry you found out this way." He shook his head in regret. "You're going to hurt yourself. Please, just hear me out, sweetheart." He stooped down to lift her from the floor but stopped short when she screamed at him to stay the hell away from her.

Her arm swung out to emphasize every word, "Get out of here, Joshua! she yelled. Just go! Get out! Leave me alone! I never want to see you again!" she sniffled, hiccupping on sobs.

He felt lost. Her pain was his own. Didn't she know that by now? "I can't," he responded. He didn't know if he was talking to himself or to her. All he knew was he couldn't leave her like this. He didn't know exactly how to proceed, so he stood there continuing to murmur words of love and apology and waited.

Eventually, when she calmed a bit, she looked up. There he stood, looking more scrumptious than ever. Pain etched into his handsome features, but it only served to upset her more. He was not hers to admire. She was done with him. She ultimately found her way back onto her feet.

"Sweetheart, I don't want you to go through this, I can explain if you," he reached out to touch her, but she would have none of it. Striking out with as much blunt force as she could muster, her fist pummeled into his upper arm.

"Don't you dare touch me!"

He sighed with regret and rubbed over the area where her fist struck him. She packed quite a wallop when determined. His eyes pleaded with hers, "I could have handled this better, Fonn."

"You think!" she spat in disgust. "I'm a damn fool for ever believing in you, Josh." She squinted at him without giving him a chance to respond, "You don't even try to deny it," she laughed to herself and then started to sob again. "It's, it's all true, isn't it? All of it!" she moaned. Nothing in her life had ever hurt this much. Nothing. Had he ever loved her? Could he have been just using her?

Maybe this was all a horrible mistake. Maybe she misunderstood something. Maybe she should let him explain. "Joshua, please, she besieged him, tell me it's all a lie, she sniffled, her voice barely above a whisper. Tell me she isn't your wife, and you don't have a child, she begged. We were supposed to have our first children together. You said you wanted to have your firstborn with me. Tell me it isn't true, Josh! She is just a crazy stalker, right? Tell me, Josh... Please! she urged him, grabbing onto his shirt tightly. "Say it! This is just an awful mix-up, right?" She dared to hope.

Maybe if she were nicer, he would tell her what she needed to hear. When it seemed he was about to speak, she incentivized him on, "I promise, I will believe whatever you say. If you tell me she was lying. I won't ever bring any of this up again. Just say this isn't true," she whimpered softly.

He stood there motionless and speechless. More than anything else in this world, he wanted to give her what she asked for. Whatever she wanted, but he couldn't give her that. He would be lying if he told her what she wanted to hear. Although he was tempted, he couldn't help but think of all the damage his omissions already caused.

He refused to lie anymore. "Fonn, Fonn, baby I," he stopped short. He didn't know what else to say. His heart seized, and he closed his eyes for a moment, remaining quiet. When he opened them again, desperation and shame wouldn't allow him to make eye contact.

The small glimmer of hope she'd been holding onto faded into obscurity as his silence confirmed all she feared. She could feel her dreams liquefying and subsequently draining from each pore. It was final. Nothing left; she recoiled away from him as if he were fire threatening to consume her. Their entire relationship now equal to a dreadful lie.

"Believe me, Fonn, I wanted to tell you everything myself. I started to," he shifted his stance, "Give me a chance to explain everything. I never expected..." he hesitated, "Or wanted you to find out like...

"You are the lowest, bottom-feeding form of life, Joshua Abbot. You are a pitiful rendition of a man." She lowered her head and wrapped her arms around herself. She felt like a fool standing there berating him yet filled with so much love for him. How could she still care for such a dreadful liar?

Remaining calm, he stared at her. "You are the only woman for me. I wouldn't be here, Fonn, if I didn't love you. There is nobody else on this earth for me. I'm in love with you and only you. I apologize for the appearance of deception. I know it looks bad, but I never meant for you to get hurt. If you give me a chance, I can make it right between us again. I can make this right, baby. Just let me explain, and I promise you, I will erase all the pain you're feeling. Ending this hurt is what you're ultimately after. I know you, and I know it's what you've been longing for these past weeks, for me to explain myself, for me reassure you about us."

She didn't answer.

"It's what I want too, Fonn." She appeared to receive what he was saying, or maybe she was just too damn exhausted to keep fighting him. "I do not have a genuine relationship. She doesn't mean anything, baby - not like you do, you mean everything," he said in earnest. "We are miserable without each other, Fonn." He gently lifted her chin, "I'm miserable without you, he choked out. I'm so in love with you, sweetheart. You are everything; she means nothing." His eyes locked on hers, "Hear me out first, then decide if you can forgive me."

"I don't trust a word out of your mouth, Josh!" She continued to rage inside, but confusion held her in a vice grip. A haze of sorrow mixed with deep longing had her off balance. He stood there, never taking his eyes off her. It surprised her he remained after she'd screamed, hit, and did her best to insult him. Yet, there he stood unmoving, waiting however long it took to break her. The tenderness and almost believable pain etched in his eyes shook her. Joshua Abbott exuded uncompromising control in every situation; the master of his universe, but the man before her looked vulnerable, exposed, and even a bit heartbroken.

She felt drained and very tired. No, defeated, was a more accurate word. She felt betrayed by everyone. Did anyone ever tell her the truth? The man she held in the highest esteem turned out to be her dad revisited. Nothing could make this better.

"Let me get you out of here?" he willed her.

"Will leaving with you make you unmarried to that woman?" she asked in defiance, trying not to show the chips in her armor.

He stared at her, with arms crossed, unmoving, daring her to continue to resist. Finally, he said, "Just come with me, Fonn."

She dropped her head into her hands and rubbed at her temples. How could he make such passionate love to her with such fervor and intensity, knowing he had a wife somewhere? It was disgusting. When she thought of the intimate things they'd done to each other, things she never let any man do to her before. Guilt and shame coursed through her. This woman's husband defiled her in so many ways. Oh Lord, please have mercy on me. I didn't know. She felt sick to her stomach. Did she know him at all?

He outstretched his hand to her again. "Come with me now, he directed. I will explain everything but – away from all these people," he motioned outside to the guests. The sky twinkled with stars, and artificial light bathed the guests on the deck. She no longer had words. Their gazes locked and played a familiar silent battle of wills.

"Fine, she shrugged and whispered, my purse is out there," she pointed toward the patio deck.

"Stay here, he instructed. I'll get your purse and say your goodbyes." She nodded quietly and wiped under her eye as she watched him head outside. She avoided Joshua whenever she got angry for good reason. This power he seemed to wield over her good sense, her judgment. She felt so helpless. No strength, no resolve. She didn't want to end up one of those women who loved a man so much he got away with doing any disrespectful thing to her.

As of now, she hadn't seen him in weeks and refused to talk to him after the scream session she had regurgitating her confrontation with his wife. But, true to form, he found a way to get to her. He stalked her in silence and waited with patience until he could go in for the kill. In honesty, was she surprised? Getting to her is what he did best. Joshua Abbott got to her in every conceivable way.

He reappeared through the sliding glass door. Their eyes rested on each other. He approached her gingerly and brought a finger to her cheek, wiping under an eye. "No more tears my love." His lip turned up at the corner of his mouth, "You are lovely, Fonn, even in the poufy state you're in," he smirked at her grimace. Her lids lowered at his soft touch. He was so close. His familiar scent filled her nostrils, pure male with a hint of rainwater freshness. It tangled with her senses. She blinked quickly to chase the thoughts.

"I will explain it all. I promise."

She felt his soft lips brush lightly against her cheek and then the corner of her mouth catching the next tear. His arms encircled her, taking advantage of her weariness. He needed her to know he would be there no matter what she said or did. He released her before she snapped again.

Josh missed her with a fierceness that surprised him over the past few weeks. He wanted to make her forget all the pain he caused.

"All I want is a chance to talk to you alone," as he held up both hands in surrender as if harmless. She almost smiled at him then. "Let's go," as he held her purse in one hand and reached out to her with the other.

She placed her hand in his and felt the charge go through her body at contact. Time away from him had been difficult when, over the last two years, they spent almost every waking moment together. Never had she experienced such powerful chemistry with another person, period. She felt swept away by him, with him, in him. It was difficult to deny the undeniable magnetism between them. She thought it to be the most genuine thing in her life. What a damn fool.

Chapter
7

He took her arm and ushered her out into his car before she had a chance to change her mind. What an awful mess. Admittedly his own fault, he thought to himself as he took a long, exasperated breath. He expected to clear up the living, breathing, disaster of his marriage. He thought he could end it before Chiffon ever got wind of it. That had been his intention – ah, but the road to hell. He shook his head. Now, he had to make her see this had just been a mistake, his mistake but only a mistake.

Chiffon came into his life like a breath of fresh air, awakening feelings, desires he couldn't describe. He took pride in the order of things, and right now, everything was out of order. Trust meant everything to her. He knew it, and he betrayed it, but he vowed to do whatever it took to make it right again. He would prove he wasn't some treacherous bastard like her father.

He was on unstable ground, he couldn't deny it, but he'd waited a lifetime for a woman like Fonn. What they shared was rare and real. A set of unfortunate circumstances would not deny him his destiny. He wouldn't allow it.

The first order of business would be to convince her to stop running like a bat out of hell when things got tough. She had to learn to work through it with him, not without him. It would prove challenging to break her from her avoidance tendencies, but he would see it done.

It made him cringe to think she could ever compare him to her dad. Not only was he not leaving her, but he also planned not to let anything, or anyone separate them again. He would make sure of it with his last breath. His dad always told him, if you don't like the results you're getting – either change what you're doing or change your mind about the situation you're in. The time for a change had come.

Silence shrouded them in a heavy cloak as he entered the highway toward Alpharetta. He fumbled with the knob, and soft jazz music started to play in the background. He kept a close eye on her as she stared off into space, never letting go of her hand. They headed in the direction of his penthouse.

She watched the familiar buildings pass. Streetlights flickered past her window in a blur. The cool leather seats comforted her burning hot rage. He was smart; she had to give him credit. He did not utter another word while still in the car. He pulled into his parking space and got out. He assisted her and led her up into his unit.

Once inside, she did a quick once over to see if there was any trace of another woman but found nothing out of the ordinary. "Can I get you some Verdi?" he asked as he stepped out of his shoes and dropped his keys on the stand. He knew her wine of choice and always kept some at his place for her.

"Yes," she murmured and emptied the glass of its contents after she took it from him. It warmed her insides and calmed her nerves. He refilled her glass and poured something for himself.

She sunk down into a plush couch, her favorite in the living room. He had a single lamp on in the corner. It bathed his stylish décor with a warm glow. The hardwood floor still gleamed under the shrouded light. He kept things meticulously clean.

He sat next to her and took her hand, kissing each finger. Electrifying shocks went through her at his touch. She didn't even try to resist him anymore. He already depleted all her reserves. She found herself tired of trying to avoid someone who refused to be avoided. She gazed at him gingerly. Her life hadn't felt right without him, but she didn't know if it could ever feel right with him again.

He drank her in with a heartfelt gaze; his beautiful Fonn. His eyes swept the length of her – her slanted brown eyes, creamy, warm, brown skin, high cheekbones, and full, delicious lips. They knew precisely how to please him. He almost grunted aloud at the thought. He closed his eyes for a moment repositioning himself.

Lust, infatuation, and love consumed him. Her smooth, soft skin always felt hot to the touch. The fullness of her hips, the thickness of her thighs, and those endless, long legs were perfect for him, perfect to him. When he closed his eyes, he could conjure up her enticing scent on his lips; his favorite delicacy, damn edible, and he jeopardized it all. He didn't blame her for being irate and infuriated with him. He deserved it, but he'd had enough already.

The time had come to lay it on the line – to tell the truth. He should have told her from the start. He had to make her understand. Please, God, let her understand. His heart thumped in his chest. He couldn't, no, he refused to lose her. These last few weeks had been a living hell. Nothing mattered. For the first time in his life, he found it difficult to concentrate on his business. He had to get through to her for both their sakes. He took her hand in his, holding it securely, and began his story.

"Candy and I have known each other for quite some time. Our fathers worked together in business, and our families became friends. We eventually ended up attending the same university. I was working on my 2nd Master's and she a Bachelors. There, we began to date off and on. Back in those days, settling down never made it onto my radar." He brought his other hand to his temple and rubbed the corner, deep in reflective thought, "I dated around. Candy ended up being more like a friend with benefits."

She squirmed a little in her seat, and he tightened his grasp on her hand. "She actually had been dating this jock guy, Terrance, but not a good relationship-rather abusive." He paused for a moment, recalling what must have been a disturbing memory.

She drank him in. It was difficult to concentrate with him in reach. Golden brown, warm, caramel skin covered Josh. His eyes were unlike any she has ever seen on a black man – green, gray, and often blue. They changed various hues depending on his mood. He had supermodel good looks and an elegant sophistication that captivated.

At 6.4, he sported a muscular build, straight, white teeth, and perfect lips that made you want to kiss them on sight. How wonderful they felt when they kissed her everywhere. She swallowed and flushed.

His eyes narrowed on her, "Are you ok, sweetheart?" He noticed her dis-ease. He got on her nerves doing that. He understood her so well.

"Yes," she whispered, "Go on."

He continued, "He wouldn't leave her alone but, she perpetrated it. It was her own fault," he said in disgust. "She kept going back to him after ending it. Anyway, he finally put her in the hospital. It was there that she found out about the pregnancy."

"Pregnancy? So, there is a baby?" her voice quivered. "She had your baby?" her voice trembled.

"No, biologically not my baby."

She let out a breath she didn't realize she'd been holding.

"Candy knew she would never get rid of him if he found out she carried his child. So, I offered to help her get a new start. I was about to graduate and needed to remove myself from my family's overwhelming influence in my life. I had to do something to show I was no longer just their baby boy. So, upon graduation, I accepted a position at an outside consulting firm, and Candy, and I got married."

Her heart compressed in her chest. Finally, he uttered the words. Finally, he admitted the truth. She reached for her glass with trembling fingers and downed the remaining contents. He wiped at the moisture on her cheek.

"I don't ever want to make you cry again. All these tears; it's why it has been so damn hard to tell you. It kills me to cause you so much pain, Fonn." He squeezed her hand, "I wish I would have done it differently now, but I finally managed to leave the family business, and, at the time, I thought it was worth it. I didn't love Candy, but I did care about her wellbeing, and I do love the child.

Candy went through hell with Terrance. I wanted to help her. Admittedly, her feelings ran deeper than mine. I knew it; she knew it, but I thought we had an understanding. We did a quick city hall thing. Our marriage was an open one. Again, she knew I didn't love her and was not in love. She didn't necessarily like it, but she accepted it. After all, it was ultimately for her protection."

Witnessing the unsteady way Fonn stared at him, he almost didn't say another word. He just wanted to hold her, to comfort her, but it was too late to stop now. He continued, "When I knew I would be moving out here, I brought up divorce, but it seemed every time I brought it up, another incident with Terrence occurred. I didn't have an immediate need to end the marriage, so I just let it linger. When a business acquisition acquisition became available in Georgia. I relocated to pursue it without her. I moved here just before you and I met. She remained in Tennessee with baby Joshua."

"Joshua? she repeated stunned, she named her baby after you?" her heart sank.

"I know how all this must sound to you, Fonn. We had to be convincing, and I didn't mind back then. He is a beautiful baby. He's the best thing in my life after you. You will love him too."

Cautiously she asked, "I'll love him too? You want me to meet the, um… your baby?"

"Of course I do," his hand grazed her cheek softly. "I don't condone my behavior, the pain it's caused you, but I'm glad it's all out now. I want you to be a part of everything meaningful in my life, my only one. No more secrets between us. Everything is out in the open now."

He went on, "So to the world when I moved to Atlanta from Tennessee without my 'wife', a separation occurred. As far as I was concerned, we hadn't been together in the first place. She is fully aware of that, Fonn."

He looked off into the distance, "I can't be sure what drove her to make herself known to you as she did. Rest assured, there is nothing outside of friendship there for me, and I'm starting to question that. It's been a long time since we even resided in the same town,"

He turned his warm gaze toward her. He brought the hand he'd been holding to his lips and kissed it softly. She warmed inside at the slight touch. "None of this even mattered until I met you. I didn't think about it very much. She had her life, and I had mine. Believe me; I never intended to keep this from you. I planned to tell you. I hoped to be divorced when I did. I am not in love with her baby. I can't say it enough. I am married in name only. It's a piece of paper to me," his eyes pleaded, "Believe me, Fonn. I would have never gotten involved with you if my marriage were real. I am not that kind of man."

She closed her eyes and took a deep breath. She was quiet.

"What is it, baby? You can ask me anything."

"Nothing you've said explains why you didn't tell me. I get it; you wanted to be divorced when I found out. When a divorce didn't happen, you continued to remain deceitful. When were you going to let me in on this? Her stomach churned. I had to find out from a hysterical stranger in the middle of a restaurant. Do you know how embarrassing it was to have your wife verbally attack me at a business dinner? I don't know how she found me, but she was on a mission to let me know that you were hers. I wanted to crawl under the table and die, but the worse part of all was not knowing this from you. You let me believe you were available," she said with disgust.

"I know I was foolish. Even though I considered myself single, the fact remained I was indeed married. But in my own defense, I didn't know how important you would become to me. We happened so fast. I did believe I would be long divorced before it would become an issue for you, I mean us. I never thought Candy would put up such incredible resistance. She refused to discuss divorce when I brought it up and when I went to confront her, she avoided me.

By the time I realized time was running out, I couldn't find the right words to say to you. All my previous attempts at resolving the matter failed. I didn't know if you would believe me. I didn't know if you loved me enough. I didn't know how to tell you. So, I tried to figure out the best approach.

He rubbed his hand over his face and held his chin. You and I fell ridiculously hard, amazingly fast, and I was afraid, Fonn. Afraid you wouldn't understand. I wanted to find the right time."

He fidgeted, picked up the glass holding the dark liquid, and took a gulp. After setting the glass down on the dark wooden table, he lifted her head. She hadn't realized she bowed again. "I know this is a lot to take in. It's a lot to believe. I tried on more than one occasion to tell you. I just couldn't bring myself to do it. I knew it would hurt you, baby, and I didn't want to lose you. I promise I've been working on getting a divorce. She is resistant. I told her she would be served. She knows I want this over. As you found out at the restaurant, she knows all about you, Fonn. I told her I was in love with you, and she should sign the papers."

He placed her hand on his chest. She felt the slow, steady rhythm pulsating there. "You have my heart. You and only you, baby. Do you understand?" He searched her eyes for a response. "You wouldn't talk to me, and it was like death. I know I created this mess, but baby, being without you, it's been unbearable.

I had to find a way to get you to at least hear me out. I wanted to be sure you were in love with me before I told you everything. I admit I was a coward. I didn't want to lose you then, and I don't want to lose you now."

He kissed her hand repeatedly, moving to her inner wrist. Everywhere his lips landed, a warm, liquid satisfaction coursed through her body. "I adore you, sweetheart, and at this point, I have enough love for us both. He breathed hotly against her skin. You came into my life like a bolt of lightning, and I have been eternally changed, ignited from the inside out. Please forgive me for not being honest with you from the outset. I apologize, baby. Let me make this right. I promise I will make it right if you let me."

She squeezed the tense area at the back of her nape and closed her eyes.

"I am an open book now." He cradled her close to him and placed his lips against her forehead. She didn't feel angry anymore, just worn out. He kissed each eyelid. "You are so beautiful. Even with your runny nose," he smirked as she hit his shoulder lightly.

"So very, very beautiful," he murmured. "My sweet love." His lips brushed against hers, lightly at first, testing the waters. When she didn't protest, the kiss became more desperate and consuming. He could exist for the rest of his life on her kisses.

With steady determination, his tongue teased and toyed inside her mouth, willing her to open to him. He was a man lost, taken to another world whenever his lips met hers. For a while, they were all heads, tongues, lips, and hands groping as if trying to devour each other. She pulled away from the assault on her mouth, needing to catch her breath. She was in trouble now.

"There is nothing else. You know everything now." He exhaled deeply and placed her hands in his, "Will you let me make this up to you?" His eyes searched hers again, willing her to allow him back in. "Can you forgive me? Will you? You still love me, Fonn?" he asked in succession.

She started to answer but abruptly hesitated, staring at this compelling man who turned her world upside down, how she wanted to believe him, to trust him. All men couldn't be as lousy as her father, could they?

When they first started dating, it was difficult for her to accept this moving, breathing, movie star-like specimen could ever be serious about her. I mean, she could hold her own, certainly not chopped liver, but Joshua Abbott, wow! No words. She found him so poised, so charismatic, and so damn pretty to look at. Those times, when he caught her staring at him, he never made her feel embarrassed about it. In full command of his magnetism, he would just wink at her.

Josh possessed a deadly combination of power, elegance, and influence that was attractive beyond measure. She didn't know how much money he made, but he appeared to hurt for nothing. She found his commanding presence intriguing, enticing, and sometimes a bit intimidating. He could have anyone he wanted, and he chose her. How fortunate she'd felt. He made her feel like she was the center of his universe.

Now, the truth at last, but it didn't change the facts. Hard and cold. She wanted nothing to do with any form of adultery. It was a sin against the sanctity of marriage, and she would be no better than her adulteress father if she participated. She never wanted to touch a married man, no matter his reasons. Josh put her in such an awful position. "Yes, of course, I still love you Josh," she whispered, gazing into his compelling eyes.

"Promise me you will never leave me like that again," he ordered softly.

"I didn't leave you, Josh. I was just hurt. I didn't feel like I could trust—"

"Don't ever do it again, Fonn, ever," he mandated in a more chilling tone, putting emphasis on each word.

She searched his eyes, the sudden briskness of his cantor startling her, "I can't promise you I won't ever get angry, Josh."

"Of course not, but you can promise me you won't ever refuse to see me or talk to me – I can't control you, but I can't be responsible for what action I take if something like this ever happens again."

"Is that a threat, Joshua?"

His lip curved up slightly on the side. "If this is going to work, you must trust me. It doesn't matter what anyone else says or does. What matters is you and me and our ability to communicate."

She agreed. She felt guilty for not talking her feelings out with him. She would never trust easily. Her father destroyed her ability to believe in a man's words. Only actions would stand up for her. Looking at Joshua now, he reminded her of a small child who just found something he thought was lost forever. The time had come for her to ride or get off this train.

Chapter 8

Close your eyes for me baby," he directed lightly. She warmed, wondering what he had up his sleeve. He trailed his finger down her cheek and traced her lips. Her breath caught in her throat as she blinked rapidly. "My sweet and beautiful Fonn. I will never let you go. I will make this up to you. I will." He took her mouth once more. This time she didn't pull away.

He eased her back into the soft cushions of the couch. She heard pellets of light rain caress the panes of the windows from outside. His hands were everywhere, stroking, teasing. She was on fire for him. Nothing else mattered.

He pulled at the buttons on the front of her dress and undid each one while his lips blazed a trail down her neck and collarbone. She felt his hand cup her breast through the silky fabric of her bra. She clasped her arms around his back and rubbed over his solid frame. Her outsized nipples were taut and ripe—ready for him.

He pushed the fabric back and took one, then the other in his mouth, suckling, and tasting, toying with the solid peaks. He savored each one until she couldn't take it anymore. The growing fire in her body longed for all of him. She clasped the back of his head and pulled him closer to her flesh. He knew just what to do. Just the right amount of pressure to apply on the thin line between pleasure and pain.

"My beautiful girl," he released her from his teeth and gazed at her, "Sweetheart, you are a vision of loveliness.

God, I've missed you. I love you," as he smiled at her, and her heart melted.

"You too are a vision," she concurred.

He grinned slightly, "Since we are all agreed here, I think it's time you got busy undressing this vision."

She smiled at him. So bossy, she thought to herself, shaking her head. She pushed him until he leaned against the back of the couch and dropped to her knees between his legs. She groped his manhood. He moaned and closed his eyes. It was thick and rigid underneath her grasp. She lifted the sides of his shirt and pulled it over his head. Faint hairs decorated the surface of his muscular chest.

She leaned in to press her lips against his skin. Again, he moaned. He smelled of fresh rainwater, sandalwood, and dusk. She flicked her tongue over his nipple and suckled there. He stroked through her long tresses as she reacquainted herself with his body. She, again, felt how solid he was for her as he undid his belt, the trouser button, and slid the zipper down. And then there he was, naked in front of her, solid and bigger than she remembered. Had it only been a few weeks?

"Fonn," he lifted her head up to meet his glistening eyes, "This is what I present to you. All of me, bare, raw, and all yours. I couldn't have been a bigger fool, and I want you to accept my apology. I haven't been with anyone else after you. It's you. It's only been you. We belong together, you and me. I will never give you up; give this up. Don't ever expect me to cause I can't, sweetheart, and I won't," he promised. "I'll do whatever you want to make it right between us again. His face softened as he wiped at the trickling tear on her cheek. No more tears, baby."

He pulled her up to her feet and made quick work of letting her short dress and undergarments fall to the floor. They stood bare in front of each other. He gently pushed at her shoulder until she took a small step backward. His eyes raked over her nudity. "My beautiful love," his eyes darkened with lust. "There are so many things I've been waiting to do to that beautiful body of yours again." Her eyes widened because she knew he was about to tell her.

"I want to take my sweet time to lick up, down, and all-around your delicious inner folds. I want to feel the pressure of your hands on my head as I bury my tongue deep inside you, tasting you, circling and suckling your clit until you clutch onto me for dear life. Only then will I sink so deep inside you, you never again forget we belong together."

She moistened her lips, biting down on her lower one. She was always taken aback when talked to her so roguishly, but it made her so wet. She used to flush with embarrassment but not for long. It soon changed. Joshua changed everything for her.

He reached out and gently rolled each of her nipples between his thumb and forefingers. She cried out from his expert touch. Their lips met again. He slid one of his hands down her flat stomach to the soft, moist curls of her mound. She gasped as he slid first one, then another finger deep inside her. She arched into his hand, squirming as he continued to invade her mouth with his tongue. He was incredibly passionate tonight. His intensity wreaked havoc with her senses. He pinched her erect nipple again, and she again cried out. She could feel the pressure building between her legs as his fingers continued their sweet assault.

"You are so wet for me, baby. I think you did miss me too a little, yes?"

"Yes!" She let out a wail as he repeatedly stroked the most sensitive area inside her. She grabbed onto his shoulders. How quickly he could take her there. She would shatter and soon. Suddenly, he stopped. He removed his hands from all parts of her body, and she gasped, gaping at him in disbelief.

He stepped back, breathing raggedly, "I want you to let it sink in right now," he peered at her.

"What?" she panted, confused by his behavior.

"It's not a good feeling, without warning, to have everything you want desperately snatched away from you, is it Fonn?"

She glared at him, bewildered. "Oh Josh," escaped her lips, his meaning sinking in. "Baby, please, forgive me." She moved closer to him and touched his face, drinking in those cautious but torturous eyes. "I didn't feel like I had a choice. What would you have done if some strange man came up to you screaming, I was his wife, and you were a whore for ever touching me?"

"I would have talked it out with you, Fonn," he sighed. "All you did was scream at me then refuse to speak to me."

Her gaze lowered, "You are right. I should have let you explain. It was a mistake to avoid you, but I did the only thing I knew."

He examined her intently. "I want you to handle your pain differently with me. Don't group me with anyone else. We could have avoided a lot of extra misery. Stop running from me." he demanded.

Like a live painting, he stood - so virile, so male. Every hard, chiseled muscle of his naked frame called out to her. She needed to feel him again, but she could tell; anger had him in a chokehold of displeasure. "Please don't punish me now, Josh. Haven't we been through enough already? We need to forgive each other," she said hopefully.

If he admitted it to himself, he'd been more than slightly disturbed by how she handled, or should he say chose not to handle, him—knowing how hot she could be in his arms and how cold she could turn when hurt had his emotions running the gamut. One minute he wanted to punish her, the next to protect her but ultimately, his love for the woman always won out.

"So, if I forgive you, what will you give me?" he teased.

"Whatever you want," she promised. He slowly slid the finger that had been inside her deeply into his mouth. Her insides clenched with heat. He took it out and put it up to her lips.

"Suck it," he ordered, and she did so hungrily. He pulled it out of her mouth and used it to point to where they had just been sitting, "Go lie down on the couch and open your legs. Spread that beautiful treasure wide for me."

She turned to do as told when she heard -

"I want your hot juices squirting all over my face while you scream out things that can't be deciphered. There is one caveat tonight." His voice hardened, "One rule of engagement."

"Rule?" she questioned, swiveling to face him again.

"Yes, one rule."

She waited.

"Tonight, you wait until I release you for orgasm. I will dictate when you can climax." He knew how very responsive she could be in bed, easily aroused at his touch, but tonight he wanted the reigns. Respect for him wasn't optional. He would show her how serious he was.

She crossed her legs to ease the throbbing ache there. How unfair, she fretted, but outside of attacking him and jumping on his staff, she didn't have a choice. Only he could put out the raging fire threatening to consume her.

"My way or no way. Your choice." he offered. Her eyes moved down to his raging hard-on and then back to meet his intense stare. She turned and went over to the couch and spread her legs as wide as she could. He grabbed his manhood, stroking it back and forth. He got down on his knees between her open thighs and rubbed her throbbing sex with one of his palms.

She closed her eyes and soon felt his incredible tongue slide up and down the length of her again. She grabbed his head and pulled him closer, "Oh, Josh," she cried out. His expert tongue took her to the edge of madness. How did he become so good at this? Did she want to know? Over and over, she arched against him as involuntary upward motions took over her body.

"Delicious, delectable, you are, baby," as he nibbled at her flesh. Her body bucked and arched back and forth faster and faster. "I love tasting your true essence. You were made for me."

"Josh, baby!" she called out to him as she pinched and rolled her nipples between her fingers. She felt a sensational pull at her core, "Oh yes!" she writhed as her eyes rolled back in her head. She was right there. "Joshua!" she called his name. "Baby, I love you! Yes!" She started to shake and tremble again. "Yes, yes baby, yes!" she wailed out, feeling the delicious moment when everything numbed before intense pleasure threatened to overtake her – and in that instant, he let her go and moved his marvelous tongue away from her body.

"Baby, what in the…!" her eyes flew open, "What… what are you doing?" she stuttered in bewilderment. Her arms unconsciously reaching out toward him as he backed away. She was in a haze of disillusioned ecstasy.

"What do you think you are doing?" he stared down at her still trembling frame. "Did I give you permission to climax?" She stared at him in amazement. Was he serious? "What are the rules of engagement here?" His eyes narrowed, "What did we just agree on?"

She leaned up and shook her head. Did he expect her to answer him? "I know you didn't give me permission yet. I couldn't help my—"

"Did I give you permission to climax?" he asked again sternly.

"No," she said, feeling like a child with her hand caught in the cookie jar. This was crazy. Ordinarily, he loved it when she lost control with him.

"Tonight, I make the rules, Fonn. I want nothing more than to bring you to your heights again but only on my terms. My terms tonight, me entiendes?" his brow raised. When she didn't reply, she heard, "Me comprendes?"

Wow, he was serious, she thought. He was multilingual, and depending on his mood, he would sometimes speak to her in one of the many languages he knew, as if she could understand him. She didn't know if he even realized he was doing it. All she knew was she physically ached for him.

"I need full control here tonight. Are we agreed?"

"Josh, I...I," she nodded affirmatively.

She would have agreed to just about anything to get his hot tongue back on her. She put her hand on her mound and started to rub it lightly. "I'm sorry," she continued to rub herself.

"Naughty, naughty girl." He dropped back to his knees and snatched her hand away, replacing it with his marvelous tongue yet again.

This time she held out long as she could until her body began to overtake her mind. He did this suckling thing around her clit while circling his tongue over it that nearly finished her. Her body shuddered, overruling anything else.

"Oh, Josh, Sweetheart," she cried out. "Oh baby," she grabbed his head as she arched up against his glorious tongue. "Please baby, please, Josh, she panted. Can I now? Is it ok?" Her head thrashed back and forth. She fought against the growing urge because she didn't want him to stop again, but this was impossible. "Please," she begged him, "Forgive me. Isn't it what you want, baby, me to give you back the control I took away? Oh, Jesus!" Her breath caught in between gasps, and she uncontrollably arched up further to meet his agile tongue swirling deliciously around her.

"That's my girl," he murmured against her flesh, "Good job; yes, baby, you can come for me now." He increased pressure on her, and before she knew it, a wild, earth-shattering orgasm overtook her. She gasped, cried out, and shook in almost violent gyrations under his amazing tongue. He continued his torment and her head thrashed against the cushions. Her eyes squeezed shut as she rolled her hips against his mouth, wanting to feel more but unable to take it. He planted light kisses on her throbbing sex and moved them steadily up her body while continuing to fondle her wetness. She couldn't speak. She was lost in the feeling she missed so desperately.

"Open your eyes for me, Fonn."

She felt the head of his solid penis at her entrance. Whenever she was in the throes of ecstasy, he wanted her to look at him, to know it was he who took her there; nobody else, only him. "Fonn, look at me, baby," he instructed. She opened glazed, hooded eyes.

He held her gaze, "You are the best thing to come into my life. I love every delicious part of you. Don't ever take this away from me again. I can't live without it. We belong together, woman, you understand? You feel it?" he stroked his cock up and down the length of her.

She whimpered and called out, "Yes, yes, Josh, I feel it, I feel it. I need you inside me now," she said in a throaty whisper. What were previously tiny pellets of rain now becoming a steady crash against the panes.

He smiled down at her, "You sound incredible when nothing else matters but you and me. I'd like to hear more." He plunged himself deep inside her, and she almost lost it again. Over and over, he sank deep inside her, filling her with his rock, hard length. She held on tight. He murmured something to her. She wrapped her legs around him as another orgasm racked her body. How magical it was to be with him again. So wonderful.

"Yes, baby," he moaned–her incredible responsiveness took him over the edge. He was unable to restrain himself. He stiffened and combusted within her as she shook underneath his weight.

"Dammit, Oh Goddammit!" he cried out. "Damn you, woman," he buried his head in her neck. "We will always be together. You are mine, Fonn, all mine."

Chapter 9

Blinding light ricocheted in through an opening of the blinds at the window. She opened her eyes and squinted taking in her surroundings.

His even breathing rose and fell moving her head up and down against his chest. She lifted her head and kissed him there. They must have fallen asleep. How did they get to the bed? She grinned; she couldn't remember. She did remember him taking her again and then again throughout the night. It was as if he was attempting to make up for lost time.

The early morning sun made a slow accent in the eastern sky. There was no trace of the torrential rain from the night before. She drank him in. This man, her man she thought as she let her finger tread lightly over his thick brows, his chiseled nose, well-defined lips, a faint, well-shaped beard, and mustache. "Can I trust you, Joshua?" she asked softly.

He stirred but didn't wake. She got up and sealed the blinds so he could continue to rest, and let him awaken to the smell of breakfast instead of harsh light. She felt her stomach growling, and his would be too, after that marathon lovemaking session. She smiled mischievously, grabbed a robe, and headed to the kitchen.

She found all the makings for a Denver omelet. She busied herself preparing everything. She caught herself humming as a slow grin found her lips. She felt happy again because it felt so good to be back in his life, kitchen, and bed. Maybe they could work out all the kinks. Maybe Joshua was the answer she'd been waiting for.

It's You

A permanent life with him is what she craved. Please be telling me the truth, Joshua, she thought to herself. No more lies, no more omissions. Everything out in the open. She could handle anything if he led with the truth from this point forward. She would support him as he obtained the divorce.

She turned the sizzling bacon over in the skillet. Unconditional love would never be easy for her, but she would try. She bent down to get a bowl out of the lower cabinet and saw a crumpled-up piece of paper on the floor. She thought nothing of it. He obviously missed the garbage can by a mile, she mused to herself. She examined the paper a little closer as she headed over to the garbage with it. It peeked her interest because it looked like a photo was inside, surrounded by the white paper of a hand-written letter.

Curiosity getting the best of her, she opened the crinkled-up paper just enough to remove the photo. She couldn't resist peeking at it. Her primary aim was to see the image. She wondered why he balled it up for trash. People didn't usually ball up pictures. She peered over to the open door of the bedroom; he still slept soundly.

Apprehension grew stronger as she approached the reveal. She took a deep breath, and with fingers trembling, she flattened the photo against the countertop and gazed downward. An image of Josh, a woman and a beautiful little baby boy, stared back at her. Her eyes rested on the woman in the photo. She was prettier than Fonn remembered; tall, slender, and very fair-skinned. She fought a surge of jealously that penetrated through her body. The woman in the photo was the same woman who assaulted her at the restaurant. It was his wife, Candice.

Now she had to read the attached letter even though a sense of quiet dread flooded her body as she unraveled it.

'Dear Joshua, how long you think I'm supposed to wait for you? You promised we could live together as a family months ago, and you were breaking it off with that damn bitch you have been playing house with out there. What is taking so long? You make so many promises when you are begging to be inside me, don't you?

She stopped reading and closed her eyes. Pushing back tears. Dammit, Joshua, she thought in anguish. Dammit. Her hands shook so much she had to put the paper down for a moment and compose herself. She continued to read.

'Just let her go like all the others toys I let you play with. Why is this one so difficult for you? You've had plenty of practice over the years. You know what to do when it's time for me to come home. No matter, I'm moving down there. Trust and believe I will be there with our baby in exactly one week. I won't be put off any longer. I hope you will have everything prepared for us; your "real family". I won't tolerate your side pieces any longer!

Chiffon glanced up at the date of the letter. It had this past Wednesday's date on it. She continued reading.

You will not carry on with her and expect me to believe in our future together. You cannot have us both. You better end it as you promised. I gave you more than enough time to handle your business. Now, be the husband and father you vowed to be to our son and me.'

Chiffon choked back a sob releasing the crinkled paper and photo to hit the kitchen floor. This woman was coming home to live with Josh in a matter of days. How could he come and get her to bring her back into this mess? She refused to cry. She bit her bottom lip and moved as quickly and quietly as she could. She turned off the fire on the stove and gathered up her belongings and dressed.

She hesitated at the bedroom door and stared at the beautiful specimen lying there with a single sheet covering his lower body. She whispered softly, "I understand why she wants you, why she loves you so much because I feel the same. I will never ever come in between you and your family. I can't do it," she choked out. She blew the man she loved a kiss and got out of there. Never looking back.

THE PRESENT

Chapter

10

He slammed down the phone in frustration, "Dammit!" he didn't have time for this shit. His overbearing father demanded he get his ass back to Tennessee as soon as possible. It appeared, Candy, had been back to her parent's home threatening to kill herself. Presently, nobody could locate her, and she left the baby at his mother's home.

He'd been trying to reach Candy all day with no luck, and it wasn't like her. No matter how upset she claimed to be when he reached out, she always responded. How he despised a manipulative woman. Candy would lose more than his friendship if she didn't get her act together. He was done with her antics.

He told his parents to keep the baby with them while he figured things out. Candy's instability increased to greater heights every day. He didn't want his son exposed to her drama for another minute. He'd never struck a woman in his life, but she pushed his limits repeatedly.

Resolving this would interfere with his plans with Fonn. He squinted at the intense rays of the sun streaming through his office blinds. He got up and looked out over the breathtaking view of the city. The colors of the sunset had him mesmerized. He shook his head as he closed the shade.

Fonn would not understand if he didn't show up tomorrow. All the progress he'd made would be in jeopardy. He was not prepared to take two steps back. If Tam hadn't intervened, he would still have a long road ahead. He knew when he arrived at the lobby of Fonn's place; he had to figure how to get inside.

He always had a talent of making a way out of no way, but the Lord himself must have intervened to have Tam walk right into the lobby as he sat there. He knew she didn't like him very much, and he couldn't blame her, but he also knew she stood in the place of a sister to Fonn. If he could make her see how much Fonn meant to him, he had his in.

He decided to lead with the truth. No games. He would appeal to something he knew every woman had at her core; the romantic sense of a love gone wrong being righted again; the fairytale image of a prince who just needed a kiss from his fair lady to sustain life itself.

Although he needed much more than a kiss from Fonn, he had to make it past the gatekeeper first. He made a mental note; they would do something nice for Tam after the dust settled.

He sat down on the edge of the huge, mahogany desk. If he took stock of his life right now, he needed two things more than the ability to breathe: number one, Fonn by his side, in his life, and his bed. Secondly, the other great love of his life, his son. How he adored that baby - he wanted them to all be a family, and stupid, silly Candy made that probability more of a possibility every day.

He just had one problem; he hadn't quite discussed his decision to get full custody of his son with Fonn yet. His parents urged him to have the conversation asap, but he wasn't a complete fool. He couldn't lie too much at her feet in the same setting. First, he needed to get himself back in; unfortunately, the timeline moved up substantially with these new developments.

He knew what he had to do. Now there was the challenge of getting his sweetheart on board. Tomorrow would be a big day for them. Fonn just didn't know it yet. When she went to bed tonight, she would have no idea the surprise he had in store for her.

Chapter
11

Chiffon med over in bed and moaned. Her alarm rang out, but it was far, far too early. She opened her sleepy eyes, rubbing them. Trying to focus, she skimmed the room for the bright light of her digital clock. 5:30 am shone brightly on display. My goodness, she closed her eyes again. Maybe she was dreaming. She didn't get up until at least 7 am and she knew she set her alarm appropriately.

Wait a minute! Her eyes shot open when she heard the shrill noise again. That was no alarm clock; that was her bell buzzing. She jumped up out of bed. "Who on earth?" She went to the intercom.

"Yes?" she breathed out. Someone must be ringing her bell by mistake. Visitors always had to see the damn doorman, and they would either be announced, or they would dial into her phone system so she would have a heads up to whoever approached—what a joke.

"It's me, sweetheart," Josh's voice rang through the speaker system.

"Josh, what are..." she buzzed the door. Did she forget something? She expected him after work, she thought. She stood there in shock. Soon, she heard the knock at her door. She opened it and quickly and rushed into his arms, delighted at the sight of him. She jumped up on him and wrapped her legs around his hips. He scooped her up in his arms and clung to her.

"Hello sweetheart," he held her tightly, laughing.

"What are you doing here this early?"

He placed her down and kissed her lips softly. "I couldn't stay away from you, baby," he pulled back and smiled, eyes twinkling.

She smiled back, "Ok, what's going on here?" she headed into the kitchen to start some coffee or tea or something. She was not a morning person, especially not a 5 am in the morning person.

"I came here to fetch you."

"To do what?" she scratched her head and yawned. He didn't even look tired.

"You are taking this week off, baby, and we're heading to Tennessee."

"What?" she shrieked, "To Tennessee? What are you talking about? I can't just…"

"Yes, baby, I know, but this is an emergency."

She walked past him toward the couch, hit the table lamp button, and sat down. The light illuminated their faces. "What the hell are you talking about?" she demanded, starting to wake up.

He sat next to her. "I've got to go to Tennessee for a few days, and I want you to come with me," his beautiful eyes searched hers.

"For what reason?" she questioned, bewildered at this sudden change of plans.

"It's JJ."

"JJ?" she repeated.

"Joshua Jr."

"Oh," she said a little too quickly.

"Candy has disappeared and left the baby with my parents."

"What?"

"Yes, apparently, she threatened to commit suicide because of the impending divorce, and then 'poof' she disappeared."

"Did somebody call the police?"

"Yes, and I also have my own team on it, but I need to go down there, and I'm not going without you."

"I can't just take off work like that," she reasoned. "I know you want me to go, but I just started my job, and I don't have vacation time accrued or..."

"Listen, baby," he interrupted her. "I have already cleared it. It has been approved by everyone, including me." He gave her a quick grin, "I just need you to get yourself packed. What's his face - your boy in acquisitions will be responsible during your absence."

"Who, Isaac?"

"Yeah, the one who couldn't take his eyes off you at the meet and greet."

Her eyes widened, "Josh, I don't think he..."

"I need you to hurry along, baby. Our flight leaves at 8 am," as he pulled her to her feet.

She closed her eyes, rubbing them again. This damn man was infuriating. "We're going to your parent's house? Are you sure you want me with you, um, now?" she asked cautiously. "Do they already know about me?" flushing with embarrassment, "I mean, who I am to you?"

"Baby, you worry too much," he stroked her cheek.

"My parents are going to adore you, and so will JJ."

"But, but… I'm, I mean we…"

He took her hands, his eyes settled upon her, "We are two people who fell in love – truly, madly, deeply in love. That's it. That's what they know. They are looking forward to finally meeting you in person."

"Finally?" she repeated.

"Yes, I told them about you a while ago when I felt our relationship intensifying. They have wanted to meet you. I just couldn't make it happen until I had a chance to tell you the truth about everything. I wasn't purposely trying to keep you from family or friends. It needed to …"

"You didn't want them to out you," she uttered painfully. "Too bad I had to be closeted like that. Now they know exactly what I am."

"What you are is the love of my life, sweetheart. Don't feel ashamed of what we have, Fonn. It's the best thing that has ever happened to me. I don't want my stupid behavior to tarnish it in your mind. Our love is pure and good. Always remember that."

His words touched her.

"My family will embrace you. I told them the truth about my debacle of a marriage soon after the ceremony. They weren't happy about it, but ultimately, they came to accept it.

It was a huge upset finding out JJ wasn't mine, but living a lie never ends well. I will correct this mess I have made. I promise I will make this up to you. One day you will find it in your heart to truly forgive me. You will trust me with your heart again. I know I need to put in work to regain your full trust. That's partly why I want you to come home with me. I want everything out in the open. My family understands it all now, including why we separated for the past few months."

"You told them everything?" her eyes widened in shock.

"Not verbatim, of course, but I was not, let's say, my best self after you disappeared on me. I had to come clean and explain my behavior." He stared into space, staring out but seeing nothing. "My dad helped me bring light to the dark. My parents have been nothing but supportive," he continued to look off into space, then snapped out of it, returning his attention to her.

"I have to be honest; I don't feel comfortable going to your parent's house. Not while you are technically still married to someone else. It's not the way I thought I would meet them."

"Not to worry, I'm taking care of it." He rose to his feet and held out his hand to her, "Let's go get you packed." She shook her head with uncertainty but placed her hand in his, nonetheless.

Chapter 12

It was early afternoon when the limo driver pulled up in front of what could only be deemed a palatial estate. The well-manicured, green lawns appeared endless. Like walking through a museum, life-size statues of eagles adorned each side of the driveway. She stepped out of the car and took in the gorgeous surroundings. Colorful tulips stood at attention like yellow, pink, and red soldiers lined up for battle on each side of the long walkway.

Josh held her hand as they ambled up to the large mahogany door of the multi-level estate.

"Oh, my God, Joshua! This is where you grew up?" she asked in awe. The beauty and sheer majesty of the place took her breath away. A warm breeze tickled her nose as she noticed a butterfly bounce from flower to flower.

"Yes, this is home." He pressed some buttons on a keypad and placed what looked like a keycard against a dark surface to gain entry. He started to walk in, and she stood stark still. She had no idea the man she loved came from such opulence. She started to understand his innate sense of entitlement.

He gazed at her with such tenderness. "C'mon, baby," he grabbed her hand. "It's ok, I promise."

They entered the large foyer. The house smelled as if she'd walked into a corner bakery. A dramatic dual staircase led up to what she guessed were sleeping quarters.

A small cream-colored dog with brown splotches came running across the luminous, horizontal tiled floor straight to Josh. "Bowzer!" he laughed and bent down to his knees. The dog barked and ran around in circles before commencing to lick all over Josh's face. Josh looked so young and innocent, frolicking, laughing, and rubbing the dog.

"Joshua, honey, is that you?" she heard a female voice coming from what appeared to be a sitting room area. The most beautiful and fashionably dressed older woman she ever saw appeared around the corner of the doorway. She was all smiles holding out her arms for Joshua.

"Mama," he gushed and embraced her planting a kiss on her cheek. Fonn couldn't help but smile caught up in the adoration every living thing in this house seemed to have for this man.

He turned to her and slinked his arm around her shoulder, "Mama, this is Chiffon or Fonn as I like to call her." The woman smiled warmly at her and held out her arms when Chiffon went to shake her hand.

"We are huggers around here, sweetheart," she embraced her.

"It's a pleasure to meet you, Mrs. Abbott," Chiffon exhaled. The woman smelled of lilies and expensive taste. She went to let go of the woman, and Mrs. Abbott took both of her hands in hers and stared, "Well, aren't you a beautiful thing. I see why my son is so enamored with you." Fonn smiled again.

"Are you hungry? Can I offer you something to drink?" The woman took her hand and led her back to the kitchen area before she could respond. She turned to look at Josh with quiet desperation – he only smiled and shrugged his shoulders.

They all headed to a dining room area to sit at a small table near a large, looming plant. Crystals of the enormous chandelier sparkled as the light from the windows bounced off, turning them into various shades of the rainbow. Mrs. Abbott sat first, then motioned for her to sit. After seating, a very neat-looking woman in a maid's uniform appeared. She smiled at Josh, "Hello, mister Josh."

"Ms. Garcia," he replied, "Good to see you again."

"Madam, can I get you anything?" she motioned to the matriarch.

Mrs. Abbott and Josh both stared toward Chiffon. "Oh, tea would be great," she offered.

Josh nodded, and his mother directed the woman to bring tea for everyone.

"Where's dad?" Josh asked while munching on some sort of biscuit or cracker in a dish on the table.

"He had some business downtown; he will be back this evening."

She could see the family resemblance in the shape of his face, nose, and eyes. His mother was striking, full of grace and elegance. Fonn liked her immediately. Her high cheekbones were amazing.

"Any new news?" he asked his mother. She glanced from Fonn back to him. "It's ok, mama; Fonn knows everything. Speak freely."

His mother appeared to relax. "Still no word from Candy. Her mother just left here visiting JJ." A knot went through Chiffon's stomach.

Josh nodded, "Where is he now?"

"He's in his nursery sound asleep."

Of course, he had a room here. Chiffon scolded herself for being shocked. He was the baby in the family; they accepted him as their own.

The housekeeper sat the tea out, and everyone busied themselves with the pouring, adding of sugar, lemon, and the like.

"You have a very beautiful home Mrs. Abbott," Chiffon said, looking around in fascination. Expensive paintings decorated the walls. Elegant sconces ordained the walls. It was so expansive and pristine, difficult to believe anyone lived there.

"Thank you, dear. I'm sure Joshy will give you the full tour after you all get settled."

"Mama, please don't call me Joshy," he requested with a look of anguish on his face. Fonn smiled while his mother sipped her tea with a grin.

"Joshy loved that name growing up."

"No, I didn't," he shook his head, but Fonn could see the hint of laughter on his face.

"Go sit!" Mrs. Abbott yelled at the dog, who was rubbing against Josh's legs.

"Oh, leave him alone, mama. He misses his only real friend in this house. Ain't that right, Bowzer? Ain't that, right?" he rubbed the dog's head again, smiling genuinely.

"Humph!" his mother snorted.

Fonn could feel her eyes welling up. She could feel all the love in this house. No family was perfect, but she could picture how Josh and his older brother and sister must have grown up. It had to be wonderful to have their parents together. She longed for such family life. It was touching to witness.

They finished their tea. Josh rose to his feet, "Ok, mama, I'm going to take Fonn upstairs to get her settled," he glanced at his watch. "I have to head downtown for a quick meeting, but I should be back before dad gets here." He went over and kissed his mother's cheek. Chiffon waved at her as they ascended the staircase.

"So where will I be staying?" she followed behind him as he passed down a long corridor to the right of the staircase.

"We'll be staying in the northeast corner of the right-wing." Wow, this place has wings. Josh grew up in a home that had wings. She followed him through a door leading to a bedroom so large that it had a full sitting room at the front. The scent of potpourri and clean linen filled her nostrils.

Staring at their suitcases on the floor, with her brow raised, "This is very nice, Josh, but why is your luggage in here too?"

He grinned and sat on the bed, "I don't understand your question, sweetheart."

"Surely you don't expect us to sleep together here," she gestured toward the bed, "In your parent's house with your parents right here?" she pointed toward the door.

He laughed out loud, then a full-bodied haughty laugh. He was laughing so hard she started to smile herself. "You are so old-fashioned. You would make me love you even if I didn't want to." Then he laughed some more.

When he finally calmed himself back down, he said, "I'm not letting you out of my sight while we are here. Together is exactly the way we are going stay."

"But, but here? In the same bed?" she asked him, horrified at the very idea. She wasn't trying to be argumentative but being respectful was important to her. Their situation was bad enough.

He stared at her for a long minute, expressionless. Then he smiled again, "Ok, sweetheart, if you want me on the couch while we're here, then that's where I'll go. I don't think that's where you want me at night," he murmured mischievously. She felt that familiar tingle through her body, collimating between her legs.

He rose to his feet and put his hands on each side of her face. They stared at each other. He pulled her closer and pressed his lips to her forehead lightly. "If I didn't have to go right now, we would christen this bed together properly right now. I don't give a damn where we are," as his lips overtook hers, suckling, nibbling, probing. She wrapped her arms around him, consumed by the passion she felt for him. His tongue mingled with hers, hot breath caught in her throat.

"Baby, sweet baby," he mumbled against her.

"Josh," she exhaled. She felt her nipples push out through the fabric of her blouse, teasing toward his chest. He pulled himself back from her and stared down into her eyes.

"You're killing me," he said, as his eyes made a slow descent down to her breasts, whose taut ends gave away her desire. When aroused, her nipples protruded much more than the average woman, practically doubling in size. She used to hide it with nipple covers, but Josh made her take them off and swear them off forever.

"Damn woman, you are downright edible. I could eat you for breakfast, lunch, and dinner."

She warmed, savoring the thought.

His smoldering blue-gray eyes went back to hers. "I've got to take care of something important," he spoke softly. "I'll be back, ok?" He stroked her shoulders.

"Yes," she nodded.

"Good, why don't you unpack and get yourself settled. Try to close your eyes for a minute. I know you must be tired. I'll be back before you know it." He kissed her lips and her forehead and headed out the door.

She wondered what held such importance he had to depart so soon after their arrival. His hard arousal pushed against her, so leaving couldn't have been easy. She also knew this wasn't a vacation, a lot of shit was brewing in the pot. He probably went to check on the latest with Candice.

She stared up at the clock on the wall – 2 pm. She went ahead and did as he suggested and unpacked her clothes. No matter what happened, she decided, she would never run again. The pain of separation just wasn't worth it. If he remained honest with her, they could survive anything. She soon drifted off into a surprisingly restful sleep.

Chapter 13

Candy, I'm here in town," he spoke harshly into the receiver, "Enough with this bullshit." He glanced around to make sure no one was in earshot of his one-sided conversation. He sat in the reception area of his attorney's office, tapping his foot against the chair leg.

He had not planned to file in Tennessee, but what the hell. "JJ is with me, and he will remain with me. Let's make this a quick process. All the hysterics are unnecessary. I will be fair with visitation. I have been with him since the day he came into the world. My name is on the birth certificate. He is my son in every sense of the word. You need to call me, Candy. Stop fucking around. Everyone is worried about you."

He disconnected and glanced at the clock, quarter to 3. He almost didn't make it here at all. Fonn's hot body called out to him in every language he knew.

He might have to move their room down to the farthest end of the hall. She got loud when they went at it, and he loved making her scream. If she thought he wouldn't touch her because of their location – well, she would need to learn the long, hard way. He smiled to himself. He couldn't keep his hands or lips off her. She was made for him.

He closed his eyes and leaned back in reflection. She had a fragrance that reminded him of fresh springtime. Every day with her represented a promise fulfilled.

He would never let her get away again. He opened his eyes as someone walked past him. He needed to handle this divorce fiasco with the utmost expedience.

Candy's absence made it difficult but not impossible. She had better resurface soon. Fonn needed to see resolution, and he couldn't blame her. He would be at the courthouse every day if he found out she was married to someone else.

He should have just been honest in the first place. When they first met, he knew she was something special. He just did not expect to fall so completely so fast. Before he knew it, they were inseparable, and his feelings consumed him. Initially, he didn't know if she felt the same way about him. He refused to risk it by laying all this heavy shit on her. He kept putting it off and procrastinating until everything caught up with him in the worst possible way.

He'd stopped in the baby's room to check on him before he left the house. He slept so peacefully. He had a love for JJ he couldn't explain. His feelings and desire to protect the child surpassed biology. He had to ensure his son's safety.

Candy hadn't been a bad mother; she was just unstable. He used to think that part of her personality was rather amusing. She was a lot of fun, but poor decision-making created extra work for him over the years.

Constantly, he had to save her from herself, and it had gotten old. He eventually made the ultimate sacrifice for his friend, and it almost cost him everything. The receptionist let him know he could enter Jake's office. He rose to his feet.

Chapter
14

Something tickled her nose. She scrounged up her face and scratched at her nose. She felt it again. She opened hazy eyes and stared into the face of a precious, little baby boy. He smiled at her and grabbed at her nose again.

She smiled back at him and sat up, "Hello, little one; you must be JJ," she looked past the child at Josh, who held him close to her face.

He also had a bright smile. "Fonn, meet JJ." Then he turned the baby to face him. "JJ, meet Fonn." He turned the smiling baby back to her. She glanced at the clock again after 6 pm. Wow, she'd been asleep for hours.

"Wake up, sleepyhead," he said softly as he bent down to kiss her cheek. She stroked his face lightly and brought her attention back to the baby.

A myriad of feelings flashed through her. She thought she would hate this child cooing at her now, but she didn't feel negative at all. His absolute gorgeousness certainly helped his cause. He was quite beautiful with a shock of dark curly hair, light brown eyes, and warm brown skin.

"Awhh," he squealed, bouncing up and down.

"Can he talk yet?" she sat up, and Josh and JJ got onto the bed.

"Yes, he mutters intelligible words but makes more noise in his own language." She smiled at them both.

The baby's eyes were glued to hers. He reached up to be picked up, and she stared up at Josh.

"Go ahead," he nodded, "He likes you." She didn't have a lot of experience with small babies and felt a little hesitant.

"Go ahead. He only has about eight teeth, and they are all in the front. "He probably won't bite you, but if he does, it probably won't hurt much," he laughed as she took the beautiful baby gingerly.

"Hi, JJ." She held him in front of her, and the baby laughed and squirmed and kicked.

"Wow!" Josh said. "He likes you; he's excited." She felt a warm sensation of tenderness fill her. She could see why Josh loved this baby, and she could tell Josh was waiting to see if she would embrace this child, his child.

She spoke to the baby, "It's a pleasure to meet you, JJ." The baby cooed some more, giggling with joy. She knew this moment would come, and she thought she would dread it. More reminders of this damn family he was a part of without her; this family she was forced to share him with.

She didn't expect to meet the baby like this but, it was ok. Josh never waited to get the ball rolling on what he wanted, and she knew the baby would be a part of their lives. She spoke at length to Tam about that very thing before she left, and she realized she could accept it. Plus, he was so doggone adorable you could just eat him with a spoon.

She didn't feel jealous. She laughed out loud at how the baby jumped around. What a happy baby, and the sheer satisfaction on Josh's face let her know this was a package deal.

He reached for the child, and the baby lifted his arms to him. "I'll be back, babe," he scooped up the baby, "I think the nanny needs to do a diaper change. Right man?" He kissed the child's cheek, and the baby giggled and held his father's face with his little hand. At that moment, she was filled with so much love for Josh. Sometimes there was nothing more masculine than a man loving on his baby. JJ wasn't even his baby. How much more would he be with their children.

"He is beautiful, Josh."

Josh gave her the warmest, most genuine smile she'd ever seen. "I love you," he said.

"And I love you," she watched him depart.

She soon heard commotion downstairs – like people were arriving. She slipped on her sandals and made her way toward the noise. It sounded like Josh's voice downstairs as well. She peeked down the long staircase, careful not to be seen. A large man, who she could only guess was Josh's dad, considering he looked exactly like him, just 20 years older. The man was striking. He had the same crazy eye color Josh had.

Mesmerized, she watched him. He was laughing and hitting Josh on the back. Another man who also had to be family was also laughing at the bottom of the staircase. Soon, a woman strolled in who bore an uncanny resemblance to the rest of them. Mrs. Abbott stood there as well. Was it a family reunion?

Josh didn't tell her everyone was coming over tonight. Thank God she got some rest earlier. Her hair swung up in a clip, but it still hung down all over her head. Second thoughts assailed her. Usually, she loved a wild hair look.

Just then, she heard Josh say, "Let me go get Fonn, and we can get started." She slowly backed away and hightailed it back into the bedroom.

Get started with what she wondered; dinner maybe? Soon he breezed through the doorway. "Come, sweetheart," he held out his hand for her. "I got some people I want you to meet."

"Who?"

"The rest of my family."

She looked at him nervously and glanced in the mirror.

"Baby, you look beautiful, the most beautiful thing I've ever seen. Let's go," he reached for her with both hands.

"Where's the baby?" she asked, grasping ahold of him.

"Oh, he's sleeping again. You'll see he spends about as much time sleeping as he does awake."

They descended the staircase, and all chatter stopped. All eyes were on her. It was extremely uncomfortable. She squeezed Josh's hand a little tighter. He glanced at her adoringly.

At the bottom of the stairs, Josh introduced her to the big man first. "Fonn, this is my father, William Abbott, dad, this is Fonn," the big man gave her a warm smile and took her hand.

He bent down to kiss it lightly. She wasn't expecting it and blushed accordingly. "Umm, nice to meet you too, Mr. Abbott."

The big man took over the introductions then. "This is my son, Gregory, and this is my beautiful daughter,

Violet." She felt like she was in some sort of movie regarding cloning. Each one of the kids had the same dark curls and those damn eyes; what a gorgeous family.

Gregory shook her hand, smiling and looking quite amused. "You can call us Greg and Vi."

Violet gave her a quick hug. "Welcome to Hazelton," she smiled at her.

"Hazelton?" she repeated. They all spoke at the same time, filling the surrounding area with many voices. Apparently, the manor had been named after Josh's birth since they all inherited their daddy's changeable eye color.

"Now that we are all here, should we do dinner first or tackle the business?" Mrs. Abbott asked the group.

"Business," they all answered in unison, and Chiffon chuckled. Apparently, eye color wasn't the only thing running in the family.

Mrs. Abbott linked arms with her daughter on the left and Chiffon on the right. "We take our family meetings in the den," she directed to Chiffon. The boys followed close behind.

"Are you sure you want me to attend your family meeting?" Chiffon whispered, feeling like a bit of an intruder.

"Of course," Mrs. Abbott responded – it affects you as well."

"Besides, you make it even," Violet interjected, "I'm tired of the boys outnumbering us." She laughed with her mother.

Inside the brightly lit den, they sat in a circle of comfortable chairs. It resembled a genuine meeting room with small tables resting alongside each station to house notebooks or refreshments. Her feet sank into the plush rug. The housekeeper appeared and asked for requests. Wow, she was well trained, Chiffon surmised. The housekeeper took note and disappeared through a side door.

Mr. Abbott called the meeting to order. "While this is an unfortunate turn of events regarding Candy's disappearance – it is important to concentrate on the well-being of my grandson." Everyone nodded in agreement.

"Candy has officially been declared a missing person. The Lake family would like the child to stay with them until Candy resurfaces, but we, of course, would like the child to stay here. This is where his mother left him."

"Dad, can I interject?" Greg asked politely.

"Sure, son."

"Shouldn't it be up to Joshy, where JJ stays?"

"Yes, ultimately it is, but we know Josh is, shall we say, in between residences." Josh flinched at his father's assessment but couldn't deny the accuracy. "Candy obviously wants to get a rise out of him – which is why she has pulled this stunt."

Josh interjected then, "JJ will stay here at least until Candy gets in touch. The Lakes are welcome to visit whenever they want. I think they already know that."

"They know it," stated Mrs. Abbott, "But it doesn't change the fact they want to take my baby away from us."

"It's not happening," Josh reassured her, being cautious about what was said in front of Fonn. He still needed to clear some things with her first.

His phone buzzed in his pocket. He glanced at it briefly. "Excuse me for a moment, I've got to take this," as he stepped out of the room, speaking in a strong but hushed tone. The housekeeper came back with their refreshments.

Mr. Abbott asked Chiffon if she had any thoughts on the situation. Her stomach twirled; she didn't know she'd be expected to participate actively. "JJ needs safety, security, and a boatload of love right now. Whatever affords him the best stability during this volatile time would be the best thing to do."

"Well said," Violet spoke up.

"I can't believe Candy. I mean, you can't force someone to love you or stay with you. Children need to be with their mother," Mrs. Abbott said; "If the situation is a healthy one." Everyone agreed.

Josh came back to his seat, looking rather ashen. "What's happened, son – what's wrong?" his dad asked.

"That was my detective."

"Yes?" his mother urged him on.

"They have located Candy?" Chiffon asked, "Where is she?"

"She is with Terrance, again."

"Oh Lord have mercy!" his mother wailed. Loud murmurs filled the room. Everyone knew the trouble Candy went through to escape Terrance and his abusive ways. They also knew he was the baby's biological father.

"She is out of her head," Greg added.

"Son," Papa Abbott motioned to Josh. "The time is now."

Josh then looked toward his beloved. He closed his eyes for a minute. "Fonn," he called to her and held out his hand, rising to his feet. She got up and took it. "Excuse us, everyone." His dad nodded, and everyone continued to talk.

"Where are we going?" she queried, trying to keep up. He walked briskly through the large house, pulling her along. He eventually turned into a comfortable living room area. He sat her down on a soft chair and bent down on his knees in front of her.

"What's wrong?" she automatically started to rub her hands through his soft, short, curly hair. She knew it had a very calming effect on him. He grabbed her hands and kissed them.

"You seem very disturbed," she hesitated and then went on, "I know finding out Candice is back with Terrence is not good news, but at least she is ok." He didn't speak for a while, just gazed at her.

She was concerned about him. He was visibly upset, and it was unusual. Where was the cool, composed man she was used to? He appeared a bit, well, frazzled.

"Baby, listen," he kissed her hand again.

"What is it? What are you trying to tell me? Just say it, don't worry, I'm all in with you now. I'm not leaving you again no matter what." She could see the wave of relief wash over him. He kissed her hand once more.

"Baby, I love you so much, and I want us to have a bright future together," he breathed out in a husky voice.

"I know that," she responded. He let her hands go and reached into his inner jacket pocket and handed her a document. She stared at it quizzically at first, then took it and opened it. Petition for the Dissolution of Marriage was sprawled at the top.

Tears clouded her eyes, "You filed?"

"Yes, baby, I filed today because I promised you I would, and I never want to break a promise to you again."

"Oh Josh," she reached out and held him. He filed. He really filed for a divorce, even amidst Candice's shenanigans. He pulled back from her. His own eyes were glistening.

"What's wrong then, Josh? This is good news, right? We are free to get on with our lives together."

"Oh yes, baby, yes I just, it's just…my son."

"You're worried about him? Don't you think she'd give you visitation? I mean, you took him in since the day he was born. Surely…"

"I don't want visitation."

"Hun? Of course you want to see your son on some form of a regular schedule. He's going to need you."

"I don't want visitation with my son," he repeated.

She shook her head back and forth, furrowing her brow. "I don't understand."

"I know," he said with a slight grin. "What I'm trying to say is, I don't want to see him periodically. I want permanent custody of him, Fonn."

Her eyes widened, "Permanent custody," she repeated, "Like permanent full custody?" she asked in surprise. He never, ever mentioned anything like this before. "You want the baby to live with you, I mean with, with... um, us, like every day?" she added.

He answered her quietly, "Yes baby, that is exactly what I'm saying. I want us all to live together every day."

"So, you want me to be like his mother?" she asked in disbelief her eyes narrowing uneasily. "You think I can be his mother?"

"Yes, his mother and my wife. My real wife not this silly bullshit I've participated in with Candy."

Dumbfounded, she held his gaze. Was he proposing to her? She was confused. "I need you with me. I don't want to do it without you. I don't want to do anything without you again baby."

She stared at him in astonishment then rose to her feet. At the terrace window, she witnessed trees swaying in unison outside. She couldn't imagine herself as a mother. He wanted her to be a mother to his child. Obviously, she knew the baby would be a part of their lives, but she did not expect this degree of well... responsibility.

Soon she felt him come and stand behind her wrapping his arms around her waist. She closed her eyes because it felt lovely. "Baby," he spoke just above her head. She could feel his warm breath in her hair. "I know this is a lot to spring on you. I know you just met JJ."

She turned to face him. "I don't know anything about babies! I don't know how to do diapers or bottles or pacifiers or babies!" she panicked.

"You were wonderful with him today. He loves you already, I can tell. I will teach you everything you need to know. JJ will teach you." She felt a little smile touch her lips then.

What was Josh getting her into? "This is all so sudden," she exclaimed.

"I know, I know it is. I didn't plan to broach this subject just yet. I wanted to give us a chance to get reacquainted, to have more quality time together. Candy has forced my hand."

He turned her to face him and held both of her hands in his. Gazing into her eyes he said, "Sweetheart, sometimes life's biggest rewards come when we least expect them, when we thought we weren't going to be ready for them. You must be ready to jump when opportunity arises. I can't let Candy oversee his well-being anymore. She is all over the page. I wouldn't be able to sleep at night but, at the same time, he touched her chin, I wouldn't be able to sleep at night without you. Support me with this baby and I will make sure all your dreams come true. I will make sure you have whatever you want."

"All I want is you Josh."

"Well, we are golden then. You have me. I'm yours - every tender morsel."

She smiled, "I…"

"Shhhhh," he placed his finger over her lips. "Don't answer right now. Take some time and think about it. I know this is a lot to lay on you."

"What if I can't Joshua. Are you going to dump me?"

"What! Of course not. We are in this for the long hall. I will implement plan B."

"What is plan B? she asked.

" Vi or my mother will take him."

"You would be ok with that?"

"I'm not gonna lose you, Fonn. Not for any reason. I would never force my child on you. You wouldn't be happy, and neither would he."

She gazed at him, he was so humble, so full of integrity. What if it were a child she loved? She would want Josh to support her, to care for her enough to stand by her. She couldn't imagine her life without him, and he couldn't imagine his life without JJ.

"I don't need to think about it Josh. I don't need any additional time."

"You don't?" he waited anxiously for her answer.

"I see how much you adore your son and frankly, it just makes me love you more. If you want him with us, then with us he will be. I can learn to be a mommy."

He grabbed her and swung her around planting kisses all over her face. She giggled. He put her down and stared at her. At first, she couldn't tell what his expression meant. Those eyes were turning a smoldering blue again. Then it dawned, she knew what the different colors meant now.

"Josh," she warned him, as he started to slowly unbuckle his belt. Her eyes widened as she glanced around quickly. "Not here," she glanced toward the open door.

"I'm going to take you right here, right now," he said unblinking, "Nobody comes in here."

She felt herself backing up. "Josh," she held out her arms to stop his approach. Just then their attention turned toward the entrance way – as footsteps could be heard coming down the hall. She exhaled not realizing she'd been holding her breath again. This man literally took her breath away. If he continued to come closer to her, she would have embarrassed herself on various sections of his parent's furniture. She shook off the thought. Coming here with him was probably not a good idea in terms of her moral compass.

"Dammit," he uttered and made the proper adjustments to his pants and belt. "Lucky you," he whispered as he smiled roguishly at her.

"There you guys are," his mother exclaimed as she entered the room. "I wasn't sure which room you went off to. Dinner is ready," she said as she held JJ in her arms. Josh smiled innocently at them both.

Chiffon went over to Mrs. Abbott and held out her arms for the baby. Hell, she figured, she might as well get started. Josh looked at his mother's confused look. "It's ok, mama. Everything is ok now."

"I trust your talk went well then?"

"Yes, very well, mother."

Mrs. Abbott smiled and handed the baby over to Chiffon, who kissed his cheek. Was it possible she already started to love him? She didn't want Terrance to get his filthy hands on him. Josh was right; the child needed to be protected.

What was going on in Hazelton? She thought as they all headed back toward the dining room. She was now becoming swept up in Josh's world, and she couldn't imagine it any other way.

They had a delicious meal full of family banter. The Abbott clan got together at least once a week for dinner. She learned his brother immersed himself in the family business as CFO at Abbott Electronics, while his sister served as VP at the main headquarters of Abbott Enterprises. Whereas Josh ventured out on his own and had no tie to the day-to-day activities like the others.

She got the distinct feeling Poppa Abbott didn't like it one bit. Josh stuck to what he did best, and that was finding new business and branding. The strings loosened on him for now, but she deciphered the underlying tension between the two men.

No matter, as it seems, whenever there was a crisis, they all banded together. Their bond was evident, and Chiffon found herself fighting envy again. Her family was scattered and barely spoke to each other. She was somewhat close to her mother, but that relationship became strained in her father's absence.

Her mother came to rely on her in an unhealthy manner. Enhancing her mom's life became her sole responsibility. Chiffon had been in no shape to fill in for anyone. Truth be told, she needed her mother to be there for her, not the other way around.

After his siblings left and his parents retired, they went in together to put JJ down. She even changed a diaper. She watched Josh feed, burb, and rock the baby, who was a little fussy as he drifted off. What a lucky little boy to have this man, who wasn't his father, fill in the role, and with such tenderness. They put the baby down in his crib and headed back to their room. Joshua stopped just outside of the door.

"Thank you, baby. Again, I know this is not easy for you. I apologize for the mess you've got to deal with now due to my choices. I tried…I intended to protect you from all of this."

She reached up and touched his face. Inspecting him, she spoke, "I don't blame you. You are a good man, an honorable one. Everything you did, you did because you cared about someone else."

"I appreciate that, baby," as he smiled down at her. They entered the bedroom, and he closed and turned the key in the door. She watched him. He went on and on about something his brother said. As he started removing his shirt, she stood motionless.

He glanced over to her, and for a moment, no words were spoken. "You're still nervous about being here with me?" She nodded. He gazed at her with slight amusement. Then eased closer to kiss her eyelids, her nose, then her lips. The kiss, light at first, probed gently. He slid his tongue gently over and around hers. Then she felt him unclasp the clip in her hair and throw it to the floor.

He massaged his hands through her hair, lifting her head back to expose her neck. His hot tongue slid down the length of it, softly biting and suckling her skin. She grabbed his head and kissed him roughly. Her hands stroked under his t-shirt, rubbing his hard-muscled torso.

A slight groan escaped his lips. He pulled back and looked down at her, "Let's not start this, baby. If you're going to make me stop because of where we are," he motioned around the room, "I'm telling you now," he breathed out heavily, "I won't have the power to stop."

She started to unbutton her blouse and let it drop to the floor. She unsnapped her jeans and gently pulled down the zipper, smiling at him. He smiled back and shook his head. She let her hand hesitate over her zipper.

"Don't stop, baby. Now is not a good time to tease me," he said gruffly. That hungry, carnal look in his eyes told her she'd better save the striptease for another day.

She slid her snug pants down her long legs and stepped out of them. He folded his arms and watched her intently. She undid her bra clasp and let it drop to the floor. She then slid her panties down and stepped out of them.

The next thing she knew, he picked her up over his shoulders. She started laughing, "What are you doing?" she squealed.

"I'm going to make you even wetter than I know you already are," he smacked her ass as he carried her.

Once in the bathroom, he tantalizingly slid her down his body. After her feet landed on the cool tiles, he turned the shower on, and the room started to steam up. She pulled his t-shirt over his head, and immediately her hands rubbed his chest. He undid his belt and pants and dropped everything to the floor. He stepped out from the pile naked. Their lips met furiously, hands, arms, legs.

Tangled in him, she whispered, "I love you so much, Josh."

"I love you more," he murmured between kisses. "You taste so good, baby, everywhere." He slid the shower glass to the side, and she stepped in. He entered right behind her. She stood closest to the stream of pulsating water that hit her ankles. She usually took great care not to get her hair wet in the shower, but she could care less right now. He pushed her lightly until she was directly under the stream of hot, pulsating liquid. She closed her eyes and let the soothing, steamy water run over her.

He cupped her breasts from behind and toyed with her nipples. She threw her head back, enjoying the sweet sensations. He turned her around to face him and covered her mouth with his own. Soon she felt his finger slide in and out of her body down there, and she cried out his name.

"What is it you want, baby?" he mumbled gruffly. "You're calling me. Do you like that?"

"Oh yes," she stepped back and let the water run down the front of her body, splattering between them.

"I want you to come apart for me." He bent down and took one of her nipples in his mouth. He suckled and bit into her tender flesh. She held him tighter as he pushed her against the shower wall out of the stream. She opened amorous eyes. The water now streamed onto his back. He lifted his head and stood as close as he could in front of her.

His long rigid staff slid back and forth in between the area just below her entrance. He cupped her breasts and rolled her nipples between his fingers. It felt so damn good.

It's You

She wanted to scream. His lips were on her shoulders, her neck, her lips. Everywhere as he continued the sweet torture. She had never seen anything as sexy as his hard body glistening wet.

"Oh!" she cried out and started moving faster around his staff, wanting him inside her. "Oh Josh," she was lost to how wonderful he made her feel. She hadn't realized he grabbed the showerhead.

She opened her eyes when she felt the hot pulsating water tantalize her breasts and nipples to a harder solid state. He then turned the dial, and the stream flowed out faster. He lowered himself to his knees and angled it between her legs. She literally thought she would lose consciousness. She writhed and bucked as he caressed one breast with one hand and held the pounding, throbbing water to her clit with the other.

"Come for me, Fonn, come for daddy," he bit into her nipple. She was out of her mind. Sensation culminated in a high fever pitch, "Oh, Joshua, baby!" she screamed as a supernova orgasm racked her body. She called his name over and over and grabbed at his neck and shoulder, anything to hold onto. She was trying not to fall while he continued this torturous assault on her senses.

"Open your eyes," he commanded softly. "Fonn," he called to her. She opened heavy lids. He then replaced the showerhead. "I want to make you come like that every single night – deliciously and only for me. He pressed his body against hers. You are all mine, baby, made for me."

"Yes, yes, I'm yours, all yours," she nodded and embraced him. She was his. Her body continued to spasm. He pulled her right leg up over his hip and thrust himself deep inside her. He filled her. Tears came to her eyes. She was lost.

"Yes, God, baby," he moaned into her ear, "Forgive me if I'm a little rough. I've been dreaming of this all day."

She couldn't speak. She nodded and held onto him as he had his way with her. Over and over, he plunged. He showed her no mercy as each thrust felt deeper and harder. This angle had him hitting her spot deliciously and continually. Soon she felt a familiar tingle – her breath catching in her throat. It was unreal how easily her body responded to him. Passion overruled everything. His explosion erupted deep inside her.

She clenched her muscles, and her teeth. Soon she was overtaken overtaken by another earth-shattering orgasm. "Goddammit!" he yelled out, still pumping away inside her. "Fonn, Fonn," he repeated her name. "You are perfect for me, baby." She held onto him, clutching and grabbing for stability. As soon as they could breathe again, they found the body wash and washed each other gently. She felt slightly sore from the assault, but she wouldn't have changed a damn thing. So much for being so timid in his mother's house.

Chapter
15

She woke up disoriented. Where was she again? She warmed all over as it all came back to her. She was with her man but where was he? His side of the bed was empty. She glimpsed around and noticed 8am on the clock. Um, maybe he went to check on the baby.

Although hesitant, she decided to check in with work. She wanted an update on an important vendor meeting. Her network app wouldn't connect, so she couldn't access work email from her phone.

She tried her secretary's number from memory, but it went straight to voicemail. She then called Isaac's cell phone number.

"This is Isaac," he answered after one ring.

"Hi Isaac, it's Chiffon."

"Chiffon, oh my God, are you alright?" he said with concern.

"Yes, Isaac, yes, of course, how is everything there?" she wanted to know.

"Good, where are you?" he asked. She hesitated, wondering how much she could share with him. She felt like she could trust him, but she figured, no, she was positive Josh wouldn't like it.

"Chiffon?" he asked, "Are you still there?"

"Yes, yes, I'm here, Isaac. I'm in Tennessee right now."

"In Tennessee?" he repeated. "What are you —"

"Something um, unexpected came up, and I have to be away this week. How did the Tinley meeting go yesterday?" she changed the subject.

"Better than expected. We had to narrow down on deliverables, but I think everyone is on the same page now."

"Good," she smiled, "I'm sorry I couldn't be there to watch you in action," she said smiling.

"Me too," he said quickly, too quickly. They were silent on the line. "Chiffon, he broke the awkward silence. I want you to know you can talk to me, you know, about anything. He spoke gingerly, "I mean, I think you know I care about you. In the few months you've been here, I, no I should say, we have become quick friends, right?"

"Yes, yes, of course," she agreed. Isaac had taken her under his wing. She very much appreciated and liked him. "I know you care, Isaac, the feeling is mutual," she exhaled.

"What I'm trying to say is, well," he hesitated, "I don't want you to get hurt."

In surprise, she responded, "Hurt? Why do you think I would be hurt, Isaac?" Did he know something she didn't? She got up and walked over to the window. "Is it something regarding work?" she asked. He didn't respond. "What do you know I don't, Isaac?"

"I don't know anything for sure, Chiffon. I just have a feeling."

"What kind of feeling?"

"Just, well, you might be in over your head."

"In what regard?" What was he talking about? "What are you trying to tell me?"

He hesitated again, "Ok, Chiffon, I'm just going to put it out there and ask you."

"Ok," she said.

"Are you involved with Joshua Abbott?"

In shock, her stomach clenched. She hesitated to respond – that was completely unexpected.

"I knew it," he said smugly when she failed to answer. "That's where you are, right? Somewhere with him? Cause he is clearly not in the office either." His tone was accusatory. Guilt besieged her. How did he know? Jesus! Did everybody know? Were rumors going around the office about them as they spoke?

"Well, I, I mean we, um," she couldn't lie. She didn't want to lie to Isaac. He was the closest thing to a friend she had at work. She was silent for a moment. "Yes," she said barely above a whisper.

"Chiffon, you need to know something. Something I don't think you are aware of."

"What?"

He didn't speak for a moment, "I'm sorry to be the one to tell you this but, but I care about you, and I don't want you to be deceived."

"Just spit it out, Isaac, please," her hand quaked.

"Joshua Abbott is married," he finally blurted out.

Oh, my God. He knew. Shame and embarrassment enveloped her. "I- I," she didn't know what to say. No matter how she responded, she would sound like a fool for knowingly being involved with a married man.

"You don't understand all the circumstances, Isaac," she said in a small voice.

"You're right. I don't. But I think it might be you who isn't quite clear, Chiffon. You deserve better, so much better than someone like that."

"It's not what you think," she defended herself weakly.

"It's not?" he asked. "What exactly do I have wrong?"

Tears sprang to her eyes, "We are in love!" she pierced out defensively.

"I see," he said coldly, "So you knew about his marriage?"

"No, no, of course, I didn't."

"So, he lied to you."

"Yes, but..."

"Sounds rather complicated, Chiffon, and you don't sound incredibly happy. Shouldn't real love bring you joy, not pain?" She didn't answer. "From what I saw at the company party, you are in a lot of pain with him."

"Isaac, no, I, I mean..." Then she became silent because he was partially right. He just didn't understand what she and Josh had found in each other. She couldn't even begin to explain it. She knew what she was doing, but it would sound like she was making excuses for Josh's bad behavior if she defended him now.

"I've got to go now," she managed on the verge of a sob.

"Listen, Chiffon, I'm sorry, I didn't mean to upset you. I shouldn't have blurted that out. I overstepped but it's just, you are such a wonderful person, and I want what's best for you. I don't want to see you get hurt. You should be with someone who can stand up and honestly be there for you. Someone who wouldn't lie to you just to get what he wants. Powerful men tend to take advantage of vulnerable women."

She wasn't vulnerable, was she? "I hear you," she assured him. She didn't want to hear anymore. "I will talk to you later," she whispered.

"I care about you, Chiffon. I just want you to have what you deserve and not settle for less. You could have so much more with the right someone. Don't be angry with me," he beseeched her.

"I'm not. I understand what you are saying," she said solemnly.

"Who are you talking to?" Josh said abruptly, startling her. She hadn't even heard him come in. She turned to face him feeling caught and uncomfortable. She hit the end button quickly.

"Oh, I um, just talking to Tam." She figured she'd better keep Isaac's name out of her mouth with Josh.

"Is something wrong? You seem upset."

"I'm ok," she sniffed and held herself. "She is just going through a rough time with her ex. I feel sorry for her."

His beautiful eyes narrowed on her, "Did something else happen?" He waited and searched her eyes for a lingering moment. She wanted to look away. She swore he could read her soul with those eyes of his.

"No, um, nothing particular – just rehashing the same options over again." She didn't make eye contact. "So what time is breakfast around here?" She changed the subject, hoping he would follow her lead. When he didn't answer her, she tightened her housecoat belt. "Where is JJ? Is he up?"

"I don't like it when you keep things from me. Tell me what's got you so upset," he decreed.

She walked up to him and wrapped her arms around his broad shoulders. She lay her head down on his chest. She could hear the faint sound of his heart beating. His arms didn't come up to embrace her like normal, and she knew she had to come up with something better than Tam's hysterics.

"Joshua," she looked up at him, "Please, believe me, everything is ok. We discussed some of the things I have been going through, and yes, I started feeling a little melancholy, but I'm fine now." He stared at her for a minute and then enclosed her in his arms.

"Fonn," he mumbled into her hair.

"Yes, darling."

"We are starting over now, right, clean slate?"

"Yes," she nodded.

"No more secrets between us."

"Right Josh."

He bent down and kissed her lips lovingly. Lifting her chin, he pulled his face back to gaze at her, "You know you can tell me anything, right? You shouldn't feel like you need to go elsewhere for solace; I don't want you turning to someone else. If something has upset you, it's my job to be your comforter and mine alone."

"Dammit, Joshua!" she said in exasperation. "What are you talking about?" her arm flared out. "I'm not turning to anyone else for comfort," she exclaimed, as she raised her eyebrow at him. Just how long had he been standing there? Did he know she had been talking to Isaac? "Women always talk to each other. We need a place for all our words. Trust me. You don't want me to only talk to you."

"You're right, he agreed, but I do want you to only come to me if the issue is about me. I'm the only one who can make it right, nobody else."

"Ok, I understand," she agreed.

"I want you to hear me," he reached around her and pulled her to him. "I've got you."

"I know Josh, I know." She closed her eyes and forgave herself for the little white lie.

The next few days were spent awaiting word from Candice or the detectives. So far, it was radio silence. Candice seemed to have vanished into thin air again, so Josh took out some time each day to show her around his hometown and some of his old haunts.

She loved seeing his grade school and high school. The suburbs were beautiful, and she didn't have words for downtown Nashville. Music was one of her first loves, and she enjoyed almost every genre. The food and the entertainment were fantastic. She could get into Tennessee, she thought.

The following morning, the baby entertained everyone around the breakfast table. He got food everywhere, in his hair, on his face, and all over his highchair. He sang and cooed and made everyone laugh.

Oddly enough, when she first awakened, her thoughts were of JJ, like she missed him. He made her feel optimistic about the future.

After they got him cleaned up, they let him scoot around. It was amazing how much he could find to get into at his age.

Josh had some work to finish, so he left the house early with his father. He warmed her heart standing in the doorway, promising he wouldn't be long like he hated to leave them.

"Boy, get outta here!" his mother yelled at him just as JJ started waving goodbye to him, and they all laughed.

Chiffon and Mrs. Abbott spent the day hanging out and getting to know each other better. She revealed Josh had been completely despondent after she disappeared – inconsolable. Both she and his dad told him he had better do whatever it took to regain her trust so he could, in turn, regain his sanity.

What a down-to-earth lady his mom was and always busy. She owned a successful direct marketing corporation. She took the morning off just to spend some quality time with her. Everyone in his family was dynamic in their own rite.

His mom admitted something didn't sit well in her spirit with the quick marriage to Candice. She always let her kids make their own decisions, but it was her opinion he could have found another way to help the poor child. "Everything unfolds as fate would have it." she surmised.

She wanted to ask her many more questions, but she figured she would have time for it later. His mother revealed photos of when the kids were young. Josh was as stunning as a child as he was an adult.

She couldn't stop staring at his pictures. She could have looked at them all day, but Mrs. Abbott had to run out and take care of a few things. She said she would be back soon and for her to make herself at home.

The baby napped, and she was alone in the huge house, except for the nanny and maybe some kitchen staff. She couldn't help but let her mind wander back to her conversation with Isaac. She exhaled deeply. You should be with someone who could be there for you – someone who would never lie to you to get what he wants. She kept hearing his pleading voice in her head. Yes, she knew Josh lied, but he apologized. He is repairing the situation. We all make mistakes. Right?

After finding something to eat and briefly speaking with Tam, she decided to head back upstairs to their room. She climbed the stairs, sauntered down the hall, she thought she heard the baby crying, or was that whimpering she heard?

JJ's nursery sat several feet from their room. The nanny stayed in there, but she thought it a good idea to check on him herself. She turned into the nursery door, stopped short, stunned, she didn't make another move.

Chapter 16

Josh sat across from his father in the nicely appointed executive offices on the top floor off the expansive, shiny, glass office building. His dad, he reflected, was king of the castle everywhere he went; relentless, respected, and revered. William Abbott was also known as a cut-throat in business. Make a grown man cry.

Josh admired the authority his father commanded while simultaneously hating it. The king never found complete satisfaction with anyone. He always expected higher and better from all his subjects.

"Nice job covering the Nano Technology conference this morning, son. Thanks for the assist. Nobody does it better." His father leaned back in his King chair and clasped his hands together. "You were born for this work."

"Thanks, Dad," Josh replied.

"It's so good to have you, home son, although I wish under better and more permanent circumstances." Green- grays met green-grays. "Once this mess is over," dad continued without missing a beat, "I want you to consider coming back home on a more permanent basis. Get back into corporate full-time."

Josh raised his eyebrow. Here we go again, he thought. "Dad, even if I considered it, Fonn and I haven't gotten that far yet. She literally just let me back into her life, and she might want to stay in Chicago."

"Yes, yes, I know, but she seems like a smart girl. She'll follow your lead, I'm sure."

Josh smiled to himself. Fonn did whatever she wanted to do when she wanted to do it. Sometimes he had a hard time figuring out who led whom.

"She seems like a good girl Joshua," he sanctioned.

"Thanks," he said halfheartedly. He didn't need or request his father's damn approval. Yes, he thought to himself, he always wanted it, but he didn't need it to survive, unlike his siblings.

"You need to expedite the matter with Candy. Let me know if you need my help," his father offered.

"I've got it under control, dad. She was served by my detectives when they located her Monday. I expect to hear something from her soon."

"Ok, ok, I'm just letting you know I'm here if you need me." Joshua loved his father, but it's a thin line when someone wants to constantly exert their control over your life – particularly a parent. It had been a strained existence for him, and as he got older, he realized he needed, no, he had to have as much independence from him as possible.

He worked extremely hard to make his own money, to become self-sufficient to make choices outside the family's approval. He didn't want to work corporately with his dad. He wanted to remain a consultant in branding He wasn't like Greg or Vi; they would do anything to make their dad proud of them. He needed more. In fact, left up to him, he wouldn't participate in the family business at all, but he never could seem to pry himself completely away.

William Abbott would never allow it anyway, so Josh continued to do his thing but on his own terms for his dad's many holdings. Josh wanted everything to remain as is. How many times did he have to explain it? He had his own businesses and investments to monitor and control. He rose to his feet, "Glad to be of assistance, Dad. Now I need to get back and check on JJ."

His dad grinned, "Who are you trying to fool, son. You can't wait to get back to that gorgeous little lady of yours."

He returned his dad's smile.

"Go on ahead," his dad waved him away, "We'll discuss this later."

He exhaled loudly. Nothing to discuss, he thought to himself as he headed out of the door.

With his head leaning against the headrest, he closed his eyes. The driver headed back to Hazelton. His dad did know him well. Fonn was never far from his thoughts, and he didn't like being away from her. The past three months had been torturous for him. He'd started to think he would never see her again, which was, well…, unacceptable.

Never a man to give up what he wanted; he found her, he had to find her. He made it impossible for her to avoid him. He knew she loved him. The depth of her reaction or overreaction solidified that, but how they felt wouldn't have made any difference if he couldn't get in front of her again. His sweet Fonn, he didn't just want her; he required her. He needed her to see the lengths he would go to possess her mind, body, and soul again. He didn't want to consider what would happen if she ever left again. He couldn't imagine it. They needed to get married with quickness.

When she put herself out of his reach, it almost did him in. He had been a fool for not telling her the truth. Thank God, she gave him another chance. He wouldn't blow it this time, and when she accepted his son, well, it was over then – he couldn't possibly love her more.

He didn't even want to think about the incredible lovemaking, so hot, so passionate – he felt himself start to swell at the very idea. He wanted forever.

All this extra noise had to be dealt with quickly. What he walked in on this morning disturbed him. Someone had upset her. He didn't know who, but he knew it wasn't Tam. She was a terrible liar. Later, he would get the truth out of her.

Chapter 17

Chiffon gawked at first, motionless. "This can't be," she muttered to herself. Rendered speechless, she watched as some strange woman clutched JJ rocking him back and forth. She sat in a big rocking chair near the baby's crib.

Chiffon's eyes widened as the horrifying realization hit her. A prickly sensation of dread tip-toed over her skin. "Candice," she whispered, as she spotted an extremely large knife resting on the side table near her. "What do you think you're doing!" she screamed out before she could catch herself.

Just then, she heard whimpering from the far corner of the room. She turned to see the nanny sprawled against the far wall, bound, and gagged on the floor. Chiffon glanced wildly around the large room to see if she'd missed anything else. Everything was neatly in place: the crib, the playpen, the body on the floor.

"Hello, Little Chiffon," Candice smiled a crazy, desolate-eyed smile at her, "We meet again. How have you been enjoying my life?" She was dressed haphazardly in pants that were too big and a blouse that was too small. Her hair fell wildly all over her head, and a strong musky scent filled the air. Candice rose to her feet and picked up the blade holding it close to the baby.

"Oh, my God! No! Candice, please!" she pleaded with her, "What are you doing?" she took a step forward. Candice screamed at her not to make another move, and she instantly stopped in her tracks.

It's You

This woman has snapped, Chiffon thought. She has lost her friggen mind. "How did you get in here?" Chiffon glanced around nervously.

"You think I'm not welcome here!" she shrieked. "I know how to get to my damn baby! This is my baby! I'm his mother, not you! Me! Me! ME!" she snapped at Chiffon, waving the knife around wildly.

"Ok, ok." Chiffon said, holding up her hands nodding.

Candice peered at the knife in her hand and whispered to her fingers, "I know how to get into the manor," she continued to stare at the blade, twisting it backward and forward as though mesmerized. Then she quickly looked to the left and right as if she thought someone was watching her from all sides.

Chiffon wondered about the other staff, who else might be in danger, or if Candice had other weapons. Candice bent down and kissed her baby, who rested on her hip. The baby smiled and reached out to her; obviously, he had missed his mother. Chiffon choked up then. She swallowed and took some deep breaths trying awfully hard not to let the tears, welled up in her eyes, fall.

"Close the door and lock it," Candice directed her, pointing the knife toward the door. Dammit, she hoped Candice wouldn't realize the door remained ajar. She shut the door and turned the lock. When Chiffon turned back around, she saw that Candice put the knife down and was talking to the baby. Chiffon wondered if she could get to the knife without getting hurt or potentially causing harm to the baby.

"You didn't answer me!" her head shot up and wild-eyed, as she stared Chiffon down. "How are you enjoying my fucking life, you man-stealing bitch?" her eyes burned into Chiffon's.

"Candice, I am not living your life, I ...,"

"Shut up!" she screamed as she sat the baby down gently in the crib and came closer to Chiffon. A wave of fear, as well as relief, washed over her. She needed to keep Candice away from the baby at all costs.

"You are here with my husband and my baby BITCH! I HAVE NEVER BEEN ASKED TO STAY HERE! How come nobody wants me?" she sniffled and began to cry. "Why can't I stay here too?" She spoke in barely a whisper. Chiffon shook her head. She didn't know what to say. She had to calm Candice down if possible.

"I'm sorry, Candice," she breathed out.

That took Candice by surprise, "You are?" she sniffled.

"Yes," she shook her head - better keep with this. Candice seemed to calm a bit. "Yes, Candice, I'm sorry. I never meant to hurt you. I swear, I didn't know about you.

"Josh lied to both of us."

"But when you found out, you wouldn't go away," she sniffed.

"That's not true, Candice. When I found out, I left."

Candice started to cry harder. She howled like a gutter animal, "Joshua lied to me!" she continued to sob and took a few more steps in Chiffon's direction. Then, suddenly, she halted. Her face instantly turned to stone. "He told me we would be a family. He wanted us to get married and be a family."

Her eyes rolled, "I trusted him and got married to him, and then," she closed her eyes and opened them frantically. "Then, I get these!" She pulled some folded papers out of her pocket and threw them in Chiffon's direction. She caught them before they scattered to the floor and peered closely. They were a replica of the divorce papers Josh had shown her previously.

"He wants to divorce me because of you! You! You BITCH!" she started screaming at Chiffon again. The baby started to cry, and Candice turned to him.

Oh Jesus! Chiffon prayed.

"Don't cry, baby. Mommy's gonna take care of everything. We will all be together again. I promise," she smiled a sickly, sweet smile at her baby and then frowned. "If your stupid daddy won't let us be together in life; soon, we'll all be together in heaven JJ. I will send everyone to heaven."

Chiffon's mouth dropped open. Her hand came up to cover it in horror. Candice wanted to kill them, and she looked crazy enough to do it. Candice went to reach down for the baby again.

She had to stop her. "Candice!" she yelled out.

"What!" Candice turned, bleak-eyed, to her again.

"You don't have to hurt the baby or yourself or anyone. I will go away. I'll leave Josh and your baby, so you all can be a family again."

Candice seemed to consider this, "You will?"

Just then, both of their heads turned to the pounding at the door.

"Why is this door locked?" Josh's voice boomed, "Fonn, are you in there? Is JJ with you?" Then he started to sound frantic when there was no answer. "What's going on in there! Fonn!" she saw the knob twisting.

Candice screamed out at the top of her lungs, a guttural scream that made everyone, including the baby, hold their breath. "You! she screamed at the closed door. This is your fault, Joshua. You are a lying bastard! You just couldn't keep your hands off her! Now you're going to lose everything just like I did!"

"Candy?" he questioned in surprise.

"She's got a knife!" Chiffon raised her voice.

"SHUT UP! I told you!" The baby started screaming again.

"Candy, open this damn door!" Josh kept shaking the handle and banging on the door.

"Get away from the door Joshua or your girlfriend here is gonna get it first. Maybe I'll start by slicing off those juicy tits you probably like to play with so much. Has he spanked you yet?" she laughed with a shrill. "Did he make you kneel before him yet?" She blinked rapidly, "He's a breast man, but I guess you know that don't you? Don't you!" she screamed. "Let me see them," she demanded to Chiffon. "Let me see what my husband loves to play with, you whore!" Chiffon was frozen. Did she really want her to take off her clothes? "Take it off!" she screamed and went to pick up the knife again.

"Candice, please," she begged her in a shaky voice. Her heart was beating frantically. "I told you, I will leave. Please, I will go. You and Josh can make everything right again." She started unbuttoning her blouse with trembling fingers. Now in her bra, she unhooked the clasps and let the garment fall to the floor.

Candice smiled at her. "You're bigger than me. Is that what he likes about you? IS THAT WHAT YOU LIKE ABOUT HER? she howled at the door. "Look at the size of those nipples!" Chiffon put her arms over her breasts.

"Candy!" Josh's voice came through the door. "I need to speak to you alone."

"Oh, now you want to talk?" she said sarcastically, "NOW YOU WANT TO TALK TO ME! YOU DIDN'T WANT TO TALK WHEN YOU SENT THOSE DIVORCE PAPERS TO ME!" she screamed again. "I'M DONE TALKING TO YOUR ASS!"

She waved the knife in front of Chiffon. "Put your hands down," she ordered. Chiffon wondered if she was high. Her eyes had a spacey, glassy, un-present look about them. Chiffon dropped her hands, and Candice took the knife tip and circled around her nipples without cutting. Chiffon gasped and closed her eyes. Her nipples hardened involuntarily.

Candice smiled and sneered. "Look at them; they're getting even longer. You like that don't you? You're a deformed damn slut! You want to fuck the entire family, don't you?"

A tear fell from Chiffon's eye. How would this end? Candice lost touch with reality. She snatched the blade away from her body. "Why did he have to meet you?" she asked pathetically, holding one hand against her heart, "We were doing fine. We were! Why are you taking him away from me?" Her voice sounded like a wounded child. "We loved each other."

Chiffon swallowed and opened her eyes again. She wiped at the tears she couldn't contain anymore. "Candice, I apologize," she gulped. "I never meant to hurt you. I will leave." Candice's eyes widened then. "I promise, Candice. I will leave you all to be together again. Will you let me tell Josh?"

"Tell him what?"

"Tell him I'm leaving him so you can be a family again. Can I call him, please? Isn't that what you want?" The nanny mumbled something. Chiffon could tell she was uncomfortable down there.

"My cell phone is in my pocket. Can I get it out and call him, so I don't have to yell through the door?"

Candice eyed her speculatively, "Go ahead." She shook her head, never taking her eyes off Chiffon while clutching the knife for dear life. Chiffon exhaled and slowly took out her phone.

Candice started rubbing her finger along the sharp end of the knife blade. She began slicing into her own flesh but didn't appear to feel it. She appeared fascinated with the droplets of blood she extracted.

It's You

Chiffon shivered and inhaled deeply. She dialed Josh's number. He answered before the first ring. "Oh, my God! Baby, are you ok? What the fuck is going on in there?"

Her eyes never left Candice. She muttered, "Everything is ok," she trembled out, "I am leaving you."

"What in the ...?"

"Shhhh," she silenced him. "Listen to me. Candice is right. I don't belong with you." Immediately he understood and told her to try to stay on the phone. So, she rambled on.

"Does she have any other weapon?" he said urgently.

"No, she is the one for you. It's always been, Candice for you, Josh, not me."

"Ok, baby, try to get her back to the door. I've called the police. They will be here any minute. I am the only other family member in the house right now. Everything is going to be ok. I'm going to get you and JJ out of there. Trust me, ok?"

"I think she will untie the nanny after I leave," she clutched the phone tighter.

"Oh Jesus," he moaned out, "I love you, baby. Just try to stay calm and get her back to the door."

"Ok, Josh, I'm glad you will accept my decision. JJ is fine," she kept talking.

"I'm about to knock this door down and kill that bitch with my bare hands!" he said angrily.

"No, Josh, Please! You belong with your family."

Suddenly, Candice snatched the phone out of her hands with her bloody hand.

"She's leaving you, Joshua! You hear me?" she screamed. Chiffon reached down and slipped her bra back on.

Candice saw her but was too busy screaming at Josh to stop her.

The good news was, in her rage, she turned her back to the door's entrance, and Chiffon maneuvered to stand in front of the baby's crib, effectively shielding him. Chiffon noticed the knife had slipped out of Candice's grasp and landed just to the side of her on the floor as she continued to scream at Josh.

It was now or never. She didn't know what this crazy woman would do next. She lunged at her just as the door came crashing in. She grabbed the knife as she landed on Candice. They struggled for it as Josh ran up to them and tried to pull Candice off her.

In her wild state, Candice had unimaginable strength. The last thing Chiffon remembered was Josh's voice screaming her name as a piercing, burning pain took over her body – then everything went dark.

Chapter 18

An awful, pungent, antiseptic smell infiltrated her nostrils. She winced and tried to open her eyes, but they were so tired. Why was she so tired? She could make out voices around her but they sounded a bit muffled. Was she dreaming? She fought again to open her eyes but soon gave up.

"Josh, man, why don't you go get some rest." Greg threw his arm around his brother's shoulder. You have been here non-stop for days. I'll stay here and let you know if there are any changes while you go and freshen yourself up."

Joshua put two fingers into the corners of each eye and rubbed there for a minute. His eyes were burning from crying, from staring. "I can't leave her, man. I just can't. I need to be here when she wakes up."

His brother realized getting Josh to leave was futile. "Ok, let me get you a sandwich or something."

"It's ok, Greg, mom and dad just left, and mama left me all kinds of food over there." He pointed to a bag in the corner of the room. "Besides, Chiffon's mother and friend Tam just left to head to the cafeteria to bring me something."

He wondered why everyone thought he needed to eat? All he needed was Fonn to open her beautiful brown eyes, to look at him again. He couldn't help but blame himself for it all. He just didn't realize how insane Candy had become.

"Man," his brother sat down on a chair next to the bed, "This is some straight-up madness. What the hell happened exactly? I've only heard bits and pieces."

Joshua paced back and forth. "I told her I was coming in. She should have just waited for me. That damned impulsive nature of hers, I wish I could chain it up somewhere and throw away the key. I know she was only trying to protect the baby. Still, she risked her life. I'm furious she did that, he said angrily. She jumped Candice just as I kicked the door in. I saw them on the floor, struggling for the blade. I started trying to pull that crazy bitch off Fonn, but she got ahold of the knife."

"The thing is, I think once she saw me, once she realized I was there, she really wanted to strike me with the blade but got Fonn instead." He closed his eyes and shook his head, "She struck her hard. There was so much blood. At first, I didn't realize who was stabbed. Then, I saw her lifeless body. Man, I lost it. The police and paramedics rushed in. They had to pull me off Candy. I was screaming, 'I'll kill you, crazy bitch!' I tried to choke the living shit out of her."

He held his hands up and gaped at them, "I never felt so much rage and helplessness at the same time. They finally managed to pull me off. They wouldn't let me near Fonn, so I ran over to get JJ. I just hope he didn't witness everything. I don't want that in his spirit, you know."

"Yeah, I know, man," his brother agreed.

He walked over to the bed where his darling was so very still. It had been four days since the incident happened.

She looked so peaceful, so beautiful lying there without a stitch of make-up. He could almost hear her saying, "You could have put some gloss on my lips or something," he smiled to himself briefly. She hadn't regained consciousness after surgery. The doctor was concerned but told him not to worry, and her vital signs were excellent, and the surgery was deemed a success. The knife had just missed her heart by a few inches.

This could have been an entirely different situation. He could be standing over her coffin instead of her hospital bed.

The doctor told him to be patient because the body knows what it needs in healing. She could wake up at any time. He hadn't left the hospital since it happened. Every night he held her gently and kissed her and prayed she would come back to him. He combed her hair and put it into a side ponytail. He felt the hot tears stinging his eyes again.

"I'm so sorry, baby," he said to her again.

She must have awakened from sleep because she heard the voices again. She detected a bright light switching from one closed eye to the other, and it was pissing her off. She moved her lips, but they were so dry, "Why is somebody shining that bright ass light on my eyes?" she whispered angrily. She started to squint, "Why won't you let me just sleep?" She tried to swallow, but it felt like a desert in her mouth.

She slowly opened the still heavy lids. She could make out what she thought to be a caucasian man in a white coat with a stethoscope hanging around his neck. He still held that bright-ass light on her. She made out Josh's figure standing next to the man.

Josh grabbed her hand and brought it up to his lips, "Baby, baby, oh my God, baby, you're back! Thank you, Lord." He smiled a beautiful smile at her that made her want to smile too, but her mouth was so dry.

"Back from where?" she barely managed, still trying to gain her focus. "Where am I?" She stared at Josh, who didn't answer her. He didn't look so good. Stubble was all over his face and his eyes looked funny to her, colorless.

"Are you ok, Josh?" she asked in confusion. Was he sick? "You don't look so good."

A look of disbelief flashed in his eyes, and then he chuckled lightly. "I'm fine, baby. I'm not the one we are worried about here."

The white man moved closer to the bed. "Chiffon, you were in, well umm, you had an accident, and you are in the hospital."

She closed her eyes again. Her chest felt so heavy. "I'm in the hospital?" she whispered.

"Yes, baby," Josh answered, still smiling, and holding her hand, kissing it.

"What happened?" she looked at him with a mixture of shock and uncertainty.

"Do you remember anything, Chiffon?" the doctor asked her.

She closed her eyes and thought back. Everything was hazy in her mind. "I don't remember," she said, opening her eyes. "What day is it?" she asked.

"It's Wednesday, Chiffon," the doctor answered. "Wednesday?" she repeated, not understanding. She looked around the hospital room. There were cards and balloons everywhere.

She saw the doctor look at Josh, who remained quiet; staring at her with an odd expression, he looked both relieved and upset. "Am I going to be ok?" she asked quietly. "Why can't I remember anything?"

"Disorientation is quite common after suffering a trauma. You will be fine. Things will come back to you soon enough."

"Is somebody going to tell me what happened?" she queried.

"Mr. Abbott," the doctor turned his attention to Josh, "I need to do a quick examination. Please give me a minute with Ms. Hartwell." The nurse walked in.

He continued holding her hand for a minute longer staring at her. "I love you, sweetheart," he mouthed to her.

"Me too. I'm going to be ok, Josh," she said reassuringly.

Josh just stood there holding firmly to her hand while staring at her, not saying a word.

Again, the doctor made narrowed-eyed, eye contact with him, and he finally let go and walked out. As he stepped into the hallway, Chiffon's mother and Tam were heading toward the room. She saw his tear-rimmed eyes.

"Is everything ok, Joshua? Is my baby ok? Did something happen?" Chiffon's mother grabbed his shoulders.

"She's fine now, he said and embraced the woman briefly. She just regained consciousness." He then turned and embraced Tam.

"Thank God!" her mother closed her eyes.

"She's going to be ok," Tam and Chiffon's mother embraced.

"The doctor is in there with her now. It shouldn't be much longer before you can go in and see for yourself."

They sat down in the chairs directly outside of Chiffon's room. "She will probably be moved from intensive care soon." He put his head down into his hands, and all the fear and tension began to flow like a stream out of his eyes.

Chiffon's mother put her arm around him, and he let it all out. Everything he had been holding in, waiting for her to wake up. "I'm sorry, Mrs. Hartwell." He collected himself and wiped under his eyes with a handkerchief.

"That is one crazy bitch." Tam spat out. "I wish I could have been there. This would have ended differently."

"Hurting people isn't the answer, Tam." Chiffon's mother put her arm around Tam, who also broke down into tears.

As she comforted Tam, she turned to Josh, "And I don't want you to blame yourself. You could not control a crazy woman."

"This should never have happened, Mrs. Hartwell," as he shook his head.

"You are probably exhausted, and please call me Ms. Lula or mom," she smiled at him.

He had arranged immediate transportation to get Fonn's mother and Tam to the emergency room. He knew their presence here would expedite Fonn's recovery.

"I can't do this right now. I'll be back later." Tam rose to her feet, turned, and walked away from them.

It was Wednesday evening, and the hospital had a flurry of visitors coming and going. Fonn had to be the most popular person on the floor. His family had come several times. Also, a few of his close friends and even Candy's parents appeared.

Candy was being held at a mental hospital for evaluation. Decisions would have to be made on the next steps. If this had been a homicide, the prosecutor's office would have made the decision to bring charges against Candy; but, since this was attempted murder, it would be up to Fonn to decide if she wanted to press charges.

Josh knew Candy needed help and wasn't sure if jail was the right answer. He had some compassion for her because she was JJ's mother; he had to evaluate this situation carefully to ensure JJ's protection.

Chiffon's mother looked down at her buzzing phone. "Tam says she's heading back to the hotel. She'll be back before visiting hours are over."

"It's probably best. She's more upset than I am if that's possible," he almost grinned.

"Thank you so much for getting us here so quickly."

"Not a problem," he smiled weakly.

The doctor and nurse walked out. They rose to their feet. "She's doing fine now," the doctor assured them. "She is still a bit groggy; she'll be like that for the next few days."

Josh shook his hand, "Thank you for everything."

The doctor smiled at them both, "Currently, her short-term memory is still affected. She doesn't remember anything about the incident, but it will return any time now. I will leave it up to the family to tell her exactly what's happened. I will move her to a private room, out of ICU in the next day or so as we discussed Mr. Abbott."

"Thank you so much," Ms. Lula said to the doctor. He nodded and walked off.

When they entered the hospital room, the nurse was changing the iv-fluid bag. They waited until she departed, then approached the bed. Chiffon's eyes were closed.

"Sweetheart," her mother called out to her placing her hand on Chiffon's arm.

"Mama?" she opened her eyes.

"Yes, baby, I'm here." Chiffon teared up then. Her mother was here. She thought she had heard her voice a while ago, but she thought she had been dreaming. This must be bad.

"What happened to me, mama? Josh won't tell me." She tried to stick her tongue out at him, but it was not working. He chuckled a bit, then he and Ms. Lula looked at each other for a long minute.

He nodded his approval. "Chiffon, sweetheart," her mother started, "You were stabbed."

"Stabbed!" she raised her voice as much as she could. "What?... When?... How?" She shifted and grimaced in pain. Josh grabbed her hand again.

"Relax, baby, he said soothingly. Everything is ok now. Just take it easy, sweetheart." She did.

"What is the last thing you can remember?" he asked.

She closed her eyes again and thought back. She remembered going to check on the baby but nothing else. "I went to check on JJ. I thought I heard him crying." Her voice was barely audible. Panic took over, "Oh my God. Where's JJ?" she questioned, looking back and forth.

"He's fine," her mother said. "He is with Joshua's family."

"Oh, thank God," she sighed. "Tell me what happened, mama." She looked from her mother to Josh.

Josh kissed her hand again. "You were trying to protect JJ from his mother."

"From his mother?" she questioned, disoriented, "From Candice?" she asked.

"Yes, somehow Candy got into the house and was threatening the baby."

Chiffon closed her eyes. It was starting to come back in jumbled pieces. Pending tears spilled, "Oh my God! She wanted to kill us all," she whispered. Her mother carefully put her arms around her and kissed her face.

"Don't cry, honey," she soothed.

"The baby. Is he really ok?" She looked at Josh, who was wiping under his own eyes again.

"Yes, sweetheart. You saved him from that maniac."

She nodded, "I'm so sleepy." She picked up the tissue her mother gave her and attempted to blow her nose; a burning, piercing pain engulfed her.

"Close your eyes, baby. We'll let you get some rest," he bent down to kiss her forehead. She closed her eyes, and they cleared the room.

"I'll drop you off at the hotel and go home and get changed," he said to Ms. Lula as they entered the hall.

"Tam will notify your driver when she wants to come back."

"Fine, I think Tam needs some time with her alone," Josh nodded in agreement.

Ms. Lula grabbed his hand, "Try not to worry, Josh. Chi is going to be all right."

Nearly an hour later, Tam entered Chiffon's room. Her friend lay there, so still, so quiet. She approached her in silence. "Chi, she called softly. Sweetie, can you hear me?" Chiffon opened her eyes and saw her friend.

"Tam, my heart," she said weakly.

Tam smiled down at her, "Chi, my heart." Tam bent down to kiss Chiffon's cheek. Chiffon reached out to hold Tam's hand. Tam grabbed it and kissed it. "You better not leave me, Chi. I mean it. I'll kill you if you do."

Chiffon smiled weakly, "I promise I'm not going anywhere. I love you too much for that nonsense."

Tam squeezed her hand, "I won't stay long; I just want to touch up your make-up."

She laughed, but it was uncomfortable. "Thank you, Tam," her lids shut so Tam could do the important stuff.

Chapter
19

Over the next few weeks, Chiffon got progressively stronger. Tam stayed as long as she could, but she had to get back to Chicago as she had her salon to run.

What a way to meet your man's family, she thought to herself as the flurry of visitors came and went.

Josh was with her every day and night. He said he secured her leave from the job for the next two months. She wanted to discuss it further but didn't have the energy. She could barely walk at first.

They removed the large wrapping from around her chest, and now it was a smaller band just under her breasts secured around her waist.

They let her see the rather large scar underneath her left breast. It was healing well, thank God. They were applying some sort of ointment that would minimize the scarring. She was concerned about how she would look in a bathing suit or even her underwear. Josh assured her it didn't matter at all to him, long as she was safe. For him, nothing else mattered. She appreciated the sentiment, but she was still concerned about the damage done to her body by that crazy woman.

The beginning of the fourth week heralded her release from the hospital. She could walk on her own, although Josh insisted on carrying her from the car into the house. His fussy cautiousness had her on edge. He needed to allow her a bit of freedom to truly get better, but she understood his protectiveness. After all, his wife had almost killed her. Chiffon still shuddered at the thought.

She was stationed in a bedroom on the first floor. Josh moved his stuff into the room with her but did not sleep with her at night. He didn't want to hurt her accidentally, he'd said. She missed cuddling as they slept, but he refused to join her. She told him they could figure it out, but he insisted on sleeping on the couch.

It's funny, she thought to herself, as she stood at the bathroom sink; she originally asked him to sleep on the couch, and he refused. Now, he refused to sleep in the bed. She shook her head in amusement.

Everyone had been so wonderful and generous to her. She really loved his family and was grateful, but she was ready to get back to her life. She wanted to get back to work. Gone for over a month now, she had bills to pay. She just needed to figure out how to tell the warden.

She also tried to talk to him about Candy and the next steps. He told her not to worry about it now. All she knew was Candy had been committed to a mental hospital and had to undergo treatment for manic depression. Chiffon didn't want to press charges. She just wanted to be sure she got the help she needed. Josh insisted they would discuss it further when she had her strength back. Well, dammit, she DID have it back. He just refused to acknowledge it.

After almost three weeks of convalescing, she went in for a follow-up. It had been almost two months since the incident occurred. She felt so much better now.

"Your breathing is excellent, Chiffon. The doctor smiled as he pressed the stethoscope to her chest. You are healing quite well; you can resume light duties at work."

Before she could respond, Josh said, "She won't be going back to work anytime soon."

Her mouth gaped open, and she glared at him. She started to argue, but the look on his face made her think a private conversation would best serve this.

The doctor raised his eyebrow and went on, "You can also resume sexual activity to the degree that you're comfortable." She smiled, and Josh frowned. She glared over at him again. She needed to give him a piece of her mind. Just wait, she thought.

As they rose to leave the doctor's office, Josh announced he had to take care of some business and would have their driver take her home. He kissed her briefly on the mouth as he helped her into the car, not letting the driver do it, and then he disappeared.

What was the matter with him? She shook her head in dismay. She was back to her old self, and she wanted her lover and her friend back. She missed him, and he felt extremely far away. She really didn't know how to get him back. He took excellent care of her, but he barely touched her, like she was going to break. He had her on a tight schedule of feedings, walking, bathing, and sleeping. The baby had more freedom over his schedule than she did.

Late one evening, she sat in front of JJ, feeding him in his highchair. The baby accidentally poked himself in the eye. He started screaming at the top of his lungs. She immediately reached out to pick him up, and Josh came out of nowhere. He pushed her hands forcefully away and picked up the screaming child. He walked away, trying to calm the baby.

She made eye contact with Mrs. Abbott. She saw the sympathy in her eyes for her. Mr. Abbott also witnessed the exchange.

"Chiffon," Poppa Abbott called her over to the table where he and Mrs. Abbott were sitting. She walked over and sat down.

"Chiffon, your accident has been difficult on Joshy," Mr. Abbott explained sympathetically, "He tries to be strong, but deep inside, he is our most sensitive child."

She put her head down and started to cry quietly. She didn't mean to; she just couldn't help it. "He won't let me do anything," she sobbed. Mrs. Abbott came over to her and hugged her.

When she let her go, Mr. Abbott continued, "He's scared, Chiffon. He almost lost you, and he doesn't want anything to happen to you now."

Her red-rimmed eyes met Poppa Abbott's "Yes, I know, but he won't let me do anything by myself. The doctor said I can resume work now, and I'm scared to talk to him about it. You both have been so gracious and wonderful to me by opening your home, but I do want to go back to my life and my house now. I have been gone for over two months on a trip that was supposed to last a week. I just started this brand-new job."

She knew she couldn't leave Hazelton without Josh's quote-unquote permission. He would hunt her down like a mad dog if she tried to leave without him.

"I'll talk to him," Mr. Abbott rose from his chair.

"Thank you," she uttered. Her eyes filled with gratefulness as Mr. Abbott went to find Josh.

"Ok now," Mrs. Abbott grabbed a tissue from the table and dabbed under her eyes, calming her. Chiffon smiled at her. How sweet she was.

"Thank you, Mrs. Abbott," she grabbed the woman's hand. They stared at each other for a minute.

"Chiffon, I've never seen Joshy quite like this before. Believe me; he loves you. He just wants to make sure you're safe and protected."

"Yeah, but who's going to protect me from him?" Mrs. Abbott smiled, and Chiffon grimaced.

Chapter
20

Mr. Abbott walked in the room as Josh laid a sleeping JJ down in his crib.

"Son, let's chat for a minute."

"Ok, sure," Josh sat down at the table where his father sat.

"How are you holding up?"

"Fine," Josh answered matter of factly.

"No, I mean really, son. I know this has been quite the ordeal for you."

Josh stared at his father. He lowered his head and rubbed his right hand up and down his face, finally grasping his head on either side. "This has been insane, dad." Mr. Abbott nodded in agreement. "I mean, one minute I'm thinking of what we might do for dinner, and the next she's bleeding out on the floor. I-I couldn't save her," his voice cracked as he choked up, "She was lying there, and I couldn't do anything. Her... her blood," he held up his hands, staring at them blankly, "I saw blood everywhere Dad; on Candy, on the crib, it was.... was on my hands," he stared at them in horror.

His father took his son's hands in his and held them securely. "Son, you have to forgive yourself. Do you hear me? Forgive yourself. Chiffon knows you never wanted this to happen. She knows your priority is protecting her."

Josh stared at his father through tear-stained eyes. It was as if he had become a stranger and he was seeing him for the first time. This man, filled with compassion for him; this man was passing his strength to him through joined hands.

"She is much better now, son. Can't you see that? She is just about ready to go back to work and..."

"No!" Josh said defiantly, "She is not!" Josh shook his head and waved his hands, snatching them away from his father's. "I definitely don't want her going back to work yet. It's too soon."

"Joshua, his dad said in a sterner voice. Her medically trained physician said she is fine, man. Candy did not kill her." He raised his voice a notch, "Do you understand me, Joshua? Candy did not kill Chiffon. You are the one who is doing that!" Josh's eyes widened. "Don't you kill her instead," his father warned.

"What?" Josh whispered in disbelief.

"You are the only one killing her now, Joshua. She is still here with you. Don't take her life away from her in an effort to protect her."

His dad's words stung like a blow. He hadn't been doing that, had he? He just wanted her to take things slowly, to let herself truly heal before she got back to everything. Her head-strong stubbornness is what got her into this mess in the first place.

"She loves you, Joshy, but you need to be present with her again."

"I'm not sure what you mean, dad," he said with uncertainty, "I haven't left her side since this incident occurred."

"Well, she begs to differ. She said you left the building and sent this ugly, mean security guard in your place."

Josh smiled a slow smile through his pain. "She said that about me?"

"Yes, she did," his father nodded. "You have been blessed, son. Your woman is still alive, and she wants a life with you, despite, well, everything. Release her and let her fly free. Chiffon has a lighthearted spirit. Don't keep her caged in. Don't run her away from you again."

That jarred him. Fonn wouldn't leave him again. She promised. Was he running her away? Josh hesitated a minute before he spoke. "She..." then he shook his head in realization, his dad was right. He had been acting crazy. The woman made him crazy, he thought to himself.

"Go to her, Joshua, tell her how you feel. Let her know you thank God she is better and still by your side." He nodded at his father. "Let her know this is a democracy, not a dictatorship." His dad got up and outstretched his arms toward his son. Josh rose to his feet. Who was this gentle, wonderful man before him? Did he really know his father at all?

He embraced him and felt himself tearing up again. His dad kissed his cheek and left him standing there dumbfounded. He had cried more in the past few months than in the entirety of his life. He couldn't believe it. He didn't cry, dammit. Jesus, what was happening to him? He had a suspicion he already knew.

In the bedroom, Chiffon folded clothes on the bed when Josh walked in. She held her breath for a moment as he closed and locked the door behind him. She wondered how it went with his dad. She hadn't seen Mr. Abbott again since she cried on his shoulder before dinner.

"Hi," she said and turned to face him. He approached her. She stared at his handsome face.

"Hi," he said back to her. "How are you feeling, baby?"

"I feel great, Josh, more like my old self."

"You look better to me," he added. "No, cancel that. I mean, you look beautiful, sweetheart," he corrected himself. She smiled at him then. He seemed lighter; his dad must have reached him somehow.

"Honey," he reached out and touched the side of her face, "I think I need to apologize to you."

"For what?" she waited.

"Well, I've been somewhat of an asshole."

"Somewhat?" She repeated, raising an eyebrow smirking.

"Hey," he said in feigned shock. "I have met with your defiance before; I couldn't have it again. Not with this. I needed you to take this seriously."

"What? Are you kidding me? Ever since you showed at my place, I have done everything you asked of me."

"That's not what I mean," his eyes clouded over.

"Ok, what do you mean then?"

"You get something in your head, and you just act! You live in the moment. Sometimes there's a heavy price to pay for that Fonn."

"Are you talking about the stabbing or something else?" she searched his eyes.

"I'm talking about you and me. You already left me twice and then… then," he hesitated, "Well, you almost left me permanently," he said pensively, his voice cracking.

She felt a warm flood of love cascade through her body. "Oh Josh, tears sprang to her eyes, "In the past. I reacted poorly. Our situation has hurt us both. I was lost back then; I didn't know what to do or believe but, I never, ever stopped loving or wanting you."

"And how would I know? You wouldn't talk to me. Christ woman!" he said in exasperation.

So, there it was. Finally, she understood. He hadn't forgiven her for leaving him, and this incident just reminded him of her leaving him again.

"You're right, Josh. We could have handled our pain better, you agree?" she asked.

"Yes, of course, agreed."

"So, let's make a promise, from this point forward, we will believe in our love first and everything else second," she went on, "Then we will be able to…"

"I promise," he said before she could finish and covered her mouth with his own. So gentle, so sweet, his lips and tongue caressed hers.

He missed this. He hadn't kissed her, really kissed her in such a long time, and he was done talking. His arms slid around her softly, carefully; he didn't want to hurt her. She pressed her warm body closer to his.

"Dammit Fonn," he exhaled deeply.

"What?" she smiled and continued to kiss him. She rubbed his shoulders and chest with her fingertips. "I've missed you so much." She murmured between his kisses. A low growl escaped him. She didn't have any idea how much he dreamed of holding her, touching her again. It took all his will power; all his resolve to stay away. She slept only a few feet from him each night, and he couldn't touch her like he wanted to. It killed him.

"Baby, my sweet baby," he said as he kissed her neck and then the open v of her blouse. He carefully unbuttoned the buttons and let the garment fall to the floor. He looked down at her bandage. He lightly rubbed his finger over it. "Does it still hurt you?"

"No," she covered his hand with her own. She dropped the bra straps from each side of her arms and twisted the material to the front. He unclasped the hooks and took it off. He swooped her up and carried her to the bed.

"Wait a minute," she squirmed, "What about my clothes?"

"I'll buy you new ones." He placed her down gently and started to remove his garments. She watched him intently as he got naked in front of her. His rigid staff was engorged. He removed the remainder of her clothes and leaned on the side of her.

Her luscious mouth and round ass had his name written all over them. He wanted to do everything to her. He parted her legs and dropped his head until he could inhale the sweet scent of her folds. He slowly circled her clit with his tongue, applying and withdrawing pressure just the way she loved it. She arched up to meet him and winced. It hurt a little, but it was so good she couldn't stop.

She grabbed his head as his tongue explored every crevice down there. He missed tasting her, and her moans were driving him mad. He lapped and tugged and swept his tongue up and down the length of her. Soon she felt a crescendo of intense feeling start at her core. It had been so long, too long.

"Josh, Josh, Josh," she pulled him closer, gyrating against his tongue. "So much, baby, I…" she felt the quickening and tightness overtake her. It happened suddenly. The orgasm was so deep, so carnal she felt as if she was losing her mind. Her body arched and shook uncontrollably. She screamed out as he continued to pull and lick on her tender flesh until she begged him to stop.

"Baby," he lifted slightly, "Am I hurting you?"

"No, no, no, she shook her head, I just…" she didn't have words.

He planted kisses on her throbbing flesh. "I think you should turn over baby, get on all fours so my weight won't be on your chest or stomach area."

She turned over and stuck her ass out. He rubbed over it. "Your ass is beautiful, sweetheart." He smacked it solidly and quickly rubbed the area where his hand struck her. She let out a yelp of pain and pleasure. He slid his fingers inside her from behind. "Your pussy is so wet. I love it." He leaned down to kiss her behind, first one cheek then the other. She arched back to meet his fingers.

She was having an out-of-body experience. Her chest did hurt. Yes, it did, but the way he made her feel. Nothing could compare to it or him. He found that most sensitive area again, and she cried out, beginning to tremor.

He was going to kill her with orgasms. "No!" he smacked her ass and brought her back to reality. "Wait for me, baby. I want to be deep inside you when you come again."

"Ok," she nodded in anticipation. He placed the head of his swollen rod at her entrance and slowly inched himself deeply into her. Methodically he invaded her.

"This is the best fuckin pussy in the world!" he called out as he stroked her steadily. "The best," he repeated. He leaned over her back and grabbed and squeezed at her nipples as he continued the assault to her senses.

"Joshua," she called out to him.

"Yes, baby," he grunted out. "Yes, yes, yes." He moved his hand around to massage her clit, while he pumped away inside her. "Thank you for always coming back to me, Fonn," he panted. "I really don't think I could live without you." That did it.

Her insides exploded in pure rapture and unadulterated ecstasy. She was on fire. It was hot and sticky – a sweet surrender she had no power to control. Soon she felt his hot, intense explosion shoot out against her inner walls, and she knew where she belonged and who she belonged to. As the orgasm shook her, she couldn't speak. Only a deep guttural sound made its way out of her mouth.

He cried out, "You are so sweet, baby, so sweet." He emptied the last of his essence inside her. When he finally slid out, he turned her over, gently placing her down on the bed. His lips met hers furiously. "Dammit, woman. I didn't hurt you, did I?" he lifted his head and then breathed into her neck.

"No, Josh, I'm not hurt."

He gazed at her. They were both breathing heavily. His eyes were piercing into hers. "You better not be lying to me. We can find a way to be more careful."

She touched his cheek. "I'm ok. It wasn't you; it was my body gyrating that caused some discomfort, but I wouldn't change a thing," she smiled. He returned the smile and rested his hand over her bandage.

He bent down and kissed the material lightly, then proceeded to kiss all around it. "I promise I will protect you, baby. Nothing like this will ever happen again."

"I know you will," she said, closing her eyes. She was falling asleep. He grinned down at her motionless frame. Guess she wasn't as strong as she pretended to be. He moved her wrinkled garments to the couch and pulled a bed sheet off a shelf to cover her body. He kissed her forehead and went to hop into the shower.

Fonn slept all night long. He checked in on her a few times before turning in. When she woke up, they could talk about the next steps. He slept beside her for the first time in a long time, and it was wonderful. He snuggled up behind her and remembered not to throw his arm around her. He snuggled as close as he could and fell asleep.

Chapter
21

Sound asleep, she snuggled into the soft mattress. He leaned down and rubbed her nose with his own. She moaned. He did it again.

She opened her eyes. "You're here," she chortled at him. "Did you sleep here with me?"

"Yes, baby, so overdue."

She nodded in agreement. Things could finally get back to normal.

"You turned in quite early last night," he said as he nuzzled her neck, and she laughed at the tickling sensation he caused. "I bet you're hungry."

"Yes, I am," she sat up in bed, "But I really need to get freshened up first."

The sheet dropped to expose her breasts. He eyed them lustfully. "Ok, do you need any help with that?" A grin took over his face.

"You want more?" she asked disbelievingly.

His eyes turned serious, "I can never get enough of you. I almost lost you. I want to feel you, to touch you as much as I can, as often as I can."

That oh-so-familiar tingle was starting between her legs again. "Oh, please, baby, I need some nourishment first. I'm in recovery, remember?" She smiled shyly.

"I'm going to give you something to recover from, he said with a smirk." He leaned in and kissed the tip of her nose. "Go ahead and get cleaned up. I'll be back in 30 to get you for breakfast."

"Ok."

It's You

She headed to the shower. She loved the water, and she hadn't realized how much she missed it until it ran hot over her body once more. She washed herself and her hair. The doctor told her she could remove the bandages when taking a shower or bath and then replace them. When she finished cleaning herself, she lightly rubbed over the area where the stitches were. It was hard, thick, and raised.

Without warning, she flashed back to that day in the nursery. She could feel the excruciating pain of the blade entering her body. She could hear the baby crying, and she was screaming. The pain was so profound. It pierced, and it burned, and it sliced open her flesh. She shut her eyes tight, trying to hold back the tears. That woman hated her so much she almost ended her existence on this earth. Both Josh and JJ would also be dead if she had her way. Chiffon had to stop that crazy bitch.

Her body tremored as unexpected, deep, gut-wrenching sobs escaped from her lips. She never allowed herself to sit with the magnitude of what was done to her. She spent most of her time trying to calm everybody else down, to show them her strength. She minimized the true impact, but she could no longer hide.

It slapped her with a ferocious blow. She had to lean against the wall of the shower for support. Her body shuddered, and she wept. She wept for herself, for the baby, for Josh, and even for Candice. She slid down the wall of the shower as the sobs racked and hiccupped her body. She could barely breathe because the rapid-fire water pelleted her in the face, but she didn't have the strength to move or stop herself from weeping. She started gasping for air as she faintly heard her name in the distance.

"Fonn, sweetheart," he called out again, waiting for her answer just outside the bathroom door. "Baby?" he called, questioning no response from her. The water was still running, and he could hear something. To his horror, he realized she wasn't responding to him because she was wailing. He crashed the door against its hinges and saw her figure slumped through the glass of the shower.

His heart beat painfully in his chest. "Fonn! Did you fall? Did you hurt yourself!" He snatched open the shower door and stepped in, fully dressed, shoes and all. "Sweetheart," he leaned down, "Baby, are you ok?" Concern etched in his face. She reached up to him and held him close. He stayed there for a minute and let her cry with water pulsating down on them.

"Come on, baby," he lifted her to her feet. He kissed her wet, swollen face. "It's ok, sweetheart. Everything is ok now." He held her up as shower water rippled across his back. He walked her out of the shower. He stepped out of his shoes, shirt, and pants and then grabbed a towel to dry her gently. He wrapped her in the towel and lifted her into his arms to carry her out of the bathroom.

He placed her on the bed and gave her tissue from the nightstand. She sank down into the mattress. "Put this on," he handed her a silk housecoat. She did as her body heaved from the heavy crying. He took off the rest of his wet underclothes and dried himself. He quickly put on dry clothes and sat next to her.

"I-I'm sorry," she continued to sniffle. He held her close to him.

"It's ok, love; always my tough girl. You have been through a great deal."

"I-I," she couldn't find the right words.

"Shhhh, he calmed her. "You don't have to say anything." She laid her head down on his shoulder, and he held her until she quieted.

He stood up, "Turn your head to the side." She moved, and he grabbed a brush off the nightstand and bushed her long damp hair. Once it was neatly together, he started to braid it into a long braid down her back.

"You're a jack of all trades," she smiled, holding her head down so he could finish.

"There," he said, "You'll find there isn't much I can't do, sweetheart. Are you ok now? Want to put on some clothes and come to eat?"

"Yes," she replied.

"I'll wait here for you." He went over to the desk with his computer on it and started plugging away while she reapplied her bandage and got dressed. She freshened up her face and went down with him to eat.

The baby bounced on her lap under Josh's careful watch. He made her promise not to lift him but sitting on her lap was approved.

The butler interrupted them as they were feeding the baby. "Sir, a package has arrived for Ms. Hartwell." Josh rose to his feet and reached for the baby as she leaned him toward his father. She walked out to the front parlor.

She saw a beautiful bouquet of yellow roses. She smiled and grabbed the card. Josh was so wonderful, she thought. He had already got her some flowers; she really didn't need any more, but she wasn't complaining. She grabbed the card, and her smile quickly faded when she saw it wasn't from Josh at all; it was from Isaac. The card read, "Feel better because we all miss you. Give us a call." The card said us, but only Isaac's signature was on it.

How was she to explain this? She hadn't spoken to Isaac since their last conversation pre-accident. What was she going to do with Isaac? She was annoyed, but a hint of a smile etched her features. She took a deep breath and walked back into the dining area. "The job sent me flowers." She held them out for Josh to look at.

"Very nice, he said and took them from her. These are a little heavy. You don't need to be carrying them. That's what we pay the staff for."

She grunted and shook her head. "I'm fine. I will let you know if I need assistance, ok?"

"Are you getting annoyed?" he asked with his eyebrow raised. She just stared at him.

The baby played in his pen. She went over and tried to get him to smile. He was such a good baby. She turned back to Josh, who was thumbing through the Wall Street Journal back at the dining table. "We need to talk," she approached.

His brow raised again, "About what?" he put the paper down, giving her his full attention.

She moved to sit down across from him. "A few things. First, I think it's time for me to go back to work." He didn't respond. His handsome face was expressionless. "I'm ready. I can't say enough how wonderful everyone has been, but I'm ready to go home."

"Your job is not in jeopardy if that's what you're afraid of," he reassured. "Everyone thinks you were in a car accident. That's what they've been told. We kept it out of the press. You can take as much time as you need."

"I know that. I have already taken as much as I need, please," she pleaded, and he let out a frustrated breath.

"I need to get back to work. It's time to pay bills, and I don't have much saved after the move and everything."

"Why do you concern yourself with bills? You have me and all my resources at your disposal. Consider your bills eradicated."

She couldn't believe him, "I don't need you to do that. I can take care of my own bills, but I need to make money to do that."

"You don't have to work, Fonn. You don't ever have to work again," he said again, without expression.

What? Was he for real? "I thought you told me that you were going to let me get back to my life."

"I am, and I will, but your life is with me now."

She stared at him in disbelief, "Yes, it is, but not to the exclusion of everything else." Let the stare down begin.

She knew this would be uncomfortable, but they needed to have it out. His eyes pierced through her, and she tried not to get lost in them like she often did.

"Are you missing your boyfriend?" he dared her.

"My, what?" she rose to her feet. She was nervous, where did she put the card, had he seen it?

"I'm not even going to dignify that with an answer. You are deflecting, Josh, and it's cruel."

Exhaling deeply, he stroked his chin, "I know you want to get back to work, Fonn."

"I do, and I want us to have some privacy again," she pleaded her case.

He appeared to consider that.

"So, Chicago is your choice. Is that final or is there room for negotiation?" he asked.

"At least for a while, Josh. I want you and JJ to come home with me. Can we do that? If it works out well, we can find a place we both like. JJ will need a big backyard and a swing set and a pool."

He chuckled at her enthusiasm. She got up and sat down on his lap. His arms immediately encircled her so she wouldn't fall.

Gazing down, she touched his cheek. "I want you and JJ to come home with me." She kissed him softly and felt the stiffness rise beneath her bottom. She pulled back and smiled at him. "Say it will be ok," she implored while simultaneously praying.

"Ok, ok, fine," he huffed out; "What else, you said a few things?"

"I want to talk about Candice." She got up and sat back down on the opposite chair so they both could concentrate.

"Candice is going to remain in a treatment facility where she can get the help she needs," he said. "Her family has signed her in since you have agreed not to press charges."

She nodded and added, "Hopefully, one day, she will be able to see the baby again."

"I think you are pretty incredible for thinking of JJ first, baby. I know that isn't easy."

"Loving him is easy, Josh."

He smiled genuinely at her.

Now, on to her next question, "What's happening with the divorce?" He held his breath for a moment. Dammit, he knew it was coming. He wasn't going to be able to avoid it ad infinitum. He spoke to his attorney, and the news wasn't good. Because he had filed in Tennessee, he had to adhere to the laws of the state. State law prohibited divorce while the other party was mentally incapacitated.

Or, at the least, state law made it exceedingly difficult to proceed with one. There was some good news, though; she signed the divorce papers before the incident (probably in some fit of anger). The bad news was she may still be considered mentally incompetent at the time. The court date was pending. He honestly didn't know how long the entire process would take.

"Well, baby, the divorce is in progress. There are a few complications due to Candy's current state, but my attorney is working through it."

She smiled, "Finally," she said and went over to hug him and sit on his lap again, "I can't wait until you are all mine."

"I can't wait either, baby. We don't need a piece of paper to declare our commitment. We belong to each other right now." She was about to reply, but just then, his mother and sister entered the dining area from some door she hadn't even realized existed.

She started to jump up, but Josh's grasp tightened around her and held her there. She was embarrassed, but she didn't try to move.

"And what have you two been up to?" his sister asked with a wink. The ladies both began to speak to them as if she weren't in a comprising position with their family member's member poking her ass.

"Joshy, I want to take Fonn to the sale at Rothchild's," his sister directed to him.

"You want to do what?" he asked his sister with a don't be ridiculous look on his face.

"Un umm!" Fonn interrupted them, "You who, I'm right here, Vi. You can ask me." Violet smiled at her and turned her gaze back to Josh. Chiffon couldn't believe it. He had the whole family under his spell.

"I don't know that she's up to going out on a shopping spree yet," he said to his sister, who started to pout. Chiffon rolled her eyes at him and got to her feet.

"Come here," she grabbed his hand and pulled him right outside of the dining area.

"Somebody's finna get it," she heard Vi say as they walked out.

"I need to get out of here for a little while. Why don't you want me to go?" she questioned; it was stare down time again.

"Ok fine," he motioned with his arm, pointing at her, "But you'd better take it easy."

Chapter
22

She glanced at her watch. She and Vi had so much fun, that a few hours had passed. She called Josh but he did not pick up the phone. Hopefully, he wasn't angry. He always picked up her calls.

She found out Mrs. Abbott planned to host an event at the manor that evening. A night of dinner and ballroom dancing. Vi was smitten with a certain someone she wanted Chiffon to meet at the shindig, and she was all for it. She loved love.

Upon their arrival back to Hazelton, they found the nanny feeding JJ, but Josh was nowhere to be found. She asked where he was and was told Mr. Josh left not long after she had.

She then went into the bedroom and locked the door. She called Isaac, who, true to form, answered on the first ring.

"Hi Isaac, it's Chiffon."

"Chiffon, it's so good to hear your voice. My God, how are you? I've been worried about you."

"I'm doing much better now," she replied.

"When will you be back? Everyone is waiting for your return."

She smiled to herself; that was nice. "Hopefully within the next week or so. I'm so ready to get back to work."

"I'm ready for you to get back too," he said. They were both silent.

She wasn't quite sure what was going on between her and Isaac, but something was. Perhaps him more than her, but she found herself entwined with him, nonetheless. She didn't know what to make of it because she was so completely and totally in love with Josh, she would never consider another man.

Isaac had gotten under her skin somehow. It frustrated her but even more so, it frightened her. There was no explanation for it, but it had to end or be tamed or something; she just wasn't sure what yet. This mutual attraction or whatever this was couldn't get any more life.

"Isaac," she hesitated for a moment, "The flowers were beautiful."

"Just like you."

She blushed, "Are you trying to get me killed?"

"What?" he laughed.

"You sent that note, and it could have been seen."

"C'mon Chiffon, the note was innocent enough, wasn't it? It was from your job."

"Yeah, but you're the only one who signed it."

"Ok, my bad. I'm sorry. I need to be more discreet."

"Look, Isaac. I know you don't like Josh or the situation I'm in, but you are going to have to respect him. He is ultimately going to be your boss and mine. Whether we like it or not."

"Is he coming back with you?"

"Yes, he is," she said quietly. Silence again.

"I'm not sure what is happening between us, Isaac, but I don't want to lead you on."

"You're not," he interrupted her.

"I want to keep you as my co-worker and my friend, but that's all I can give. I have been in love with Joshua for a long time."

"Has your love filed for divorce yet?" he said sarcastically.

Her eyes widened. "Um, well there are a few, um, complications with the divorce, but I know it is going through Isaac." Still silence.

"Ok, please say something."

"So, you want me to keep my distance from you?"

"Yes, I mean no." She didn't know what she meant.

Isaac represented something comfortable, peaceful, and stable. Something about him drew her in. She shook her head in uncertainty.

"Look, I want you to respect my relationship and be my friend. That is what I want. Will you do that, please, Isaac? I really like you, and I think we'll be able to accomplish some great things together if we don't mess it up with…, I don't know, with other stuff."

"If that's what you really want, I will try Chiffon." They were both silent again.

"Why don't you give my friend Tam a call?" she blurted it out before she knew it.

"Who?" he asked.

"Tam, she's like my best friend in this world, and she thought you were a hot Afro Latino mix," she laughed, trying to convince herself this was a good idea.

"Tam, huh?" he said. "Yeah, I remember her now."

"Yes, but only if you really would like to get to know her, Isaac; not just to, to um …"

"To not think about you on the regular?" he interrupted her.

Her grasp on the phone got tighter. She closed her eyes. What another hot mess, she thought.

"Ok," she breathed heavily, "Do you want her number or not?" she waited. "Isaac?"

"Yes, give it to me."

She gave it to him, then switched the conversation back to work. "Now, tell me what the hell has been going on in my absence."

She talked to Isaac for about an hour. He made her laugh and forgot all the other stuff that had been on her mind.

"Ok, Isaac, I better go now." She thought she heard sounds right outside her door.

"Ok, he said reluctantly, just tell me one thing before you go."

"Yes?" she huffed impatiently.

"Are you really ok?" his voice was etched with unease again.

"Yes, I'm ok, Isaac. I don't want you to worry. Something sharp entered my chest during the accident, and it was touch and go, but I'm fine now; ready to get back to work." She crossed her fingers for massaging the truth a bit.

"Well, I, I mean we really do miss your presence around here. You made this a better place to come to each day."

She exhaled deeply. She felt the same way about him. She kind of missed him too, but she wouldn't dare tell him.

It's probably the reason she kept calling him, she reflected. "Ok, please tell everyone I said thanks for the cards and letters and, well, their overall patience with me."

"You're worth it." Silence again.

"Goodbye Isaac, talk to you later" she disconnected the line before he could respond.

"Fonn! why is this door locked?" She heard the almost panic in Josh's voice outside of the door.

"Oh shit!" she immediately put the phone down. "I'm coming," she yelled and walked toward the door and opened it.

"What are you doing?" he asked, standing there in all his delicious glory. He changed into black shirt and slacks; it intensified the beauty of his face and the expression in his turbulent eyes.

"Oh, I'm sorry, honey. I was going through some, um, private paperwork, and I didn't want anyone to just walk in on me." He glanced around the room. "I had just wrapped up." He walked in, and she left the door open.

"So, how was your excursion?"

He sat at the table that held his laptop. She came up behind him and wrapped her arms around his neck. "Thank you for not being too upset with me. It was wonderful." She kissed the top of his head into his soft curls. "I love your family, and I love you." She felt the tension start to leave his body. I even saw something there that I just had to bring back for you. She started to kiss the back of his neck, and he closed his eyes.

"Oh really, and what was that?"

"Me!" she laughed and continued to kiss his neck. This woman was going to be the end of him. He just knew it. She insisted on putting herself at risk.

"I made it back to you in one piece," she held him tightly from behind the chair he was sitting in. She kissed his ears and then his neck again, running her tongue over his hot skin.

He rose suddenly and stared at her face to face. He grabbed her shoulders. "If we don't have two yeses', it's a no, Fonn. Didn't we agree to that?"

"Yes, but...,"

"No buts."

His wonderful, soft lips took over hers. She wrapped her arms around him. "I can't lose you, Fonn. If I could lock you up in a room indeterminately, I would do it."

She laughed at him, and it didn't escape her; he wasn't laughing. "Josh, sweetheart, you can't panic every time I'm out of your sightline – neither one of us is going to be very happy."

He nodded at her, "You're right. I know you're right, and I'm trying, baby."

"I know you are." She took both of his big hands in hers. "I'm not going anywhere. I love you to distraction, Joshua Abbott. You and baby Josh are my life."

"Ok," the tension eased around his eyes, "I believe you, and if you're ready to go back to Chicago, we can, but you need to know, I did go to see your doctor today."

"You did? Really?"

"I needed confirmation that it was ok for you to travel and exactly what could you do in terms of work."

Oh Lordie, she thought to herself, this man, this man, this man of mine. "He already told you all that."

"I know, but I needed to hear it one more time."

"And the verdict?" she asked.

"He said you had healed nicely, and as long as you didn't overdo it too soon, you should be fine. So, this is what I'm proposing ..."

Oh boy, she thought and walked over to the bed where they sat down, still holding hands. He continued, "We can leave here this Friday. If it's ok with you?"

"That's fine," she said, with excitement etched in her voice.

"We'll wait a few weeks before we bring JJ up. I need to clear some things with his other grandparents. It could prove challenging, but I'm not too concerned. They knew this day was coming. We need to secure a live-in nanny and ..."

"Live in nanny?" she questioned. "We don't need that."

"Yes, we do. You are not fully recuperated, and we both will be going back to work."

"What do you mean we will be both be going back to work?"

He smirked, "Don't look so panic-stricken, baby. I told you I wouldn't interfere with your job, but obviously, I will need to go into the office periodically. A lot of what I do can and has been handled remotely, but I need to show my face from time to time as a new partner. I've already missed a few important meetings I couldn't video conference in to." He stared into her concerned face. "Don't worry baby, no one will know I lick you from head to toe every chance I get."

She gasped and flushed as a hearty laugh escaped his throat. She hadn't heard him laugh that way in a long time. The sound was infectious, and soon she started to laugh too.

"I have a big surprise for you, my shy little kumquat. You'll see, everything is going to work out fine."

Oh boy, she thought to herself. The last time he had a "big surprise" for her, she ended up here at the manor, and it wasn't easy to escape.

Chapter 23

With the ballroom dance in full swing downstairs, she and Josh finished getting ready. He didn't give her a hard time about wanting to attend. She figured since he could keep his ever-watchful eye on her she was "allowed".

She observed herself in the full-length mirror. Josh had this "buyer" lady come by the house a few weeks prior and take her measurements. She came back a few days later with a full wardrobe for Chiffon. Before she could fuss at him, he reminded her she hadn't brought enough for a lengthy stay, and since she was starting to feel better, didn't she want to look better. He won.

She put on a short, sparkling cocktail dress. She let her hair hang down in soft curls around her shoulders. If people didn't know, they wouldn't think anything ever happened to her.

As for her man, what could she say, but damn! He had the nerve to add a royal blue bow tie to his tux. It made his eyes a dazzling bluish color. Was he trying to kill her? He walked up to her and kissed her forehead. "You look stunning, baby. Umm mmm mmm," he mumbled. "Nobody is going to be able to take their eyes off you." He nuzzled her neck.

She laughed, "Thank you, darling."

"Let's go," he grabbed her hand and led her to the ballroom. He made her put on shorter heels, and she secretly thanked him. She hadn't walked in heels in a long while, and it wasn't easy getting acclimated.

She mingled and danced a slow dance with Josh. She was having a great time. She felt her phone buzzing in

It's You

her clutch bag. "Excuse me for a minute," she left Josh standing with a small group. She was a little reluctant to leave because this one woman, a "friend" of the family, was a little too "friendly" with her man.

Every time she looked around, Miss Millicent was somewhere near Josh. It wouldn't be so bad if she wasn't so damned pretty. She smirked at her and headed outside the ballroom doors. "Hello?" she spoke into the receiver. It was an unknown number. Just when she thought those days were through.

"Ms. Hartwell?" the voice asked. "Yes, this is she. Can I help you?"

"This is the fraud alert department from your financial institution, First Bank."

"Yes?" she asked, curiosity peeked.

"We don't mean to alarm you, but first, can you verify your code?"

"Sure," she gave the numbers.

"What's happened?" she wondered cautiously.

"Ms. Hartwell, this is highly unusual. This call is regarding certain activity on your account."

"Ok..." she said, urging her on, still puzzled.

"We confirm all your bills with on-time payments have been paid in full, and a large deposit has been placed into your accounts."

"What? she was confused. I'm sorry, what are you saying?"

"I apologize for any confusion, Ms. Hartwell, I'm calling to confirm all your balances have been paid in full and a rather large sum has been placed into both your checking and savings accounts."

"What do you mean, large amount?" she asked, eyes widening.

"Sorry, ma'am, we aren't allowed to give that information over the phone, but these amounts were paid within the last few weeks." Her mouth dropped open.

"You can log in to your account and check the balance at any time. Also, feel free to call us back anytime to discuss investment packages."

"Ok, ok, thank you," she said as she hung up the phone.

"He didn't," she shook her head, "He wouldn't."

She called her automated banking service. Her checking account had an available balance of $750,000.00 and her savings a balance of $850,000.00. She hung up and called back to hear it again. The phone slid right out of her grasp. She retrieved it and immediately called each of her creditors. Every single balance had been paid in full. She called her student loan corporation; over $80k in loans were paid in full. Unbelievable.

She sat down in the nearest chair outside the ballroom with her hand up to her chest to still her wildly beating heart. Joshua not only paid off all her bills, but he also deposited more money than she had ever seen at one time in her life into her accounts. It was over a million dollars total! He made her a millionaire and didn't even tell her.

How was it possible? Could you just go and pay other people's credit cards off? Can you deposit whatever you want into someone else's account unbeknownst to them? Don't you need permission or something? She put her head in her hands and started to rub her forehead. She didn't know whether to run in there and cuss him out or to run in there and hug him in gratitude. She grinned to herself. He left her feeling that way quite a bit. Apparently, he didn't realize the fraud department is alerted when "any" kind of suspicious activity occurs on your account, even positive activity. She laughed to herself; even the bank knew she was supposed to be broke.

She had a sudden overwhelming desire to see JJ. He always made everything better. She had fallen in love with that baby and couldn't imagine her life without his smile or high-pitched cry. He had taken over her heart just like his father. Josh was right. Biology meant nothing. She risked her life for the child, and he felt like her own. She was all he had for a mother.

She walked back into the ballroom and found Josh, oh and of course, Millicent, nearby him. She whispered in his ear. "I need to step out for a minute. I'll be right back, ok?"

"Is everything alright? Do you need me to accompany you?"

"No, no. It's fine. Just need to get away from the music and step out of these shoes for a minute."

He nodded, "Ok baby, patch me if you need me."

"Ok," she smiled. He was so weird, always saying 'patch' instead of text. What was a patch anyway? She giggled and headed to the nursery. She had been in there several times since the incident. At first, it was a bit unnerving, but Josh suggested thinking of it as the place where she saved JJ's life, not the place where she almost lost hers, and it worked.

The baby was sleeping soundly. Josh would kill her if he knew what she was doing. She bent down and slowly lifted the sleeping baby. He didn't open his eyes but did a crazy, contoured baby stretch, puckering his lips while sticking out his little butt, which Fonn found adorable.

She kissed his sleeping cheeks. "I love you, JJ," as she felt hot tears come down her face. She kissed the baby repeatedly. He and his daddy were her family now, and she didn't know how she got picked to be so blessed. Josh had given her everything. His heart, his baby, and his money.

She wasn't angry, in fact, just the opposite. More love is what she felt. Nobody had ever taken care of her the way Josh had. Sure, her man had heavy-handed tactics for sure, but his heart was good. She couldn't love him more than she did at that moment.

She smiled down at the baby. She'd better put him back down before Sargent Abbott appeared in the doorway. She gently laid the baby back down and headed back to the ballroom.

Just as she entered, Vi came and took her by the arm. She pointed out a gentleman who was holding a drink in his hand speaking with a woman. "That's him," she whispered to her. Chiffon knew exactly who 'he' was. Vi had spoken about him constantly earlier that day. He was a bank executive who oversaw and approved a lot of Poppa Abbott's financial transactions. Vi only interacted with him on a few occasions, but to her, he was the one.

"Why don't you take me over there, Vi, and introduce me? It would be a great way to start a conversation, right?" she smiled at her deceptively.

Violet laughed, "Um, great idea." She pulled Chiffon over to where the man was standing. He turned to see them coming and smiled a wonderful smile at Vi. Chiffon's heart warmed.

"Hello again, Edward," she reached out to shake his hand. He took it and kissed it, still smiling. By then, Violet had turned all shades of her name.

"And who is this other vision?" he asked Vi.

"This is Chiffon, she said nervously. Chiffon, this is Edward Ballist." He took her hand and kissed it as well.

She smiled at him. "Well, you're quite the charmer, aren't you, Mr. Edward Ballist."

"Tough job," he continued to smile at her. He did a quick glance around the ballroom. "Are you both at this Abbott shindig all alone?" he asked, looking at her but soon turning his attention to Vi.

Before Vi could answer, they all heard, "Unfortunately for you; she is not." Joshua's voice came out of nowhere as she felt him slip his arm around her waist. How did he keep sneaking up on her like that? She turned to glare up at him.

"What's up, man?" Edward immediately took a step back and reached out to shake Josh's hand.

"This is my lady," Josh said accusingly.

"He wasn't talking to me; he was talking to Vi," she whispered, trying to keep her composure.

He didn't take his eyes off Edward, "She disappeared some time ago," he turned to her, "Good to see you've made it back." Oh boy, she forgot she was under surveillance.

"Joshy," Violet interrupted them, "I wanted Chiffon to meet one of our VIPs in the banking industry."

"You did, huh?" he questioned. "And why is that?" They all looked at him with a bewildered look on their faces.

Chiffon exhaled, "Come on, Josh." She took his hand. "Let's let these two catch up. It was a pleasure to meet you, Edward." She turned, practically yanking him away.

"What's your problem?" she bit out as soon as they got out of earshot.

"My problem?" he countered. "Mr. financial had his hands all over you."

"What?" she said in disbelief. "That man kissed my hand, that's it. He did the exact same thing to your sister, and I thought he was rather charming," she smiled defiantly.

"Did you now?"

"Yes, I did." she snapped.

He raised his brow at her. "He was taking off your clothes with his eyes."

"Oh, my God, Joshua, your sister has a crush on that man. I was trying to help her."

"Well, you were doing a deplorable job."

"Dammit, Joshua, that's it! If you don't stop it with your ridiculous jealousness or possessiveness or whatever the hell is going on with you, we are going to have to seek some counseling."

"Counseling?" he repeated.

"Yes, counseling because you are acting crazy."

"Protecting you is not crazy."

"Protecting me when there is absolutely no threat is crazy, Joshua."

It was stare-down time again. He held her gaze in silence and began slowly undoing his bowtie. Then, unblinking, he began unbuttoning the button at his collar.

"What in the hell are you doing?" she asked in exasperation.

"I'm doing the only thing we seem to agree on."

"What?" her eyes widened in horror. "You're kidding?"

He threw his bow tie to the floor, never taking his eyes off her.

"This place is full of people!" she warned him, glancing around.

He then slipped out of his suit jacket, and she turned and took off running.

She was hot and out of breath as soon as she started. She ran out of the ballroom and headed straight upstairs. He was two steps behind her, and she tried to close the door on him. It didn't work. He came in and locked it.

She was out of breath and completely turned on. Her panties were saturated. Joshua drove her crazy. The current between them remained set to high. Her belabored breathing caused her to bend over, gasping deeply. She couldn't say anything. When she finally caught her breath, she looked up. The man had stripped down to his boxers.

"You're crazy!" she yelled at him.

"About you," he lifted her straight up like she was JJ.

"Don't ever run from me, Fonn," he held her up against him, gazing intently into her eyes.

"Are you about to shake me into submission?" she cocked her head to the side.

He placed her down in front of him. "I've got something else in mind." His mouth covered hers, devouring her. She gripped his shoulders, so she didn't lose her balance. "Nobody gets to undress you with their eyes but me. Nobody gets to undress you with their hands but me."

She moaned into his mouth and started tugging on his boxers. She moved her kisses to his neck, shoulders, then to his nipple. Her tongue teased the hard pebble.

Feverishly they groped each other like they were both starving. She kissed down his chest and stepped out of her shoes. She bent down further and winced a little. A shooting pain burned through her chest area. He lifted her to an upright position and moved to sit on a stool.

She got down on her knees in front of him. She moved in and wiggled her tongue in and out of his navel area, leaving hot, wet kisses in her tongue's wake. His hands massaged through her hair. She grabbed his hard cock and stroked it through the light fabric of his boxers.

"Dammit Fonn," he closed his eyes and put his head back. She lowered his boxers and stroked the full length of his solid staff. She stuck out her tongue and circled the tip. He clutched her head tighter, and she let it slide fully into her mouth. She suckled and flicked her tongue on the underside of the tip until he started to gyrate. Slow, gentle thrusts converted into deeper, faster ones.

He was stroking into her mouth, and she loved it. She tried to fit all of him down her throat. She felt him grow even stiffer. She wanted him to explode all over her face.

"Oh baby," he called out. "Suck it. Goddammit."

She licked him up and down and groped his balls. She loved the feel of the veins that distended down the length of him.

She could tell he was near the apex. He panted, moaned, and pumped into her mouth. Suddenly, his motion stopped. He gripped her head as he shouted her name in complete erotic pleasure. He spurted wildly, and she suckled at his seed. It squirted everywhere. In her mouth, on her face. She continued to lick.

"What on earth are you doing to me, woman?" He pulled her head back and looked at her with a sexy satisfied look. He slid himself out of her mouth and went to get a towel. He wiped himself off with one edge and gave her the other to wipe her mouth. Once clean, she smiled.

Back on their feet, they gazed at each other. He turned her around and unzipped her dress. It slowly slipped down her shoulders, landing in a puddle at her feet. His wet kisses touched where the fabric had once been. She wasn't wearing a bra, and he stroked the hard, sensitive tips of her nipples. A surge of pleasure engulfed her as he suckled at her neck.

She could feel his penis rising again against her ass. "How insatiable," she chortled. He slid her panties down and helped her out of them. He sat down on the stool again and, with her facing him, pulled her over him until she straddled him. She angled herself over his rod. With a light push, he entered his tip inside her. He was suspending her with his hands under her arms. He prevented her from dropping down on him like she wanted to.

"Josh," she called out, "Baby, please. I need to feel you inside me," she moaned out.

He moved the head of his penis around and around her entrance, then started sliding it up and down the length of her hitting her clitoris. She was going crazy.

"Sweetheart, please let me have it," she cried, throwing her head back again when he took her breast into his mouth.

She was on fire. She wanted him inside her. No, she needed him, had to have him. She wriggled, and slowly he inched himself up into her tight channel.

"Mine, baby, all mine," as he thrusted himself harder and deeper.

"Yes, sweetheart," she called out, "I love how you-"

Her insides throbbed, and instantly all sensation disappeared before it came rushing back in a flood that infiltrated her soul. So fast, it happened. It took her by surprise. She screamed out through an unimaginable vortex of pleasure. It was almost painful in its torturous hold. She shuttered, quivered, and shattered. She could lose consciousness from pure bliss.

He gripped her tighter and unloaded inside her with a guttural cry. It only made her orgasm stronger. Finally, she bent down over his shoulder, completely spent. If something hurt, she wasn't aware of it. The sex was getting hotter and more passionate between them. He held her securely. She felt a tear come down her cheek. It was so overwhelming this love they had, and it seemed to be intensifying for them both. Scary territory, she thought.

Finally, he kissed her shoulder and pulled her back to look at her face. "You're crying, baby. Why? You have to stop me if I'm hurting you," he stroked her hair. "You promised to tell me."

"No, no, nothing like that. You didn't hurt me."

"Good," he smiled. "So, what's wrong? Why the tears?"

"Nothing, baby; everything is right."

He smiled again and kissed her cheek. "So want to clean up and go back to the party?"

She chuckled, "Cool," and they did just that.

Chapter 24

The end of the week arrived, and before they knew it, they were saying emotional goodbyes to the family. She developed such a kinship with the Abbotts; they were her family too.

She couldn't, or wouldn't, let go of JJ. Joshua had to pry the child from her arms. She thought they could find a way to take him now, but Josh insisted they make proper preparations first.

Of course, he was right, but she didn't expect to feel as sad as she did, leaving everyone. Even Poppa Abbott got a little choked up. They promised a return soon. Joshua held his brother for a long embrace.

"Two peas in a pod." Vi shook her head and wiped under her own eyes. Excitement mixed with a little trepidation filled her. Let the games begin.

Joshua held her snuggly against him for the ride from the airport. She was exhausted and drifted off with his arm around her.

"Baby," he kissed her forehead, "Baby," he kissed her again. "Wake up, sleepyhead." She grinned up at him opening her eyes. Were they home? "Now, close your eyes."

With incredulity, she asked, "Did you just wake me up to tell me to close my eyes again?"

"Yes, I did," he snickered, "Now close them." She did, and she felt him slip some sort of blindfold over her head to cover her eyes.

"What are you doing?"

"I have a surprise for you, and I know you will peek even if I tell you to keep your eyes closed."

She heard the hustle and bustle of the city traffic around them as he led her out of the car.

"Are we home?" she asked nervously, holding onto him for dear life because she couldn't see a thing. He walked closely behind her through a revolving door.

This felt like her building, but she had been away so long she couldn't be sure. They waited for the elevator. Once inside, she felt his lips cover hers. Her arms came up around him. How wonderful he tasted. Oh my, how enticing with the blindfold on. What was he up to?

The doors opened, and they parted lips. He led her down the hall, and they stopped. He pulled keys out of his pocket and opened a door. He pushed her in. She cautiously entered and heard the door close behind her. He stood directly behind her. She could feel his breath on her neck, sending shivers through her body.

"Welcome home, sweetheart." He took the blindfold off. She blinked rapidly to get a clear focus.

"Have mercy," she muttered, taking in the scene before her.

She stood in her unit, but it had been beautifully and tastefully renovated. It looked like something straight out of a showcase magazine.

"Wow," her mouth dropped open. Spectacular. All her furnishings were still there but rearranged with some noticeable additions. She left him standing there and went to look around. It was beautiful. She turned back to face him, "How did you manage to do this."

He looked at her with a hint of amusement mixed with mischief. "It wasn't easy, but I know what you like, and I figured since we're merging, I could help."

When she took a second look around, she noticed some of his furnishings from his penthouse had been moved in. She went into her bedroom, and her office, and all the boxes had been unpacked. They didn't remove any original pieces but made them better.

Apparently, she and Josh would be sharing the office space. His section was off to the far corner of the room facing left, and hers had been pushed closer to the door facing right.

She shook her head in amazement. "Incredible," was all she could muster but when he told her to look at guest bedroom, she couldn't hold back tears. It had been turned into a nursery. While the bed remained, everything else was set up in shades of aqua and blue for JJ.

"Do you like it, baby?" she heard his voice come from the doorway.

She jumped into his arms, "It's absolutely beautiful." She held him tightly. When she let him go, she raised an eyebrow, "I'm not exactly thrilled about strangers going through my unpacked boxes," she wiped under her eyes.

"Don't be upset, sweetheart. I knew how much work remained here, and I wanted to make things easier for you." She wasn't even going to ask how in the hell he got access like he did, not to mention, the bastard already had his own set of keys.

Her place was spacious, and she remembered thinking how it was probably too big for her. Now, she could see it was going to work out fine.

"The people I hired are discretion personified, don't worry about your privacy." She walked around again, polished hardwood floors, granite countertops, repainted walls, all updated. Amazing.

She knew her unit was a condo, but she was only a renter. She didn't know what to say, shocked at what he accomplished. It was also a bit intimidating. He did whatever he wanted without consulting her, and she didn't love that. This was her personal space, after all.

He couldn't tell if she was completely thrilled. He knew this risk could backfire. Although he knew her to be extremely private, it seemed worth it. Her healing had just begun, and she would have been trying to move things and lift things, unpack things and redecorate things.

He decided to assist whether she liked it or not. On top of preparing the condo, she insisted on getting back to work and taking care of JJ on her own after his arrival. Not on his watch. He couldn't stop her from going back to work, but she would heal properly and take it easy at home.

Soon they heard a knock at the door, and Joshua went to get it. The bell person must be dropping off their luggage, considering there was absolutely no notification from the front desk again. While Josh attended to it, she found her buzzing phone in her purse. She walked to "their" bedroom for some privacy.

She observed Tam's smiling face on the screen and smiled to herself. "Hello, baby bubba," she said with a grin to her friend's hello.

"Are you back yet?" Tam said anxiously.

"Yes, we just got in."

"So, mister man is there with you, I take it?"

"Oh yeah," she replied. "Boy, is he with me," as she went on to explain her apartment upgrade.

"Wow!" Tam breathed out loudly. "That damned Joshua." They both laughed. "Well, girl, I just wanted to welcome you back home and tell you I received a surprising call yesterday."

"Oh yeah?" Chiffon said, sitting down on the bed kicking off her shoes.

"It was from fine ass, Isaac." Chiffon's eyes widened, and she felt her stomach turn a little. She didn't respond.

"Girl," her friend kept talking, "He wants to go to dinner."

"He does?" Chiffon closed her mouth, which was left slightly ajar. Unreal, he really called Tam and asked her out.

"I couldn't believe he called. I just wanted to thank you, girl. He didn't say it, but I know you gave him my number."

"Umm, yes, I –"

"We are going out this week."

"Really," Chiffon said.

"Yes."

Her friend sounded so excited. She should be happy for her; she set them up after all.

"That is excellent news, Tam. You'll have to let me know how it goes. Is it ok if we chat later, though? The bellman just brought our suitcases up, and we just got home."

"Oh, yeah, girl, of course. Let's chat later."

She disconnected the line and stared at the phone in her hand. Well, he certainly didn't waste any time, she thought to herself. What was she talking about? She shook her head dismissively. She told him to. He did what she insisted on; whatever he needed to do to free himself, but it stung.

She could never be what Isaac wanted. Joshua had her too entangled and entwined. Anything felt for anyone outside of him was residual and probably downright unfair. It would be ordinary. She looked up to see Josh leaning against the doorway, staring at her.

"What's wrong?" he eyed her quizzically.

"Nothing," she shook it off and rose to her feet. "Let's get unpacked."

She eventually reamed him for entering her private domain and making decisions all over the place without her. He explained what he was trying to accomplish and promised to let go of the reigns more. I mean, he did let her go back to work, for Christ's sake.

Couldn't she see he was trying, he asked. A slight grin touched her lips at the memory.

The prospect of returning to work filled her with excitement and trepidation. She usually drove herself to work each day, but Josh insisted that she use "their" driver from now on. She tried to protest, but eventually, she made him promise to have the driver drop her off first and drop him off separately.

She knew he thought it ludicrous, but he promised to keep their relationship private until she was ready to reveal it. She couldn't have anyone witnessing them arriving to work together.

The driver pulled up in front of the office building and started to get out to let her out. "No, Brandon! Stop!" she yelled out to him. He paused with the door slightly ajar. "You don't have to assist me. In fact, I will always let myself out." She saw Brandon make eye contact with Josh through the rear-view mirror.

Josh nodded at him, and he closed his door without getting out. She looked at Josh in his dark charcoal suit, crisp white shirt, and dark red tie. How handsome. He smelled of cedar and sandalwood. She hoped they could get through this day together.

She leaned over and kissed him briefly. "Have a nice day, Mr. Abbott," she smiled.

"Have a nice day Ms. Hartwell," he grinned. She jumped out and headed to the elevator.

"Hey Monica, I'm baaaaaack," she smiled as she approached her assistant.

"Oh, Ms. Hartwell," Monica jumped up and gave her a warm hug. Then, she abruptly let go. "Oh, I'm sorry, Ms. Hartwell," she blushed.

It's You

"No, no, Monica, don't be silly. Hugs are always welcomed." Monica was a bright, friendly Caucasian woman with a cheery smile. Very competent and discreet.

"Give me about an hour to get myself together, and we can meet and catch up."

"How are you feeling, Ms. Hartwell?" she said with concern. "You don't look like you were ever in an accident."

"Thanks for that, so much better now, Monica, thank you."

"Ok, well, you have a quick status report out with the project team at 10:30 am, but otherwise, your calendar is pretty clear."

"Good," she smiled and headed into her office. She eyed the many files on her desk and shook her head. She figured she had at least 1 million emails to respond to, things to sign, and people to contact. Better get at it.

Joshua leaned back in his chair after eyeing some specs on the Rollindar project, a critical client of the firm. Fonn's name was all over it. Apparently, she had started it before she, well, they left town. From what he'd seen, she had done everything right, but this account would require a lot of additional work on her part. It wouldn't qualify as the light-duty she promised.

He tapped his pen on the desk and considered this. He had already been reprimanded for making decisions for her without her. She was so damn stubborn, he thought. He had Molly run a report on all her assigned projects; this was by far the biggest one. He then had her run a report on all projects with manager assignments. He wanted to alleviate suspicion and perhaps make a few adjustments.

Chiffon left her office to drop off some diagrams to a colleague. As she passed the breakroom, she saw Isaac standing by the copier. Obviously, he was having an issue with a paper jam. Her stomach somersaulted at the sight of him. She would never understand the visceral response she experienced with him. He looked so adorable in his confusion. He scratched his head, trying to lift a lever that wasn't moving.

"Such brilliance in the board room and such goofiness in the copy room," she mused. He turned to look up at her, and his face brightened.

"Chiffon Hartwell," as I live and breathe. He rose to his feet and gave her a big hug. He held her just a tad bit too long, and she pulled back first.

"I see you still have everything under control around here," she motioned to the copier and folded her arms with a smirk.

He laughed, "I wasn't sure if you would be in the office today. I would have stopped by." She stared at him and wondered if she should bring up his upcoming date with Tam. She decided against it. Better keep it professional, she thought.

"How are you feeling, Chiffon? Are you sure you're ready to be back?" Her brows furrowed. He sounded like Josh. Didn't anybody believe she knew her own limitations? Geez.

"Yes, I'm fine. I'll follow up with my new doctor here, and I'm sure he will agree with Dr. Thomas. I'm on light duty," she made the quotes signal with her fingers.

He stared at her, not saying anything for a moment. She could literally feel him eyeing her up and down. After a few moments passed, she called to him, "Isaac?"

"Um, yeah," he snapped out of it. "So, can I take you to lunch? We've got a lot to catch up on," he said quickly before she could protest.

She glanced at her watch. It was 11:30 am. She wondered what plans Josh had for lunch, not that she could or would expect to go with him; she just wondered. It was difficult knowing he was somewhere in the same building, and she couldn't touch him, be near him, or even acknowledge him.

"Hmmm," she considered it. "I'm only in the office a few days a week, and I really have a lot to catch up on."

"Come on, Chiffon – strictly business," he promised.

"Ok, fine, Isaac," she huffed.

"I'll pick you up at your office in 15?" he questioned.

"Ok," she went up to the copier, lifted a lever and removed the paper jam, and handed it to him. "You're buying," she smiled, turned, and walked away.

He wasn't kidding when he said they had a lot to catch up on. He chattered away as they rode down in the elevator. Engrossed in what he was saying, she didn't pay attention to where she was going and literally bumped smack dab into Josh at the revolving door. Her heart jumped in her chest at the sight of him. His eyes burned into hers. He looked from her to Isaac and back to her again. She inhaled a deep breath, and she had to maintain her cool. This was ridiculous.

A slow smile came over his face, "Ms. Hartwell, welcome back. I trust you are feeling better." Everything and everyone else disappeared at that moment. "How are you feeling? I hope you are taking it easy, it being your first day back. Isn't that correct?" His beautiful mouth said something to her, but she honestly couldn't make out what. She nodded, not saying a word. The way his eyes devoured her, she felt owned and captured.

She would give them away if she uttered a sound. Everyone would know how she clutched at his hair, screaming out his name while sitting on his face the night before. She swallowed hard.

Max took her hand and shook it. "We are so glad to have you back."

"Thank you," she managed.

"If you have some time this afternoon, maybe you can join us for the executive weekly. You can get caught up on anything you've missed over the past several weeks. I know you're only here on a part-time basis right now."

"Technically, I will be in the office just a few days a week, but I will still be working from home otherwise." Her eyes moved to meet Josh's direct stare and she quickly looked away.

"Good, then we'll see you at 3pm then." Isaac said his hellos to both Max and Josh but as he shook Josh's hand, she could feel the tension between the two men. Their eyes stayed on each other after the quick handshake, sizing each other up.

Josh glanced at her again. "We'll expect you at 3pm then, Ms. Hartwell."

"Yes," she murmured softly as Isaac started leading her toward the revolving doors.

Chapter 25

They sat across from each other looking at the menus. His entire disposition changed. Their vibe was gone. Now he was all business.

Oh, Jesus, she thought to herself, is this what she could expect with Josh in the building? He started talking about the various new accounts he was trying to land.

Although he looked directly at her, their connection was gone.

"Isaac," she stopped him mid-sentence, "Why are you angry with me?"

"I'm not angry, Chiffon."

"Yes, you are. Ever since we saw Jo…, I mean Mr. Abbott."

"Is that what you guys are calling each other? Mr. this and Ms. that?" he grimaced, "Who do you think you are fooling with the false pretense? It's all over that cocky bastard; he owns you, and it's all over you; you wouldn't have it any other way."

"What?" she exclaimed, eyes widening.

"How long do you think it will be before everyone knows just why you were hired?"

She flinched, "Ok, Isaac, wait just a cotton-picking minute," she said angrily. "Are you saying you think I am incompetent or unable to perform my job responsibilities?" her eyes narrowed. "You believe I don't deserve this position, and Josh is the only reason I got hired?" her voice rose steadily.

"No, I'm not saying that Chiffon. I know you will kick ass at this position and any other you choose. What I am saying is what everyone will think once they realize you are screwing the new partner."

She flushed. If she could have turned bright red, she would have. It was a dagger through her.

"Isaac!" she was horrified, "This is not your traditional unsuspecting subordinate meets superior, and an affair ensues"

"You're right, he said. It's worse because Josh infiltrated the company just to get at you. He doesn't give a damn about Reynolds, just you, only you."

She shook her head, "That's not true. I mean, you've only got it partially right, Isaac. Josh doesn't make bad business decisions, not even for me. Their family business is centered around electronics, marketing and acquisitions."

"Christ Chiffon, there you go again. Josh is a manipulative, arrogant, controlling bastard. You are blind because you are mesmerized by him and under his spell. Anyway, it doesn't matter what the truth is; perception rules." The server came to set down bread and butter and took their orders.

After the server departed, Chiffon bit into a piece of bread. She needed it to calm her stomach. She sank down into her seat and spoke barely above a whisper, "Nobody knows anything about our relationship, and you promised you wouldn't say anything."

"And I won't because I think you can achieve great success at Reynolds, and dammit, I care about you, Chiffon, but you need to face reality. Anyone who spends any time around you two when you're together will know. Don't kid yourself; Max and George aren't stupid."

"Josh promised he wouldn't interfere with my job."

Isaac lifted his eyebrow, "Really, Chiffon, wasn't he the one who secured your time off? Didn't he notify everyone of your accident? Jesus Chiffon, you both came back here on the same day."

"Both Max and George know that Josh and I were previously acquainted, that we…," then she grew silent, abruptly ending her rebuttal. Why bother? He was right; her job would be in jeopardy if the truth ever came out. Their food came, and they ate in silence.

"Look, Chiffon," he reached out and grabbed her hand across the table. She felt it in the pit of her stomach. "I'm sorry I said that. I didn't mean it. I just…, it's just…, you just," he stammered, and they both started laughing uncomfortably. He put his head in his other hand for a minute. "I'm kinda transparent huh?"

"Well…" she answered, still smiling at him. She liked Isaac, she enjoyed his company. Yes, and a weird attraction existed between them, but even more, she wanted his friendship. He had become special to her for some reason, and it was obvious how much he cared for her. She couldn't put her finger on it, but he became important to her. If it weren't so, she was confident she would have already slapped his face.

"Can you forgive me?" he squeezed her hand, massaging one of her fingers. It felt intimate. She knew she should move her hand out of his, but she liked it. No wonder he was confused. She was confused.

"I'm sorry, Chiffon." The tenderness in his eyes moved her.

"It's ok, Isaac. I'm a big girl, and I will deal with the consequences of my choices."

"I'll make you a deal."

"Ok," she replied.

"I will try to be respectful of your situation, but I want you to answer one question first. Then, I'll leave it alone." Curiosity peeked, she agreed.

"I need to know for sure I'm not just imagining this thing between us; cause it's very real for me. If you weren't involved with him," he gazed at her intently, "Would you let me lick those crumbs off the corner of your mouth?"

Her eyes widened. She had just taken a drink of water, and she almost spit it out. She swallowed uncomfortably and coughed. "Isaac!" her mouth fell open, and she attempted to compose herself.

"Just tell me, Chiffon, I'm a big boy; I can take it. Would I have a chance with you?" She didn't know what to say. She wiped along the sides of her mouth. She had to proceed with caution. Her first thought was yes. Yes, she could see herself with Isaac. He was gorgeous, funny, talented, and successful in his own rite. Their connection was undeniable. He was just the kind of man she should be with – available, unmarried, and uncomplicated.

Why couldn't she have met him first? She knew it wasn't fair to string him along, and she really wasn't trying to. He had information that could destroy her reputation if he chose to use it, but she didn't think he wanted to. She figured Isaac felt the energy between them, and his question was fair.

"Isaac, I..." she started, but her phone buzzed. "Excuse me a sec," and she took her phone out. Oh boy! It was Josh calling. Her pulse quickened. Ever since her accident, it always felt like he was somewhere around, monitoring her actions. She held up a finger to Isaac, letting him know she needed just a minute.

"Hello," she breathed quietly into the receiver.

"Hello, Ms. Hartwell," he said evenly.

Her heart skipped a beat. "Hi," she responded.

"Are you enjoying your little outing with your boyfriend?"

She swallowed, "Um," oh wow, she thought, "Yes, um, I mean no, listen, you've caught me at a bad time. I'm out to lunch with a colleague. We were just wrapping it up. Is it ok if I call you back?"

"No need, I will see you later."

She closed her eyes. Was that a threat or a promise? She couldn't tell, and she just couldn't address it now. "Ok, I'll see you then." She ended the call. She would deal with him after the meeting.

Isaac glanced at his watch. She knew he was waiting for her answer, but Josh's call had thrown her. She didn't want to say too much. "Isaac, we had better head back." He waited, unmoving. "The short answer to your question is yes. I would want to explore our um, this um, thing between us. I don't want to go any deeper than that right now. It will never be my first choice to date someone I work with. As you have pointed out, it just complicates everything," she said with bitterness.

"Ok, he put up his hands. I needed to know if you felt me too." She had no response.

The waitress brought the check. He paid, and they headed back to the office. She was quiet on the way back. She gave his hand a quick squeeze as she got off the elevator on her floor. She needed to jot down a few things before this afternoon's meeting. She was staring at her phone's calendar when she entered and closed the door.

When she raised her head, she gazed directly into Josh's stormy eyes. His presence filled her office. He was leaning against the far wall next to the window. Her breath caught as she inhaled him. She loved the smell of him. "Joshua, what… are you doing here?" she whispered.

She stood motionless, waiting. He stared at her, reeking of importance and damn fineness. She must have really upset him if he risked coming to her office.

"So, how was lunch?" he asked, unblinking.

Was she in trouble? She wondered, "It was fine… I mean, there was a lot, we, I needed to catch—"

"So, tell me, what exactly is going on between you and Mr. Mergers and Acquisitions?"

"Nothing," she exhaled, but she felt nervous and defensive. He glared at her in disbelief. She walked over to her desk and dropped her purse and phone down. "Nothing is going on,

Joshua," she said in a calmer tone. He remained still, arms folded in front of him, taking her in.

She could feel the distance, the stiffness all over him, and it was uncomfortable. She walked over to him. She reached up and touched his lightly bearded face with the back of her hand. "Do you think you might be overreacting to an innocent lunch? You know I'm not interested in anyone else. Don't you?"

He continued to stare at her, softening a little. "Yes, I know who I am in your life, but you must be aware, it doesn't preclude other men from desiring you. You are a beautiful woman, baby, and the way that motherfucker challenged me," he stiffened again.

"Challenged you?" her brow furrowed, "When did he do that?"

He didn't answer her. "Does he know about us?"

She put her hand down and fisted it to her side. She didn't know what to say. If she told him. he would know just how close she and Isaac had become. With the mood he was in, it just wasn't a good idea.

"I don't think anyone knows about us, Josh. He may suspect something, but I'm not sure."

"You need to let your friend know he doesn't want to fuck with me. He doesn't want to go 'a round' with me. He will lose."

"What are you talking about? He wouldn't try to challenge you. He respects your position."

Josh didn't respond, just continued glaring at her.

"Besides, he's going out with Tam," she revealed before she could stop herself.

His eyebrow raised in suspicion, "Is he now?"

Exhaling deeply, she added, "He's my friend. That's all. Please don't read anything else into it. Tam really likes him, and they are going on a date. I told you he was kind to me when I first started here. We became friends. We are allowed friends of the opposite sex, right?"

His brow raised, "Of course, as long as everyone is clear on the boundaries, I don't have a problem with it, but if anyone needs clarity, I'm happy to provide it." He wasn't stupid. That bastard wanted his woman, and it simply wasn't an option. He had gone through too much to get her back, too much in almost losing her. Nothing was coming between them again. Nothing.

Thankfully, she would only be in office sporadically. He was going to keep it like that long as possible. Not because he didn't trust Fonn, but because he knew the effect she had on the opposite sex. For some reason, she wanted to believe Mergers was completely innocent in this. Not to mention, she seemed to really like that bastard, which pissed him off more.

He grabbed her chin and covered her lips with his own. Her wonderful soft lips, he could drown in the taste of her. Her arms came up around him partly because she couldn't help it and partly because she needed to hold her balance since the kiss was so forceful.

She involuntarily pushed her body in closer to his. A low moan came from his throat. His tongue stroked the inside of her mouth, and he suckled on her tongue. The kiss took her breath away. It was so passionate, so primal. She had to gasp for air as their lips parted. She put her hand up to her mouth.

They stared at each other. She murmured, "You know we can't do that here, Josh."

"I know, I couldn't help myself," as he smiled a charming smile at her. "I'll leave you to your work." He moved in close to her mouth again. He felt her tense and wait. He kissed her lightly, pulling her bottom lip between his teeth, and she gasped. "I'll see you later." He cupped her face with both hands and dropped a quick kiss on her nose. He turned and walked out of her office. Her hand moved to cover her lips again.

She watched him until he was out of her sightlines. If she ever went out with Isaac again, she would meet him there. She couldn't have Josh coming to her office to mark his territory again. She sat down and rubbed the back of her neck. She prayed Isaac would honor his promise to keep quiet. She had to trust him.

By the time she arrived, the room was filling. Mingled voices filled the air. She spotted Joshua standing with a group of managers from various departments. She felt his eyes on her while he continued to speak to them. As usual, he had the entire group riveted to his every word.

She sat down at the far end of the long, sleek table. Isaac came in and smiled at her. She grinned quickly, nodded politely, and pretended to look through her notes. He sat directly across from her.

The meeting came to order, and they reviewed executive slides sent by each department. It was extremely informative. Lots of new developments were underway at Reynolds and Baker; eventually, some of them would affect her directly. It would take a while before major changes were implemented. Normally, she would not even be invited to these executive meetings, but it was the best way to get her caught up on company-wide projects.

When the slide presentation ended, Max rose and stated, "We would like to acknowledge Chiffon Hartwell and officially welcome her back to the fold. We know you are going to do great things here, Chiffon."

She smiled and thanked him and everyone for their well wishes during her recovery. Josh leaned back in his chair. He watched Isaac look at Chiffon longingly. Maybe she really didn't get it. The man was practically panting and salivating. He didn't report to Josh, and that was best.

He promised he wouldn't act on his suspicions, and he wouldn't if they remained only suspicions. He certainly couldn't kick every man's ass that showed an interest in his woman; especially, when they weren't aware she was off the market.

Something told him she and Mergers shared more than she let on. He personally couldn't wait to let the world know they were together. The women were already circling him like vultures. He was used to it, but notification he was officially off the market could help matters.

Fonn was so worried about keeping this damn job and making it happen on her own. He could set her up with her own company in a heartbeat if she let him.

Providing for her gave him great pleasure. He would rather have her home with JJ anyway. Her job could be taking care of her man and their baby. She could do charity work or something. One thing was for sure; he was done with this sneaking around. He would take matters into his own hands and soon. As always, he had a plan.

The meeting ran long, and ended at 5 pm, the same time the place was shutting down, so people were scrambling to get the hell out of there. She rose to her feet and picked up her materials.

"Ms. Hartwell," Josh spoke to her, and she met his heart-stopping gaze. "I'd like to see you for a moment. Can you wait?"

She looked toward the door as the last of the people were departing. The sleek room felt bigger with just the two of them occupying it. "Sure," she answered nervously.

She walked over to where he was standing.

"Did I tell you how beautiful you look today Ms. Hartwell?" His eyes raked over her snuggly fitted dark pencil skirt. His eyes danced from her lips back to her eyes. "I have a proposition for you."

She swallowed, "Yes?" He looked toward the door and held up a hand to signal he was going to close it. She swallowed again. How was this ever going to work out? She could not be alone with him at work. As soon as

It's You

they were alone all she could think about was riding him, clawing at his back in ecstasy, and it was impossible to concentrate on anything else. He closed the door and turned the lock. He took off his jacket and threw it on the conference table.

She glanced around anxiously, "Um, Mr. Abbott, must we talk here?" she asked as he approached her.

He smiled warmly at her. "You don't want to discuss work at work Ms. Hartwell?" He stood directly in front of her looking down at her. She closed her eyes for a minute. The electricity between them was palatable. He touched under her chin sending electric shocks all over her body. "I have a proposition for you baby." He was standing so close she could feel his hot breath on her face as he spoke. She blinked up at him.

"Within the next 30 to 45 days we will be splitting off the Project Management Office (PMO) to Skokie, Illinois."

Her eyes widened and she took a step backward, "The new office location has been solidified?" "Yes."

"Skokie?" she replied confused. "I thought this was months away. How long have you known about this?" she muttered accusingly.

"Splitting out the PMO department has been an agenda item for a few months now. It was recently decided it would be a definite go."

"So, we are moving to Skokie," her eyebrow raised.
"Yes, some of you."

"Why didn't you tell me this before?"

"I'm telling you now," he furrowed his brow. "You're the one who insists we don't mix business with pleasure. He leaned against the conference table. While you were convalescing, business went on. You are aware I can't share everything with you."

"Yea, but—"

"Listen sweetheart, you are the first employee I'm sharing this with.

I'm preparing you. Nobody else knows this is happening so soon."

"So, what's the proposition?" she questioned with her hands on her hips.

"Take your hands off your hips and come here," he commanded. She stood her ground for a minute. Her emotions ran the gamut with him. One minute she was completely in love, the next she was angry, then longing, then hopeful, then scared, then she could barely breathe

Without him. She couldn't keep up with how ragged he made her feel sometimes.

He opened his arms, "Come here honey. Don't be upset." She stepped into his arms. They encircled her warmly.

"The project management office (PMO) is going to need a manager, Fonn, I think you should head it."

"What?" she stepped back again.

"That's the proposition," he stated. "The job is yours if you want it."

"Manager of the PMO?" she asked.

"Yes, baby, George and Max both think it would be a great idea since they've never had anyone fill the role in the past. And before you even ask, I did not tell them to offer you the role. They were throwing a few names around and when yours came up everyone agreed."

She leaned against the table next to him. "I have only worked here for about… she looked at her watch, let's see, all of 10 minutes. How can I get promoted over the other people who have been here for the long haul?"

"You are a brilliant, dynamic, educated woman. Why wouldn't you be promoted?"

"I'm also your girlfriend," she turned and stared out the window not responding.

He took her hand and kissed it, "Why don't you have faith in yourself honey? This isn't because of your connection to me. They wanted you. In fact, when in the interviewing process, they knew you would also be a candidate for this upcoming role. It was just a matter of when."

"Will you be there?" she asked not sure what she wanted his answer to be.

He smirked, "At the Skokie office?" she nodded. "No baby, I won't have an office there, I think Max is going."

"Good," she smiled. He grabbed her shoulders and buried his head in her neck, her breath caught in her throat as she started to laugh. Suddenly they heard a knock at the door. They immediately let go of each other and stepped away. She smoothed out her clothes and sat down in one of the chairs.

"Yes," he said loudly.

"Mr. Abbott, you have an important call." It was Molly, one of the executive assistants.

"Think about it sweetheart. You would be fantastic. We can discuss this further, I gotta run," he kissed her cheek and departed.

She let her head rest in her hands for a minute. What a first day back. Suddenly, she felt very tired. She had too much to think about and catch up on.

Once back in her office, she saw a text from Josh telling her to call their driver and go home without him. He had to put out a fire. She wondered what could be going on, but it was ok. She could close her eyes in the car and think.

He went on to notify her that a section of the office was expanding to Skokie, IL, and she was picked to head up the project management arm. It was surprising because she was so new to the company. It would definitely cause a stir. He insisted he had nothing to do with it, but she knew better.

Upon entering the condo, she headed to the nursery and lay across the bed. She missed JJ. They called him every night. Josh said it would be a few weeks before they could secure him. She didn't understand the delay. He was holding something back from her. How many times did she have to tell him she could handle the truth?

He also was very vague about the divorce. She didn't plan to continue to live with and spread her legs to another woman's husband no matter how much she loved him. It didn't sit well in her spirit. She wanted her life to have God's favor, not his wrath. She knew Candice's institutionalization would delay things a bit, but it had been a few months since everything went down. She needed a solid status report.

She made dinner, steak, wild rice, and butter rolls and put them in the warmer. It was 7:30 pm, and Josh still hadn't made it home, so she went ahead and ate dinner.

Even though they had only lived together for a short while, the place felt empty without him. Where was he?

She went into her office and tried to put more of a dent in the million or so emails. The more she thought about the relocation, the better she felt about the whole thing. It would put the distance she needed in place with both Josh and Isaac. Necessary distance from Josh, because she wanted him too much, and Isaac, because she didn't want to want him.

An hour later, she heard Josh coming in. Soon, his solid frame rested against the doorway of their office space. Her heart warmed at the sight of him. "Hey gorgeous," he smiled, loosening his tie. She smiled back at him. "It smells wonderful in here, babe."

"I made dinner for a change," she smiled.

He chuckled and held out his arms. She stepped into them. "I get to eat twice," he smiled and covered her lips with his own. She forgot she'd been worried.

Chapter 26

Over the next few weeks, she avoided going to the office as much as she could. She didn't want to run into Isaac or deal with water cooler discussion on the office move but the time had come for her to see her new doctor for a follow-up. She didn't tell Josh about it because he would take it over with all his questions and self-imposed directives. She would head to the office, leave a little early, go to the doctor, and come back. Brandon could pick her up at 5 pm, as usual, none the wiser. Josh would not be in today, so she could pull it off.

Hopefully, the doctor would have great news on her progress. She certainly felt good and strong. Restrictions could most likely be lifted, but her physician had to sign off.

Sitting at her desk, she scarfed down a delicious sandwich she brought for lunch. Overcome with a sluggish feeling; she headed to the breakroom to retrieve her favorite creamer. A cup of coffee would give her the jolt she needed. Peering in the fridge, she didn't see it. She moved her head toward the back of the bottom shelf when she heard, "Lawd, have mercy woman."

She rose and turned to see Isaac leaning against the counter behind her. His head cocked to the side with a wide grin.

She couldn't help but smile at him, "What are you doing on this floor Isaac?" She smoothed down her skirt, acutely aware of his penetrating gaze.

"I'm enjoying the view."

"Isaac!" she admonished him.

He laughed, "I have a meeting up here, but Frank is not in his office."

"Oh, I saw him earlier. He's around."

They stared at each other in silence. She had to give it to him; Isaac was a handsome man. He's a more reserved beauty. He didn't exude all that in your face; everybody take notice, gorgeousness that Joshua did, but he didn't need to. He could hold his own. He would make some pretty babies, she thought.

"Did you find what you're looking for?" he grinned.

"Huh?" she queried.

"In the fridge," he pointed to the appliance.

"Oh," she blushed. "No, no, I didn't. Apparently, someone around here likes coconut caramel too."

"I know I do," he said without a smile.

She exhaled, so the good news was, there was no pressure between them anymore. It was lighthearted and fun again. The bad news was his extreme flirtation was constantly present, more so now than ever before. He remained professional, but when they were alone, well, not so much.

She had mixed feelings – part of her wanted to tell him to stop it, put an end to the behavior, and the other part wanted to let the chips fall where they may. It was fun and served as a bit of a reprieve from the intensity of Joshua. It perplexed her.

"You are staring at me again, Chiffon."

"What?" she snapped out of her thoughts.

He smirked, "Admit it, you want this," as they held their gaze. "You just can't do anything about it, can you?"

"I, I, haven't—"

He held up his hand. "It's ok. I can wait."

"What are you talking about Isaac, wait for what?" she scrunched up her face questioningly.

"Wait for you. Joshua Abbott is going to disappoint you, he's going to let you down again, and when he does, I'll be there to pick up all your beautiful pieces. I'd like to give each piece my individual specialized attention."

Her mouth dropped open just as someone else entered the kitchen. "Um, I gotta go," she turned to leave, and he stepped in front of her, blocking her way.

"By the way, I have a date tonight. I'll give Tam all your love," he spoke slowly and methodically. "It has been a bit of a challenge for us to coordinate our schedules, but finally, we worked everything out. Tonight, is the night."

Her eyes widened. She had forgotten about them, about that. Clearly off-balance, she mumbled, "Well, um, have a great time." She angled around him and got the hell out of there.

He watched her retreating figure with a smirk on his face. "I will have you Chiffon. Maybe not today, but one day you will wrap yourself all around me," he whispered.

In the back of the cab, she squeezed the back of her neck, trying to rub out the tension building there. Again, she told herself, she had no right to be so jealous. Tam deserved to be happy with a good man. That move to Skokie couldn't happen soon enough.

It's You

Her phone vibrated. She looked down at it. Josh. Should she answer? Yes, she decided. "Hello dear," she tried to sound like she was still at work.

"What's going on, baby? Where are you?" he questioned. "Where am I? You know I'm at work today," she said nervously, looking around. Could he see her?

"Yeah, but you're not in your office. There are no meetings on your calendar. Where are you?"

"How do you know I'm not in my office?"

"Well, let's see, I just called and was told you were out at an appointment."

Good grief, she forgot to tell Marcie to say she was in a meeting. Why did she always feel like a child caught with her hand in the cookie jar when talking to him?

"Joshua," she said with exasperation, "I have a follow-up with Dr. Hall." There was silence on the line.

"And I'm just hearing about this. Why?"

She took a deep breath. Why did she bother trying to keep anything from him? "Because I wanted to take care of it myself." He was quiet again, too quiet. "Please don't be mad at me. I can handle an appointment on my own."

"Where?" was all she heard. She gave him the address.

"I'll meet you there," he hung up. She stared at the phone. Did he just hang up in her face? By the time she arrived, checked in with the receptionist, and turned to find a seat, he was walking through the lobby with his eyes glued to her.

Did he see all the heads turning as he sauntered through? What a specimen, she thought to herself as she watched him approach her in a light gray designer suit with a green and gray speckled tie. Rephrase. What an angry specimen. He bent down and kissed her cheek chafely. He grabbed her hand and led her to some empty seats at the far side of the room. After they sat down, he picked up a magazine, not saying one word to her. He started thumbing through the pages.

She studied his profile. Her love, her life he represented, she thought. Not fair for him to have this much control over her emotions. When did she lose her mind? She tried to think back to a time when Joshua didn't matter, and she honestly couldn't remember one.

She fidgeted, "Ok, I'm sorry," she said quietly.

"Are you?" he continued to thumb blankly through the pages without looking up.

"Yes, dammit. I apologize," she said, raising her voice a little this time. He peered over at her, taking her in.

This damned woman was driving him crazy. Such defiance. What was he going to do with her? He didn't know, but he knew what he wanted to do to her. For some reason, he had never been so turned on. She appeared so innocent, her dark lashes blinking over her beautiful brown eyes.

Those luscious lips parted slightly, just waiting for his. Her long tresses hung down on her shoulders, curling slightly at the ends. And the way her hands were clasped on her lap like a little schoolgirl. He could devour her on the spot.

He wasn't necessarily angry. He just wanted her to stop keeping things from him. How was he going to protect her if she didn't keep him informed? Nothing would ever happen to her again, not on his watch, and he planned to always be watching. He didn't care how upset she got with him. It was for her own safety, end of story.

He'd already made himself clear, "Don't keep things from me, Fonn; important things or any things. You got that?" he said impatiently.

"Yes, I got that. I was going to tell you," she exhaled, nerves calming.

"Yeah, after the fact, what did you think I was going to do bribe your doctor or something? Tell him to put you back on bed rest?"

"No, no, nothing like that. I just wanted to handle it on my own. You treat me like I'm so fragile. Like I'm going to break, but I won't. Can't you see I'm strong – I'm a survivor," she hit her balled-up fist against her chest.

Yes, he saw it; it was one of the things that made her so scrumptiously attractive to him in the first place. But she took that whole strong and independent thing too far in his estimation. Her appointment sidetracked him from his original mission. He had important news to share today.

Instead of spilling now, he decided to wait until after the appointment.

"Ms. Hartwell," the nurse called out her name. She got up and reached for his hand. He got up and took hers, and they headed to the back.

The doctor gave her a thorough examination and let them know she was healing well. Josh asked him one million and one questions, but he didn't seem to mind. He agreed she should remain on light duty for the next 30 days, and then if all is well, she could get back to her life full-time. The stitches were removed before she left Tennessee, and she wasn't in any real pain.

Departing from the doctor's office, she saw Brandon waiting on the curb for them.

"I assume you need a ride back," he glanced down at her.

"Yes, I do."

"Will you be going home or back to the office?" He seemed to still be a little testy with her.

"I have my laptop. That's all I need. We can go home."

"Good," he said and motioned for Brandon to get the door for them. Once settled in the limo, Joshua pressed the intercom button and told Brandon to continue to drive until he directed him to head to the house. He pressed the button for the dark privacy glass to drop.

She squinted her eyes at him, "What's going on?" she asked.

He took her hand in his and hesitated.

"What is it, Joshua?" His serious demeanor made her feel anxious.

"Honey, I have some rather unpleasant news to share."

"What?" she questioned, "Is JJ ok?"

"Yes, he's fine. It's not that."

She held her breath as her heart started to hammer in her chest.

"Honey, Candy's family has checked her out of the facility."

"What? You can't be serious, she shrieked. How is that even possible?"

"They want to bring in their own doctors to treat her."

"So, she's back on the street, free to roam?" her hand covered her mouth in shock. "But she's still insane!" she cried.

"Well, I wouldn't say free. She is under constant guard at her parent's home."

"They can't do that." Chiffon stared out of the window, tearing up. He pulled her close to him and wrapped his arm around her. She breathed into his neck, "She almost killed me," she trembled. He rubbed her face soothingly.

"Shhhh, nothing's going to happen to you. I promise, baby. I'm not happy about this news either, but the Lakes are immensely powerful people. The good news is, I know they want their child to get better. She is not going to go untreated."

"But she shouldn't be free, out just like that. What if she escapes or something?" She looked up at him, "She could come after JJ again. Can't we protest or get the authorities involved? Have her remanded again?"

"I suppose we could, but I assured them we would not."

She recoiled from him, "You what?"

"I had no choice."

"That doesn't make any sense whatsoever, Josh," she hissed.

"The only way to get the divorce sign-off was to agree not to fight them," his voice raised.

"What does one thing have to do with the other?" she queried.

He went into detail about the delay in divorce processing. He ended on, "As her guardians; I need their signature on her behalf. They forced my hand. If I demand her institutionalization, they could hold up the divorce – possibly for years."

"For years?" she repeated disbelievingly. Her head dropped into her hands. So, the only way Josh could be free was to let a homicidal maniac roam the streets again. Let an attempted murderer back on the loose? A shiver ran through her. "What about JJ?" she looked at him through tear-stained eyes. "Will we still be able to get him?"

"Yes, JJ is still coming to live with us. I demanded it."

Her eyes lit up, "Is he, really Joshua?"

"Yes, it's just going to take a little longer than I originally anticipated."

"How much longer?"

"By the time you relocate to the Skokie office, we should have him."

"But that's nearly a month away. This was only supposed to be for a few weeks."

"I know, this complicates things more. Also, I should make you aware of something else."

She furrowed her brow, "What?"

"Terrance showed up at my parent's house demanding a paternity test."

"This can't be happening," she cried out.

"Yes, apparently, Candy told him the baby was his prior to her breakdown."

"So now he wants him too?"

"It appears so."

"This is unbelievable." She was holding on by a thread, but Josh remained surprisingly calm. "Why aren't you more upset about this?" she wiped under her eyes.

His head tilted slightly. "Because I know everything has a natural path."

"There is nothing natural about any of this. You feel level-headed cause you've had time to digest this already, time that I wasn't afforded," she rolled her eyes.

"I would have shared this sooner, but I needed something concrete first. Baby, listen to me," he took her hands; his smoky gaze searched hers. "Don't look at me like that. I have told you everything now. I couldn't lay all this on you while you're recovering. I didn't want anything to impede your progress. Forgive the delay darling," he kissed the inside of her palm and let his mouth linger. She felt the current go through her. "Don't be angry," he pleaded against her skin.

"I'm tired of forgiving you, Josh."

He chuckled, and she closed her eyes when he kissed the sensitive area once more and sucked gently.

"Oh God," she let out a soft moan.

"Do you believe me when I tell you I'm going to keep you safe?" he held her hand against his cheek. "I just forgave your delay in revealing your appointment today, didn't I?"

"That's not the same."

"Withholding is withholding, isn't it?" he planted light kisses up and down each finger.

"I guess, "she said, barely audible. She found it challenging to concentrate on anything but his moist lips against her skin.

"I'm going to make sure nothing interferes with our dreams. I will protect you. I promise. I love you, baby. Nothing will stand in the way of us having, or being the family, we've planned. I won't let it. You trust me?" She stared into her love's eyes. She trusted him.

"I will rectify the situation, so let it drop from your lovely head. Now, if you want to concentrate on something, concentrate on all this," he motioned to himself.

Suddenly, she felt tugged upward until she found herself on his lap, straddling him. Her skirt inched up over her thighs. Their lips met fiercely. She suckled on his lips and tongue, so warm, so wet. She heard the low growl from his throat and felt his hard length pressing against her dampness.

"I can't get enough of you," he whispered.

Sometimes he feared he might swallow the woman whole.

Sucking on his tongue reminded her of his shaft in her mouth. She mimicked the motion as he gripped her ass, pulling her even closer to him. His hands moved underneath her blouse. In one swift motion, he had it off. He frantically unclasped her bra, and her aching breasts fell free. He pushed her back, parting their lips. His hand lifted her breasts, pushing her nipples toward the other. He bent down and grabbed them both in his mouth at the same time. Her nipples were so long and hard, and it was easy.

"Oh Josh," she cried out with her fingers clasped behind his head, pulling him closer as she squirmed on top of him. He suckled at the hard peaks making them more solid and sensitive to his tongue. Exquisite pleasure crept down her spine.

She reached to slide off his suit jacket and pull his shirt out of his pants. She threw her head back for a moment, caught up in pure sensation.

"I need to be inside your hot, wetness, baby," he murmured, "I want you to throb tomorrow from my penetration today."

She yelped his name.

He then assisted her in unbuckling his belt and moving his trousers and boxers down to let his solid manhood free. She stroked it with her hands as he ground his hips up and down. "Oh, Fonn, sweet baby." He slid his hands on either side of her skirt and pulled it up over her hips.

Their lips met again as he ripped her panties off. She squealed in delight when his rock-hard staff entered her fully, roughly, deeply.

"Yes!" she cried as she pumped her hips, meeting him thrust for thrust. His own eyes closed, he moved forward to suckle at her taut nipples again.

She held onto his shoulders as he controlled the timing of his penetration. "I will do anything for you," he murmured against her hot flesh. "Whatever you want," he took one hand and circled her sensitive clit with his finger.

"Oh, sweetheart… I, you… baby," she moaned out, trying to tell him something, "I…" she felt the tension building inside. "Baby, I… it's, it's so…gooooood!" She cried out his name as a tremendous orgasm racked her body. She thrashed and writhed about wildly as the earth-defying torment took her over. A million stars exploded inside of her – she tightened her muscles around him.

She felt him stiffen and then cry out with the same abandon as she did. "Goddammit," he held her hips tightly. "Dammit, woman."

She kissed him as he spurted inside her, filling her. They held each other tight with him buried deep within her. He kissed her neck and her cheek. After a while, he pressed the intercom button and directed Brandon to drive them home. They slowly put their clothes back on, still kissing and holding each other. Eventually, she nestled herself on his lap and closed her eyes.

Once home, they got out of their work clothes and showered. She just settled down on her oversized, comfortable recliner to flip through her Easy Living magazine when Josh came out of the home office dressed in jeans and a black t-shirt.

"Soooooo," he smiled down at her, "Will you be accompanying me to Max's event tonight?"

She looked up at him curiously, "What event?"

He sat down on the floor in front of her, facing her. She was in jean shorts and a tank top. He rubbed up and down her legs. Damn, that felt good. She loved it whenever he touched her.

"I thought you might have forgotten. He has invited everyone to a garden party this evening."

"Really, and you want us to go um…together?" she queried with an eyebrow raised.

"Yes, I do," he shrugged his shoulders, "If you're up to it."

"You know we can't attend together, right?"

He stared at her intently and let out a frustrated sigh. "This is insane," he removed his hands from her. "We need to get married already because once we do, this I spy shit ends." She narrowed her eyes at him. He went on, "This sneaking around you want me to do, is getting ridiculous."

"I want you to do?" she questioned.

He let his forehead rest on her leg, "I know I agreed to keep this, us quiet –"

"Yes, you did," she challenged.

"I'm finding it difficult and frankly, rather disturbing, he looked back up at her, "I don't enjoy games."

"Disturbing, hun?" she questioned with a slight grin.

"Well, you literally turn green whenever you see me at the office. You insist I don't enter your office, and you damn sure won't come to mine. We barely ride into work together without you freaking out and putting the fear of God into Brandon."

She laughed aloud then. It simply wasn't possible to scare Brandon. He was a big, burly bodyguard/chauffeur, but she got his point.

"Soooooo...," she dragged out the word. "Is there a marriage proposal in there somewhere? It almost sounded like you want us to get married."

He grinned at her, "You already know I want to marry you."

She shook her head, "No, I don't. How would I know that? You have never officially asked me. You just assumed we would be married one day. No proposal and no actual date necessary."

"Well, I'll be," he said as the realization hit him. Let me make myself clear then. As soon as I get the official notification the divorce is final, I want to marry you, Chiffon Hartwell. If I could do it today, no, yesterday, I would."

He rose to his feet, pulling her up as well. He then got down on one knee in front of her and took her hand.

"I have loved you since the day I first saw you standing in Handover Park by the fountain," he kissed her hand, reminiscing, "You would stand in the same spot daily, letting the wind blow through your hair. You'd close your eyes and turn your head up toward the sun. Every day you would come to that fountain around noon, right around the same time I was en route to Edgewater Consulting."

He grinned, reflecting on the crazy workaholic he was back then. She shook her head affirmatively.

"You were so beautiful, Fonn. You took my breath away then, just like you do now. I remember leaving a little early each day to have a few extra minutes to sit on the bench on the other side. I waited for you and was mesmerized each time you arrived. I was late on more than one occasion caught up in you." Her eyes welled.

"I made up my mind you were going to be mine one day. I had to have you. Remember when I finally walked up to you and told you just how gorgeous you were." She smiled through her tears. She remembered just like it was yesterday.

"I have loved you, baby, from that day to this one," Josh continued.

"Oh, Josh," she choked, tears falling freely.

"Forgive me for being so presumptuous," he kissed her hand again, "Will you marry me, Fonn?" he asked, his own eyes sparkling. "I'm expecting the official divorce papers any day now. Then I want to put a ring on it. As far as I'm concerned, we can go straight to city hall. The sooner you are, Mrs. Abbott, the better."

"City hall? You're kidding, right?"

"We can make it official first, and then we can have a huge ceremony for friends and family later. I don't want to wait for a big wedding. I want the world to know you belong to me." He stared up at her with moist eyes and stroked her chin, "I want you to know it too."

That touched her. This beautiful, wonderful man loved her, and it meant everything. She stroked across his neatly cropped beard.

"I do know it, and my answer is yes."

He jumped up and lifted her off her feet and swung her around. She laughed and held him tight.

A wide grin took over his face, "I knew it was a yes."

"Shut up!" she pushed lightly at his shoulder.

"I already have your ring, sweetheart. I've only been waiting for the appropriate time to present you with it. He kissed her lips again. "And you are never going to take it off," he smiled wryly.

"Never," she repeated. She stared at him quietly for a moment and then moved close to whisper in his ear, "So what time are you gonna meet me at this party?"

He jerked his head back, shook it, laughing heartily.

Chapter 27

She left the apartment about 30 minutes after his departure and hailed a cab to Max's place. Josh promised to be on his best behavior and keep his distance as much as possible, but for some reason, she didn't believe him. She didn't see him when he left the apartment because she was still getting ready.

As she approached the front entrance, a greeter stood directing visitors to a side entrance. Striding toward the back fence, she could hear music, voices and smell delicious food. Plush gardens surrounded her as she followed a stepstone trail leading to the festivities.

When she turned the corner, a dramatic scene awaited her. A long, white table housing several bouquets of flowers marching down the center. An assortment of food and desserts surrounded the floral arrangements. Lanterns swung above the table, adding a soft glow to the area. A live band perched on a stage in the far corner—what a beautiful backyard. The green grass was perfectly manicured, and a large fountain bubbled with what looked like champagne flowing out. Servers dressed in black and white tended to every need.

A warm sense of satisfaction washed over her. She smiled and waved at some familiar faces. Her eyes scanned the lawn for Josh. She didn't see him, but she knew he was there, she could feel him.

After making small talk with co-workers, she made her way to the champagne fountain. She stopped drinking altogether after her injury due to the pain medication but was much better now, so she decided to partake. She picked up a glass and held it under the bubbly stream.

Soon, she felt someone come to stand directly behind her. "Don't turn around," she heard him say. Her muscles tensed, it was Joshua, and he was so close behind her she could smell the familiar fragrance of his cologne. She closed her eyes for a moment and inhaled his masculine scent.

"Since I'm not allowed to be near you tonight, standing behind you to get a drink shouldn't be too suspicious, 'J'ai raison, n'est-ce pas'?" he finished his statement in French. She crossed her legs to ease the throbbing ache she immediately felt.

Every hair on her body prickled up at his voice. He knew how crazy it made her when he spoke in French. His fluency in a few other languages, popped in at random. Multi-lingual bastard, she chuckled. He said it was paramount for business.

She had it bad, and he knew it. Boy, did he know it, she thought.

"I just wanted to tell you; you look beautiful tonight, damn scrumptious. The way that dress hugs your curves and flairs in all the right places. I can't wait to peel it and everything else off you."

Her eyes involuntarily closed.

"I want to place my tongue everywhere my hand touches to get you naked."

Oh my God, she thought with every nerve fiber on alert. She opened her eyes suddenly when she felt the liquid in her glass overflowing onto her hand. She hadn't even realized; her cup runneth over. She snatched her glass away and found a place to sit it down.

When she finally turned back around, he'd already departed. She grabbed some napkins and cleaned up the mess she'd made. She took a few deep breaths and emptied the glass in one swallow and refilled it again. Hmmm, delicious, she thought as she sipped even more. A warm, liquid cascade ran through her entire body. How nice, she thought and then hiccupped.

Startled, she giggled aloud.

Better get some food, she figured and joined a few of the other project managers near the buffet. They were discussing the upcoming split of the PMO to the new location. Grace turned to her and asked how she felt about it. She hesitated for a moment, not sure how much she should divulge.

"Umm," she thought for a moment, "I think ultimately, the expansion will be good for the company."

"Yeah, maybe," Grace interrupted her. "I figure it's going to take at least a year before anything actually happens. They've got to secure the lease and get everything moved."

"Yeah," John chimed in. "I think they are creating new positions and everything for that office."

"I heard a few rumors about that," Grace added. "Well, I know if any promotions are handed out, I should be at the top of the list." Leslie added, "I've been here the longest."

"You know they don't make decisions based on length of service," Grace added.

"Yeah, but they should, Leslie insisted. Maybe if I could get Mr. Abbott's ear," she smiled widely.

"You want more than his ear," Grace laughed, and Leslie nodded.

"A girl's gotta start somewhere. His ears are as beautiful as the rest of him."

Chiffon grimaced and inhaled deeply. She surveyed the lawn, wondering how many other women were lusting after her man, probably all of them. Her eyes found and lingered on him standing near the bandstand. He was dressed casually for him but immaculate all the same. The cream-colored linen pants with a matching shirt just made him more beautiful.

It's a wonder, anyone, women, men, children, could get anything done when he was around; breathtaking, she stared. Sometimes it was difficult for her to get her bearings, to use her words when he looked at her in that special way he had. He knew how to make her feel like she was the only woman on earth. The only woman for him.

It seemed anyone with functioning eyesight wanted his attention. She figured he had the homosapiens locked down for this lifetime. Joshua possessed an inherent elegance that was so commanding, so authoritative, it was almost out of your hands, that desire to please him.

No one wanted to be on the wrong side of Joshua Abbott. No way, no how, and he didn't make it easy to find yourself on his good side. It had to be earned and well deserved, but once you were in, God help you. He would give his life for you. Quite delectable, he was, on so many levels. She imagined either people were scrambling to please him or hoping to get the chance. She knew because she was first in that line.

"Things are really moving and shaking since Abbott joined," John said, shaking his head affirmatively. She remained quiet.

"I'd like to move and shake on him," Leslie added with a laugh. "He is super, duper, duper fine."

"Yeah," Grace joined in. "He is, but I think he's married."

Chiffon's heart squeezed painfully at those words. Oh boy, is he married, she thought. Ya'll have no idea.

"A man that beautiful couldn't be single, Grace continued, somebody surely has snatched that up, but he doesn't wear a ring if he's hitched."

"Everything stops when he comes into the room," Leslie sighed and glanced at Chiffon, who was not doing such a good job of reigning in her jealously, tight-lipped, and quiet.

"What do you think about him, Chiffon?" she asked, "You're awfully quiet. Ain't he fine?" All eyes turned to her. "Didn't you know him before you started here?"

Could anyone say – hot seat?

"Umm, yes, she cleared her throat. He did some consulting at the firm I worked for in Georgia." she retorted a well-rehearsed reply, "And, of course, I think he is a very handsome man indeed. He seems to be excellent at what he does. He usually comes in and turns a company around." she smiled at the group.

That seemed to satisfy, and they continued to chatter as they fixed their plates.

"I heard he is the one who insisted the company split the PMO to another location," John said, all knowingly.

"Really?" Chiffon asked him.

"Yeah, they weren't considering doing anything like that right now. They have been focused on getting new business, not restructuring current business."

Her brow raised. She wondered just how much she could rely on office gossip. She would have to ask Josh about that later. Why would he care about splitting the PMO off so soon if it weren't a part of the original corporate initiative? She hoped it wasn't just for her to take that promotion. She knew him well. If he wanted something, he didn't wait for it to happen. He made it happen. Let the casualties fall where they may. Collateral damage, he would call it.

Accepting the position wasn't definite because another posting held her interest. She was good at developing training materials, and there was an opening for a training manager she considered applying for. She just had not told Josh yet.

Most of all, she wanted baby JJ with them. She wanted to go back to Tennessee and get him with something akin to desperation. She never mentioned it to Josh but thought about it daily. She needed JJ to know he was safe.

She got the feeling he saw everything that went down that awful day, and she wanted to make sure his little inner man was ok.

The baby sounded happy, but he wasn't getting the chance to see Candice or Joshua. He was probably wondering where her nose was as well. She smiled to herself, recalling how he used to grab at it and try to kiss it and/or bite it all the time. She wanted her baby now, sometimes even more than she wanted anything else. It was amazing how he changed her life already.

She fixed her plate and walked with the group to sit at a table. She sat next to John on her right and one of the senior managers, Eric, she thought his name was, on her left. The party had a large turn-out. People were dancing on the make-shift dance floor near the bandstand.

She made eye contact with Josh a few times. She noticed him at the far end of the table with some of the other executive types. Birds of a feather, she thought to herself. He was never alone. There was always someone talking to him or waiting to talk to him.

He handled it all with the cool diplomacy she admired. She wondered if he ever felt lonely with all the attention and responsibility he held.

Some lady sat next to him, enthralled by his every word. She couldn't blame her really. How could she get upset when he wanted everyone to know they were a couple, and she wouldn't allow it? It didn't seem fair, though. The next time she caught his eye, he winked at her, and she flushed, quickly turning away. She figured she would get him later for that. He knew better, she thought. When she saw the smirk on his face afterward, she knew she was going to get him.

John got up and asked her if she would like to dance. She considered it for a moment. Why not? She thought Josh wouldn't like it, but he was busy with his hoard of worshippers. She glanced over at Josh with an 'I'm just keeping up the pretense' look. She got to her feet and took John's hand.

She noticed Josh's impassive look turn to a scowl. This was one of her favorite Luther songs, So Amazing. She couldn't dance with Joshua, so she went for it. Besides, she had a little too much champagne and wanted no needed to have some innocent fun. Let Josh wonder who was circling her for a change.

What the fuck? He immediately tuned everyone else out. What the hell was she doing? He saw them head toward the dance floor. If she wanted to dance, he was right there. This was some bullshit. The guy leaned down and whispered something in her ear. She giggled, putting her arms on his shoulders. Who was that anyway? He didn't see Mergers and Acquisitions yet and had already prepared himself to watch him panting and salivating upon arrival. That, he was prepared for, not this, her letting someone else, anyone else, put their hands on her. In front of his face, no less. Unacceptable. He inadvertently shook his head in dismay.

"Right, Joshua?" Max said again, following his steady gaze to the dance floor. Max slapped him on the back and jarred him out of the trance-like state.

"Oh, I'm sorry Max, I was, well um—"

"Man, he leaned over closer to Josh's ear. You've got it bad." Josh's jealous green gaze met Max's. A slow grin took over Max's face. He leaned in and whispered, "The no fraternizing policy is for employees in the workplace. Not enforceable outside of the office. Why don't you just go on and ask her to dance."

"You mean cut in?" he asked.

"You might as well. You're no good for anything here, are you? You've been, shall we say–distracted all evening."

Josh smirked. He was caught, and he didn't have any defense, no wisecrack or quick comeback.

"I don't want to be well, um – inappropriate."

"Man, do you see the dance floor? Everyone is inappropriate. It's a party. If it makes you feel better, I'll get Margaret, my assistant, and ask her to dan..."

Before he could finish, Josh was already on his feet, appreciating the opening Max gave him. He didn't care how it looked. What he cared about was his woman being in another man's arms, even for a minute. He didn't want anyone else touching her. He was having a physical reaction to it. He lightly touched John's shoulder.

"Mind if I cut in?" he asked coolly. Chiffon met his cool gaze. Even though he was talking to John, his piercing eyes never left Chiffon. Ute ole, she thought to herself. She was in trouble now. Why did she always underestimate him?

She bit her bottom lip.

"Oh," John stepped back, "No problem, Mr. Abbott," he smiled briefly at Chiffon and quickly departed. They stood there and stared at each other for a long, torturous minute without words.

"Josh, I...," she was about to explain when he held his arms out for her to step into his grasp. Helpless to resist, she shut her mouth and reached around his waist. He held her close to his solid frame, and she thought she would melt right there.

"Such insolence, Fonn," he said evenly. She shook her head and started to say something. "Shhhh," he quieted her. "You wanted me to come and get you, didn't you? You say you don't want anyone to know about us, and then you dare me, beckoning me to come and get you in front of everyone."

"No, I...,"

"Shhhh," he shushed her again. "I thrive on dares, you know that. You knew as soon as you let another man touch you, I would react. You know I don't play that shit."

She started to say something but shut her mouth instead.

"It's ok, it worked," he answered for her, "Because now I get to hold you in front of all these people. Max even directed me over here to dance with you because I couldn't take my eyes off you."

"What?" she started to pull back, but his grip got tighter.

"Don't move," he ordered in a soft but serious tone. She immediately stilled. "I don't think you want to make a scene out here, do you, sweetheart?"

She sighed, closed her eyes, and rested her head on his shoulder.

Why fight? No point trying to hide it now. She never thought he would be bold enough to cut in, to risk a dance with her, to risk exposure before they were ready. Then again, Josh did what he wanted to do, didn't he?

Maybe she did try to get a rise out of him, seeing all those women fawning all over him. No pun intended. The song ended, but he held her there. She couldn't move; she didn't want to.

"How do you think bad girls should get punished for poor decision-making?" he asked, stepping back and looking down at her intently. She closed her eyes again; grateful another song came on. She stepped back into his embrace.

"Should I spank that beautiful ass of yours?" he whispered near her ear. "Should I bury my face in-between those cheeks?"

She felt her nipples tighten into hard peaks through the soft fabric of her sundress.

"Josh, please," she whimpered against him.

"Shhhh," no more talking for you. I think you have already said enough with your actions, don't you?"

She didn't respond. She was caught up in the feel of him, the smell of him, the nearness of him. She hated when she upset him. It always left her with a price to pay.

"Can we go inside?" she whispered softly. He raised an eyebrow. "I'm ready to accept whatever punishment you deem appropriate," as she looked up at him with smoldering eyes.

She tugged at his heartstrings when she looked like that, all compliant and ready to give it up. "Shit!" he exhaled. They were both about to get fired.

He released his tight grasp on her.

"Go inside, and I'll meet you in the gallery. It's to the right, down the corridor." She smiled at him lightly, thanked him for the dance and walked into the house.

She made it to the dimly lit gallery in a flash. She left the lights off and found a bench at the far end of the room in front of a large sculpture. She removed her panties and put them in her purse. She leaned back on the bench and closed her eyes.

Josh grabbed a drink off one of the serving trays and downed it quickly. He scanned the lawn and made his way inside the residence unnoticed.

Chapter
28

When he approached, she looked like she was asleep. His rock-hard staff was throbbing against his leg.

How beautiful his Fonn. He wanted this woman constantly. He stood above her motionless. He couldn't believe he was doing this.

There was no door on the gallery entrance. Anyone could walk in, and he really didn't give a damn. All he wanted, all he cared about, was being inside her again. To be engulfed in her hot moistness. He craved her. Nothing existed like the feeling she gave him. He would risk anything, risk everything.

He wanted to be her husband, to openly declare his love for her, never to let her get away from him again. No woman had ever affected him as much or incited such emotion from him. For the first time in his life, he was truly in love.

He knew he wasn't an easy man to deal with. He was demanding and controlling, and at times all-consuming. He knew it, but he also knew that she understood him better than anyone else. She forgave him of his faults; and made him want to do and to be better. He wanted to be a better man for her.

They had already been through so much. His thoughts went back to seeing her bloody body on the nursery floor. He winced at the painful memory, and his eyes instantly welled up. He almost lost her forever then. The rage he still felt burned like hot coals in his belly, and he really could have murdered Candy. He would have easily ended Candy's life for attempting to take Chiffon's. He shuddered at the impact of that realization.

She opened her eyes, feeling that he had been standing over her. "Josh? she questioned. Honey, what's wrong?" She sat up, looking compassionately at his tear-stained face. He didn't speak – just stared at her with a haunted look in his eyes. Those beautiful eyes filled with tortured emotion. She reached up and touched his face with the back of her hand. She had never seen him cry like this. Tears immediately came to her eyes as well.

"Sweetheart," she rose to her feet and held him tightly. "Did something happen?" she said into his neck.

"No," he choked out, squeezing her tight.

"Oh baby," she spoke quietly, sensing what was wrong from the intensity of his hold on her. "I'm fine now, baby. You have made sure of that. You have taken excellent care of me. I know I'm safe with you."

He just held her saying nothing. She remained in his arms, knowing he just needed to hold her in that moment. No words were necessary. He didn't make a sound, but she could still feel hot tears running down his cheeks.

"Let me get you some kleenex honey," she looked up into his eyes. They were a color she hadn't seen before, almost violet. She moved to get her purse, and his grip tightened on her. "Honey, I'm not going far. See my purse on the floor right there she pointed. One second, ok?"

He stared at her expressionless and then nodded. She kissed his wet cheek and slowly moved out of his grasp.

Her hands were trembling as she reached into her purse to grab tissues. She turned back around to see him wiping under his eyes with a handkerchief. She handed him the tissue, and he blew his nose. He dropped everything to the floor. She felt so guilty. She was just kidding around by dancing with John. She didn't know it would incite this kind of reaction from him. Take him back to such an ugly place.

She put her arms around him again, "I'm sorry, baby, I never meant ...,"

"You didn't do anything wrong," he pushed her back, staring down at her. "I'm just overprotective and a little crazy when it comes to you. I don't know why I went back to that place just then. I guess I saw you lying there, and it reminded me of that horrible time."

He shook his head, "It didn't have anything to do with your dance. I don't want you to think you can't enjoy yourself at a party or dance or have friends. I'm not that much of a brute," his eyes squinted, "Although, I don't take too kindly to seeing anyone else's hands all over you. If you need to be in a man's arms, I'm here."

She shook her head affirmatively. "I know that Josh." This wasn't the time to lecture or try to teach him to practice letting go of the reigns. Right now, he needed assurance that she was ok and here to stay. She could give him that.

She reached down to his instantly solid manhood and stroked it over the material of his pants. He let out a groan. She kissed him, ever so deeply. She held onto him for dear life, with hot tongues mingling, searching each other. Didn't he understand she would never leave him again? Not if she could help it. He had her so deeply entrenched in him she couldn't leave now if she wanted to. She wouldn't even know how. He was like taking her next breath. She needed him to feel alive. He reached down to lift her long flowing skirt.

"Oh, my God," he exhaled when his hand cupped her bare buttocks. "You're not wearing any panties!" he broke off the kiss. "Did you leave the house like that?" he breathed out, clearly taken aback.

She laughed, "No, silly, I just took them off before you got in here."

A flicker of a smile came over his face. "You better be telling me the truth," he lifted her, and she wrapped her legs around him.

"What's wrong with no panties?" she asked, unbuttoning his shirt.

He laughed, "The thought of you bare this entire evening; you're trying to kill me."

She rubbed her hands under his t-shirt. His frame was so hard and muscular, so wonderfully Joshua. He carried her and sat her down against the far wall. She reached down to unclasp the button on his pants while he unzipped them.

She found the opening in his boxers and released him, stroking him softly as he pointed into her stomach.

"We don't have a lotta time, baby," he murmured between kisses.

"I know," she managed.

He lifted her, and she wrapped her legs around him again. Slowly he lowered her onto his pulsating rod. She squealed in delight as he filled her.

"You are incredible," he buried his face into her neck and suckled behind her ear. His hands circled both of her breasts and found the hard peaks beneath the material of her dress. He pinched them both, and she cried out. Faster and faster, he pummeled into her tight crevice. Instantly, she started to feel herself crescendo. Higher and higher. So wonderful, so damn good.

"Oh yes – oh baby yes!" he pumped away, and she wanted to shout. Out of nowhere, a rocket shot off inside her and exploded into a million fragments. She tried to quiet herself, but it wasn't possible. The orgasm had a life of its own, and it was taking her over the edge of sanity. She faintly heard voices outside of the gallery door getting closer and closer, but she couldn't stop gyrating or crying out.

He knew her well. His hand instantly went up to muffle her cries as he continued inside her. She clawed at him, tears coming to her eyes, her body spasming, tantalizing pleasure seeping through her core. The voices and shadows appeared at the entrance of the gallery. Her heavily hooded eyes could barely make out the images.

The rush of sensation overtook him then. He clinched and bit down to stifle his own cry as he emptied inside her. He couldn't stop if he tried – the sense of danger and overwhelming lust catapulting him forward.

"Ahhhhhh, baby sweet baby," he whispered, still shaking and holding her against the wall.

They both noticed their violent juddering started a small, glass vase on a stand next to them to teeter back and forth. Fonn couldn't stop quaking, and just as it fell off the stand, Josh reached out to quickly catch it.

They had both been holding their breath. He removed his hand, covering her mouth, and placed a finger there, signaling she should continue to remain silent. She whimpered, trying to still herself, still feeling him deep inside her.

He placed the vase back on the stand, and she held him and waited. The voices soon moved from the entrance. They realized Max must be giving people a tour of the house. Thank God they didn't walk in. Thank God the vase didn't crash to the floor. He let out a long sigh and looked down at her. His lips lightly covered hers again.

"What am I going to do with you, woman?" he whispered against her mouth.

She suckled at his bottom lip. "More of what you just did, I hope," she smiled and felt him do the same. He slowly eased out of her, and she gasped at the emptiness.

He reached down and grabbed the hanky and wiped between her legs and then over his still semi-hard staff. They quickly regrouped.

"I will head out first," he said. "You wait about 10 minutes and ease out." He kissed her cheek and murmured, "Thank you, sweetheart."

"For what?"

He shrugged his shoulders, "I don't know, for putting up with me and all that comes with me."

"I love you goofy. I think we put up with each other."

He smiled that gorgeous smile, heart-warming, gut wrenching. "Later, baby," he grinned.

"Yes, I have my instructions," she saluted him. He chuckled and strode out of the gallery.

She smoothed down her hair and clothes and stepped back into her undergarments. She sat down on the bench and put her head down into her hands. This was insane. You would think the way they went at it, that she didn't sleep with the man every night. They had just been together not a few hours before in the limo.

The more he gave to her, the more she wanted. He was her obsession. She wouldn't let anything, or anyone take him from her again. She might do anything for him, to him, to ensure his happiness, and it frightened her a little. Josh told her over and over he felt the same way. It was heartwarming and a little scary, but she couldn't imagine life without him. It was like they would risk everything, risk anything for each other—dangerous territory for them both.

She glanced at her watch; almost time to rejoin the party. She had better find a washroom and get freshened up. Of course, all he had to do was button and zip, and he was instantly back together again, instantly beautiful again. She, on the other hand, needed a little more assistance.

She tidied up the area and went to find a washroom. After turning several corners, she found one. She took care of business and got herself presentable again. She was glad she looked at herself before rejoining the party. Josh put a huge hickey on her neck. She tried to cover it with make-up. She couldn't believe it. When the hell did he do that?

She reviewed their lovemaking in her head and honestly didn't remember him sucking her neck like that. She did remember him kissing her neck. "Wow," she said, exasperated, then she smiled. In the words of Tam, "That damned Joshua."

She rejoined the party and slid right into a conversation with her peers. She was laughing at a story one of her colleagues conveyed when all the light drained from her eyes. Darkness penetrated her insides and squeezed at her heart. Isaac entered the party with Tam, draped on his arm. What was he doing here? And with her? Her mind raced. A million questions flooded her senses. Her breathing became erratic. Was she having a panic attack? This long day was about to get longer.

Isaac mentioned earlier, his date with Tam was tonight. She had been so caught up with Josh; she hadn't given it a second thought. She never expected them to show up here, though. That old, familiar guilt coursed through her body again.

With the extremely intense session just occurring with Josh, how could she be so jealous? It didn't make any sense. Was she crazy? What was wrong with her? She didn't understand it. She felt shame for it, but more than that, she felt an incredible culpability for avoiding Tam. She hadn't spoken to her friend since she announced Isaac asked her out.

Chiffon had been careful to return her calls when she knew Tam wasn't available to talk. Perhaps Tam wasn't suspicious, but it was unlike them not to have spoken at least a few times a week. Tam was like her sister, and she felt horrible. She seethed a little on the inside because Isaac and Tam looked so damn good together. They made an attractive couple.

She was ready to go. She didn't need Josh and Isaac getting into it, and she especially didn't need Tam to witness any of it. She sent Josh a text ...,

Her: Babe, I'm ready to head out. I'll see you at home.

Him: Are you sure? The party is just getting going.

Her: I know, but I've had enough small talk for one night.

Him: Ok then, baby.

Her: Don't be in a rush to leave on my account, sweetheart. Stay and have a wonderful time. Probably be easier for you without me here.

Him: Nothing is easier without you.

Her: *smiley face*

Him: I'll hang around for a little bit more. Got a few people I want to talk to. Then I'll see you at home."

Her: Ok, I love you.

It's You

Him: From here to eternity.

She glanced around the large outdoor space and tried to figure how to ease out without acknowledging her friend. It was terrible, she knew it, but it was just easier. Right now, she could use easier.

She kept her back to them as Isaac introduced Tam to some co-workers. She bobbed and weaved through a group of guests. She was just a few feet away from the exit. She turned to head in that direction when she heard Tam's voice ring out, "Chi, girlfriend, Hey!" She closed her eyes painfully.

Damn, she'd been spotted. She swallowed and turned around. Tam was waving her arm and smiling her pretty smile at her. "Tam," she exclaimed and went straight into her friend's arms.

"Hey, you." she smiled. She did miss her and felt terrible for putting her off.

"Girl, where in the world have you been? I told Isaac they have been working you way too hard when we can't even touch base outside of voicemails."

"Yeah, I know. I apologize, Tam." she smiled genuinely at her friend. She purposely did not make eye contact with Isaac.

"How are you Chiffon," he finally said to her. "You look great this evening." She smiled at him briefly and thanked him. Tam was holding onto Isaac's arm casually. Obviously extremely comfortable with him.

Chiffon took a deep breath. This was crazy! Her heart banged frantically in her chest. She was visibility

337

affected by them being together, and she had to get herself together. Had she taken leave of her good senses? If Josh got an inkling of this, there would be hell for her and for everyone to pay. He did not like Isaac and the way she was behaving, and she couldn't blame him. She had to reassure him on more than one occasion; nothing was going on between them. She needed to get out of there – now! She glanced around nervously.

"Were you leaving Chi? her friend asked, "I was hoping we could catch up. You don't mind, do you, Isaac?" she glanced at him adoringly.

"Of course not, far be it for me to come in between friends," he smiled mischievously.

Tam grinned and, Fonn exhaled. Isaac was obviously enjoying her discomfort a little too much. She hated him then, for existing, for having any kind of effect on her at all. She was madly in love with Joshua, and she did not want anyone else. She knew that in her brain, but her heart was filled with jealousy, with envy, with something she just couldn't comprehend. What was it he elicited in her so profoundly?

It was as if she craved Isaac and every ounce of his attention. She wanted him to want her and only her even if she couldn't or wouldn't give it back. She wanted everything else to stop existing for him when she was in the room. She loved how he made her feel, and she wanted it to continue. It was sick. Nothing could come of it. How did he get in her bones?

It's You

All at once, in the middle of her self-chastisement, a profound realization slapped into her. It hit her with so much force she lost her balance for a second. She stumbled backward. Her eyes widened as the truth saturated her being. It couldn't be. She reeled on her feet, looking for something to hold onto.

Isaac was practically a damn replica of her father. His gait, his mannerism, his character reminded her so much of her father. It was as if he could be his twin. Isaac was just lighter in complexion and slightly taller. She hadn't seen her dad in so many long years.

But, Isaac, his easy smile, the way his eyes lit up when he saw her – his unassuming handsomeness. The similarities were uncanny. Why hadn't she realized this before? It was so obvious to her now. She had been so young when her dad left. Unintentionally, she'd longed for what had been missing in her life for years, and to a certain degree, Isaac had stepped in and filled that space.

She always thought her draw to Isaac was friendly and flirtatious, but it was so much more for her. There was a physical need for him. She needed him to want, need, and feel love for her like her father never did. Was she losing her grip on reality?

It was more emotional than physical, but it felt extremely physical as well. It was deep-seated, confusing, and all-consuming. Whenever his attention was focused on her, it filled up a place in her heart that was vacant for so long. It was as if her daddy cared about her again.

Memories of her father intermingled and intertwined with this attachment to Isaac. It was crazy. She believed her dad left them to be with another woman, another family. He decided to cheat and destroyed their lives. Hence, her absolute aversion to ever be with a married man. She vowed never to be that selfish; because she knew firsthand the havoc, it wreaked.

Isaac represented a resurfacing that bewildered her. With him, the little girl inside her had a piece of her daddy again, and her little heart wanted to hold on tight. When he comforted her, smiled at her, touched her, it meant something, much more than it should. It was as if her father accepted her again. Yep, she was convinced. She was losing her mind.

She thought back to her dad patting her head, saying she was his good little girl. The feeling that it evoked; Isaac duplicated that sensation for her every time she was around him. Her father approved of her again, loved her again. She shook her head in disgust. This was some sick shit!

She had to get out of there. She turned to Tam, "Enjoy your time with your, um, date," she forced a smile, "I have already been here for a while," she kissed her friend's cheek and held her a little too long.

"Are you ok, Chi?" Tam pulled back from her, breaking the embrace.

"Yes, yes, I'm fine, girl."

Tam knew otherwise, "What happened? You can tell me." She stared into her eyes, "Do you need me to come with you?"

She stared at her friend, her sister. She loved her so much, but she did want to talk to her. She just couldn't do it today, not right now. With this realization, she needed to sit for a while. Everything she'd suffered over the past year had tentacles back to her father. Who he was, what he did, and what had never been resolved.

Now it was clear why she left Joshua when she loved him so much, why she believed the letter instead of the man. Why she quickly cleaved to the baby because his parents were a train wreck together. But most of all, how she missed her daddy so desperately, she'd transferred feelings for him to another man. Outlandish, outrageous, and incomprehensible.

"Tam, she said slowly and evenly so her friend would get it. I promise you; I will talk to you later. Please stay here and enjoy your evening with your..., your date."

Her friend smiled warmly at her. "Thank you, Chi. He is great," she whispered. "I understand, and I will wait to hear from you." They embraced again. She quickly said goodbye to Isaac and headed for the door.

As she headed to the curb, she realized she forgot to call Brandon for a pickup. Maybe it would be better to call a cab? She pulled out her phone but noticed the limo parked across the street. Brandon motioned her over. She smiled in return as Joshua took care of her so well. Sometimes she didn't even have to think, and right now, that was perfect.

She climbed into the back and put her head back on the cushion and closed her eyes. She twirled her hair around her left index finger. Josh always knew something was bothering her when she did that, and right now, she couldn't stop. She told Brandon to keep driving for a while. She wasn't ready to go home.

Chapter 29

Joshua took a long swig of his drink. What the fuck was going on between Fonn and Mergers? He pretended to be listening to Max talk again and witnessed the entire exchange. Fonn retreated, clearly upset at seeing him there with Tam. Tam seemed oblivious to what was going on right under her nose. Now that he thought about it, Fonn's sudden departure was all about Mergers' arrival. She hadn't been ready to leave until then.

He asked her repeatedly about him over the past few months, and she always denied any feelings on her part. So why was she so upset? He knew how much Fonn loved him, only him. There was no doubt about it. Before they arrived, she officially agreed to become his wife. The way she clung to him in their private time together, he knew she loved him completely. So, what hold did Mergers have on her?

Bastard! He was damn conceited with it. Had they been intimate in some way before he arrived? The thought of it made his blood boil and his skin crawl. The thought of him touching her, kissing her, licking her, he was simmering, just about ready to explode. He inhaled and exhaled deeply. He would get some answers tonight.

He excused himself from the group and made his way over to where Tam and Mergers stood. Tam saw him coming and smiled and held out her hand. "We meet again," she shook his hand enthusiastically, "How are you?"

"I'm well," he smiled genuinely at her. He would always be grateful to her for her assistance in getting him back together with Fonn. She knew his relationship with Fonn was private, so she let the greeting stand.

"So Merg..." he stopped short and chastised himself. Damn, he called the man Mergers and Acquisitions so much in his mind he almost said it aloud. "Yea, Isaac, how are you?" he held out his hand for a quick shake.

"I'm good." They shook hands and stared at each other for a moment.

"Can I have a word?" Josh motioned to the door of the house.

Isaac glanced around quickly, "Um, sure," Isaac squeezed Tam's hand briefly, "I'll be right back.

Tam watched the two men walk away, not sure who she enjoyed watching more. She smiled to herself and wondered what they needed to discuss in private. It would be a lotta fun to go out on a double date soon. They must have some work-related items to discuss, she thought. Otherwise, she didn't think they had a personal relationship.

They stepped inside the glass patio doors, and immediately all outside sound dissipated. The men looked at each other for a moment, each wondering just what the other one had that charmed Chiffon so much. Isaac was polished, fair-skinned, lean. Josh was taller, broader, and a few shades darker than Isaac.

"Let's be seated," Josh motioned to the chairs facing each other to the right of where they were standing. Isaac sat down, and Josh sat across from him. Always in command, Isaac thought. He admired and hated him.

Josh jumped right in, "Are you aware of the connection between Fonn...pardon me, I should say - Ms. Hartwell and myself?"

Isaac stared at the self-assured bastard. Yes, I know your screwing her and have been for quite some time, he wanted to say. "Yes, I am Josh. Aren't you the reason she was hired in the first place?"

Josh's eyes widened a touch, "Absolutely not. Incorrect. Ms. Hartwell was hired on her own merits and qualifications."

"Oh really," he smirked. "So, the fact that you are now part owner had nothing to do with her job offer? You didn't follow her here to force her to get back together with you?"

"Force her?" Josh inhaled again, "M... Isaac, I would like to know how you know we are involved?"

"Anyone can tell something is going on between you two. Although you try to hide it, it is obvious," he hesitated for a moment. "Also, Chiffon finally admitted it when I asked her."

"And why did you feel the need to ask her about her personal life, Isaac?"

Isaac's gaze narrowed.

Umm, Joshua thought, just as he'd suspected. "Well, let me make something clear here, Isaac. There is more than just 'something' going on between us. I have asked her to be my wife, and she has agreed."

Isaac winced at the impact of his words and then spat out, "So tell me, I'm curious as to just how you plan to accomplish that, seeing as though you're already married? Aren't you Josh?" he bit out.

Josh's eyes narrowed, "Look, Isaac, fuck the pretense, I want to know exactly what's going on between you two. Since you know we are in a committed relationship, what are you trying to accomplish? What is your end game exactly?"

Isaac chuckled, "I don't have an end game. There is nothing going on between Chiffon and me."

"Is that so? Anyone can see something is going on between you! She is visibly upset whenever you're around. Isaac grinned, and Josh wanted to punch his lights out. Smug little jackass, it was taking every bit of restraint he had to sit and try to talk to this asshole civilly. He had to get to the truth.

Joshua took a deep breath, "Man to man, did something happen between you two before I arrived in town?"

Isaac stared at him, "Ask your girlfriend, or should I say, fiancé," as he leaned back in the chair. "Didn't she answer all your questions yet?"

"You know what she told me, and I'm not asking her. I'm asking you."

Isaac wanted to inflict suffering on him, take him off his friggen expensive-ass high horse. However, he could see the bastard was dying inside. It was killing him to think something happened between them. The poor little rich guy couldn't stand thinking he screwed his woman.

Knowing he had been festering over that for the last few months would have to serve as reward enough. Besides, he really couldn't articulate what was going on between him and Chiffon. He had his own questions to find answers to. He really couldn't understand it himself. He knew that it was carnal and explosive. So much so, he made up his mind to do some investigation into her past. Maybe if he found out where she came from, it would help him figure out why she was under his skin—anything to help him understand why he was inexplicably drawn to her.

He never felt this way about anyone, ever. It was as if they were meant to be together, and he knew Chiffon felt it too. He could see it in her eyes. She just couldn't admit it. Hopefully, the background investigation could bring them both some peace. He would never be able to move on if he didn't get past this with her.

He reflected on Chiffon's prior advice to him. He didn't really want this bastard as an enemy, especially regarding something that never occurred. He worked too hard to obtain the level he had at Reynolds to have it jeopardized. They would never be friends but didn't have to be enemies. At least not yet.

"Listen, man," he leaned forward in the chair and let out an exasperated breath, "Chiffon is gorgeous, and yes, I'm attracted to her. Yes, I think she deserves the stability missing from her romantic life." Josh flinched. Isaac continued, "But she doesn't want it from me. She turned me down flat. It appears she only wants you. We decided we would be friends and leave it at that. I have no choice but to accept it. I never touched her."

Josh rubbed his chin and sat back in the chair, letting sheer relief settle over him. He respected the fact that Mergers told him the truth. He could see it hadn't been easy for him. At least he came clean, but he was still greasy as far as he was concerned.

"You couldn't have Fonn, so you take up with her best friend? You're a real class act, aren't you, Isaac?"

"Fuck you!" Isaac rose to his feet. "How self-righteous you are," he pointed. "How could you have the audacity to ever judge anybody?" he bristled. "At least I'm not leading her on while I remain married to another woman. You are dragging her heart through the wringer, making her your mistress. I have never lied to her or risked her life."

Josh rose to his feet then, "You don't know a damn thing about my fiancé or me!" he spat out. "What goes on in my relationship with her is none of your mother fucking business. You have the unmitigated gall to criticize me about my treatment of her while you try to torture her by dating her friend? All the while knowing how bad you want her for yourself?"

"It wasn't my idea to date her friend!" he rattled. "Chiffon insisted on it."

"What? You're insane."

"Believe it, she told me to do it," she practically pleaded. "Tam is a beautiful woman, so I figured I would give it a try. It made sense to get to know her."

"So, you could remain close to Fonn, I take it?" Isaac bristled.

Josh took a deep breath and took a step back, feeling they were about to come to blows. "Listen, I really don't give a damn who you decide to date. What I give a damn about is Fonn. If you hurt Tam, you hurt Fonn, and if you hurt Fonn, you hurt me. I wouldn't fucking advise it."

Just then, both of their attention turned to a figure standing just in the doorway with the screen door shutting behind them. Tam stood there looking devastated and completely stunned.

Her gaze went to Isaac. "I just came in to check on where you guys were," she said, barely audible. "George was looking for you..." she hesitated for a moment, "So, it wasn't your idea to call me Isaac?" she asked him, her voice quiet and broken.

Isaac blinked his eyes, "Oh, my God. Tam, please, you misunderstood. That's not it at all. How much did you hear? Of course, I wanted to call you, get to know you." He walked toward her, and she stepped back. He paused.

She turned to Joshua. "Josh? What's going on?" Her eyes began to well up. Was everyone lying to her? Was she a pawn in a sick game for Chi's affection?

"Jesus," Josh muttered under his breath. Hurting Tam was what he had been trying to avoid. He had to make this right for her. If he didn't, Fonn was going to kill him.

"Listen, Tam. I don't know how much you heard, but don't be angry with Isaac. I attacked him, and he was just defending himself. I mistakenly felt jealous of his friendship with Fonn. I thought it was something more.

You heard me raging. Tell me exactly what you heard so I can clear it up. I promise you will get the truth from me."

Isaac was speechless. Tam looked at him and then back to Josh. "I heard Isaac say Chi insisted he ask me out, and then you said so he can still be near her. A single tear fell down her cheek.

"Listen, Tam," he walked up to her and placed his hand on her shoulder, "I can't speak for Isaac, but I know how much Fonn loves you. She likes Isaac, and she did tell him to call, but that's as far as it went. Everything else that has transpired between you two has been of your own doing. You walked in on the tail end of a disagreement between us. I was accusing him of something I just realized he didn't do. I was blinded by unfounded jealousy, and I apologize. I behaved irrationally because I didn't have all the facts – please don't you do the same thing."

She looked over at Isaac. She hoped Josh was right because she really did like him. From the first time she saw him at the meet and greet, she thought he had the potential to be especially important in her life. She wanted him to be. Chi knew that, and that's why she thought she fixed them up. No one could make her believe Chi would ever throw her under the bus. So, she must have heard something wrong. She sniffed.

"I'm sorry you heard that Tam, Isaac spoke up. I think Chiffon just wants everyone to be happy but don't doubt that this is real. I'm not thinking about anyone but you while we're together. I have been having a wonderful time with you. No one can force me to do anything. Josh and I have reached an understanding," he looked over to Josh, and he nodded. "I'm sorry your name ever came up. It really wasn't about you at all."

Josh nodded again, "He's right, Tam. I'll leave you two to talk." He hugged Tam briefly, kissed her cheek, and whispered in her ear, "I think he's ok." That strangely comforted her. Josh wasn't quite sure if he wanted them to work it out or not, but he had bigger fish to fry. Confusion loomed heavy regarding Fonn's reaction to Mergers now. His unanswered questions remained.

Brandon, take me to O'Hare Airport." Chiffon stared out of the window at the tree-lined street.

"Yes, ma'am, he nodded. Are we picking someone up?" he queried, realizing this was way off the itinerary.

"No, just drop me off." She hit the button for the privacy glass to go up. She knew exactly what she needed to do to calm her topsy turvy emotions down.

She promised Josh she wouldn't ever just take off again, and she meant it, but she needed to get away from everyone for a minute. All of them with their demands and expectations of her. She needed to do something that would bring her some peace.

None of this would have ever happened had Josh been truthful regarding his marriage in the first place. Therein was the catalyst that brought her back to Chicago. If Josh had been free, she never would have met Isaac.

Who meets someone, and connects with them on another level, only to find the pull is rooted in pain, confusion, and rejection. All of this while providing an unexplainable sense of comfort, satisfaction, and acceptance. Her link to Isaac was spiritual and beyond her comprehension. She certainly couldn't explain it to Josh if she couldn't make sense of it herself.

If only Josh hadn't stirred up that open wound in her heart, she wouldn't be so jacked up right now. She wasn't mad at him but couldn't go home to him right now. She had to take care of her soul before she could truly face what she'd discovered. Leaving was her only choice.

"What do you mean you dropped her at the airport?" Josh raised his voice at Brandon.

"I did as instructed, Mr. Josh."

"Where did she say she was going?"

"She didn't."

"No message left for me?"

"No, Mr. Josh."

Josh leaned his head against the headrest of the backseat. He stared at his phone again; no messages from Fonn. He closed his eyes for a minute. She promised him she would never just take off again. She knew what it did to him.

He called and left several messages. He tried to patch her countless times, but no reply. Had her encounter with Mergers been so devastating, she had to escape from Mergers just as she had to leave him before?

This was making him crazy. His stomach was literally in knots.

How could he think he was fine before he met her? Sure, he had a "situation" with Candy, but it didn't interfere with anything. He flourished in business. Casual acquaintances got the job done. He didn't want a relationship or need one. Candy was an excellent front to keep the many women at bay. He used to wear his wedding band as a deterrent, but everything changed when he became intrigued with Fonn.

When she came along, and he took the meaningless ring off for good. She changed his life, changed his perspective, and changed his mind about love and relationships. Now there was nothing he wanted more than to be in a committed relationship with her.

"Dammit, Fonn," he said aloud, "You better not be leaving me again." He didn't think he could survive it, and she wondered why he kept her so close to him. This, this was why, dammit.

Just then, a text came through with her name. A wave of relief washed over him.

Her: "Josh, sweetheart, I'm ok. Please try not to worry. I just had to get away for a little while. I'm going to see JJ. I'm sorry I didn't talk to you first. Please forgive me. I just need some time to myself to clear my head. I will be back by Wednesday. Please secure the time off for me. I will call you when I arrive."

Him: "Are you sure you're ok? I'm worried about you. Thanks for letting me know where you are. I was going crazy. Tell me again you're ok."

Her: "Yes, yes, I'm ok, forgive me. I love you. I'm on the plane, and I should shut my phone down. I will call you after I arrive."

Him: "Kiss JJ for me. I love you too."

She shut off her phone and held it close to her heart. She missed Josh already. She didn't like being away from him, but she had to figure this out. His presence in her life had a life of its own. She couldn't think clearly around him. She was both surprised and relieved he didn't seem angry.

Sometimes it was hard to tell the tone via text. Could he finally be letting go of the tight reigns? She had to get herself together. She wasn't going to be any good to him or anyone else until she dealt with these mixed-up feelings. Tam would have to be told the truth. Hopefully, she would forgive her. It was stupid of her to offer her friend up like some sort of sacrificial lamb in her stead. Now she had to watch their relationship unfold.

"Crazy, stupid, idiot," she chastised herself. She would have to tell Josh everything as well. Who knows how that would go.

She called Mrs. Abbott to let her know she would be arriving around 3 am. They sent a car to pick her up from the airport. She needed to see her baby. She didn't care who thought he belonged with them. She remembered the pain of that blade slicing through her flesh, and she knew who that baby belonged with. She needed to see him, to smell him, to feel him. Her attachment to the child was as real as her own heartbeat. JJ would help her figure out her next move.

She arrived at the house to find Mr. and Mrs. Abbott waiting at the front door for her. She rushed into Mrs. Abbott's arms first and then embraced Mr. Abbott.

"What a wonderful surprise," Mr. Abbott said, taking her hand and kissing it. He gave her goosebumps just like the first time he did that. She chalked it up to him, looking so much like Josh. She giggled, blushing again.

"Where's my son?" Poppa Abbott asked. "Isn't he with you?"

She quickly glanced at Mrs. Abbott. "Um, he had business at home. This is just a quick trip for me to visit the baby. I missed him so much and you guys too, of course."

"Hard to believe Joshua let you come here without him."

"He didn't really have a choice this time," she smiled sleepily. It was after 4 am, and she felt horrible for arriving at such an awkward time.

"I'm so sorry for waking you both. You really didn't have to get up before dawn to greet me. I know my way around now."

Mrs. Abbott laughed, "Don't worry about it. We are used to last-minute things coming up with our kids." Chiffon felt warm love squeeze at her heart. Did they consider her one of their children? She sure hoped so. She felt tears approaching again, her emotions on high alert.

"Where is your luggage?" Mr. Abbott inquired. She looked at Mrs. Abbott again. She had let her know this was a spontaneous trip, but she obviously hadn't relayed that to Mr. Abbott.

"Um, well," she stammered for an answer.

Mrs. Abbott jumped in. "She still has clothes here from her last visit. She didn't need a suitcase for a short trip, dear."

"Oh, ok," he agreed.

"Come on," Mrs. Abbott grabbed her hand, "Everything is still down here in the room you and Joshy shared. You need to get some rest." She shook her head in acquiescence, suddenly very weary.

Mr. Abbott headed up the stairs stating, "I'll see you later, dear."

"Ok, thanks, Mr. Abbott," she nodded at his departing frame.

They headed to the back bedroom. Mrs. Abbott entered with her. She turned to Mrs. Abbott filled with such appreciation, and she embraced her. She held the motherly woman ever so tightly.

"Oh, sweetheart. It's ok." Chiffon started to cry lightly. "Shhhh," Mrs. Abbott comforted her. "It's ok Fonn. We're here, and Joshy loves you very much. You know that, right?"

"Did you talk to him?" she sniffled.

"Yes, he called. He is concerned about you, honey,"

She shook her head. "I know. I didn't mean to worry him. I just..., I needed to see JJ. Is it ok if we move his crib into my room later? Just for the few days that I'm here."

"Of course, dear, that won't be a problem. He needs to be with you and his father as much as possible. He misses you both. Don't hesitate to ask for anything you need."

"Thank you," she kissed the woman's cheek and started to take off her shoes.

"Ok, sleep now, dear. I'll call Joshy and let him know you made it. We will take care of everything else later this morning after you get up."

"Thank you," she removed her clothes and climbed into bed. She was asleep before her head hit the pillow.

Chapter
31

You don't seem to understand," he gripped the phone. He leaned back in his chair crossing his leg on his desk at the ankle. "Unacceptable. It must arrive by tomorrow night!" he barked. "Yes, I realize it is the weekend. Do you realize the repercussions if you don't make it happen as instructed? Good, finally, we understand each other." He ended the call.

Good help was difficult to find. His people always found a way to make it happen. Failure was not an option this time.

It was 10 am, and he still hadn't heard from Fonn. He glanced at the clock on the wall. He remained in constant touch with his mother, and on her last check, Fonn was still sleeping. He didn't sleep last night. He finally just got up, went into their shared office space, got on the phone to start barking orders at people. That always made him feel better. He would apologize later.

He felt surprisingly calm about her departure since he knew where she was. She was with family, and it made all the difference. They did need to talk, though. He didn't want to pressure her, but it had been exactly an hour since he last spoke with his mother. Fonn should be up by now. He went to the kitchen to fix something to eat. The place felt weird and empty without Fonn buzzing around making noise in the kitchen.

He smiled to himself. He didn't want to be without her. He just hoped she still felt the same. She could eat, love, and pray right here with him.

He felt his phone vibrating at his hip. He quickly picked it up. "Sweetheart," he smiled into the phone, a tidal wave of relief washing over him.

"Hi," she spoke quietly.

"How are you, baby?"

"I'm fine now," She glanced over at JJ sitting on the bed playing with a toy. He was all-consumed in his play trying to talk to the small bear. She had just dressed when Mrs. Abbott brought him to her. She held him, kissed him, and hugged him. He remembered her. She smothered him with kisses, and he seemed to be as excited as she was. It was exactly what she needed.

"Your son's attention span is increasing," she noted.

"Our son," he said evenly.

She smiled. "I-I'm sorry I left so, so abruptly. Please don't be angry with me."

"As long as you are ok, I'm not angry. I love you, baby. I just want to understand what's happening with you. I'm not clear on what happened at the party. What literally set you off? Can you tell me what happened?" he leaned against the counter.

"I-I, well, I," she was having trouble trying to figure out where to start. She decided she didn't want to keep anything from him anymore. He was going to be her husband one day, and she needed to be honest about all of it, everything.

"You can tell me anything? You know I won't judge you, sweetheart. I want you to understand you never need to go through anything alone anymore. We are two, but we operate as one. Do you understand what I'm saying?"

She was quiet. She closed her eyes, hoping she could make him understand, understand something she didn't quite understand herself.

"I need an answer. Do you understand me?" he waited for a moment, "Well, baby…do you?"

"Yes, I understand," she breathed out in a gush.

"So, tell me what's going on and what part does Mergers and Acquisitions play?"

She opened her eyes, looking at JJ. She could hear the slight edge in Josh's voice. She knew she was testing his patience with this stunt. "Are you sitting down?" she asked him.

"Good Lord!" he exclaimed. "Do I need to be? What the fuck is it about him, Fonn? Are you in love with him!" he demanded.

"No, of course not. You are my love, Josh."

"Well, then what the hell is it you have going with him? What the hell can it be?" he asked impatiently. It's driving me up a wall. I'm going crazy here, baby, please," he lowered his voice again, realizing he was getting loud. He didn't want to scare her off.

"I would rather talk to you in person," she said, barely above a whisper.

"I would too, but you made that impossible, didn't you?" he said with annoyance. Silence held them for a long moment.

"He let out a sigh, "I'm sorry, really…please just put me out of this misery. I'm dying over here. Help me understand, baby. Talk to me."

"Ok," she started, "Remember what I told you about my father?"

"Your father?" he said puzzled, "Yes, of course, I remember. He left you when you were quite young."

"Yes, and my mother fell apart at the seams, especially when she found out he went to live with another family. Instead of getting counseling or going to church, she turned to me to make everything ok. It was too much responsibility for a child."

"Yes, we agree on that." He sat down on the couch, getting the feeling he should sit after all. What did her worthless father have to do with anything?

"Well, I did the best I could with all of it," she continued, "I harbored a lot of resentment toward my mother and hatred, as well as a deep longing for my father; a yearning to have him with me, to know why he left me. This longing apparently remains in the present day.

"Yes," he urged her to continue, slightly agitated.

"When I realized you were married, it brought a flood of emotions to the surface. Feelings I thought were long dead and buried. Certain feelings I had around my father. It all came rushing back to the forefront then. You know, a man leaving his family for another woman, people getting hurt." She went on, "A wound I managed to band-aid started bleeding out again. I didn't know what to do with my feelings because I had never fully addressed them. I hid them much like my mother did; mine just presented in a different way. So, whenever issues around mistrust and dishonesty surface, I behave poorly. I didn't handle any of it very well."

"It's not your fault," he interrupted her, "I blame myself. I apologize for hurting you."

"It was too much for me. I couldn't trust my instincts anymore. I was that little girl lost again. Anyway, when I left Atlanta, I wanted to make a new start. I tried. I was on a mission, determined to make some sort of life for myself without you. I thought I could do it, but the misery overtook me. I thought about you every day, every night, and every minute in between. It wasn't as easy as I thought it would be."

"Believe me, I know," he reflected.

"When I started the job, my life, well…, at least I established some sort of order to chaos. From my very first day, Isaac took me in. He made sure I needed for nothing. He took the time out to show me the ropes, and I appreciated it. I appreciated him. He was nice to me, and I felt strangely comforted by his presence. He became more than just a casual co-worker.

Joshua swallowed hard and closed his eyes. It wasn't easy listening to her talk about how another man took care of her, met her needs. He flexed his free hand open and closed to release the building tension inside him.

"I started to realize he represented something in my life that had been missing; something I didn't realize had been missing. It was misguided but very real and strong."

"Did he replace me for you?" he asked.

"No, no, not like that; I never even saw him outside of work. It wasn't exactly sexual but more emotional for me. I couldn't figure it out. I felt drawn to him. I found myself looking forward to each day at work because I knew I would see him, or he would be somewhere around."

"Goddammit, Fonn," he exclaimed, unable to control his reaction.

"I'm sorry," she paused, afraid to continue.

"No, no, I'm sorry, go on. Finish, please."

She waited for another second and continued, "I was confused. I love you, Josh. You are the only man for me but for some reason, Isaac had some sort of a place. I couldn't figure it out because it really didn't make sense. Once we got back together, I thought it would dissipate, but nothing changed." She heard a loud exhale from him. She wiped under her eye. "The realization hit me last night."

"What realization?"

"The connection, what it was. It, it was my father," she sniffed back more tears.

"Your father? What does your father have to do with it? I don't understand what you're trying to say."

"It's Isaac, Josh; he looks like him, acts like, sounds like, even smells like him to me. His mannerisms, his stance, his everything, he is so much like him, it's uncanny."

"So, what are you saying to me here, baby? You think Mergers has been reincarnated as your dad or something like that?' he said quizzically.

"I know it's crazy, it, it's sick," she was crying freely now. "I-I know he's not my father. I mean, I, I … I know this sounds, sounds insane," she hiccupped tears.

"Shhhh, Fonn. Ok, please, baby, just calm down. Stop crying; it's ok. I wish I could be there with you to put my arms around you. Please don't cry anymore." She was breaking his heart in so many ways. He closed his eyes. This shit is serious, he realized in dismay.

"All my, my life," she cried on, needing to get it all out, "I've been waiting for my fa-fath-father to come, to come back," she hesitated at a loss for words, overcome with emotion.

"And Mergers came along at a time when you were most venerable, taking care of you, being there for you.

"Yes," she whimpered.

"I wasn't there, so he took advantage of you," he bit out.

"No, no, please, I'm not defending him, but he wasn't trying to take advantage. He had no idea. I think for him, he was just, well, attracted to me."

"Shit! Shit! Shit!" he shook his head. "How can I compete with that Fonn?"

"You…you don't. I mean, I don't expect you to. You don't need to compete. I know this is…, this sounds insane, but I just wanted you to understand the draw, the pull he has on me. That's what you've been noticing. It's not what you thought. It's not because I choose him over you."

"But you do want him in your life."

"Yes, I mean, no," she faltered. "Listen to me. I want you in my life. My life is with you. You and JJ are my endlessly. I don't dream of Isaac's touch or his kiss. I don't long for him deep inside me."

"Oh, Fonn," he let out a deep breath.

"I only want you, Josh. I dream only of you." Silence on the line again. She waited for a moment. "Joshua? Josh baby, are you still there? Please don't be upset," she pleaded, "I was afraid to share this with you, but I don't want anything, any secrets between us. We promised full disclosure when we got back together."

"I'm transferring his mullato ass first thing Monday morning," he said unapologetically.

"No," she warned, "You don't have to do that."

"Apparently, I do! Goddamn bastard has a hold on you that's gonna take years of therapy to absolve."

"No, I'm the one who will leave Joshua."

"What are you talking about you'll leave? You're not going anywhere," he said affirmatively.

She grinned through her tears. He was still so bossy. "No, I mean you don't have to transfer him. I will leave Reynolds. It's what you've wanted all along, and I think it will be best for everyone."

He considered that for a moment. Her leaving wasn't going to solve the real issue, but it would be his pleasure to get Mergers' egotistical ass out of Fonn's life for good. What bullshit. He tried to calm himself.

"He's been with the company for a long time Josh. I don't want to be the cause of him losing his job, his livelihood. I would never forgive myself. He shouldn't be made to suffer because I'm messed up inside. It's not his fault."

Joshua exhaled deeply again. What the fuck was he supposed to do with this? On the one hand, he was relieved that it wasn't what he feared most, but on the other hand, he was horrified because in a different way, it was much worse.

"He's not the problem. I am. Don't transfer him. He has done great things at Reynolds. I will do whatever you want, whatever you say, please," she begged him.

He finally got it. It all made sense now if that was the proper word for it. "Give me some time to absorb all this. I'll think about it and let you know what action I think best."

The baby started to fuss, "Hold on, let me get JJ."

She went to tend to the baby, and he heard them. She was singing to him, and he quieted down. They were his life, his heart. All this mess was his own fault. He leaned back against the cushions on the couch. He blamed himself for it all. He wanted to blame Mergers, and he did blame him, but really, it was his lies that sent Fonn over the edge.

Did he really drive all the women around him crazy? Did he make them go insane? He shook his head in disgust. Is that the price any woman who fell in love with him must pay? This was some sick mother fucking shit, and Fonn didn't want him to get rid of his ass. What good was having the power if he couldn't wield it when necessary? He needed a drink—a strong one.

"Josh," she came back to the phone. "Say something to JJ." She put the phone to the child's ear, and Josh must have been saying something good because the baby started laughing and grabbing at the phone. He was trying to talk to his daddy. It was adorable.

She took the phone from him. "You're a hit with him," she smiled into the receiver.

"Yeah, but am I still a hit with you?"

Her eyes welled up again, "Yes baby, yes, of course you are. She closed her lids, and the hot tears dripped down her cheeks. "I am yours. I need you to know this thing with Isaac is misplaced, misguided, and a lapse in judgment. You are not. I will do whatever you want; I will accept whatever you decide."

"Do you mean it, no arguing? You get your kicks going toe to toe with me," he gawfed.

"Yes, I mean it." They were silent again. She opened her eyes. "I'd better get the baby some food or his bottle. He's a little cranky this morning."

"Fonn," he paused for a moment. "Thank you."

"For what?" she asked.

"For loving JJ and for loving me. We…, well…, I don't deserve you."

She felt the knot in her throat. How could he even think that after what she just told him? She was the only one who deserved questioning as to who deserved what.

"I know we can get through this together," she said.

"I believe in you, honey, in us. I just need a minute to take this all in."

"I know," she said. "We can talk later. I think Vi is coming over to take us all out to lunch."

"Ok then, I miss you, baby, so much."

"I miss you too," she made a kiss noise. They hung up.

Chapter 32

Fonn enjoyed hanging with the Abbotts. She loved each one of them. Josh's brother stopped by with his girlfriend as well. He said they were heading to a movie and heard she was in town. She had never experienced that kind of closeness and family love. It was a joy to be with them.

They purposely didn't discuss Candice. Nobody brought her up and she smiled inside. She needed this trip to be lighthearted. She had plenty of heavy stuff to deal with later.

She waited until bedtime to call Joshua back. "Hi, sweetheart," he greeted her.

"Hi, honey," she paused for a moment. "I have never taken so much time off from for a job within the first six months."

"Don't worry about that, baby. I've taken care of it." "I should be back by Wednesday morning," she said.

"I can just work from home that afternoon if that's all right with everyone."

"Whatever you choose to do is fine. Just get what you need while you're there."

"Your family is great, Josh. They have been exceedingly kind to me."

"They'd better be."

"They are, and I know you told them to."

"Who me?" he said with a smile in his voice.

"I know you did," she smiled.

"They love you. I didn't have to tell them anything. My mother raised her voice at me because she thought I did

It's You

something to upset you. Trust me, they have embraced you on their own. I think they forgot which one of us they birthed,"

She laughed at that idea, as they had no doubt Josh was theirs.

"Are you in bed yet?" he asked her, glancing at his watch.

It was 11 pm. "Yes, I was just about to climb in."

"What are you wearing?" he asked seductively.

She smiled, "Be good. The baby is in here with me."

"He is?"

"Yes, I had his crib brought in."

"Too bad…but shouldn't he be knocked out by now."

"He is, but if you are thinking of doing what I think you are over the phone," she smiled.

"I know, I know, you can't be quiet."

"No, I can't, and I don't want to be quiet with you."

"Can't you try?" he asked hopefully.

She snickered at his pleading tone, "I will be home in a few days, and then I will be at your disposal."

"I don't think I can wait that long."

"I'll be back before you know it."

"Ok, sweetheart, get some rest, and I'll talk to you in the morning. I love you."

"I love you too, baby." They hung up.

He was done waiting. The plan was already in motion.

He arrived in Tennessee before dawn, early the next morning. The day was spent solidifying the final schedule.

Everything should go off without a hitch or with one, depending on how you viewed it. His family was doing an excellent job of keeping Fonn occupied. She was so completely unaware. By nightfall, he was close to wrapping it up.

It was no easy task, but June 17th was going to be a special day for them. He would turn it into a life-affirming day, not what it previously represented. It was June 15th, so he only had two days to make it happen.

He said his goodnight to Fonn by phone at bedtime. Once he thought she was asleep, everyone got busy setting up at the mansion. Unbeknownst to her, he had been headquartered in the basement since the wee hours of the morning. Although it was well after midnight, the house was still abuzz with activity.

By 3 am, he felt satisfied with preparations. The house was so massive; his siblings would go unnoticed. Everyone departed to their sleeping quarters. He requested staff move the baby back to his nursery after Fonn fell asleep.

He quietly entered the bedroom. She was sprawled sideways across the bed. Her head was closest to where the crib would have been. His heart melted at the sight of her. Her hair was fanned out, covering her face. She was on her stomach in what looked like one of his t-shirts. It swallowed her. He quickly dispensed with his clothes. She was knocked out, so he didn't rouse her when he slowly turned her onto her back.

She must have fallen asleep right after they spoke on the phone because it was still clutched in her hand. He removed the phone. He slowly rubbed up her legs and found she was not wearing anything under the t-shirt.

He grinned mischievously, like a schoolboy. She was the way he preferred her - butt ass naked. He gently opened her legs and started to plant kisses slowly up her thigh, how he loved to taste her soft, fragrant flesh. She was so warm, so beautiful, so inviting. Making her scream his name was his favorite pastime. She was so damn delicious and so damn responsive to him.

He didn't just want to be inside her; he needed it like breathing each day. He needed Fonn. Everything was incomplete without her. She didn't know what she did to him, how she changed his life. She constantly challenged him, and he admired her for it. He needed someone to balance out his gruffness.

She moved a little but did not awaken. He stared at her beautiful mound and lightly rubbed his palm up and down her sex. She was wet. He closed his eyes, savoring the feel of her, and repeated his strokes. She tightened her legs over his hands and moaned lightly, but she did not wake up. He lightly opened her legs again.

Gently he dipped his head and circled her sensitive bud of nerves with his tongue. With soft strokes, he lapped at her opening. He inhaled her. He loved her erotic smell. He teased and licked up and down the length of her opening, continuing to circle the sensitive area until he felt her hands cover his head and her breath quicken. He placed one hand on her hip to steady her.

Her eyes were still closed. He slid one then another finger deep inside her, and when he massaged her g-spot, she let out a sexy gasp and started to whimper. Her grip tightened on his head. She pulled him closer to her, arching to meet his hot, wet tongue.

Her head sunk down into the pillow; her head turned left then right. She began to mumble something. He slid his hand up her body to rest at her breast. He stroked over her nipple until it hardened solidly. He then squeezed it tightly between his fingers rolling it back and forth.

This dream was so vivid, so real, she thought. Oh, my God, she felt a rush of pleasure start to build at her core. Oh! This dream was so damn real she was about to climax. The intensity overtook her. She bit her lip and arched her hips upward.

Her eyes opened franticly, staring out into the darkness, trying to get her bearings. Letting go of the grasp she had on his head, she gripped at the sheets on either side of her to steady her quivering frame.

"Hello, baby," he said against her spasming flesh.

She saw him. Was this real? "Josh? Oh, my gosh, Joshua, are you here?" she gasped, unable to catch her breath. Confused, she patted his head. This didn't make sense. She wasn't at home with Josh.

"Oh baby, oh," she felt him pinch at her nipple with his free hand again, and she yelped out with pleasure. "Joshua?"

He was here. He licked her like a man trapped in the desert, discovering well water. She quickly glanced around and didn't see the crib. Of course, he moved the baby out. She closed her eyes again, caught up in unimaginable, exquisite pleasure. She had so many questions, but she couldn't think of what they were right now. She felt him everywhere; every sensitive spot on her body was being licked or massaged or caressed.

Her body lifted to meet his mouth faster and faster. In a whirlwind of pleasure, her body took over. She was along for this incredible ride. She just needed to hold on. He took her to places she had only imagined, only dreamed of with another person. "Joshua," she murmured his name.

"Yes, baby, it's me. 'Tu es belle' I couldn't stay away from you. I couldn't stay away from this. I'm right here, baby, between your legs where I belong."

She shrieked out uncontrollably as first a stillness; a numbness enveloped her core. Then a crashing, throbbing, penetrating orgasm took her completely over the edge. Her toes curled, and her mind curled. Her body heaved and thrashed in the throes of an overwhelming orgasm that took away her breath.

Joshua loved how she responded to his touch. Even when she was angry, that wet, tight, delicious pussy never disappointed. She was a hot, sexy number, always ready for him, even in her sleep.

He wanted, no, he needed to be more involved with this intense orgasm she was having. He moved and quickly entered her as she continued to lose her mind. He did it because he had to because there was no place in the world for him but deep inside her. She was home for him, and there was no place like home.

"Fonn baby," he kissed her mouth as she tried to still herself. "Baby, baby, baby," he murmured, plunging farther and deeper, untamed, and uncontrolled. He buried himself inside her as he thrusted forcefully and wildly. He filled her completely. She writhed and called out his name, pulling him closer. He appreciated the agony, the ecstasy she experienced because the same damn thing was happening to him.

"'Je vous'aime tant, Fonn!'" he yelled out as his own explosion quickly joined hers. He gripped her as convulsions rocked him from his soul.

"I love you too," she responded, remembering what that meant. Then she writhed and shook underneath him as a second rocket blasted off inside her tightening around his staff.

They grabbed at each other and held on for dear life. Exhaustion took him over, having not had any sleep in days. He moved onto his back, taking her with him, still inside her. He laid her across him and encircled her in his arms. She nestled herself against him, and they both fell asleep.

She opened her eyes and rubbed them. Joshua was still sound asleep with his heavy arm draped around her smaller frame. She smiled to herself, what was he doing here? He really couldn't wait 'til she got back home? She shook her head and grinned. She was glad he didn't wait. She was glad he still loved her despite her confession.

She peered over at the clock. It was almost 11 am. Half the day was gone. She didn't want to spend precious time sleeping instead of enjoying JJ. She eased his arm off her and got up. She turned back to look at how sexy he looked. His strong legs tangled in the sheets. She felt blessed. One day they would have it all together. She would get her mind right, and they would get happily ever after.

It was heavy shit she laid on him. She hoped it wouldn't change things. Intimacy between them had always been passionate, but just because he wanted some didn't mean he wasn't upset with her. She had to find a way to make Josh understand he was enough. She would make him believe.

She hopped in the shower and got dressed, careful not to wake him. He must be truly exhausted to sleep so long. He was always up before her. She let him sleep. She felt like he never got enough anyway.

She peeked in the nursery, and the baby wasn't in there. She headed down the staircase. A lot of activity took place in the house for Monday morning. Maybe something was scheduled she wasn't aware of. JJ's nanny gathered his blocks as he sat in his playpen in the living room. "Hi Anna," she smiled at the woman. They shared an unspoken closeness, a kinship after the awful ordeal with Candice.

"Hi, Ms. Hartwell."

"Call me Fonn, I told you."

"Fonn," she smiled at her.

"What's going on around here today? The staff seems to be on full throttle."

The nanny hesitated and smiled to herself. Everyone knew but Fonn, and it was exciting. "Nothing special I know of. Possibly Mr. A's birthday coming up soon."

"Oh," Fonn shook her head affirmatively. She would have to be sure to wish Mr. Abbott a happy birthday. She picked up the baby and planted kisses all over his chubby cheeks. "Hello, my man," she laughed as he giggled his goofy baby giggle.

"Da da - da da - da da - da da" he repeated.

"Your da da is not up yet."

"He's not?" Mrs. Abbott sauntered into the room. "I'll have Taylor go and get him." Fonn eyed her quizzically.

Recovering quickly, Mrs. Abbott said, "Yes, he asked last night to make sure he was up before noon."

"Oh, ok, she said. I can go get him if you—"

"No!" she said abruptly, then caught herself. "Sorry, no, no dear, our staff can do that."

She headed to an intercom on the wall and gave Taylor his instructions. "You enjoy JJ. I'll have Ms. Garcia get you some breakfast."

"Ok then," Chiffon stared at Mrs. Abbott, wondering why she seemed a little intense this morning. She quirked an eyebrow and turned to play with JJ.

"Mr. Josh, uh um, Mr. Josh!" Taylor called out to Joshua's sleeping frame, "It's 11:45, sir."

Joshua opened sleepy eyes, "Taylor? he looked around. Where's Fonn?"

"She is downstairs with mister JJ having breakfast, or perhaps lunch now, sir."

Joshua smirked. Good old Taylor, never one to misappropriate proper usage of time. "Thanks for getting me up." Taylor gave a slight bow and left the room.

Josh quickly showered, tightened up his beard and mustache, and got dressed in black slacks and a salmon-colored shirt. He added a lightly striped black and salmon tie. It was Fonn's favorite color combo, so he figured he would go for it today. He took the stairs at a record pace.

"Good afternoon," he said to everyone as he entered the living room where Fonn, JJ, his mom and dad, and Anna were all gathered. He was greeted as he went to kiss first Fonn and then his mother's cheek.

"You look nice," Fonn noticed his color choices. He would look good in a brown paper sack, but particularly fetching in her favorite colors. He smiled brilliantly at her.

"All for you, baby," he turned to JJ, "You'll see," he picked him up and kissed him, "One day, you'll be dressing in weird colors for a girl." Everybody laughed, and the baby jumped in excitement.

"Da da -da da -da da," he sang, and Josh smiled proudly, laughing, "I miss you too JJ." He held the child close to his chest.

As if on cue, Ms. Garcia brought a plate of steaming food to the table for him. He smiled and thanked her. Anna took JJ, and Josh went over to the nearby table to eat.

"Fonn sweetheart, he called to her between bites, come here for a second."

"Sure," she jumped up and approached him at the table. She sat across from him.

"Do you have any specific plans for today?" he asked, biting into a piece of toast.

"Well, she looked in his parent's direction, um, no. Just hanging with JJ."

"Good because I want us to do something special for lunch later."

"Like what?" she asked.

"It's a bit of a surprise for you, so go ahead upstairs and get changed," he eyed her relaxed attire. She looked down at herself.

"I can't wear this?" She had on dark slacks and a white blouse.

"No, baby. What I have in mind will require," he hesitated for a moment, "less casual attire."

She squinted her eyes. "Well, what did you have in mind? We won't be hungry because we just ate.

"It doesn't have anything to do with food, baby."

She felt a blush color her cheeks.

"Not that either," he lowered his voice, "not yet anyway," he grinned.

"Well, what then?"

"Just head on up to the bedroom and get dressed. Everything has been laid out for you already."

"You picked out my clothes?" she said in surprise. "Yes, now off with you," he pointed in the general direction of the staircase. "We don't have much time."

It's You

She rose to her feet nervously. "Ok, but I still want to know where we're going."

"Did I say we were going anywhere?"

"But you want me to get dressed." She glanced over to his parents, who were pretending not to be listening to them. "Ok, then why do—"

"Sweetheart," he put his hand up. "Don't make it so difficult to surprise you. Now, off you go!" he punctuated every word and pointed toward the staircase again. "Put your hair up the way I like it."

She narrowed her eyes at him. What was he up to? In fact, everybody was acting weird. Did this have something to do with JJ or Candice? "Ok, ok, fine," she shrugged her shoulders and headed upstairs. She moved from the downstairs bedroom to be closer to JJ's nursery. Even though she brought the crib to her room, all his necessities were still in his nursery.

She entered the bedroom, and instantly, her eyes were drawn to a beautiful, light salmon-colored dress lying on the bed, matching shoes, jewelry, the works. It was breathtaking. Where was he taking her?

Surely, he wasn't dressing her up like this to stay home. A surprise party for his dad? If so, why keep it a secret from her? She got dressed and put her hair up into a beautiful clip dripping with pearls and crystals. She stared at her reflection in the mirror. She looked like she was in a wedding party. All she needed was a bouquet; she laughed to herself.

Her head shook sullenly. Who knew how long it would be before they could get married. It was hold up upon hold up when it came to the divorce. All she could do was continue to pray about it.

She descended the staircase. Josh waited at the bottom for her. He slid on a suit jacket. Scrumptious, she thought. Her stomach twisted into a knot upon the sight of him. He reached for her and kissed her cheek when she got to the bottom.

"You look beautiful, baby. 'Vous prenez mon souffle,'" he stared at her with such intensity, she touched his face.

"What did you just say?"

"You take my breath away, sweetheart."

"You take my breath away too," she smiled then peered at him more closely. "Why do you look so serious, Joshua?" he didn't respond. "Well," she outstretched her hands, "Now can you tell me where we're going? Are we all dressed up with no place to go?" she laughed nervously.

"Come on," he led her down another long corridor toward a room she hadn't been in before.

"Where is everybody?" the house seemed unusually quiet. "What's going on? Is it your dad's birthday celebration?"

He pulled her by the hand to step inside a room decorated in dangling crystals and pearls. Sheers draped the ceilings, and chairs were gathered around facing the back windows of the room. Soft violin music started to play. She wondered where it was coming from, and four violinists came through a door on the left of the room.

Her eyes filled with tears. She looked up at him, "This is beautiful... what is all this for?"

"Come with me, baby." He led her on her shaky feet to the far end of the room. His hand raised, and his entire family and some of the staff members entered the room from another side entrance.

Her heart pounded wildly in her chest. Everyone sat with their eyes glued to them. They were on display. She covered her mouth with her hand. He wiped underneath her eye and took her hands in his. Just then, JJ started chanting, "Da da - da da - da da," and the place filled with laughter. They had him dressed in a little miniature baby suit. She couldn't even look at him because she was 'bout ready to collapse as it was.

He glanced over at the baby, "Just a minute JJ," he said softly to the baby, "Daddy has something important to do."

He turned back to Chiffon. "Chiffon Hartwell, you came into my life like a burst of sunshine. You have warmed my heart and my soul, and I can't imagine my life without you. It's funny how you can live each day unaware you have been surrounded by darkness. You go on unconsciously until a beautiful light shines on you. A light that exposes who you are and what you genuinely want. I really didn't know true happiness. You taught me, Fonn. You have shown me love and light and unspeakable joy."

"Oh, Joshua," she said in a quivering voice. "What are you doing?" she sniffed and looked around at everyone. "Everybody is staring at us."

He smiled warmly, "I know, baby, they were invited to be a witness to me inviting you to share the rest of my life." He got down on one knee and took her trembling left hand. His father got up, took a ring box out of his pocket, opened it, and gave it to Joshua. She gasped. It was a beautiful, emerald-cut, canary yellow diamond with chipped diamonds all around it. It was breathtaking, sparkling, gorgeous.

Joshua held the ring box toward her like an offering to the heavens. "Chiffon Hartwell, I was wondering if you would agree to share my life and become my beautiful wife. I love you completely and totally," he paused, choking up. The audience ooo'd and awed at him.

He sniffed, "You, you accepted me with all my faults, you love my son as if he was your own." His voice cracked, "With you, I am complete. Together we are complete."

She opened her mouth to speak, but there were no words, no words to express the love, belonging, and sheer joy Joshua brought into her life.

"I-I," she stammered. He smiled his beautiful smile at her, took the ring out of the box, and placed it at the tip of her finger.

"I've got you," he whispered to her.

"Yes, Joshua, a thousand times yes," she blurted.

He slipped the ring on her finger, rose to his feet, and turned to the audience. "She said yes!" He fist-pumped, and everyone laughed. He turned back to her and kissed her delicately. Everyone got up to hug and kiss them both. She thought she would melt right into the floor.

They were all in on it. She couldn't believe he went through all this to propose to her. He kissed her again, and when their lips parted, she said. "I love you. I would be honored to be your wife and become a part of your beautiful family." She turned to face the barrage of onlookers again, "Even though they all tricked me." Everyone laughed again. She couldn't remember being happier.

The violins started playing again, and light refreshments were served on trays. "Now, you can never say you weren't officially proposed to," he muttered, pulling her close.

"I can't believe you did all this."

"This is just a fraction of what I want to do for you."

"We have yet to talk about the money you showered onto me."

He winked at her, "I have another surprise for you."

"I don't think I can handle another—"

He raised his arm up again, and the music stopped.

The mingling ceased as everyone went back to sit. She didn't think she could take much more.

"Joshua?" she questioned. One of the servers rose and brought out a large rose-colored envelope on a silver tray and motioned for her to take it. "What's this?" she lifted it and opened it. She pulled out papers and stared at them. With shaky hands, she saw it was the final divorce decree. She looked up at him.

"I'm a free man, baby. The divorce is final."

"But," she said. "I thought—"

"Un un…" he shook his head. "No more delays. I am a single man now, and I want to marry you as soon as possible, like tomorrow."

She laughed audibly but quieted when she saw he did not smile. "You're serious. Tomorrow?" she said in shock.

"I would do it today if there wasn't a mandatory 24-hour waiting period. I want to marry you. I will not spend another day not being your husband. The time has come to share my life, my family, and my heart with you indefinitely, Fonn, and one mo' day," he smiled.

"Come here, cuz," he called to his cousin seated among the crowd of onlookers. A tall, Abbott-looking fellow walked up to them.

"Hi Fonn, I'm Randall. I work for the county clerk's office, and if you agree to take this joker to be your husband, I have all the necessary paperwork ready to sign. I can get it processed by the end of the day, and you can be married whenever you choose. Tomorrow could even work too," he winked and grinned at her.

This was overwhelming. She turned to Joshua, "Are you sure?" she asked him.

He knew to what she referred. "Fonn, I have never been surer about anything in my life," he hesitated, "I'm sure about the love we share. I'm sure nothing else matters. Don't worry; we can have an official shindig later, as we discussed. Whatever you want, just say you'll marry me now."

She smiled at him. This man had her heart, love, and her body. Everything she had to give was already his.

It's You

"Well..." she turned to the family. "What do ya'll think? Wanna watch us jump da broom tomorrow?" Yells and claps came from the crowd. She turned back to him, "My answer is absolutely yes, but you know we can't share the news with everyone until we can –"

"Hell no. Un un," he stopped her. "No more keeping anything quiet.

"Don't ask, don't tell?" She raised her eyebrow, and he chuckled.

"We'll figure it out, baby," he kissed her again. The next few hours were spent laughing, drinking, and celebrating with the crowd. After they filled out the necessary paperwork and sent Randall on his way, of course, she warmed inside because he still loved her despite everything. He didn't care about her confusion.

Tam needed to be with her. Pulling his jacket, she leaned in to ask if she could send for her friend, but he seemed a bit hesitant. "Let's talk about it when we get some alone time." She was baffled at his response. He knew how much Tam meant to her.

For that matter, she had better get her mother as well. Was this celebration only supposed to be with his family? When she checked her watch, it was nearing 6 pm. They had celebrated twice already, and she wanted to spend some alone time with her fiancé for a day. They needed to talk.

Things started to quiet down. "Can we go upstairs now?" The baby was knocked out. They had a great time, but she needed to figure out what the deal was regarding Tam.

"Sure, baby," he kissed her forehead. "You go on up, and I'll be right there."

"Ok." She kissed and hugged the remaining people and headed upstairs. She took off the beautiful gown and shoes and put on more casual fare. She sat on the bed and waited. Twenty minutes passed, and she wondered if she should go back down and get him. Upon her departure, she'd witnessed a group of the Abbott men gathered near the windows. They were having a good time, but she needed to talk to Josh like now. The clock was tick tick-ticking, and this would be extremely short notice.

At the 30-minute mark, she went ahead and called Tam. "Chi?" Tam answered questioningly.

"Tam, hey girl, yeah, it's me. How are you?"

"I'm fine, how are you?" she said coolly.

"Tam, I know your upset with me, but you shouldn't be.

"Oh, really, I shouldn't be? Is that right?" she said indifferently.

"I'm sorry I haven't been available, Tam, I've just been, well, going through a lot."

"Would that be a lot with Joshua or a lot with Isaac?" she questioned bitterly.

"What?" Chiffon asked in astonishment. "What are you talking about, Tam?"

"I'm talking about Isaac, Chi. You remember Isaac right, the one who is apparently madly in love with you!" she snapped. "But then you knew that right when you sent him my way."

Chiffon shook her head, "Tam, where on earth is this coming from?

Who told you—"

"Really, Chi, you mean Joshua didn't tell you?"

"No, tell me what?" The line was quiet. "What would Joshua have to tell me, Tam?"

"You need to talk to your man Chi, or should I say one of your men and ask them about their little discussion I overheard. Then you can call me back." She hung up.

Chiffon grimaced and stared at the receiver. Did Tam just hang up on her?

Chapter 33

Joshua sauntered in, "Sorry sweetheart, I had to put some finishing touches on tomorrow." He looked at her folded arms and tapping foot and knew he was in trouble. "What's wrong baby? I got up here as fast as I could."

She walked past him and closed the door. She stood in front of him, careful not to get too close because Joshua could easily distract her from the task at hand. At what she figured was a safe enough distance, she asked him, "What the hell happened between you, Isaac, and Tam?"

He exhaled deeply, "Which one of them told you?"

"Which one of them?" she repeated, brows crinkling.

"Why would I be talking to Isaac now?" He looked at her with a knowing look.

Realization penetrated her, "Now that's hitting below the belt, Joshua."

"You're right, Fonn, I'm sorry, listen…," he took her hand and led her to the couch. "What did Tam say to you?"

"Not much. She told me I should talk to you right before she hung up on me."

He ran his hand through his head of soft curls. "I didn't get a chance to talk to you about this because, well, you'd left before I could, and then I had more pressing things on my mind."

"Ok, so start talking now. Why did my best friend hang up in my face?"

"Probably because I confronted Mergers at Max's party. Her eyes widened.

"Well, Fonn, it was before you told me what the hell was going on. I saw you leave after he arrived and well, I lost it. You wouldn't tell me, so I confronted him."

"You confronted him?" she repeated. "What happened?"

"I asked him what the hell was going on between you two, and basically, he told me nothing happened. He admitted you turned his advances down. Oh, and he thinks I'm an adulterous asshole who doesn't deserve you."

"So far, so good," she said bluntly.

A hint of a grin came to his face, "What did you just say about below the belt?"

"Touché," she said. "Go on."

"Well, things got a little heated cause I accused him of only dating Tam to be near you."

"You what?"

"Yeah, yeah, he gets on my fucking nerves. I told him he was shady for using her to stay close to you after you refused him."

"Really?" she folded her arms.

"Yeah, and unfortunately, Tam came in, right at the end, and heard us."

"Oh no! She did?"

"I know. I regretted it the minute I said it. I just wanted him to know I would kick his ass if he hurt her."

Fonn unfolded her arms and didn't say anything. He peered at her intently. "Are you angry with me?" When she didn't answer, he asked, "We still getting married?"

She smiled, "You're not getting rid of me that easily, mister. And yes, I'm angry with you, but mostly I'm angry at myself. I'm the reason you were scrambling for answers. All because I wasn't completely honest."

"So, you're still going to marry me?" he wanted to hear her say it.

"Of course, you are stuck with me, darling. Plus, we already promised your mama and 'nem."

He sighed with relief and hugged her, "I think I can get into this full disclosure thing if you promise to always handle it like this."

"Well…you're lucky today because you just made me the happiest woman on the planet." She pulled back, "Now you are going to continue on that path and help me get my mama and my best friend here to witness our nuptials."

He held up his hand, "Whatever you want, wifey."

She shook her head, "I think I did a very stupid thing, setting those two up. I don't really know how to fix it."

"Well, I don't know how you feel about me saying this, Fonn, but I think he really does like her. His apology to her seemed genuine. He didn't deny his feelings for you, but he let her know he enjoyed getting to know her. I thought he was honest. He got two points for that."

"Only two?" she smiled.

"He's lucky to get that."

"I'll talk to her. I really want her to be here. If she knows I'm marrying you, that's got to make her feel more comfortable, right?"

"It should. Look, I'm going leave you to it," he rose to his feet. "I'll be back in a little bit. Holla, if you need me."

"Ok."

"Hey," he turned at the door. She looked up from her phone. "I love you, Mrs. Abbott."

She smiled and replied, "From here to eternity." he departed.

She dialed her friend and took a few deep breaths while the phone rang.

"So, did you speak with him?" Tam answered.

"Yes, I'm so sorry."

"For which part," she said sarcastically.

"For every part." She went on and explained everything to her. When she finished, her friend was silent.

"Tam, listen to me. If I thought for one minute, he wouldn't be sincere in his pursuit of you, I would not have given him your number. I made him promise."

"Yeah, but you were trying to get rid of him, to get him off you."

Chiffon closed her eyes. "Ok, that is partially true, Tam, and I am apologizing for that. Sincerely."

"So, what are you going to do about your... your feelings for him, Chi?"

"I'm unsure outside of counseling, I don't know what else I can do."

"So, he has no idea about this?"

"No...God no!" she clutched the receiver. "Please, don't say anything, Tam. I want him to move on. Once he realizes I'm married, I know he'll let go and –"

"Married! Did I just hear you say you're married?" her friend squeaked.

"Yes, I mean, no. I didn't mean literally, um, look, the reason I was calling you in the first place is that Joshua just surprised me. He proposed, and he wants us to get married tomorrow.

"Tomorrow!" her friend exclaimed.

"Yes," Chiffon laughed.

"Oh no, you are not getting married without me."

"I know, Tam, that's why I'm calling you silly. He finally got the divorce, and I'm getting married tomorrow. I want, no, I need you to be there, to be here with me. You know Joshua is the only one for me. I want to be his wife as soon as possible."

"Wow, girl, Josh doesn't let the grass grow under his feet where you're concerned. Engaged today, married tomorrow."

"Will you come, Tam? I want you and my mother to be here. We will still have a big ceremony later, but we want to do this now."

Tam was quiet again.

"Tam, please. Will you stand beside me? I need my great loves near me—you and Joshua. I know I did a stupid thing, but I would never purposely hurt you, Tam. I think Isaac is a good man. I want you to find some happiness. I know everything you've been through."

"The jury is still out on him, Chi. I could never be sure he wasn't looking at me, wishing he were looking at you."

They held the phone in silence.

Tam sighed, "I'm not sure about him, but I am positive about you. You better not get married without me there."

"Yes!" she yelled out. "Joshua will make the arrangements for you to fly in tomorrow morning or tonight or whatever you want. Can you take time off?"

"It shouldn't be a problem."

"Ok, I'm about to call mama."

"Good, Chi, she should be there too."

"Yes, and Tam?"

"What?"

"I love you."

"I love you too." Tam's voice cracked out, "Damn you, Chi, we can't be infatuated with the same guy. It didn't work while we were growing up, and it's not going to work now."

"I know that Tam, and I promise I will not get in your way." Chiffon leaned against the desk, eyes downcast.

Her friend hesitated for a moment. "Well, it does help that you're getting married. So, do you have a dress already or what?"

"Oh my!" she said in horror. "I don't have anything. This is so last minute."

"Look, I'll try to get there tonight, and we'll figure it out."

"Thank you, Tam. I didn't want to do this without you."

"See you soon," she said.

They hung up. "Whew," Chiffon closed her eyes for a minute. That was close, too close; one down, one to go.

Next, she called her mother. "Mama, I have some big news for you," she said at her mom's hello.

"What baby, what you up to?"

"I'm getting married."

"What? To Joshua?"

"Who else, mama? Yes, he proposed earlier today, and I said yes."

"Congratulations, honey. I know you will have a beautiful ceremony."

"Yes, mama, but there is a small catch."

"Oh, he's still gotta work out that marriage stuff out with the crazy woman?"

"What? No mama. He is divorced now. The nuptials are going to be held tomorrow in Tennessee."

"Tomorrow!" she shrieked, "In Tennessee?"

"I know it's short notice, mama, but I need you to come here by tomorrow morning. I need you with me. Josh is making all the arrangements."

"Oh, my God. You're doing this tomorrow. Why so fast, baby?"

"I wanted to marry him six months ago, mama. I don't need or want a long engagement. He doesn't either."

"I see, so this was his idea?"

"Yes, and if I could live without him, maybe I would have suggested we wait until we could plan a real wedding. I can't risk losing him again. I can't go through the pain I had without him again, mama."

Her mother was quiet. "So, you're ready for all that comes with a man like him, his kind of power, not to mention wealth? You didn't know just how much money he had when you started dating him. It will be a different world than what you've been used to. You will need to fight for your voice with him.

Also, he's an extremely attractive man; you will deal with women who will be very jealous of you. And on top of that, we both know how controlling he has proven to be. He wants what he wants when he wants it. He does whatever it takes to get it. It sounds like he's already taking over everything."

She closed her eyes. She knew her mother was right. "Mama, no relationship is perfect. Joshua is not perfect, but he always gives me a voice. He doesn't always do what I want, but I know he hears me and loves me. His main goal is to protect me. It's out of love, not just control."

After a bout of silence, she sighed into the receiver, "Let me put it like this, mama, the next time I cry over Joshua Abbott, I will be crying over my husband, not somebody else's."

Her mother let out a long breath. "Ok, fine. When do I need to get there?"

Chiffon smiled, "We want to get you and Tam here either tonight or tomorrow morning. The wedding won't happen until sometime tomorrow evening." She ended her call with her mother and went to find Joshua.

The house was still a-buzz, and she loved it. Josh's family adored him, and they fully embraced her. She started to tear up at the very thought of it. Hopefully, having them all as her own will help with some of the inner turmoil she battled.

She ran smack dab into Vi, munching on a tart, in the nicely appointed kitchen. Her future sister-in-law hugged her tight, "I'm so happy for you both."

"Thank you, Vi. Where's your brother? I've been walking in circles looking for him."

"Oh, he's in dad's study with him."

"Oh, damn, I wonder if I should interrupt that?"

Vi shrugged her shoulders and looked at her watch. "They've been in there for a while now. Dad has always got some business to discuss. He also knows we are in the middle of a momentous occasion."

"Ok, I really need to talk to Josh, so maybe Poppa Abbott will let me borrow him for a quick minute."

Vi hugged her again, "This family has been overdue for some good news. I'm so happy for you, Fonn."

"Me too," they hugged once more, and she headed toward the study.

She heard several voices as she approached Poppa Abbott's study. She heard Josh, his father, and another unfamiliar female voice. The door to the study was slightly ajar. She put her arm up to knock on the door when she heard Josh's voice rise. "I don't need to protect myself from Fonn!" he snarled at someone.

Her hand froze; she dropped it and listened.

"Mr. Abbott, this is standard procedure for a man with your level of wealth." she heard the female voice say. She peeked through the opening of the door.

It's You

Joshua turned to his father, "A prenup is necessary to divide assets in case of a divorce. Fonn and I will be married for life. No divorce, ever."

"Son," Poppa Abbott shook his head, "I know you love this woman, hell, we all love her, but you need to be reasonable. If something should happen to your mother and me, do you realize how much money is at stake?"

"At stake?" Josh looked appalled.

"You will inherit a third of my fortune. When you couple that with your own assets, the amount reaches, I don't know, somewhere near the stratosphere."

"So what? Fonn doesn't care about my money. She didn't have a clue how much I could be worth until I invested in Reynolds. In fact, I still don't think she really knows because frankly, it never came up."

"Again, son, you know how this works. If she doesn't care, she shouldn't have any problem signing. I can't let you marry her without a prenuptial agreement signed."

"Let me? Are you serious?"

"I'm dead serious. We didn't have this issue when you married Candy. You already had one. So, I am aware you understand the significance of the document. You want Fonn to have everything, but what about your son?"

"Fonn loves JJ. She has been the only real mother he has known for the last few months of his short life. I have no doubt she will take excellent care of him."

"Mr. Abbott," the woman in the room interrupted him, "Do you think she won't sign?"

He turned to her and tried to calm himself. "I wouldn't ask her to sign this shit you have put together. She is going to be my wife, not a casual acquaintance I met on the street last week."

"Ok, Mr. Abbott, I can change the wording. If you divorce, she will get half of whatever you earn during the marriage. Everything else will be bestowed upon your death as your original will dictates."

Joshua closed his eyes and inhaled deeply. It was taking much restraint for him not to completely snap.

"Dad, I'm only going to say this one more time. What I choose to give to my wife is my choice, not yours. I do not need or want an 'in case of failure press here' contract. If, for some reason, we divorce, my life will be worthless anyway. Money won't replace her for me, so if you don't want to leave me anything, so be it. Greg and Vi have been your more obedient children anyway. I have more than enough to provide for my family during our lifetime and then some."

Poppa Abbott's eyes narrowed on his son. Before he could reply, Fonn pushed the heavy door open.

All startled eyes were upon her as she entered the room. "Hi ... hi, baby," Josh quickly rose from his seat, taken aback. "Were you looking for—"

"I heard everything," She put up her hand to stop him from talking.

"What did you hear?" Poppa Abbott inquired.

"I heard everyone, but my fiancé, wants me to sign a prenup."

She turned to Josh. "Honey, just when I thought I couldn't love you more, you top yourself." She put her hand up to his face, "I will sign whatever is necessary to become your wife. That's all I care about. Don't give up your birthright for me. I would never forgive myself or you if you did that."

He stared down at her lovingly, "I don't care about any of this Fonn. I just want to make you legally mine. I don't give a damn about these formalities. I trust you with my life."

She smiled at him and kissed him quickly. She made eye contact with Poppa Abbott, "Make whatever adjustments you and my future husband can agree on. Make sure he will still receive his inheritance. Whatever is decided is fine with me."

"Fonn," his father turned to her, "I'm sorry you heard all this. It's not personal; I think you will be a great asset to our family. Particularly now," he smiled genuinely at her. "Don't worry about any of this. Joshua and I will come to an agreement."

Her eyes narrowed on the lawyer just because she was there. She turned on her heels and started to walk out.

Josh reached out and grabbed her arm, "You don't have to do this."

She put her hand on his chest, "I love you, Joshua Abbott. I would do anything for you."

He smiled at her, and her heart warmed over. On her tiptoes, she kissed his cheek and embraced him. She whispered in his ear while hugging him, "I was looking for you to tell you I got Tam and my mom on board."

"Thank God," he whispered back. "Instruct Taylor to make the arrangements. I let him know he probably would need to."

He turned and looked at his dad and the lawyer, then back to Fonn. "I won't be long, baby."

She smiled at him and shut the door behind her. Her heart pounded out of her chest as she let out a long breath. She leaned against a wall in the hallway. Jesus, how much money did he have? She really didn't even know. He wanted her to have it all, no stipulations. The way he stood up for her to his father. She didn't care if he was destitute. She would marry him in a heartbeat, and she wouldn't make him sign anything either. She laughed aloud to herself then, as if her paltry salary could even compare.

She found Taylor and gave him the instructions. She thought it best to fly her family in that night, so they would already be with her when she got up in the morning. If everything went as Taylor planned, everyone would arrive between 10 and 11pm. She glanced at her watch. She didn't have a whole lot of time until then.

She went to the nursery to spend some time with JJ, who was up from his nap. If they were getting married tomorrow, did that mean they could take the baby home with them, she wondered? Joshua was keeping everything a big secret, and it was killing her. If they could take their baby, everything would be perfect.

She sat on the nursery room floor with JJ. He was taking steps but falling. Occasionally, he managed to stay on his feet after wavering. She was delighted and clapped for him every time he achieved it.

She must have lost track of time because when she turned back toward the doorway, she saw Joshua leaning against it. She smiled at him, "How long have you been standing there?"

"Hi baby," he came in and bent down to kiss her cheek.

"Hi man," he reached down and scooped up the baby.

He kissed him and started talking baby to him. She got to her feet. Anna was on the couch reading. They kept her there 24/7 now because no one wanted to leave JJ alone. The nursery door no longer had a lock.

Josh handed the baby to Anna.

"Come with me, sweetheart," he reached for Fonn's hand, "We've got to talk." She took his hand, and they headed out.

He led her into one of the small, brightly lit sitting rooms. They sat down, and he handed her some papers.

"Is this the prenup?" she asked.

"Yes, such as it is. Take your time and read it carefully. If you disagree with anything, I mean anything, tell me, and I will have it changed."

She stared into his green liquid pools, "Give me a pen."

"Fonn, I want you to read it first."

"Give me the pen," she demanded.

He reached in his shirt pocket and took out a pen. She flipped the pages to the back and signed the document and handed it back to him. He stared in disbelief. How did he get so lucky, he wondered. If he ever believed in God, in a Higher Power, he believed now. She was crazy but completely made for him. He would provide for her for the rest of her life, no matter what happened between them.

He finally got that point across to his father. They both compromised, and in the end, his inheritance was protected, but his own assets were not. She would receive half of his entire fortune if the marriage ended. He also stipulated a payout of $450,000 each year she remained his wife. He wanted her to know she didn't have to work unless she wanted to. He wanted her to have more, but his father convinced him he didn't need to stipulate it. He could just do it during the marriage.

He held up the document, "I want you to read this. You could have just signed your life away to me."

"I don't care. I'm about to give my life to you tomorrow, so what's signing it away tonight."

He stared at her unblinking for a long while. "What's wrong?" she asked. "Why are you looking at me like that?"

"I want you so bad right now that I physically ache," he said in a husky voice. He reached toward her breast, and she jumped up.

"Un...un, you've gotta wait until your wedding night to taste these morsels again.

He laughed, "Dammit, I knew you were going to say that," he grimaced.

"Yep," she nodded.

"So, that means we don't sleep together tonight?" he questioned with pain etched on his face.

"Exactly. Tam and my mom will be here," she looked at her watch, "In about an hour or so, and I'm going to have them in the room with me."

"Well, you know that's a pretty big bed we could all fit."

"Don't even try it. Now, what can you tell me 'bout tomorrow? It's killing me not knowing anything."

He rose to his feet and pulled her close to him. While he held her, he explained he wanted everything to be a surprise tomorrow. He had her dress and accessories all picked, and they should have been brought into their bedroom already. They were getting married at 4:30 pm in the ballroom, and the staff had strict instructions not to show her anything, so she shouldn't bother trying to look. She pouted then.

They would have the same people there tomorrow as they had today, apart from her mom and Tam. Dinner would be served after, and then, they could do whatever she wanted. Once he made an honest woman out of her, he'd share another surprise. Joshua and his surprises she shook her head.

She was along for this ride. This initial mini wedding celebration would be at his direction, but the biggie would be all hers to control. He mentioned, he was already practicing how to say, "Yes, dear."

At this point, she just wanted him. How strange, she didn't care so much about work and what people would say or think anymore. She just wanted to spend her life with him.

His lips met hers. The taste of him was intoxicating. She started to moan and pull away from him. He held her tightly. "Josh," she whispered against his soft lips. "I need to go upstairs. I would like to wash my hair and whatever else before my mom and Tam arrive. I need to get myself ready for tomorrow."

He reluctantly dropped his arms., "Just let me know what you need, and I will have it brought to you."

"The servants can't do this for me, honey. I can take care of it. This will be my day, my way." She put her finger up to his mouth before he could protest. "I will see you tomorrow at 4:30 pm sharp. I'm going upstairs now. Don't give me that face," she smirked, "Getting married tomorrow was your idea."

"Fine," he grimaced. "Can I see you later, at least, like before the clock strikes midnight?"

"Maybe," she smiled at him, reached up to kiss his cheek, and left the room.

Joshua decided to have a copy of the signed prenup sent to Chiffon's room. Her mother would make sure she read it, no doubt. Nobody dictates to him what he could and couldn't do for his wife. Not in this lifetime.

Yes, his wife – he liked the sound of that. He never experienced a real marriage before, and he wanted it to be perfect. Fonn was a brilliant force of nature, and he planned to have her work with him in the business. He knew she wanted to do her own thing, separate from him. She thought he was too controlling, but together they could rule the world. He just had to convince her. He would bide his time on that one. He usually got what he wanted, and his new wifey would be no exception.

Chapter 34

Fonn couldn't believe it was happening so fast. She peered down the hallway toward the ballroom. She wanted to go in there to peek desperately.

She pouted again. It wasn't fair. She saw one of the staff members in the hall and approached him, "Hi Larry," she noticed his nametag on his lapel.

"Hi Miss Chiffon," he smiled.

"I think I dropped my earring in the ballroom entrance earlier today when Josh was showing me where the wedding would be held. Is it ok if I run in there quickly and retrieve it?"

Larry stared at her suspiciously, "We are under strict instructions not to let you enter the ballroom."

"Yes, I know, but I think I want to wear those earrings for the ceremony."

"I will have the staff do a sweep and bring them to your room if found." He stared at her pouting face, unblinking.

"Please?" She put on her most adorable face, but it wasn't working. Damn, Josh had the staff on lock. She slumped and headed back up to the bedroom.

Just as he mentioned, a beautiful empire waist, sparkling, cream-colored dress, and all manner of accessories and shoes had all been provided. His taste was impeccable. Impressive, she thought. Obviously, she would have rather picked out her own garb, but with less than 24 hours, she never could have accomplished what Joshua did.

She climbed up on the bed and closed her eyes for a minute; what an overwhelming day for what would be an overwhelming life. She drifted off and soon after found herself groping around aimlessly for her buzzing phone. Still groggy, she picked it up, "Hello?"

"Chi, girl, we're pulling up in front. Oh, my Lawd, this place is incredible!" Tam exclaimed.

Fonn sprang up instantly awake, "Ok, I'll be right down." She hightailed it to the stairs taking them two at a time.

When she got down to the main floor, she saw Taylor standing at the open door. First, her mother, then Tam, stepped in. She embraced and kissed her mother first, and then she and Tam stared at each other silently. "Tam, I," her eyes filled with tears. Tam opened her arms, and the two women held each other. No two sisters could have been closer. She would slit her own wrists before she would purposely hurt Tam. "I'm so sorry," she held her friend tightly.

"It's ok, Chi. I don't want to talk about it now, ok. This is your time. Let's get you hitched."

Chiffon leaned back and wiped under her eyes. Tam's eyes welled up as well.

"I love you, Tamara."

"I know, silly rabbit. I love you too." She hugged her again and took her mother's and Tam's hands and gave them a tour of the house. She introduced them to everyone she could and then back upstairs to her bedroom.

While Tam went to use the facilities, her mother turned to her. "So, what's going on with you and Tam? She was unusually quiet on the way up here. Is she having a hard time sharing you?"

Oh boy, she thought. What an understatement, "She's just got to get used to the idea that I'm going to be married. She's feeling better now."

"Good," her mother nodded. "Honey, I must say, I've never been in a place quite this fancy before. It is stunning." She glanced around the room.

"I know, right? Josh never told me or even hinted he grew up with servants and guards or in such opulence; I found it nerve-wracking at first, but the Abbott's are wonderful people, mama. I think you and Mrs. Abbott will hit it off. They are very down-to-earth. Not snobbish or standoffish, only regular people who love each other very much."

Her mother nodded, but Chiffon wasn't sure she was convinced.

Tam came out of the washroom. "Chi girl, this shiggity is crazy!" she laughed. She was her old self again, and Chiffon was thrilled.

"Welcome to my in-law's place," Chiffon grinned.

Tam picked up the gown and whistled, "Did he pick all this out for you?" She took in the accessories and shoes.

"Yes, he is providing everything for this wedding. He assured me our 'real' one would be up to me."

"You can't pull this kind of thing off overnight," her mother sat on the chair facing them.

Tam interjected. "Right, mama, this was definitely pre-planned. He knew your answer would be yes."

"He couldn't have," Fonn spoke up. "Ok," she backtracked, "He might have been sure I would say yes, but he had no idea if I would agree to do it in 1 day."

Tam shook her head, "Poor Chi, she still underestimates her man." Fonn hit her playfully on the butt.

"Time for a group hug, ladies." They gathered and held each other. Fonn released them, wiping under her eyes again. "Are you guys hungry? We can head down to the kitchen, or I can have something brought up."

"I think I'd like room service," her mother stated. They laughed, and Fonn ordered up.

As they finished eating, Fonn noticed a band of rolled-up papers sitting on the dresser. She picked it up, slid the rubber band off, and flattened out the papers. Her mouth dropped open. It was the prenuptial agreement. Her hands started to tremble.

"What is it, Chi?"

She met her mother's eyes, "It's the prenuptial agreement."

"Prenuptial agreement?" Tam asked, "You signed one?"

"Yes, and I've been afraid to read it."

"Afraid to read it!" her mother stood up. "You signed something you didn't even read! That's the craziest thing I've ever heard."

"Mama, you don't understand," she handed her mother the papers. "I overheard him screaming at his father over it.

He didn't want me to sign anything. In fact, he was going to give up his inheritance from his parents so we could be married tomorrow without incident."

"Wait a minute," Tam interrupted. "So, you're saying the prenup was his father's idea?"

"Yes."

"And Josh didn't want one, but you signed one anyway?"

"Yes, that's what I'm saying. Listen, before you two call me every kind of fool, I made him promise he wouldn't give up his birthright on a principle. I know what we have is real. I don't care about his money."

"Sweetheart," her mother stopped her. "Yes, you do. You care very much about his money, your money. I told you, this is a different world you are entering with the Abbott's. You need to know exactly what you are dealing with. This is not about love. This is as much about a business transaction as it is about a marriage ceremony. You should make sure your interests are cared for. Just like you did before you married, you must do the same while you're married, and God forbid, after the marriage is over as well. People are only human. We can't control how they feel from day to day. Nobody wants to think about their great love ending, but you and I both know it happens every day. I raised you better than that, Chi."

Chiffon shook her head, "You're right, and I know it, mama. He told me to read it, and if I wanted anything changed, to let him know."

"Well, let's see what you've agreed to, shall we?" her mother started to read the document aloud. She began, "This prenuptial agreement is made on this date by and between Joshua, Jason Abbott, husband, an adult residing in Atlanta, Georgia and Chiffon, Lacie Hartwell, wife, an adult residing in Chicago Illinois, in consideration of the contemplated marriage of the above-named parties, this agreement shall not be effective until the marriage contemplated by the parties is solemnized."

Her mother went on to read the entire 9-page document. They all fell silent after her mother finished. Chiffon sat down on the soft bed, visibly struck, shaken, and floored.

Her friend sat down next to her and took her hand. "Wow," she said under her breath. "I have never been at a loss for words, Chi, but I honestly don't know what to say."

Her mother interjected, "This is unbelievable," she waved the document back and forth. "Joshua Abbott is an amazing man."

"He puts his money where his mouth is. I have added respect for him," Tam said in awe.

Chiffon smiled hesitantly, "How could I have not known the magnitude of his wealth?" She was dumbstruck, a deer in headlights. His net worth was in the triple digits in terms of millions of dollars, not to mention the inheritance from his parents, which couldn't even be estimated. Her mother got up and poured some water from the pitcher and gave it to her. He always had priceless things and dressed impeccably, but nothing made her think he was a kazillionaire.

She remembered wondering how he could have her entire apartment redone when she was just a renter. How he could, just like that, sit at the table with the owners of the advertising firm as a partner; and how he could effortlessly pay off all her bills and put more money than she had ever seen in her entire life into her bank accounts. She knew he was wealthy, but damn.

Some of the gifts he gave her over the past few years; jewelry, clothes, shoes, were strikingly beautiful. She remembered how she would try to give the presents back to him at first. He refused and if she wouldn't take it, he would find a way to leave it somewhere for her to find later. She didn't ever consider the cost. He was a class act, so it wasn't shocking he gave wonderful gifts. But this…

In the prenup, he was willing to share everything with her. Everything. He was even going to give her an astronomical "allowance" each year just because she remained his wife. He didn't really ask for anything in return, just that she try to give him plenty of babies. The only thing that appeared off-limits were some real estate holdings to the tune of about 50 million.

She took a large gulp of the water. She didn't want to read the prenup even though she knew she should. She knew everything would become extremely real.

"What am I getting myself into?" she spoke aloud without realizing it.

"Chi," her mother gazed at her intently. "If you really are in love and you are ready to legally enter this world," she motioned around her, "Marry him."

She turned a confused look towards Tam.

"This man can literally have anything he wants, Chi, and he wants you. Don't hesitate to make it legal, girl."

It's You

Just then, they heard a rap on the door. "Yes?" she said loudly.

"Ms. Fonn," she heard Taylor's voice. "Mr. Josh wanted me to notify you it is nearly 11:45 pm, and he would like the pleasure of your company before the clock strikes 12."

She turned to her mother, who was looking confused. She held her hand up to the side of her mouth and whispered to her. "I told him he couldn't see me on our wedding day until the ceremony, so this is literally the eleventh hour."

"Oh," her mother smiled in understanding.

She opened the door, "Thank you, Taylor. Yes, I want to see him."

"Very well, Ms. Fonn, may I take your guests downstairs? I would like to get their input on a few matters."

She glanced over at them, "Sure, ok."

Tam linked her arm with Chiffon's mother, and they followed Taylor out of the room. As soon as they departed, someone came in with a cart and cleared their food and dishes.

She stood staring at the open doorway. Soon, just as she suspected, he appeared. Her stomach clenched at the sight of him. So athletic, so masculine, so beautifully put together and well, just damn pretty to look at. She couldn't believe he was all hers. He was everything she'd ever wanted. She could pinch herself.

He sported a fresh haircut and neatly faded beard and mustache. He took her breath away.

"Hey, baby," he said softly. Their eyes searched each other's.

"Hi," she replied.

"Did I make it in time?" he advanced into the room. Her eyes filled with tears that spilled over and down her cheeks. He rushed to wrap his arms around her trembling frame.

"Sweetheart, what's wrong?" He held her tightly. "Don't cry, baby. It's not twelve yet. I'm not in violation."

She shook her head. "No, that's not why, I, I'm crying."

He leaned back and stared at her face. "What's wrong then? Why are you so upset?" He bent down to pick up a napkin left over from dinner. He wiped under her eyes and kissed her cheek. "Tell me. I know you're not having second thoughts. I'm not canceling that big ass cake."

She managed a small giggle then. "You are crazy," she whispered.

"About you," he watched her with concern. "So, what happened?"

He took her hand and led her to the couch to sit. "Is it your mother or Tam? What upset you?"

She grabbed a tissue, blew her nose, and took a deep breath, "Are you absolutely sure, Joshua?" she inquired.

He eyed her quizzically, "Sure about what? About you? About us?" She nodded. "I've never been surer about anything in my life. I take it you read the prenup." He turned and eyed the papers laid out over the bed. She nodded.

He grabbed her chin and lifted it. His eyes were a soft blue-gray trained on her brown ones. "You are staying married to me until you die, you hear me?" he said with a hint of laughter in his voice. "Everything I have is already yours. You are stuck with me. We will never need to use that document, but I want you to know I am sharing everything with you. You are the love of my life," as he wiped underneath her eye again.

"You don't have to pay me a stipend every year I stay married to you. You don't have to entice me. I'm not going anywhere."

"Damn right, you're not going anywhere," he rebuffed. "I want to take care of you. You don't have to work unless you choose to. I want you to have your own money – out of my control, to do with whatever you please. You can stay home, take care of JJ and our other babies, start your own business, continue working at Reynolds, or come to work by my side. It really doesn't matter to me, as long as you are happy and all mine."

She nodded, "I am happy, and I'm already all yours."

He smiled a brilliant white smile. "Good answer, because as you've noticed, I'm slightly possessive. I want you to consider working at the Abbott Enterprises arm with me. Now that I'll truly be a married man, I need to set down some roots. Besides, you are about to become Mrs. Chiffon Abbott. I want you to seriously consider the family business."

"Chiffon Hartwell Abbott," she said defiantly.

He smirked at her, "That's my baby. You get a kick out of it, don't you? The defiance. You know I'll let you win sometimes, huh?" as he tapped her nose lovingly.

"Yep," she smiled sheepishly, "And you better let me win most of the time."

He grinned boyishly at her. They stared at each other.

"I love you so very much, Joshua."

"Good baby because I'm about to lock that in for all time. I don't want you to have any doubts, and I need you to know I have none whatsoever. We are a team, you and I. Nothing is going to come between us." She reached up to touch his face and saw the hint of moisture in his eyes. He closed them and placed his hand over hers.

When he opened them again, he said, "No matter what, I've got you, Fonn. I will never leave you uncovered as your father did. I will be your umbrella. Do you understand me?"

"Yes," she exhaled, mesmerized by his beauty, transfixed in those eyes, absolutely taken by the intoxicating power of his affection.

He kissed her hand, "I want to shelter, protect, comfort, and provide for you from this day forward. If anything ever gets to be too much or too hard, I want you to talk to me, baby. Promise me you will never let anything else fester inside you, eating away at you from the inside out. You don't have to be afraid anymore, baby. I will guard your heart.

When you give the cue, I will close every window and shut every door. I will shut out the big bad world and hold you until you're ready to face it again. That is my job and my honor. I vow to not let anything ever hurt you like, like…" he stammered.

"Shhhh," she moved in and kissed him lightly. The charge of electricity that shot through her body at the touch of his lips melted her soul. She trusted him with everything, her body, her heart, her very life. Never did she think herself capable of that with another person.

The kiss intensified. He pushed her down into the cushions of the couch. She whimpered in protest. She knew they were headed for trouble, but she had mixed feelings, confused due to the intense need she had for the man and her desire to wait.

"Josh," she managed against his soft lips. "Baby…we," she fell silent when his fingers circled her nipple, instantly hardening it. She let out a moan of pleasure.

"I know you want to wait, baby," he trailed kisses down her neck, drinking in her sweet scent. "I understand."

She held him, wrapping her legs around him. She could feel his solid arousal against her. Her eyes were closed, and she was lost in her desire for the man. So quickly, she lost her good sense. She groped his stiff length.

"Dammit, woman, you're asking for trouble," he pulled away from her. "Since these were your rules, I don't want you to have any regrets."

He rose to his feet and glanced at his watch, "I only have a few minutes left."

She peered at his tall frame through heavily lidded eyes.

"Your family will be back here any minute and well…I won't be able to stop myself once I touch you there," his eyes dropped to where her legs met. "I'm making my exit, baby, before I tear your clothes off."

She sat up. "But I don't want you to go. I think I've changed my mind about the rules."

He smirked, "You are such a naughty, naughty little girl, Fonn – and so very perfect for me." He bent down and kissed her briefly, holding her bottom lip between his teeth, causing her to moan against him. "I want to bite you, to lick you everywhere, you know that," he exhaled. "Until tomorrow, love." He released her lip and started to back up toward the door. "I love you, baby."

She sat up, watching his retreating frame.

"I will show you how much tomorrow, I promise," he whispered to her, still walking backward.

"I can't wait," she mouthed the words quietly. Then he was gone. The ache between her legs was undeniable. She found herself breathing deeply, just from the man's kiss and gentle caress. What shape would she be in if they did more? She had to get herself together. They had the rest of their lives to please each other.

She calmed herself and stood up. So much for her and her rules. No wonder he never took what she said seriously. She smiled to herself; she wasn't particularly good at holding her ground with him. She gathered the prenup, re-banded it, and placed it in a drawer.

She unzipped the clear garment bag and ran her fingers over the silken fabric and folds of her beautiful gown. It was exactly midnight. She was getting married today. How she'd longed for her father to walk her down the aisle one day like in the fairy tales she'd read as a little girl. Who gives this woman to married to this man? I do. Her father would say and turn to kiss her cheek. She sat down on the bed, laid back, and closed her eyes, dreaming of what could not be.

Soon Tam and her mother came bursting through the door. "Girl," Tam waved her hands all around. "Joshua outdid himself. I'm telling you. I've never seen anything so damn fantabulous!"

She smiled anxiously at her, "Can you tell me anything?"

"No," her mother stated firmly. "We are under strict instructions," she made a motion simulating, zipping her lips and throwing away the key.

Chiffon laughed. Her mother was so good, too good at keeping secrets.

"Please, mama, what can you share?"

"Just that you're gonna love it. Let's get some sleep. We've got a huge day ahead." Her mother went to her suitcase and retrieved her pajamas.

"I want you both to stay in here with me. This bed is huge."

"Really? Tam asked, there are more than enough rooms here."

"I know, but please humor me."

"Fine with me, her mother said. Your last night as a single woman might as well make it memorable."

The next morning when she opened her eyes, she found her mother's arm draped across her shoulder and Tam's leg lying across hers. Whose idea was this to sleep together anyway, she mused to herself. It wasn't possible to untangle herself without waking everybody up, so she woke everybody.

She sat up, and they moaned and groaned. "Wake up!" she clapped her hands together and climbed over Tam's still frame. "I'm getting in the tub." They both mumbled something. She laughed and headed for the tub.

When finished, she saw breakfast had been brought up. She couldn't eat much; anxiety had a vice grip on her insides. Her mother made her eat the fruit cup at the very least, which she did painfully.

After the ladies dressed, she summoned Taylor to get the car ready for them. She had to find the perfect ring for Joshua. She wouldn't dare let him supply that when he supplied everything else. She needed her own touch to this beautiful, glorious day.

Careful to avoid seeing him, they slipped out. She sent him a text letting him know she had a quick errand. He tried his best to get her to elaborate on plans, but he would just have to wait. He said he had an appointment for them at 1 pm, so she'd better be back by then.

They arrived at the jewelry store just as it opened. A lovely blonde woman led her to the men's rings. Two equally beautiful women, one black, one Asian, were standing behind the counter. Impressive, she thought. It had to be a sales tactic. They all stared down into the glass case. Immediately she saw the ring that spoke to her.

"I want to see that one," she pointed to a platinum square-shaped, sliding diamond wedding band with a finish in the center that was a mix of coarse, heavy sandblast. It had a high-polished finish around the perimeter and baguette-shaped diamonds. It was stunning. The lady took the ring out and handed it to her. Speechless, she peered at it closely. She'd never seen anything like it before.

"Jesus Chi," Tam reached out for the ring, and Chiffon handed it to her.

She scrutinized it, "I love it."

Her mother reached for it then and gaped, "This is very nice, Chi, very elegant and sleek."

Tam smiled, "Just like Joshua Abbott."

"Joshua Abbott?" The pretty, black saleswoman repeated. They all looked up at her.

"Yes, that's who my girlfriend is marrying today."

"Today?" the sales lady looked horrified and stared at Chiffon. "Joshua is getting married? Today?" she whispered as if she couldn't believe it.

"Do you know my fiancé?" Chiffon asked her briskly. "Yes, I, I mean, we knew each other in college."

"In the biblical sense?" Tam asked her.

"No, no I—"

"Oh," Tam said, you just wanted to, huh?"

Completely embarrassed, Chiffon said, "You seem surprised Josh is getting married," she stared the pretty woman down.

"Well, um, yes, I don't mean any harm. It's just he never struck me as the settling down type."

Her mother interjected then. "Perhaps that held true until he met my daughter. The poor man pleaded with her to marry him."

"Wow," the saleswoman exhaled. "Well, this ring is upwards of $20,000," she clipped.

Chiffon refused to show any emotion. "Do you have it in size 11?" Tam and her mother looked at each other, then back to Chiffon.

Just then, a Caucasian woman came up. "Tracy, I'll take it from here," she said tightly. Tracy vanished. "My apologies, Ms? Ms...,"

"Hartwell," Chiffon answered.

"Ms. Hartwell, please let me go and make sure we have the ring in the appropriate size. I'll be right back." She left them all standing there. Chiffon turned to Tam.

"It doesn't matter where I go; somebody either knows him, knew him, or wants to know him. It appears my husband to be, has been quite popular with the ladies around town." Chiffon smiled slowly then, "I guess it's my duty to make sure his fine ass is officially off the market."

"Somebody has to do it, girl – might as well be you," Tam laughed aloud. It made Chiffon relax.

The sales manager, Veronica, came back with the ring. "Yes, Mrs. Hartwell, here it is in size 11."

She picked up the ring. She had never made a purchase this costly in her life. This ring cost more than she'd paid for her car.

"Can I get something engraved in the inside of the band today, like right now?"

"Um, well, it usually takes a few days, but our engraver is on the premises today. I will take care of it for you at no extra charge."

"Thank you," she wrote what she wanted on the inside of the ring and gave the paper to the woman who disappeared with the ring again.

"Chi," her mother grabbed her shoulders, "You're about to pay $20k for that ring?"

"Yes, I am."

Her mother shook her head.

"She's rich now, mama," Tam chimed in. "It's like paying $200 for it."

"Humph," her mother snorted. "You're not rich yet. I know you don't have that kind of money on your own."

Her mother was right. "Momma, Josh had funds deposited into my account a while ago. He didn't even tell me he did it. He paid off every bill I had and left more money than I have ever seen in both my checking and savings accounts. So, because of him, I can be generous just like he was with me." Her mother's eyes narrowed, and she did say another thing about it.

The sales lady brought out the ring in a beautiful velvet box. Chiffon pulled out her debit card and prayed as the woman took it up to the cash register. Approved appeared on the screen, and they all let out a collective breath. She fought the urge to ask Tracy a few more questions about her previous relationship with Josh, but she represented the past. Chiffon represented the future. Nothing was going to ruin this day for her.

After a few additional stops, they arrived back at the house, where they were immediately ushered into one of the upstairs rooms. She couldn't believe it. An entire staff of people were there to pamper them—hair, makeup, massage therapists, nail techs, you name it.

She felt like a princess. Lunch had been brought in, and Mrs. Abbott and Vi joined them for the treatments. They laughed, joked, and fussed over Chiffon.

She received another text from Joshua.

Him: "How is it going in there?"

Her: "Crazy. Thank you, honey, for all of this. Everyone looks beautiful."

Him: "No one could outshine you, baby."

Her: *smiley face with a veil*

Him: "Go to the door and open it."

Her: "Now?"

Him: "Yes, right now."

She tightened the robe she had on and went to the door. A uniformed man stood there with a bouquet of beautiful flowers. Gratitude filled her as she grabbed the flowers. "Thank you," she turned to get her purse, and the man held up his hand.

"No need for a tip, ma'am, been taken care of already."

"Oh, yes, ok, thank you again," she typed on her phone.

Her: "If you don't cut it out, I won't be in any shape to get married today. This is already overwhelming."

Him: "Welcome to the rest of your life, baby."

Her: "I love you."

Him: "You know."

It's You

She laughed and sent him a final text letting him know she couldn't spend any more time texting. She had a special appointment this evening to get ready for.

Him: "Until then, Mrs. Abbott."

After being tucked, plucked, massaged, and manicured, she went back to the room alone. She only had about 30 minutes before everyone would be coming in to help her get dressed. She got down on her knees and leaned over the bed. She prayed a prayer of thanksgiving and covering over their new lives together. This is real, it's really happening, a sense of pure contentment oozed from her soul.

She rose to her feet and gazed at herself in the full-length mirror, her final hour as Chiffon Hartwell. She was about to embark on the biggest journey of her life. She opened her robe and stared at her naked frame. It was no longer going to be hers. Who was she trying to fool? Ever since she met him, it had no longer been hers anyway. They were about to become one in the realist sense, and she wanted nothing more.

Chapter 35

Joshua sat in one of the large rooms with a host of fellows. His dad, his brother, a couple of his favorite cousins, and one of his good friends, who had just arrived. Taylor and a few of the other house staff members were making sure everyone had anything and everything they needed.

He glanced at his watch. It was almost time. He had already put on his slacks, cummerbund, shirt, and socks. He just needed his tie, jacket, and shoes, and he was ready to go. The men were all in various states of dress. He wasn't going to rush anybody. Today belonged to him and Fonn. They were the only two people who needed to be ready on time as far as he was concerned.

"Man, it's almost over," his buddy, Ty, hit him on the shoulder with a smile.

Josh leaned back comfortably into the cushions of the chair. "Man, it's just beginning for me. Not ending."

"Wow, man, I can honestly say, I've never seen you like this, and I've seen a lot," his friend, Ty, hit him on the shoulder.

"I've never felt like this man. Trust me, I had to come to terms with a lot during this relationship, and all I know for sure is I can't live without her," a slight grin took over his features. "I want to make her happy, not just today, but every single day from now on. Every move is for her and JJ, to secure our future," he continued wistfully, "Sleep is merely formality to get to the next day, the next adventure with her. I can't explain it, man."

Ty tapped his shoulder, "I think you're doing a pretty damn good job, Josh, and if you start singing or crying right now, I swear I'm outta here," they both laughed heartily.

Gregory Abbott slid on his tux jacket and walked over to his little brother and held out his hand to pull Josh to his feet. They stared at each other in silence for a moment, forest green to green grays. There was a kinship, a bond beyond being family the two men shared. Josh always looked up to his big brother, and even though he didn't always agree with him, he was one of the only people in this world whose opinion mattered to him.

"I'm proud of you, Joshy. You have found an unbelievable woman who loves you. I see it in you. You are finally ready to settle down. It's an incredible journey you're about to embark on."

Josh nodded his head in agreement.

Greg exhaled deeply, "When I think about how that woman, your woman, risked everything. Her safety, her very life," he hesitated and choked up.

Josh felt it to his bones and let silent tears fall.

"For you, you, and your son," Greg went on emotionally, "I can't think of a greater gift, my brother. There isn't too much you could do or give to her."

"I know," Josh embraced his brother tightly then.

There wasn't a dry eye in the man cave.

Poppa Abbott came over to them both. "Dammit boys," he dabbed under his eye with his handkerchief, "You are worse than two damn chickadees."

Resounding laughter erupted then. "We are all proud of you, son." His father slapped his shoulder. "You stood your ground with me, and I know that was challenging. I know she's with you for the right reasons. You have your mother's and my blessing."

Ordinarily, Joshua would shun his father's approval, but today was different. Today it meant everything to him.

"Thanks pop," they embraced, and Joshua cleared his throat. He had to get himself together, or he would never make it through the ceremony.

"Ok," his father stood back and looked him up and down. "Gentleman," he announced to the group, "Let's finish whipping this boy into shape."

Chiffon glared at her mother, "Don't you dare, mama," Chiffon urged her mother not to start crying. If she did, Chiffon would lose it. Tam placed the veil on Chiffon's head, and she had to admit, she was the picture of a beautiful bride. She hugged her mother, and her mother wiped under her eye.

"Chi, you look stunning," Tam hugged them both.

Mrs. Abbott and Vi came over and hugged them too. "Really?" Chiffon said to them. "How am I supposed to not cry, here? My makeup is going to be a hot mess."

They disengaged. "Let's get you down to the outer door of the ballroom," Mrs. Abbott spoke, "It's almost time."

They all headed down. Everyone dawned their prettiest pastel dresses. The small wedding party was perfect. Josh sent her an I love you text just before she finished getting ready, and she replied, 'From here to eternity.

She remembered she and her mother would get the musical cue and walk down the aisle together. Mrs. Abbott, Tam, and Vi would follow her and stand to her left after her mother and Mrs. Abbott were seated. That seemed easy enough.

Her stomach was in knots; she couldn't believe this day was finally happening. She stared at her ring and thought about the man it represented. A flush of warmth and gratefulness penetrated down to her core. She heard the music and tightened her grip on her mother's arm as the large doors opened.

Pale peach roses filled the room. Their scent invaded her nostrils. Dozens of large, transparent baskets and vases held colorful bouquets. Endless streams of rose-covered garland ribbons hung down from the ceiling, and a long table, placed against one wall, was draped in a lace fringe with towering silver candelabra. The edge of the table was lined with rows of sparkling crystal flutes.

Several silver trays filled with various hors d'oeuvres were stacked at either end. A red carpet flowed down the center of the room to meet an ornate arch draping with pearls and crystals and green vines. She gasped at the sheer beauty surrounding her.

"Oh, Joshua," she whispered to herself as she saw him standing at the far end of the room under the archway of flowers. His tux hugged his masculine frame. He had that special gift of making anything he wore look better.

Everyone rose to their feet as she slowly made her way toward him.

Tears filled her eyes as she realized the song was one of her all-time favorites. All I Want Is You, by Surface. Her mother squeezed her arm tightly to steady her. When they arrived at the end of the aisle, the officiate asked, "Who gives this woman to be married to this man?"

"I do," her mother resounded. Chiffon smiled. Josh held out his arm for her, and her mother placed her arm in his. He was so cool and calm, the picture of distinction and grace, she thought. While she could barely stand there without trembling, he was the picture of elegance and resolve.

"Hi, baby," he whispered to her.

"Hi baby," she smiled nervously at him through the sheer fabric of the veil.

"You look breathtakingly beautiful," he mouthed. She smiled wider, feeling a strange calm wash over her and the ceremony began.

"Dearly beloved, we are gathered here today to witness the union of Joshua, Jason Abbott to Chiffon, Lacie, Hartwell."

The preacher eyed each one of them and continued to speak. "Today, you begin an amazing journey of the joining of your lives together. Now, you are individuals standing before me. When you depart, it will be as husband and wife. Your families will merge, and your commitment will encapsulate individuals whom you both love independently of each other.

A successful marriage unifies two bodies, two hearts, two souls, and one God. Your bond will strengthen based on the love you have and share with each other."

The pastor looked pointedly from Josh to Chiffon, "As you sail upon this journey, remember to open your hearts to each other, pay attention to each other and most of all, trust each other. Disclose how you feel about the big stuff, the little stuff, and all stuff. You won't always agree, but believe it or not, you were never designed to. That's ok. You are different people; you won't see everything out of the same lens." So, make happy medium your mantra and guide.

Then he turned to Josh with his brow raised, "She doesn't always have to agree with you, Joshy."

The onlookers burst out in laughter, and Josh winked at her, smiling. The pastor was a longtime friend of his parents and knew him very well.

"May you delight in your lives together, and at the completion of each day, take comfort in each other. Be each other's soft place to land. I wish you a home of joy, peace, understanding and an everlasting friendship that is planted on fertile ground. May it bloom and blossom now and forever more.

Joshua and Chiffon, when the darkness comes that all marriages confront, remember the force and power that initially brought you two together. Recall the love that compels you to join your souls right now. It will sustain you when the going gets tough. Like any overcast day, even though you can't distinguish the sun's rays, it doesn't mean it has vanished from your lives. Illumination is around the bin. Become the brilliance for each other until it returns to view.

Put respect for God and each other at the forefront of your relationship. Take responsibility for making the other feel safe and cared for. Remember, sometimes tenderness, kindness and willingness to be wrong can go a lot farther than the satisfaction proving you are right in the moment. Joy comes in the morning if you can get through the night together.

Take full responsibility for the quality of your lives together and exercise your faith. Always remember God is the ultimate ruler of your house, not either one of you. Ok, the lecture portion is now concluded," he grinned and winked at them. Josh smiled back at him. She was too busy trying to stay upright to acknowledge him.

"Joshy and Chiffon, your love shouldn't only fill a void but introduce true fullness. When challenges come, forgive one another as Christ has forgiven us. May you know joy and understanding and everlasting love. May it show up in your daily interaction with one another."

"This is a glorious pairing of two souls. Marriage is not to be entered into swiftly or without counsel. It is an infinite lifetime obligation of the highest order. May God add a blessing to the joining of your hearts, the blending of your families, and this honorable love commitment."

"Now, Joshua has a special announcement for his bride-to-be."

It's You

Joshua tightened his grip on both of her hands and stared down at her. His life was wrapped up in the woman; how he loved her. He still wondered when it happened. When did she steal his heart, his mind, his soul? She held the key to everything he locked away for so long. There were parts of him he never planned to expose to anyone. Not only was every closed space now open, but every part of him felt free to give her love and receive love in return.

"Fonn," he said and cleared his throat. His voice heavy with emotion. She rubbed her thumb inside of his palm, and instantly it calmed him. It was their secret way to say they had each other's back. He smiled at her, "June 17th will be the day we celebrate our years together every year from this day forward. I know it hasn't been a particularly good date for you in your past because society at large usually celebrates Father's Day on or near this date."

She started to tremble, no words.

"I want to turn this day into one that will make you happy from now on. A day that will now fill you with a sense of joy, not loss."

"Oh, Josh," she mouthed the words as she let the tears fall.

Four men stood up in the front row and walked up to the left of him, all facing her. Then she heard the music from 'We'll Be United', by the Intruders begin to play.

She put her hand up to her mouth in surprise, as Josh began to sing to her.

"I'm tired of running around. Me and my baby's gonna settle down. I'm gonna make her my June bride, we gonna walk down the aisle side by side, (then in perfect harmony all the men sang) 'cause I love her, and she loves me that's the way it's gonna be and baby you just wait and see we're gonna be united."

The crowd cheered as Josh and his backup finished the song in perfect harmony.

Speechless again, she parted her lips, but nothing came out. It was one of her favorite songs, and he had just sung it to her in front of everyone. She had always heard him fooling around singing here and there, but she had no idea he could sound like that.

She was glad the veil was covering her face 'cause she started doing the ugly cry. She would never ever forget this day. She had already forgotten it was Father's Day. Leave it to Josh to fix it for her. He grabbed her and held her tightly as everyone ooohed and ahhed.

"No fair," she whispered to him.

"All is fair in love, baby." He held her for a moment longer, rubbing her back. He gave her his handkerchief, and she got herself together as best she could. She turned to the audience and gave the thumbs-up sign, and everyone laughed.

The preacher interjected, "Wow, well done, Joshua. We are now ready to have the presentation of the rings."

Joshua's friend Ty stepped up and gave Joshua the elegant, glittering band and turned to give Chiffon a ring for Joshua, but Tam stepped up to give Chiffon Joshua's ring.

Josh looked puzzled for a moment, "That's where you were," he whispered to her, and she nodded.

Something washed over her soon-to-be husband. It presented as shock, joy, or plain ole love, but whatever it was, it touched her.

"Do you Joshua Jason Abbott, take Chiffon Lacie Hartwell to be your partner in life, sharing your path, equal in love, a mirror for your true self, promising to honor her, cherish her, and be faithful only to her through good times and bad, giving only unto her until death do you part?"

"I will, and I do," he said with his gaze steady on her.

"Place the ring on her finger."

He took her left hand and kissed it, and then placed the ring on her finger.

"Do you Chiffon Lacie Hartwell take Joshua Jason Abbott to be your partner in life, sharing your path, equal in love, a mirror for your true self, promising to honor him, cherish him, and be faithful to him through good times and bad, giving only unto him until death do you part?"

"I will, and I do," she said.

"Place the ring on his finger."

She took his hand and slid the ring on. Her hands were trembling. He covered her hand with his and smiled at her. It's like there's no one else in the world when he smiles at me, she thought. She calmed.

"Is there anyone here who can show just cause why these two should not be joined in holy matrimony, let them speak now or forever hold their peace?"

Both Josh and Chiffon made a grimacing face and turned a hard look out into the crowd, daring anyone to say a word. They turned back to each other smiling, engulfed by the laughter of the onlookers.

The preacher cleared his throat and continued, "Wedding rings are made precious by your wearing of them. Your rings say you have chosen to be bound together. It's a physical representation that love is considered a circle of true happiness. May these rings always remind you of the vows you pledged to one another today. And now, by the powers vested in me by the State of Tennessee, I hereby pronounce you husband and wife. You may kiss your bride."

Josh lifted the veil to his crying bride and lowered his head, and pressed his lips against her soft, luscious mouth, wet with her tears. "Now you are mine," he breathed against her.

"Yes, she responded, "And you, sir, are mine." She slid her tongue into his mouth. She didn't care. He kissed her back passionately.

"Woman, we are about to put on a show in front of your mama. Watch yo self," he breathed against her mouth. She broke off the kiss laughing. He gave her his handkerchief again, and she quickly wiped under her eyes. He used it to wipe under his eyes as well.

Cameras flashed, and the crowd rose to their feet as she and Josh turned hand in hand to face the audience of well-wishers. She then heard another one of her other favorite songs—United Together by Aretha Franklin. Tears sprang to her eyes again, and she hugged Joshua tightly.

"You have made this day so special for me Josh, you have thought of everything," she whispered in his ear. "I'm not sure I'm going to be able to top this."

"Just wait until you see the rest of your life."

Before she could respond to him the preacher said, "Ladies and gentlemen, I present to you Mr. and Mrs. Joshua and Chiffon Abbott."

Cheers sprang up from the crowd. A storm of confetti sprayed upon them. She walked down the aisle with her hand in his. Their bridal party followed them out, and they posed for photos. She had JJ on her hip and took a few photos with just her, Josh, and the baby.

"Honey, I'd like to go upstairs to change before we have dinner."

"Ok," he kissed her cheek, "Hurry up," he smacked her on the ass, "Or I will come and get you."

She ran up the stairs and changed into a sparkling, ivory short dress. She let her hair down and refreshed her makeup. "I'm a married woman now," she smiled, staring at herself in the mirror in a moment of silence, and turned to head back downstairs.

When she rounded the corner to head back to the ballroom, she distinctly heard someone calling her name.

She turned a full 360 but didn't see anyone. Then she heard it again. Ok, was she losing it?

"Over here," the voice said. She turned back toward the dining area.

She saw a movement by the heavy drapes, "Who's there?" she called out.

"It's me, Chiffon," the voice said. She slowly approached the windows. A sense of foreboding was making her skin start to prickle, raising her hackles. Who was hiding there? She couldn't make out if the whisper was male or female.

"Who's there?" she called again. He stepped out from behind the curtain, and her mouth dropped open in shock and a bit of horror, "Isaac," she whispered, her stomach somersaulting double time. The effect he had on her was still very real and quite disturbing. He was the last person she expected to see here.

"How did you get in here, Isaac? What are you doing here?" her voice quaked.

"I have to talk to you privately, Chiffon."

"Right now?" she questioned, raising her voice. "Isaac, Josh and I just got married."

"I know that," he nodded, "I just watched you marry him."

She shook her head in disbelief. This had to be some sort of joke. "How did you know about today? I didn't even know until yesterday. Josh will kill you if he finds you here, Isaac. You have got to get outta here right now!" she insisted.

He approached her, and she inadvertently stepped backward. "I didn't know you were getting married today, Chiffon. I flew out here because I was worried about you. You didn't come back to work, and you wouldn't answer my calls. You didn't look so good the last time I saw you. I figured you would go to see your baby.

When I rang the bell, a staff member thought I was here for the wedding and ushered me in. I came here to apologize for hurting you, Chiffon. I'm ashamed of myself. The last thing I wanted to do was cause you pain. While I knew you would be uncomfortable seeing me with Tam. I didn't know it would turn into something akin to anguish. I had to find you and apologize. I had to. I haven't been able to sleep, Chiffon, and I'm sorry. Please forgive me."

"You can't be here, Isaac," she was shaking her head. Literally and figuratively, she thought. Not today, not today!

"Listen to me, Chiffon. I received some extremely important news we must discuss. It will change our lives as we know it. I came to find you to tell you in person."

She glanced around quickly. A tightness crept around her heart, and light perspiration broke out at her hairline.

"I had a detective do some research into our pasts to figure out why or if there was some sort of connection between us. Anything to explain why we have been so inextricably drawn to each other."

"A detective?" she repeated, completely confused. "I'm sorry you've wasted your time, Isaac. I already know what the connection is. It's all my fault. I have been mixed up, and I apologize. I have misplaced my feelings for you with feelings I had for my father. It's all been a huge, misguided mistake." She looked around again. "I'll have to explain it to you in detail later, Isaac. I really have to get back to my husband before he starts to worry."

He approached her faster than she could back away. He placed his hands on her shoulders, griping them tightly, "I can't just leave you here like this, Chiffon." He kissed the top of her forehead and stared down at her, "Look at me," he instructed. "You have to hear me out first, and then I will go. I promise."

She was speechless and stood there motionless.

"It's no accident we came into each other's lives. Can't you see, we were fated to end up finding each other? I feel the same pull and draw to you, you feel toward me."

She shook her head, "No, Isaac. We can't do anything about that. It's wrong and –"

"It's not wrong, Chiffon!" he bristled.

Frightened, she pleaded, "Please Isaac, for God's sake. This is not the time!" She had to get away from him. She could feel herself being sucked back into that vortex, the unexplainable hold he had over her. It was as if he had a magic spell cast over her sanity.

"Chiffon, I know you love me, and it's ok."

She shook her head, "No, no, I don't. I don't, Isaac."

"Yes, you do, Chiffon. You love me, and I love you.

Very much so. There's a reason we feel like we do, sweetheart, and it's not what you think."

This was not happening. This was a bad dream. Lord Jesus, please make him stop. Don't prove our connection today. Not today, Isaac, she pleaded to herself.

"No!" she shook her head again. "There's no good reason Isaac. None of it makes any real sense. There is something wrong with me!" she raised her voice at him.

He reached out and touched the side of her face. She couldn't move. "Please don't touch me, Isaac," she whispered, gasping on strangled breath. "Please don't." Her eyes were welling up with tears. She couldn't run, and she couldn't scream. She was paralyzed.

"I don't know how else to tell you this, so I'm just going to say it. I just found out Isaiah Hartwell is my biological father. I am your brother, Chiffon. We have the same father."

She gaped in disbelief, "What did you say?" Alarm and horror caused a staccato beat in her heart. No sooner than the words were out of her mouth, with lightning speed, Josh's fist connected with the side of Isaac's head, and he hit the floor. Josh dived on top of him, with fists flying. Chiffon screamed for Josh to get off him. "Please!" she wailed.

"Stay away from my wife!" she heard Josh yell out as Isaac tried to scramble to his feet.

"Joshua, sweetheart, please! Stop it!" She forced herself between him and Isaac, trying to hold him back.

"What the fuck is he doing here!" he yelled at her accusingly.

She shook her head.

"I-I don't know! I don't know why he's here. I didn't invite him. Please, baby, please don't hurt him."

A look of pure torment appeared on Josh's face. His eyes narrowed on her. "Are you defending him right now? He just crashed our special day, and you don't want me to hurt Him?" Bewildered and pissed, he asked, "You want to protect him today?"

Tears were flowing freely down her face. "No, no! I'm not defending him, Josh. You are my husband. I love you. I'm defending you!" She stared at her husband, their eyes transfixed. She willed him to listen to her, to believe her.

"This is our wedding day, Joshua. He could press charges if you hurt him! I don't want anything to take you away from me. You must stop. You can't hurt him because I can't lose you, Josh, not now that I finally have you. It took us a long time to get here. This is our day. Don't let him ruin it, please, Joshua," she pleaded with him.

His eyes softened on her as relief washed over him. He pulled her into a tight embrace. "Oh baby," he kissed her forehead and looked down at her. "I'm sorry, I'm so sorry," he squeezed his eyes shut for a moment. "I just saw him with his hands on you, and I just went crazy. I lost it. He's an asshole for showing up here today."

She quickly glanced over at Isaac as she held onto her husband for dear life. She didn't want Joshua upset, especially not today. Today had been perfect, and she knew her husband's temper was nothing to toy with. She had to focus on him first before she could deal with all the other emotions rumbling just beneath the surface.

She managed to get through this entire day without thinking about Isaac. She couldn't believe he was here laying this on her now, today of all days. It only served to make everything even more confusing. If what he was saying had any truth to it, not only did she have this incredible guilt for how she had been feeling about him, now she could add shame to the mix.

Her brother, could he really be her brother? No way. Was this even possible? It would explain a lot. It would give a voice to how attached she felt to him without knowing him. However, it was hard to give Isaac any credit for anything right now. She was pissed he showed up here today, but she had to respect that he waited until the ceremony was over. She noticed a flash of something outside near the drapes that Isaac stepped out from. She peered closer, and she couldn't believe her eyes.

On the tree limb, just outside the window, there sat a nest with a tiny bird and a slightly bigger one inside. Above the nest, two larger birds were circling and snapping beaks at each other. She rubbed her eyes. No way this could possibly be the same birds from Chicago. No way.

"I'm sorry for this intrusion," Isaac said, now back on his feet. "I apologize to you both for showing up this way, but you need to hear this too, Josh." He rubbed over his jaw and moved it from side to side. "Even though I was here, I did not interrupt your nuptials. I could have, but I didn't." She held

Josh's hand as they gave Isaac their full attention. "Chiffon and I are related. She is my biological sister."

"What?" Josh's brows creased as his mouth fell open. "That's the connection Chiffon, and I felt. I just found out Isaiah Hartwell is my biological father. It appears I was named after him." He pulled some paperwork out of his pocket and handed it to Chiffon. "We have been drawn, connected to each other for a reason unbeknownst to us, Chiffon. I knew there was more to what had been happening, more than just physical attraction. It was too strong, too deep."

She felt Josh tense at his words, "Let me see that." He snatched the papers and looked them over.

He then looked from Isaac to Chiffon and back again. "I'll be dammed," he said more to himself than anyone else. He could see a slight resemblance between them, something in their eyes and cheekbones. Christ! Things were getting increasingly insane by the minute. The paperwork appeared to be in order. Unbelievable. He would never get this motherfucker out of his life now. Unreal.

Chiffon took the paperwork from Josh and looked it over herself. She then stared at Isaac, saying nothing for the longest time. "When and how did you find out, Isaac," she finally managed. She shuddered, and Josh put his arm around her, pulling her into him, making her feel secure. His hand rested on the side of her waist.

"I never knew my biological dad, Chiffon. Manuel Ruiz raised me since I was about ten years old. It appears Isaiah moved in with my mother when he left your family."

Her eyes widened. It couldn't be. "My father lived with you?"

"Yeah, for a short while, apparently, our parents dated for a few years prior to him moving in because I vaguely remember calling him dad."

Chiffon gasped out loud, "So, he was seeing your mother while he was still married to mine?"

She and Isaac were nearly the same age – perhaps a few years difference. That means while her mother was pregnant with her, her father already had a child outside of his marriage. She held her rumbling stomach.

"He didn't stay with us long, Chiffon. I vaguely remember him."

"So, you could be my brother?" she whispered, shaking her head.

"Yes, I believe I am." They stared at each other, invisible tentacles encircling them tightening silently around them.

"I hate to break up your little family reunion," Josh interrupted, "But this is our wedding day, Isaac. There will be plenty of time to deal with all this later. Your incredible audacity is…is; he took a deep breath, he was two seconds from beating his ass again. "Can we do this at a more appropriate time? Your sister," he said with disgust, "Was very happy before you arrived."

Isaac gazed at Chiffon, "I understand, and Chiffon, please forgive me for interrupting your day. I really didn't know anything about a wedding. I only came to apologize for the other night and make sure you received this information as soon as possible. I thought it would, it might um, help you.

I'm sorry I, I mean, I'm sorry we considered, um..." he hesitated at a loss for words. "Contact me when you get back to Chicago, he said quickly. I'm hoping we will get a chance at a new start. I would like to work at being family."

"Humph," Josh mumbled, smirking under his breath.

"I will contact you, Isaac," she said evenly. "This is a lot to take in. Right now, my focus is on my husband and the start of our lives together," she didn't make eye contact with him.

"I know," he shook his head. "I know you love him. Despite our obvious issues, I think he is a good enough fellow. That's the reason I waited until after the ceremony to tell you, but I couldn't wait any longer Chiffon. I finally discovered what was going on between us, and I figured you needed to know. Do you understand?" he pleaded.

"I understand," she nodded in agreement.

She could feel Josh watching her intently. She didn't know whether to hug Isaac or shake his hand or what. Sensing her unease, Isaac briefly placed his hand on her shoulder, "I know this is overwhelming, Chiffon, but we will figure it out. Together. Congratulations to you both. It was a touching ceremony."

He looked briefly at Josh, who was now standing with his arms folded. She nodded at Isaac, and he left. Josh stared at his new bride. She was clearly shaken, hell, he was shaken, but he wasn't going to let Mergers ruin this beautiful day for them, whoever the hell he proved to be.

It's You

He approached her, lifted her chin, and stared into her eyes. "We will deal with this later," he said firmly. "I don't want you worrying about it. Especially not today. Today I refuse to share you with anyone."

She smiled at him and said, "My husband has a selfish streak."

"Don't worry about any of this. I'll have it authenticated, and we'll deal with it then." That calmed her. He knew just what to say to her. She knew this couldn't be easy for him to deal with, but he was diplomatic and fair, showing his usual grace under fire.

"Ok," she nodded, "I love you, Joshua Abbott."

"And I, you, Chiffon Abbott," he kissed her lips quickly before they headed back into the ballroom for dinner and dancing.

Chapter
36

Her body fluttered and vibrated. She didn't think she could hold it back any longer. She panted and held his head against her throbbing, swollen, vaginal walls. If her husband wanted to lick her until she forgot everything, anything else but him, he was doing an incredible job because she was lost.

He was determined to make this day, this night only about the two of them. Her scent, her extreme arousal whenever he touched her, turned him on like nothing else in this world.

"That's it, baby," his tongue circled her clit with quick successive strokes. He then sucked on it while flicking his tongue across the sensitive bud of nerves. She felt his finger at the opening of her anus.

"Josh baby, wait," but she was lost in sensation. His finger penetrated her slowly but deeply. Undone, her body arched up to meet his hot tongue. She couldn't control herself. The build pulsated through her core. "Baby, yes!" she started to buck and gyrate against his beautiful mouth. She rode his finger like it was a penis. "Joshuaaaa!" she screamed out his name in an explosive, mind-numbing orgasm.

She didn't know if it was because of her husband's expert ministrations or if it was just a necessary release from the stress of the day, but never, ever had she come so hard. So intensely. Tears came to her eyes as she continued to convulse and heave upward.

"Yes, baby, come for your husband," he whispered against her soft quivering flesh. She tried to move away from that magical tongue of his, but he held her hips tightly and would not let her go. He continued his assault on her senses until slowly she came down from the summit. She whimpered against him as spasms had her continuously gasping for air. He moved light kisses up her stomach and took one of her nipples into his mouth.

She immediately wrapped her legs around him. She loved grabbing his head, pulling his lips closer to her hot flesh. His hair was so soft and curly. He took her nipple between his teeth and bit down lightly. She screamed out in pleasure and pain. Soon their tongues met furiously, trying to eat each other alive.

"I love you, baby. Only you, Joshua," she cried.

"I know. I know, and I don't doubt you, sweetheart," He rubbed his penis against her hot moist folds, and she almost came again. "Inside you is where I plan to be, where I want to end each day from now on." He raised up over her balancing himself on his arms. "Forever," he looked down at her heavily lidded eyes.

She nodded in agreement, "Forever." He plunged deep into her causing her to scream out his name again. He pounded forcefully into her. Everything he had been dreaming of, all that he wanted to feel, was squeezing around his prick. He was surrounded by Fonn, and he wouldn't have it any other way.

"Fuck!" He squeezed his eyes together as pleasure, need, desire, and passion took over his body. The feeling was so intense, so animalistic, and a guttural cry escaped from deep inside him. He came with an absolute force that frightened him. He continued to plunge deep, needing to feel her as long as possible.

He immediately opened his eyes to see if she was ok. She was in her own world, gripping him and taking every inch of him.

"You belong to me, baby," he whispered. "You hear me," he grabbed her face, forcing her to open her eyes, "Look at me, Fonn."

She tried to focus. She was having another orgasm, and she honestly could not see for a minute. "Yes, yes, Joshua," she managed, shaking uncontrollably. "Yes, I'm yours!"

"Forever," he demanded.

"Forever," she focused on him.

He leaned up still inside her. "You make me so happy, baby. 'Je veux passer le reste de ma vie avec toi', Fonn." He lay all his weight on her hugging her close to him. "Thank you for being my bride," he kissed her neck and nuzzled his face there.

"You're speaking in another language again, sweetheart. What did you just say to me?"

"Oh, just that I want to spend my life with you."

"Thank you for being my groom Josh. It was a wonderful wedding," she smiled, reminiscing.

"I couldn't wait to get inside you again as your husband. It wasn't easy enduring all the after-wedding formalities."

She smiled, "I don't have words for what just happened between us, Josh, but I know with you is where I belong."

"Damn right," he agreed as he kissed her cheek, her nose, her eyes. She snuggled up against him and fell into a satisfied sleep.

Epilogue

Something was hitting her on her face. She squinted, "Ouch," she said opening her eyes looking right at her baby boy who was laughing and striking her face. Joshua placed JJ next to her on the bed, where he was sitting up reading the newspaper.

"Hey, you," she sat up smiling. She grabbed JJ and started to plant kisses all over him. The baby's arms and little legs flared out in delight. She smiled at her husband, "Good morning Mr. Abbott."

"Good morning Mrs. Abbott," he returned her smile and kissed her lips. "Somebody wanted to see you when they woke up."

"I can see that," she eyed the baby with affection.

"I want to take you away. Just you and me," he sat the paper down.

"Ok, where do you want to take me exactly?"

"Well, that's gonna be a surprise. When we get back, you, me, and our son can head back to Chicago. I know you want to get back to work."

"Really! We can?" she grabbed his hand and kissed it, still holding JJ with her other arm, "Do you mean it?"

"Yes, baby, we have full custody of him. That was my other surprise for you. We are taking him home."

She closed her eyes, trying to still the flood of emotions threatening to overtake her. All her dreams were coming true. They were finally going to get a chance to be a real family. She pulled his hand up to her lips and kissed it again.

"I like that baby," he smiled. "There isn't anything I wouldn't do for you, Fonn."

"I know Joshua."

He wiped under her eyes with a slight grin on his face, "Don't cry, baby. We are finally going to have the life we have always wanted. Everything we have fought for."

She stared at him wistfully, "We still have some challenges to face, Josh. Promise me you won't ever let anything come between us. Promise me you will always forgive me. Sometimes I don't always get it right." She closed her eyes and placed the side of her face in the open palm of his hand.

"I don't need to promise you, Fonn. You are already forgiven, just like I am. You are my wife. I am your husband. It's more than a contract. Our commitment to each other is on an entirely different level now. Nothing will come between us because we won't let it. I have finally found what I've been searching for all my life; you and JJ, you mean everything to me. We can get through anything together."

She opened her eyes and stared into her husband's beautiful eyes. She could look at him all day, every day, and that's exactly what she planned to do. The next chapter of their lives was about to begin, and she couldn't be happier. If they were together, they could achieve anything.

"Mom-ma," they heard, startled; they both looked down to JJ and then back at each other.

"Did he just say, momma?" her heart was thumping in shock.

"Mom-ma," he said it again. Her mouth dropped open as the baby stared at her.

"Well, Mrs. Abbott, it sounds to me like you're stuck with us," Josh wiped across her cheek. She took his hand and slipped off his wedding band.

"Hey, what are you doing? I'm under strict orders never to remove that."

"Look at the inscription," she held it up to the light for him to see. He read it aloud, slowly turning the ring. "Joshua and Fonn, From Here to Eternity." His gaze then locked on hers, and she could feel the muscles of her core start to clinch again. He placed the ring back on his finger, never breaking the gaze between them.

"I think it's time for the nanny to feed JJ."

She smiled at him seductively, "Me too."

Authors Note

Dear Reader,

Thank you for selecting It's You by Dee Dee Welch, for your reading pleasure. I hope you found it an enjoyable escape. Be on the lookout for the next book in the reciprocation series coming soon! Updates on the newest release will be posted to my website at, www.dromancewriter.com

Feel free to browse, join my mailing list, get upcoming event info, or post a message. If you are part of a book club, feel free to post some of your answers to my page. You can friend me on Facebook at D-Romance Writer or find me on Instagram at deedeewelch9030.

Again, thank you for taking this wonderful ride with me. I appreciate your continued support. Keep reading!

Book Club Guide

Here are some thought provoking discussion questionsbased on It's You.

1. Would you define Chiffon and Joshua's relationship as a healthy one?
2. Do you feel there was a connection between Isaac and Chiffon from the start?
3. Do you think Chiffon was true to her friendship with Tam? What about Tam to Chiffon?
4. How often do you think a woman makes romantic decisions based on the relationship or lack thereof with her father or a father figure?
5. Tam let Joshua into her apartment without Chiffon's knowledge. Did Chiffon have a right to be upset or should she have thanked her?
6. What do you think was really behind Tam's motives? Did Tam deserve to be forgiven?
7. Did Joshua go too far to win Chiffon back?
8. Chiffon's mother seemed ill at ease with the marriage. Do you think her concerns were valid?
9. After successful treatment and rehabilitation, should Candice be allowed to see her baby again?
10. What about Terrance? If so, under what circumstances for them?
11. Papa Abbott likes to keep his children close. Do you think he will ever let Joshua go?

12. Can Isaac flip the switch and change his relationship with Chiffon, or will he always want more?
13. Should Tam pursue her feelings for Isaac?
14. Do you think Chiffon could handle it if Tam and Isaac got together?
15. Joshua wants Fonn far away from Isaac. To that end, should he force her to quit her job?
16. What could prevent Chiffon from being a good mother to JJ?
17. Who is your favorite and least favorite character in the novel? Why?
18. Which character would you like to see examined more closely in the next book in the series.

CPSIA information can be obtained
at www.ICGtesting.com
Printed in the USA
BVHW091850060522
636356BV00015B/453